IMPOSTOR SYNDROME

ALSO BY MISHELL BAKER

The Arcadia Project
Borderline
Phantom Pains

MISHELL BAKER

IMPOSTOR SYNDROME

THE ARCADIA PROJECT

3

SAGA PRESS

LONDON SYDNEY **NEW YORK** TORONTO NEW DELHI

SAGA PRESS

AN IMPRINT OF SIMON & SCHUSTER, INC.

1230 AVENUE OF THE AMERICAS, NEW YORK, NEW YORK 10020

SAGA PRESS and colophon are trademarks of Simon & Schuster, Inc.

For information about special discounts for bulk purchases, please contact Simon & Schuster Special Sales at 1-866-506-1949 or business@simonandschuster.com.

The Simon & Schuster Speakers Bureau can bring authors to your live event. For more information or to book an event, contact the Simon & Schuster Speakers Bureau at 1-866-248-3049 or visit our website at www.simonspeakers.com.

Also available in a Saga Press hardcover edition

The text for this book was set in Chaparral Pro.

Manufactured in the United States of America

First Saga Press paperback edition March 2018

2 4 6 8 10 9 7 5 3 1

Library of Congress Cataloging-in-Publication Data

Names: Baker, Mishell, author.

Title: Impostor syndrome / Mishell Baker.

Description: First Saga Press paperback edition. | New York : Saga Press, 2018. | Series: The Arcadia project ; 3

Identifiers: LCCN 2017019627 | ISBN 9781481451949 (trade pbk.) | ISBN 9781481480185 (hardcover) | ISBN 9781481451956 (eBook)

Subjects: | GSAFD: Suspense fiction.

Classification: LCC PS3602.A58665 I47 2018 | DDC 813/.6—dc23

LC record available at https://lccn.loc.gov/2017019627

For Wren Wallis
My Echo

1

The British declared war in January, just after my boss's twentieth birthday. Of course 99 percent of America just kept going to work and doing laundry and wishing creative deaths on their noisiest neighbors, because it was the Arcadia Project that was at war, and we'd done a damned good job of remaining invisible.

Inspiration had to flow to keep the world moving, but there was no polite way to hold a press conference now and say, *Hey, there really is a secret society that's been controlling human progress for centuries, and as of three months ago it's falling apart, and you all might die.* So anyone without a blood-signature on one of our contracts enjoyed the privilege of blissful ignorance.

My friends and I, though? We were screwed.

I'd taken a crash course in Project operations since opening a vein for them last October. I knew what the structure was *supposed* to be. A hundred ninety-eight nations, including us, reporting to Dame Belinda Barker at World HQ in London. America, being huge, was split into Western, Central, and Eastern regions, with offices in the three Gate cities: L.A., New Orleans, and New York City.

But that all got shot to hell when Alvin Lamb, our National head in New Orleans, found out that a couple decades ago Dame Belinda had authorized the abduction and torture of a U.S. citizen, aged eleven months. Once that bomb dropped, Alvin invoked the Philadelphia Protocol, which, if you're a history buff, means pretty much what it sounds like: *Fuck you, England. America's gonna do its own thing now.*

It might even have worked, if Tracy Wong in New York hadn't decided to believe Dame Belinda when she told him that Alvin had lost his last marbles. Tracy hadn't been there, like Alvin had, when we'd surprised Belinda into defending her atrocity. She'd had time to pull the mask back on, the one we'd all fallen for. Alvin had fallen harder than anyone until that moment—he'd been dripping Belinda-flavored Kool-Aid from every pore—and I think that's part of why he cut ties so hard and fast.

And now here it was—January. We should have been expecting that Dame Belinda would patiently wait to line up the precision shot from cover; she'd been a World War II sniper, for God's sake. But we weren't ready, not even a little. My boss, Western Regional Manager Caryl Vallo, had been the abductee in question. She was kind of a mess. Alvin was back in New Orleans trying to keep the Central regional manager from panicking and joining New York. My partner, Tjuan Miller, was trying to get a fourth Gate operational at Valiant Studios while simultaneously writing a hit television show there. Meanwhile, I, thanks to a backslide in my mental health, was pissing everyone off, repeatedly forgetting my basic training, and nursing a paranoia about the Residence manager's pet crow.

It could be argued that my intense level of crazy was, in a roundabout way, the only reason Tjuan got wind of what was about to happen to him. He'd been practically living at Valiant, and if not for me and that damned rubber suit, he'd have been right there in the line of fire when the news broke.

The suit arrived late on a Saturday afternoon—Caryl's birthday of all days—neatly packaged with a Louisiana return address. (By this time the shot had been fired, mere hours ago. We just didn't know it yet.)

Alvin had an in with someone who made diving suits near New Orleans, and he had put in a custom order. In theory this thing would let me wander around Arcadia without all the local spellwork being blown to bits by the excess steel that held the jigsaw puzzle of my bones together. In practice, I realized as soon as I took the suit up to my room and started pulling it on, there were problems.

Good points included the lightweight neoprene, the relaxed fit (I wasn't planning on swimming in it), and the way they'd stitched the legs of the suit right into a pair of rubber-soled hiking boots just the right size for my main pair of prosthetic feet. But when I started to pull it up to get my arms into it, things got weird.

The suit was one big piece that opened in the back and, despite my daily stretching regimen, I still didn't have the range of motion to get the zipper up on my own.

I didn't like the idea of having to ask someone for help every time I needed to put the thing on or take it off. As I stood there with the back gaping open, I asked myself a question that would indirectly end up buying us two weeks of planning time: *What if I need to pee?*

At first I was picturing a scenario where I was in the Residence and forgot to use the bathroom before putting the thing on. But then an even worse train of thought started barreling down the tracks: Were there bathrooms in Arcadia? Did fey even have bladders?

I'd been through the Gate in Residence Four's tower only twice, for brief local errands. I'd stayed away from fey civilization, from anywhere that might be laced with fragile spellwork, and so I had no idea where the fey actually lived or what their accommodations were. Was I going to have to squat in the wilderness? And if so, would I have to strip naked to do it?

I wasn't just being dainty. Ever since my semi-deliberate plummet off a seven-story building a year and a half ago (how deliberate can a person be when blackout drunk?), I'd only undressed with the lights on for one person, and that was my Echo, Claybriar. Getting naked for him was like getting naked in front of a mirror, which, don't get me wrong, had been hard for a while too. But there was no damned way my scarred and shattered self was going to strip down in a foreign land where God only knew who or what might creep up on me.

To make matters worse—and I actually tried this, there in my room—I couldn't figure out how to manage a squat with my prosthetic legs. I planted my feet apart to give myself a more stable base, but every time I tried to lower myself, I could feel an uncomfortable threat of torsion in the silicone sheath that held the stump of my left thigh. I worried the whole thing would wrench loose, send me toppling to the floor.

When I'd been released from the hospital to the loony bin

nearly a year ago, I'd quickly figured out how to do the basic stuff—getting in and out of the shower, on and off toilets, up and down stairs—and I'd confined my activities to those things. Now, for the first time in months, I was faced with a thing I quite possibly needed to do and could not come anywhere close to doing. I was *broken*.

That last bit, of course, was my borderline personality disorder talking. When people with BPD are dysphoric (think "bad mood" to the tenth power), they have a hard time balancing complexities. My dysphoria did not permit me to consider the vast and ever-changing spectrum of ability we all experience throughout our lives. My dysphoria told me I was as worthless as a shattered iPhone. It took me fifteen minutes to control my crying enough to get dressed and leave my room.

I descended the grand wooden staircase into the two-story living room where bored people in Residence Four usually hung out. My goal was to find Residence Manager Song, the most soothing human being alive, but, fortunately, even the mindful act of making my step-over-step descent as "normal" as possible helped scoot me back from the edge of hysteria.

And then I heard singing. Opera, to be exact: "O mio babbino caro," sung almost absently, light and sweet as clover honey.

I can't truthfully say it was the most astounding voice I'd ever heard, given that I'd been hypnotized by the siren Queen Shiverlash just a few months ago. But it did knock my socks off. I drifted toward the kitchen, expecting to find a new fey creature or maybe a Disney princess.

Instead, I saw espresso-colored curls trailing down a broad back. *Her.* Alondra Serrano, the new girl.

Short, fat, golden brown, and gorgeous, Alondra was my age, maybe a little younger. She was one of three refugees from New York who had reacted badly to Tracy Wong's November ultimatum of "stand with London or get fired." Getting fired meant having huge portions of your memory wiped, so the trio of rebels had played along while conspiring to flee.

They took almost nothing with them when they left, so as not to raise their Residence manager's suspicions, and headed straight for Penn Station. The iron train tracks kept the headquarters alarm from going off when they crossed the Gate perimeter, and the three of them showed up thirty hours later in New Orleans, half-starved, because Tracy had canceled their credit cards as soon as he realized they were gone.

Alvin had put two to work in New Orleans and sent the other one to Residence Four in L.A., since we were down two agents. Now our little refugee was at the tiled kitchen island, singing as she cut a delicate slice of Caryl's strawberry birthday cake.

Alondra had BPD, like me. In fact, she seemed to exist entirely to prove that I wasn't all that special. I'd attempted suicide? She'd attempted suicide *twice*. I had a boyfriend and a half? She'd left two boyfriends and a girlfriend behind in New York. My parents were dead? She'd *found* her parents dead when she was seven. And apparently she could sing like a fucking angel. This new information didn't do much to appease the resentment I'd been feeling from the minute she'd moved into my dead partner's old room.

"Oh!" she said when she heard me, turning and putting a fluttering hand to her bosom. "I didn't realize there was anyone here!" She avoided my eyes as though I'd caught her masturbating and not eating cake.

"Does that mean Song's not here?"

It wasn't that hard a question, but she looked like I'd strapped her to an interrogation chair. "I—I think she took Sterling to the park."

"Damn it."

I hadn't even raised my voice, but Alondra flinched as though I'd struck her.

"She'll be back soon, I'm sure," I said, annoyed that Alondra had manipulated me into soothing her when I was the one who'd come down needing comfort. It was always like that with her. Her feelings were always bigger, more urgent.

She took the slice she'd cut and sat down on a barstool at the island. "Do you need any laundry done?" she asked, apparently to the cake.

"You're not the maid," I said. I'd actually been trying for nice, but then I realized it wasn't the best thing to say to my new Puerto Rican housemate, and that only made me crankier.

She gave me a plaintive glance from under her long lashes. "I like doing laundry," she said. "I've been doing Stevie's and Phil's. It . . . centers me."

"Well it doesn't center me to have other people poking through my underwear," I said. "They're my clothes—I'll wash them when I'm good and ready."

"I wasn't trying to—"

"I need some fresh air," I said, and walked out of the kitchen.

I could hear myself becoming an asshole, playing alpha dog, but it was Alondra's weird obsequiousness that was triggering it. I knew exactly how she'd constructed me in that splitting, splintering borderline mind of hers. Lacking a stable sense of self, Borderlines tend to become whatever's expected of them, and so it was dangerous for us to be around each other. We kept playing into each other's expectations of bully and victim. When the world stopped falling apart, I was really going to have to talk to Alvin about the idiocy of rooming two random Borderlines together.

I undid the excessive locks on the front door and let myself out onto the porch. It was cool enough to justify my hoodie, which is about as wintry as L.A. gets. Song had recently had someone clear the leaves from the yard, and she'd bought a couple of cheap rocking chairs to replace the rotting love seat that had parked there for who knew how long. Neighbors had been complaining, and Song knew it wouldn't do to draw too much attention.

I settled into a rocking chair to await Song's return and took all of two calming breaths before I saw her goddamned crow.

It had been October when he'd smashed into a tree or another crow or whatever dumb thing he'd done when he and eleventy billion of his brothers had been driven to a frenzy by Queen Shiverlash. Three months, and still the little turd *walked* around the yard, waiting for more scraps from Song. He cocked his creepy head at me and stared.

There is nothing worse than knowing you're paranoid but having no control over it, and this crow had been driving me straight-up bonkers. I couldn't get over the fact that even though the rest of the flock had dispersed as soon as they'd finished gorging on the carnage, this one *would not leave for love or money*. Ostensibly Shiverlash was on our side—or at least on my side, since she saw me as her liberator and fellow revolutionary—but was it possible she'd left a little spy?

Or what if Dame Belinda were using it somehow? She had access to all sorts of magic. The Seelie Queen and the Unseelie King were still firmly on her side, since they were both *sidhe* and Dame Belinda was heavily invested in the idea of *sidhe* being in charge of everything. I had no idea if fey magic could allow a human to look through a bird's eyes, but it didn't seem any more far-fetched than any of the other crap I'd seen magic do.

I took a deep breath and forced myself to focus on my current problem, which was getting an answer to my concerns about Arcadia's restroom facilities. Waiting for Song was too passive to keep me calm, and she'd never been to Arcadia anyway.

Caryl would know, but even as I slipped my phone out of my pocket I reminded myself that it might be too soon to text her. Tjuan had taken a long lunch and invited her over for birthday cake; she'd left just a couple of hours ago. I had to be so careful with her.

My boss had been pretty easy to deal with when she'd been stuffing all her emotions into an iguana-size invisible dragon, but it becomes a bit harder to use one's familiar as a constant emotional crutch once you realize he's actually sentient and might want to do other stuff with his life.

Elliott was still with Caryl constantly, still acted as her familiar in many respects, but now she was trying to deal with her emotions on her own via therapy and, to be honest, not doing much better at it than I was. She had a huge crush on me, and I didn't exactly *not* have a crush on her, but I had a lot more experience to clue me in that it was a bad idea. Texting her two hours after we'd been together seemed like a mixed signal.

But she had answers, and I needed them, so I did it anyway.

U there? Have a q

We need to talk regardless, came her immediate reply, scrupulously spelled and formatted as always. *I shall come to the Residence.*

Uh-oh. Nice move, Millie.

2

I was still sitting on the porch when Caryl arrived, her short, well-groomed curls appearing a dark olive-blond in the romantic light of L.A.'s golden hour. Elliott was perched on the shoulder of her brown blazer; he'd gotten good at projecting his chosen image into multiple minds. More than about three, though, and he started losing his wings or tail at random.

Elliott was the first to greet me, which meant he wasn't holding her emotions for her; he always stayed mute when playing the role of trauma container.

"Is it all right," he asked me, "if I go inside to visit Caveat?" He'd adopted a voice of his own in recent months, a cute cartoonish thing that still retained a touch of Caryl's rasp.

It took me a minute to remember that Caveat was what our shy little house spirit was calling herself. "Sure," I said. "She's probably lonely."

Elliott spread his batlike wings and made it look as though he were flying through the closed window behind us into the house. He liked these little presentational touches. The nature of the construct Caryl used to confine him ironically gave him more freedom of movement than unbound spirits had in this world; he could move through and perceive anything within a sort of "shouting distance" of Caryl.

Elliott had been trying for three months to recruit more spirits to our cause, because their cooperation was necessary if we wanted to cast spells humanely. So far Caveat was the only taker.

We'd had access to a whole book full of bound wraiths that might have been interested in helping us if we'd explained that we were trying to end spirit slavery, but we'd foolishly let Dame Belinda flounce out of that last meeting with all but one of them in her purse, and the only person—well, manticore— who knew all their true names had exploded in our front yard, so we had no way of calling them back. The last wraith, an unrepentant murderer calling itself Qualm, had been possessing an unlinked human facade before the rebellion. Belinda had explained that much, and we'd assumed her people had somehow trapped it in there, since it had made no move to escape.

Unfortunately, we'd assumed wrong. Caryl had thrown the incarnated Qualm into the basement of Residence Five (Neither Tjuan nor I wanted it anywhere near us), and after a couple of weeks of playing the sullen prisoner, the thing had one day just vanished.

Let me tell you, there is nothing more awkward than an empty facade. They don't breathe, they don't blink . . . but they don't get that waxy corpse look, either, and they stay unnervingly *warm*. Since we couldn't risk any uninitiated people seeing this inexplicable phenomenon, the Residence Five guys dragged it through the LA5 Gate. Once it was in Arcadia, they set fire to it to make sure Qualm couldn't "reactivate" it.

The poor handling of Qualm was a huge source of tension

between Alvin and Caryl, what with Qualm having murdered Alvin's best friend and all. Alvin was hugely suspicious of Caveat, since she'd shown up offering to help a few weeks after Qualm's disappearance. But Caveat was fey, and therefore couldn't lie, and she'd said that the first she'd heard of the Arcadia Project was when Elliott had told her about it a few days before.

Because prolonged stillness was torturous for a spirit, and because they couldn't move on their own on this side of the Gate, Caveat usually cast herself onto a cat collar, which we placed on the Residence Four mascot, Monty, much to his annoyance.

"Does she seem unhappy?" Caryl asked, context suggesting she meant the lonely little spirit. My boss seemed almost shy as she climbed the porch steps.

"She says she's fine," I said, "but she's hard to read. She's certainly cooperative. She's done everything we've asked so far. Even made herself into a ward when Song hired cleaners, to keep them from going upstairs."

Caryl sat down in the other rocking chair and drew in a slow breath. She wasn't flushed, but her fingers were curled inward, not quite fists. Stress level 5: Tense. I had a whole system, borrowed from my therapist, Dr. Davis, to monitor her, because right now her moods were even more dangerous than my own. After months of study, I knew all her tells.

"Are there bathrooms in Arcadia?" I blurted before she could start in on whatever Personal Unburdening she was going to try this week. The contents of her mind were fascinating, but there was only so much I could take.

My question drew her up short, as I'd expected, and

knocked her down to a level 4: Alert. I kind of missed the days when she'd been mysterious.

"No," she said, lowering herself tentatively into the other chair. "Fey biology does not work the same way as ours."

"Didn't Claybriar use our restroom before he left last time?"

"He was using his human facade, and he had drunk three caffè mochas."

"That was a fun day," I said, trying to cover a renewed spike of anxiety. "Who knew the Seelie King became a five-year-old after a certain amount of caffeine?"

"Is there a reason you're asking this?"

"Just curious." I no longer wanted to think about it at all, since the answer was exactly what I'd feared. I let my gaze drift across the street to the row of pastel Victorian homes, their perfect lawns and gardens that made Residence Four look like a mangy mongrel at Westminster. "What is it you wanted to talk about this time? Love, or war?"

She gave me a wry half smile. "War," she said.

I managed not to say *thank God* out loud. "How's the effort going?"

"As of today Tjuan and Inaya have officially abandoned plans to make the Gate at Valiant Studios functional."

"Damn it," I said. "Why? I thought Valiant was key to our strategy. Financially, arcanely, the whole nine yards."

"It was, but Inaya and Foxfeather have not been each other's Echoes long enough to serve as builders, despite their unusually strong bond. And even if they could, it seems the Gate can't be made operable by merely removing pieces, as we'd initially surmised. We'd have to add new materials, and the Medial Vessel is locked down in London, of course."

"The Medial Vessel?"

"To oversimplify: a container of infinite capacity."

"Is that the thing Alvin was trying to get someone in New Delhi to smuggle to him in November?" That hadn't worked out; it seemed everyone on the planet was afraid to incur Dame Belinda's wrath.

"Yes," she said. "He's still a bit obsessed with its loss. Gates can't be built without it, which means our Project will be limited to those Gates already existing."

"And if someone manages to damage them, we can't repair."

"Precisely."

"A Bag of Holding, though, wow. Dame Belinda could use that to screw with us in all sorts of ways."

Caryl examined one of her gloves. She still wore them out of habit, said she felt naked without them. "Likely not," she said. "The Vessel is another of those ancient artifacts whose construction secrets are lost, and it's so vital to our Gates that Barker has always been strict about limiting its use." Caryl had stopped calling her Dame Belinda around the same time she'd found out that the woman was responsible for her unspeakable childhood trauma.

"I think all bets are off right now," I said. "Someone who knows more about this than I do might want to consider how she could use it to fuck with us."

"Fair enough," said Caryl. Still at a 4, though. Which was weird.

"Why are you so calm?" I said. "So far I've heard nothing but bad news."

That half smile again, this time a little smug. "I was saving the good news for last. King Winterglass has agreed to meet with us on Monday."

"Uhh," I said. "This is good news how? Last time I saw him, he exploded Brand and then helped corner my Echo into becoming king out of pure spite."

Caryl pushed up the sleeve of her blazer, exposing a forearm still riddled with ugly pale pink scars. "As you may recall, he 'exploded Brand' to save my life."

"That wasn't Brand's fault."

"There wasn't exactly time for debate. My point is that I find it very difficult to imagine that His Majesty will be able to look me in the eye and tell me that we're on our own."

"You think you can win him over to our side?" Suddenly I started to put together what she was getting at. At the moment we had the Queen of the Unseelie and the King of the Seelie on our side. If she could turn Winterglass . . . "We'd have the whole Unseelie Court. She'd never dare fuck with us if it would piss those guys off."

"More than just that," Caryl said. "Her Project would have no access to Unseelie magic whatsoever. She'd be forced to cooperate with us just to get permission to interact with anyone in the Court."

"What would she need Unseelie magic for anyway?"

"Not all inspiration is uplifting and beautiful, Millie. Fear and anger, channeled through human restraint and ingenuity, can be a powerful force for change. Some of the greatest artists in history have had Unseelie Echoes. King Winterglass himself—"

"Dostoyevsky, I remember, yeah. I get it. So suppose we get him. Suppose Belinda stops threatening to bring us into line and honestly lets us run our own show over here. No one's told me how we're actually planning on doing that."

I watched her climb instantly to a 6: Stressed. Oops. "You've been with us for three months," she said. "I'm not obligated to bring you in to every discussion."

"I know you aren't obligated," I said in as soothing a tone as I could manage. "I'm not yelling at you for keeping things from me. I'm asking you to give me at least a general idea, now, so I can help."

Still at a 6—anything above 5 meant a flush started to creep into her cheeks, but her hands weren't shaking yet—she took a deep breath and considered for a moment. "New Orleans would remain as the United States headquarters, as it is the most central of the Gate cities. But we'd be setting up Valiant Studios as a new international hub."

I sucked in a breath between my teeth. "You don't just want to cooperate with her. You want to replace her. Does she know this?"

"Not unless Alvin has told her. You are the third person to know."

"What makes us qualified?"

"We're not, particularly. But we're also not evil and insane. If we can get more of the world to believe our side of the story, we'll have a wider pool of people to choose from to take her place."

"Are we having any luck with that?"

"Alvin says that Mexico City and New Delhi may be persuadable—Nayantara in particular would be a tremendous international leader—but as of now they both fear they'd simply get destroyed along with us if they show sympathy."

"Not Toronto?"

Caryl shook her head. "Dominic and Tracy have always been very close. Dom would never turn against New York."

"And Alvin can't convince New York."

"Barker has done quite a number on them. Also, Alvin worked in New York in his youth, when he was a bit less . . . stable, and Tracy was there too."

I sighed and raked a hand back through my hair. "If we have the Unseelie Court, though?"

"Other nations will line up behind us in droves," she said. "Even the ones who dislike us. They all need their Unseelie Echoes."

"I can't believe we're pinning our hopes on King Puppykiller."

Her flush deepened, and I saw her hands begin to tremble, just a bit. We'd reached 7: Frazzled. "He—he cares for me, deeply. If we make this personal, we may be able to overcome his complacency."

"If you say so," I said. "So I assume you're here because you want me to attend the meeting?"

"It . . . it would help me to have you there." She looked at her hands.

"Just use Elliott," I said.

"I will. But . . . Millie, you've been the source of our best ideas over the past several months. I value you tremendously, and not just because . . . because . . ."

Her unspoken words pushed me up out of my rocking chair and away. "I know," I said, putting distance between us.

"I don't expect anything from you," she said quietly. "But I also can't change what I feel."

I slid both hands into my hair, massaging my scalp, trying to mitigate the disproportionate panic I felt rising into my throat. I didn't want to be the center of her universe right now; I didn't want my every word examined, every flicker of my face interpreted and reinterpreted. Not now.

"What should we do?" said Caryl.

"I don't know," I said, turning back to face her. "What I know is what we don't do, which is keep talking about it right now."

"Do you anticipate a better time?" The question would have worked better in her old tone, dry and emotionless. Now it just sounded petulant.

"Don't push me, Caryl," I said. "I'm serious. Contract or no, you know I'll just bail, regardless of consequences. Look at my history. You know that's what I do."

Caryl gave me a long look, then got up from her rocking chair. Elliott reappeared on her shoulder as she walked back to her SUV.

"Caryl," I said, gritting my teeth. I didn't want to talk anymore, but I hated her walking out.

"I expect you at the meeting on Monday," she said, without looking back. She went around to the driver's side, got in, and slammed the door.

"Happy birthday," I said.

I wanted to chase after her; I wanted to break her windows; I wanted all kinds of things, but I just leaned back against the house and closed my eyes and turned my attention to my breathing. In and out, in and out.

Her car started; I heard the tires squeal as she pulled out. Shit. Driving at a 7 or 8, not good. She was going to get herself killed.

Almost before I realized I'd done it, I brought both fists up and struck myself, twice, knuckles to forehead, hard enough for the pain to linger like the high sharp note of a bell.

I went back to the rocker and sat on my hands, breathed some more. Elliott would realize she wasn't driving safely. He'd ask to help. She'd let him. She wasn't stupid. And even if she did crash her car, it wouldn't be my fault. She was a grown woman. Sort of.

I couldn't seem to calm down, which only upset me more. I hadn't been this bad in months. Knowing I'd been doing better and then watching myself slide backward made my self-loathing all the more intense. The white-hot need I felt to punish myself, to physically demonstrate how very deeply I knew I was horrible—it was like the voice of the siren queen.

I opened my eyes and found myself meeting the beady gaze of that damned crow. It cocked its head to one side.

"I don't have any food," I said to it shakily.

"Caw," it said. And then strode decisively toward me.

The surprise was enough to shock me out of my spiral. The stupid bird hopped right onto the porch steps and stared at me.

"Nevermore," it said.

No. It just said, "Caw." But six of one, half a dozen of the other, at this point in my delusion.

"Can you understand what I'm saying?" I asked it. "Did you hear me say 'food'?"

"Caw." It lifted its wings abortively, then let them fall. Almost a shrug. Except it wasn't. It was a bird being a bird, and I was crazy.

Unless I wasn't?

I resisted the urge to hit myself in the head again. Instead I stood up and went into the house where the damn thing wouldn't be able to stare at me anymore.

3

Tjuan didn't get home until around nine thirty that night. I desperately needed his take on what to do about my suit, because I knew until I solved that problem my dysphoria was just going to escalate, but I knew better than to jump right on him the second he walked in the door.

Phil knew better too, but didn't seem to care. Phil was the grouchy bearded pianist who'd been dating Tjuan's previous partner when she died. He was also the second-highest ranking agent in the house, after Tjuan. Tjuan and Phil seemed to have a long history, but as neither was particularly fond of opening up to me, I didn't know much about it. Their familiarity made them talk in elliptical half thoughts to each other, making eavesdropping pointless.

"Did you sign them?" Phil asked, literally before Tjuan had even finished putting his keys back in his pocket. I was sitting patiently on the living room couch, scratching behind Monty the cat's missing ear.

"Fuck off," said Tjuan.

"It's been three weeks, Teej."

"Sign them your own damned self."

"Gotta be the senior agent."

Ah, that's what this was all about. Alvin had promoted Tjuan over Phil in October, and Phil was still pissy about it.

"Just file an X-2," said Tjuan.

"X-2s aren't worth the paper they're printed on right now."

"Deal with it, Phil. Find a way. I don't have time for this shit."

I had no idea what they were talking about—Caryl had known better than to assign me to paperwork duties—but whatever it was sent them both back to their separate rooms in a huff. Phil shut his door pretty hard.

I looked down at Monty, who was purring fitfully, like an old-timey pencil sharpener. "This seems like a good moment to hit him with my thing, right?" I said to him. I'd taken to talking to the cat recently, since Caveat was usually bound to his collar and I figured she got lonely.

I waited a few moments, then put Monty on the floor, headed back to Tjuan's room, and gently knocked on the door.

"Go away," Tjuan said.

"It's me."

"I know."

"Tjuan, how do you pee in Arcadia?"

There was a moment of silence. Then he said, "I whip out my dick, like everywhere else."

"Tjuan, I'm serious."

The door opened just wide enough for my partner to glare at me with merciless obsidian eyes. "Millie," he said very slowly, in the sort of three-deep-breaths tone you use with children. "I . . . do . . . not . . . have . . . time . . . for . . . your . . . shit . . . this . . . evening."

"I'm having a bad spell, Tjuan, and I just—I just feel like if I had an answer to this problem I would sleep better. I'm chewing on it and I can't let go. I've tried, but I just—I'm stuck on it."

He exhaled, rubbed a hand over his eyes, and leaned against the door frame. "Stuck on what exactly?"

"They've made me a suit, like a diving suit, sort of, that I can wear to keep spellwork safe in Arcadia. But . . . you know, it zips up the back, and I—it—"

"You'd have to peel the whole thing down," he said. This was a thing he'd started to do recently when I was fumbling. Part of me hated being interrupted, but another part of me liked being understood, anticipated.

"Also," I said, "I can't really . . . squat? Not anymore."

"Get one of those portable toilets hikers use, fold it up and carry it with you in a backpack or something. They're like thirty bucks."

"Oh." I looked at him in astonishment. "But . . . I'd still have to get naked."

"Why's your suit gotta be all one piece? Just grab some scissors, snip snip, pants and a shirt."

We stared at each other for seven cold seconds.

"Okay," I said.

"Now will you leave me the fuck alone?"

I smiled a little. "Hard day?"

He snorted. "When I showed up at the writers' room, someone had taped a sign above the door that said 'Abandon Hope, All Ye Who Enter Here.'"

"That's . . . pointed. What's going on?"

"The usual. Ever since that demon-dog of Naderi's kicked the bucket, she's grown three rows of teeth to replace his."

"Oh, she's always had those."

Tjuan and his boss, Parisa Naderi, had never been best buddies; neither had she and I, for that matter. If not for their connection via the Arcadia Project, Tjuan would probably still have been making unsteady money doing uncredited script rewrites. Naderi herself certainly wouldn't have been elevated to partnership in Valiant Studios if we hadn't found her Echo—and then promptly gotten him killed. Technically it was King Winterglass who'd exploded Brand, but if you traced the tragedy back far enough, it was pretty much my fault. My sickening guilt over it had kept me from being the comforting friend I'd hoped to be to her afterward.

Unsurprisingly, relations between Naderi and the Project had been tense after that. But Tjuan, better known in Hollywood as T. J. Miller, was a damned good writer, and Naderi hadn't risen to the pinnacle of power in the biz by failing to recognize talent.

"Any chance of you taking the day off on Monday?" I asked him.

He let out a sharp "ha" that wasn't quite a laugh. "I'm sorry," he said. "I just heard 'any chance of you taking your thumb off that grenade?' Why the hell would you ask me that?"

"Caryl's arranged a meeting with King Winterglass," I said. "She wants me there, but—" I felt my eyes start to sting, gritted my teeth, fought it. "Tjuan, I'm really not doing well. I know it seems like I'm okay—"

"It really doesn't."

"—because I'm not bursting into fountains of tears and self-diagnosing fatal illnesses like the new girl—"

"She's been here two months; you know her name."

"—but inside I'm a series of small constant explosions. I'm afraid that if something goes wrong in that meeting—"

"Fine," he said. "I'll be there. Now please leave me alone." And he closed the door in my face.

Just before dawn on Sunday I woke to find a gorgeous Greek woman in my bed. I was less excited about this than I might normally have been, because I recognized the facade. It had been made by Prince Fettershock of the Unseelie Court just before that fateful meeting with Dame Belinda when everything had gone pear-shaped. It belonged to the improbably named faux-human Phrixa Vourdoulas, a.k.a. Shiverlash, Beast Queen of the Unseelie Court.

She was sitting on the edge of my new queen-size mattress—which had until this moment never had an actual queen on it—staring at me with unsettling lichen-colored eyes. Her true form was blind, and so she hadn't quite gotten the hang of polite eye contact. I think visual input unsettled her, though she'd learned to use it to help navigate our world. In her own world, she sensed things much as her friends the spirits did, but without magic, our world was a wasteland to those extra senses.

Aside from the staring, she wasn't actually being rude. Not that she gave a damn for Arcadia Project protocol anyway, but monarchs were allowed to come and go through the Gates whenever they pleased without filing paperwork. And my door hadn't been locked, since it wasn't usually necessary. I was going to have to reexamine that assumption.

A slender and slightly paler version of Elliott appeared on the Unseelie Queen's shoulder. Caveat. I felt a frisson of unease.

The little spirit had caused everyone in the house to shit bricks a month ago by almost perfectly copying the construct spell Caryl had invented to contain Elliott. She'd used it to escape Monty's collar when he fell asleep for too long. The only difference was that she'd replaced Caryl with Monty as the center of the construct's travel range. This was beyond astonishing. We'd already known she had a particular talent for copying spells, but constructs weren't supposed to be possible for fey at all, only for humans. Caryl had told me this when I first met Elliott, and it had been reiterated in my basic training.

"I just copied Elliott" was Caveat's only explanation. She hadn't even realized it was supposed to be impossible. And even after we told her so, she didn't seem bothered or motivated to explain.

"I'm here to translate," she said now. Even her voice was similar to Elliott's, but she used a more casual cadence—I assumed because it was the kind of English she heard most often at the Residence. "Queen Shiverlash wants to talk to you."

I didn't have to ask why Caveat was suddenly doing the queen's bidding; Shiverlash had always had a deeply intimate relationship with all of the spirits, and Caveat was Unseelie to boot, which gave her no choice but to obey any command the queen gave her.

"What can I do for Her Majesty?" I asked Caveat, pretending my stomach hadn't just tied itself into a sailor's knot.

"If it's okay," said Caveat, "I'll transmit your words into her mind and help her answer you directly."

"Whatever you prefer," I said, rubbing the gook out of my eyes and trying to claw my hair into order.

Caveat seemed to vanish, and Queen Shiverlash took on a distant, intent look that reminded me of the alien way she'd scented the air when I'd first released her into this world.

"You are in danger," she said at last. Even her human facade had a mesmerizing voice, deep and smooth. "The human queen prepares to strike."

She meant Dame Belinda. "What have you heard?"

"Only whispers," she said. "But the time to act is now. We must free the spirits, and put an end to the *sidhe*."

I sighed and massaged my forehead. I had to be careful here, and I was still barely awake. "What exactly is it you want me to do?" I asked.

"You are to release, with your iron touch, every spirit the usurper Winterglass and his ilk have imprisoned."

"Wait, what?" My spine straightened. "We're starting in Darkest Unseelie Wherever? I figured you'd go after Dawnrowan first."

"I trust your faun Claybriar to deal with the Seelie Queen," said Shiverlash. "But there is no one fighting the usurpers in my land but I. I need you, and so you will be under my protection. Together we shall make of the false king's realm a shattered ruin."

"That sounds great," I said, remembering the way she'd ripped open Parisa Naderi's face a few months ago. "I'm all for it, absolutely. I love shattered ruins. But here's the thing. I kind of need Winterglass to think I'm on his side for the next little while."

Something cold and terrifying flashed through her pale eyes. "To deceive him?" she said. "I envy humans this power. But to what end? Do you have a plan to betray him?"

"Sort of," I said. "It's complicated. But basically, if Dame Belinda thinks that both you and he are on our side, she'll have to negotiate with us."

"The usurper Winterglass will never join you unless you renounce me and support the enslavement of spirits. And if you throw in with the *sidhe*, our alliance is at an end."

"Yes, I remember our deal," I said. "But all I need is for Dame Belinda to *believe* that the whole Unseelie Court is behind us. I swear on my life, my goal is to free the spirits. It's just that humans sometimes have to do things a little more indirectly. You're thousands of years old or something, right? Can you not wait a little while longer?"

"It is not my lifespan that is in question," said Shiverlash, "but the lifespan of my trust in you, human." She rose, and I could almost see those great oily black wings of hers spreading menacingly behind her. But she was only human, for the moment. "Watch for my return," she said. "This is the second time I have allowed you to defer my vengeance. There will not be a third."

And then she left me there wishing, not for the first time, that I had never let Caryl Vallo tempt me out of the loony bin.

4

The meeting took place at the Omni hotel in a small meeting space they sometimes made available to us during off hours. The Arcadia Project only had a couple dozen official employees in Los Angeles, but since we sometimes had random needs like fake uniforms, on-site medical care, crime scene cleanup, et cetera, we were of necessity supported by a network of businesspeople willing to not ask too many questions.

The recessed lighting and pastrylike color scheme of the meeting room were incongruously soothing as we waited at a white-draped table for the monarch to make his appearance.

Alvin Lamb was newly arrived from New Orleans, and from the look of him he'd taken a red-eye. His silver hair and goatee were perfectly groomed and his pinstriped button-down pristine, but his face looked as though it had been punched gently in a few places. He sat next to me, Tjuan on my other side, making Alvin seem even shorter by comparison.

The King of the Unseelie Court was fashionably late. Despite my irritation, I had to resist the impulse to rise to my feet when he entered. Whatever variety of pain in the ass he'd been to me, he'd reigned for a century and a half, and before that he'd been Dostoyevsky's Echo.

His scepter of office was disguised as an antique walking stick, and as always he wore a dramatic dark coat. He used the facade his son had designed for him in the fall; Prince Fettershock lived mostly in Hong Kong and had made his father into a *wuxia* hero with flowing raven locks.

"We meet again," Winterglass said to Caryl, because God forbid anyone from the Unseelie Court should sound like anything other than a Bond villain.

Tjuan and I remained seated, but across the table from us Caryl rose, elegant as always in a trim charcoal-gray blazer.

"Your Majesty," she said. Wisely she'd requested that Elliott take over his old role for the meeting. He was not currently visible other than via the complete lack of emotion showing on Caryl's face.

"Please be seated," said Winterglass as though it were he who had called the meeting.

Once the king ascertained that the chairs were made of wood and therefore unable to disrupt his facade, he lowered himself gracefully into a seat at the opposite end of the table from Alvin. As soon as Winterglass had settled, Tjuan got up to close the door; it had been propped open so that the fey wouldn't have to touch it. The handle seemed to be made of brass rather than spell-shattering steel, but I'd been led to understand that most metals gave fey a bit of a queasy feeling regardless.

Winterglass did not wait for Tjuan to return to his chair before speaking.

"I shall not waste time," he said. "I am here to warn you, as acknowledgment of my part in the chaos that was released into both worlds last autumn, that this meeting is the last chance you will receive to come back to the Project peacefully."

"We had hoped," said Caryl, her voice like dark velvet, "that *you* would come back to the Project."

Winterglass arched a brow, giving Caryl the most elegant *bitch, please* look I'd ever seen.

"Let's look at this logically," said Alvin in his warm, friendly way, his eyes crinkling at the corners as though he and the Unseelie King were old friends. "London has historically been the center of the Project's operations, but only because no one has ever questioned it. For you, it makes no sense. London is just a Gate away from the seat of Seelie power. Los Angeles is every bit as powerful an international travel hub, just as profound a center of popular culture, but without the geographical bias toward one Court or the other."

"Your Gates open onto Skyhollow," said Winterglass coolly.

"That land was granted to a Seelie duke by Queen Dawnrowan. Who is, again, based in Daystrike. The Daystrike/London monopoly has slanted the entire Project in favor of the Seelie. Wouldn't you like to see that change?"

"The Seelie are a nuisance at worst," said Winterglass with an air of weary patience. "They are not my largest problem."

"Because they're led by *sidhe*," I said. "As long as the *sidhe* control everything, you're happy."

Tjuan cleared his throat; that was enough to shut me up. But the king's wintry gaze came to rest on me, making me shiver.

"It is easy to demonize those who hold power you feel you deserve," he said. "It is easy to ignore the ordered backdrop

that those in power have wrested from chaos. You pretend outrage at the *sidhe* method of spell casting even as you reap ben-
efits that would have been impossible without it."

"You can *ask* spirits, you know," I said, taking care to keep
my voice calm, deferential. "They can do all sorts of wonderful
spells when they aren't coerced."

"And they can abandon those spells whenever they choose.
In some cases this could be disastrous."

"We're getting a bit off topic," said Alvin uneasily. "We're
not here to solve the spirit problem right now. We're here to
try to find common—"

"But isn't that the whole reason we split off in the first
place?" I said incredulously. "Because we realized London was
fine with enslaving an entire species?"

"I can't speak for everyone," said Alvin, "but the reason *I*
split with Dame Belinda was that she ordered the abduction
and prolonged torture of a human infant. You're aware of this,
King Winterglass?"

"I am aware that she has been so accused by your faction.
But I am not particularly skilled at working out which humans
are lying."

My blood pressure suddenly skyrocketed. I turned my
focus to Tjuan sitting next to me, glanced at his still, impassive
face, tried to keep my mouth shut.

"Your Majesty," said Caryl, her voice smoothing over the
tension in the air. "Have you truly allowed Barker to convince
you that she, and not I, would tell you the truth?"

His eyes turned to her and held; something in his expression snagged at my heart.

"Your people started this war," he said quietly. "Every other

Gate city across the world stands with London. All of the Arcadia Project's most valuable resources are under London's control."

"Including you," Caryl said gently. "Do you not see? You could be an even more powerful resource for our side. Millie has earned the loyalty of Queen Shiverlash by freeing her, and if you joined us, we'd have the whole of the Unseelie. The other nations would have no choice but to negotiate with us."

Winterglass hesitated for a moment. "Understand," he said finally, "that your words are persuasive. Know that while I think you are foolish to traffic with the sorts of creatures you have begun to befriend, I respect your intelligence, and I do believe that you mean no harm. It grieves me personally that we are on opposite sides of this. I wish—"

"If it *grieves* you so much," I interrupted, "why refuse? Are the fucking *sidhe* politics more important to you than what happened to a girl you supposedly—"

Tjuan laid a hand on my forearm, just briefly, arresting me mid-sentence. It was the first time he had ever touched me voluntarily, and only after that shocked me out of my anger spiral did I notice that the king had risen from his seat.

Winterglass stared me down. My blood pounded in my ears.

"I'm sorry," I said.

I wasn't even sure what I was apologizing for, but when I lowered my eyes, the king once again took his chair.

"If it were merely my politics," he said dryly, "I might be swayed. I have not reigned as long as I have by refusing to adapt. But among Dame Belinda's resources are two things I hold dear."

"What things?" I asked carefully when he didn't elaborate.

"Suffice it to say I cannot anger her any more than she can anger me while I have the Unseelie nobility united under my command. What was the phrase Americans used, when your people and mine threatened to annihilate each other?"

His people? The Russians, he had to mean; his palace was located at the Arcadian equivalent of Saint Petersburg.

"Mutually assured destruction?" ventured Alvin, who'd been alive at the time.

"Precisely. Even if Dame Belinda were not destined for victory, I still would not dare betray her." He turned, then reached across an empty seat for Caryl's gloved hand.

To my surprise, she gave it to him, her face expressionless.

"Child," he said to her softly, in a way that suggested that everyone else in the room had disappeared. "Come to my Court. Do not make me watch what she will do to you."

"You already have," said Caryl calmly. "Does the lingering magic of my blood not allow you to remember? A filthy wooden crate? A seven-year-old child screaming until her throat bled? That was my childhood, and Dame Belinda its architect. You betrayed her, without knowing it, by rescuing me. If you stand with her now, I cannot stand beside you."

Winterglass squeezed his eyes shut as though a fire truck were roaring past, then bent over Caryl's hand, pressing it fervently to his lips. By the time he released her, his expression was cool, distant.

"So be it," he said. He rose and turned for the door, not even waiting for one of us to open it. There must have been some steel in the handle after all, because for a moment we saw his true form, great pallid antlers rising from the smooth round skull, skeletal wings folded neatly against his naked ribcage. Then his hand was on the wood of the door, slender and beautiful once again, and he was gone with a swish of his black coat.

"Well," said Tjuan. "We're fucked."

"I'll confess that was disappointing," said Caryl.

Alvin seemed deep in thought.

"What about Queen Dawnrowan?" I said. "She's not *against* us so much as she's *for* Dame Belinda, and one of her dukes has already pledged himself to our cause. If we can turn her, wouldn't having the entire Seelie Court serve the same purpose?"

Alvin narrowed his eyes at me. "What motivation could she or any of the *sidhe* possibly have to betray Dame Belinda? Duke Skyhollow and Baroness Foxfeather only swore fealty to Claybriar because the guy happens to be staying at Skyhollow Estate, and it would have been awkward otherwise."

And, I was pretty sure, because they were all sleeping together, but that was neither here nor there.

"Can't we just explain to the queen that we're the good guys, freeing slaves and whatnot?" I said. "Aren't Seelie supposed to be *good*?"

"They're creatures of beauty and joy," said Alvin, "but that doesn't mean they're selfless. Fey on the whole are driven largely by self-interest."

"The queen's also *very* interested in Claybriar," I said. "We could use that."

Tjuan snorted. "You just want to see your Echo."

"I do. But it's worth trying, isn't it? Winterglass isn't the only one who's making it sound like Dame Belinda's about to go on the attack. Queen Shiverlash said the very same thing yesterday. What could it hurt to try?"

"It could hurt my job," said Tjuan. "I'm working half a day today, and now I ask for more time off?"

"I wasn't saying you should come."

He and I were both aware how improbable it was that he had gotten a job in entertainment again, much less landed supervising producer on a hit series, after his last writers' room had witnessed his possession by an evil spirit.

Tjuan shook his head slowly. "I'm not letting you near another fey monarch on your own."

"Clay will be here."

"He was here when you set loose the Beast Queen, and if I hadn't been here today, Winterglass would have snapped your damn neck. You piss people off, Roper. The only things you've got going for you are that you're good at solving puzzles and you shut up when I tell you to."

"Come, or don't," I said. "But don't use work as an excuse for this meeting not to happen."

"If it's happening, I'm there. But you've got to give me permission to tell Naderi why, so I don't lose my damn job."

"We can figure something out," said Alvin. "Naderi knows at least a little about what we're dealing with, and if that's not enough, I can get Inaya to lean on her."

It was happening! Claybriar would be coming here! I felt as though a weight had fallen away. If my Echo couldn't fix me, fix all of this, no one could.

"Who were you thinking about that time?" asked Zach later in the evening, his voice lazy in the dark. I was sprawled on a cheap mattress on the floor of his bedroom; he could have afforded better if he cared. He set his teeth into the inside of my thigh—the right one, since I hadn't removed my prosthetic legs, and the AK socket on the left didn't expose enough skin to be worth a nibble.

I squirmed and gave his thinning hair a little scratch as though he were a dog. "Would you believe," I said drowsily, "the Fairy King?"

"Wha-at?" His laugh was a puff of warm air against my skin. "Oberon?"

I was surprised he even knew that much. I hadn't told him word one about the Arcadia Project, including my complicated relationships with my boss and my Echo. "Actually," I said, "his name's Brian."

Zach laughed again; his laugh was my favorite of the handful of things I liked about him. "Brian the Fairy King," he repeated, then kissed his way up over my bony hip, my scarred ribs. I frowned. He'd been taking his time lately, lingering over tertiary parts of my anatomy.

I closed my eyes as he settled himself on top of me.

"Hey," he said quietly.

I opened my eyes. In the dark I could just make out the leftward list of his nose.

"Look at me this time," he said with such confidence that I felt a flutter of excitement. It faded quickly, though.

"No," I said, and closed my eyes again.

He rolled off me onto his back.

"What?" I said sharply. "This is how it works."

"I figured things would be different by now," he said to the ceiling.

"I didn't promise some expiration date for my issues, Zach. Come on, it's your turn. Otherwise it feels like I'm using you."

"Like you say, that's how it works."

"We're supposed to be using *each other*. This way I just feel like an asshole."

"Good."

I rolled off the mattress, cat quick despite my aching bones, groped for my clothes on the floor.

"I'm sorry," Zach said. "That was shitty of me. You've got enough problems."

"Fuck you and your pity," I said. "Give my best to your hand."

"Whoa," he said. Then: "Nah, I guess that's fair."

"Fuck fair," I said. "Nothing's fair."

I got dressed without turning on the lights and then left. I waited for my cab at the edge of the street, shirt inside out under a chilly, starless January night.

5

If we'd known what was coming, there's no way Tjuan would have volunteered to open a vein for that meeting. It wouldn't have made a difference, but it's the *principle* of the thing.

King Winterglass had snacked on baby blood for long enough to untangle his thoughts pretty permanently, and King Claybriar had his Echo to ground him, but Queen Dawnrowan was a typical *sidhe*: coherent enough to lead the fey, but not quite coherent enough to hold a productive conversation without the "intoxicating" influence of iron-laced blood. Basically, Tjuan's job was to get her drunk in reverse. Last time we'd met with Dawnrowan, I'd been the booze in the cocktail, but now I was being told that it was a bad idea for a fey to consume any one human's blood too often.

"What does it do?" I asked Caryl in the kitchen of Residence Four as Stevie removed the tourniquet from Tjuan's arm and taped a square of gauze over the inside of his elbow. Stevie's profound autism limited the types of tasks she was assigned, but she was precise with first aid and seemed unbothered by it, which made her the go-to for the otherwise unpopular job of drawing blood.

"You've seen King Winterglass," Caryl said. "It creates something like an Echo effect, though not mutual."

As Stevie moved away, Tjuan flexed his arm, testing the tape. Tjuan had nice arms, which I usually tried hard not to notice. I spent a lot of time trying not to notice things like that about people.

"Echo effect is a good thing, though."

"But it binds him to me," said Caryl as Stevie handed her the syringe and then disappeared into the back hallway. "He is drawn to me, aware of me on some background level at all times."

A casually ironic voice behind me added, "Just like Millie's always aware of me."

I strained my spine doing an about-face toward the doorway to the dining room.

King Claybriar leaned against the door frame wearing jeans, a pair of bright blue doctor's gloves, and a gray shirt with one more button undone than was strictly traditional. I made a half-muffled squeak, fumbling for the colorless latex gloves I'd stuffed into the pocket of my slacks earlier that morning. I slipped them on before crossing the room to him, and he smiled in a way that turned his dark eyes as sweet as sundae syrup.

"Good to see you, Hurricane," he said. His gloved hand went to my hair, smoothing the layered strands where I'd carefully disheveled them. I didn't mind. I stroked my fingertips over his goatee, and he dipped his head to kiss them.

"How long have you been here?" I said.

"Just a few minutes," he reassured me. "If you were saying terrible things about me, I missed it."

"I'd never insult you behind your back, Majesty."

"More fun to do it in person," he said, giving my hair a little yank. He must have seen the look in my eyes, because he took a deep breath and let go of me with the air of an alcoholic pushing away a drink.

"Who's driving?" I asked to get my mind off the many things I could never actually do without putting my Echo in a coma. Fey of importance traditionally entered through the Gate at Residence One, so another Arcadia Project employee would have the job of getting Dawnrowan to the meeting.

"I'll drive," said Caryl.

As soon as she had prepared an Arcadian screwdriver with blood and Valencia orange juice, we loaded ourselves into her SUV. Claybriar sat in the back with me and held my hand most of the way, which sounds innocent enough, but the things he was doing to my palm with the pad of his thumb were clearly calculated to dismantle higher thought. It was a nice distraction from carsickness, and from the misery that awaited me.

Claybriar's ravishing queen was already waiting in the meeting room for us when we arrived, as though striving to be the exact opposite of Winterglass in every way. Her hair was like a waterfall of eggnog over a silken dress the exact bright blue of her eyes. Laid across the table in front of her was what must have been her scepter of office, not even disguised: a twisted wooden wand with a gem-encrusted head that was just this short of garish by Earth standards.

From the way she rose when we all entered, her face drawn with mingled fury and longing, it would seem that it had been a while since she had seen her erstwhile lover.

"Drink this," said Caryl to Queen Dawnrowan by way of

greeting, briskly placing the thermos of gory OJ down in front of her. "When Alvin arrives, we'll begin."

"I won't play translator today," said Claybriar aloud, even though he didn't need to speak to communicate with a *sidhe*. "I don't want her inside my head." He placed himself at the opposite end of the table from the queen and took a seat.

He must have sent the thought to her as well, though, because she sat down as though she'd been kicked in the back of the knees. I almost felt sorry for her as I settled myself at Claybriar's right hand. Tjuan took my other side, and Caryl sat at the king's left.

"Claybriar," said Caryl. "Let your queen know she has my permission to use my mind as her lexicon, but tell her to leave everything else in there alone."

Claybriar's gaze shifted reluctantly to Dawnrowan; this time he said nothing aloud. The queen said nothing either, just drank her orange juice, her summer-sky eyes never leaving Claybriar. Alvin arrived not long after us and sat down beside the queen at her end of the table, extending his hand.

"Thank you for coming on such short notice," he said warmly. When Dawnrowan offered her hand, he drew it respectfully to his lips, making her smile. Jesus, that smile; it was all I could do not to get up and go sit in her lap. I gave my head a brisk shake and looked away. Claybriar, I noticed, was studying the recessed lighting.

"Your courtesy becomes you," said the queen in a honeyed voice. She rose and, before Alvin could get back to his feet, slipped her slender white fingers into his silver hair and bent to kiss him on the mouth.

All right, then.

Alvin looked as surprised as I felt, which was reassuring, but he didn't pull away. To be fair, who would? The queen's flaxen hair slipped over her shoulders to fall against his crisp white shirt. When she drew away, she looked directly at Claybriar. Clay was still not looking at her, which seemed to infuriate her. She fell back into her chair like a dropped bomb.

"Okay," I said, because if I hadn't said something I'd probably have started screaming. "Should we start, or should I maybe grope Tjuan a little first? Not sure of protocol."

"Millie," said Tjuan, low and stern.

"If we're finished with . . . greetings," said Caryl dryly, "perhaps we can arrive at why we are gathered. My hope is that I can facilitate a reconciliation between the King and Queen of the Seelie."

"That isn't what you told me," said Claybriar, straightening in his chair.

"It isn't what you heard," Caryl said smoothly. Elliott was on the job again. "But I did say we need to bring her to our side, which means that the two of you would need to cooperate."

"I don't see why that's a necessity," said Claybriar, eyes narrowed. "She has the *sidhe*, I have everyone else. I say we split the Seelie Court into two kingdoms. As long as we both cooperate with you, why would we even need to speak to each other? I thought our objective here was just to get her out of Dame Belinda's pocket."

"I have no loyalty to Dame Belinda," said Queen Dawnrowan. Everyone turned to stare at her.

"Why do you seem surprised?" She toyed with a strand of her hair. "Nothing ties me to her but habit, and habit is dull. I might consider another alliance, if it were worth my while."

Alvin leaned forward cautiously. "What do you require of us?"

"My goal is the same as yours," the queen said sweetly. "A united Seelie Court. Unfortunately, aside from Skyhollow and a few others, the *sidhe* refuse to bow to this new king. To have no undisputed Seelie King would break the agreement with the Unseelie Court, which is, for now, keeping the two Courts at peace. Therefore, we shall have to find a new king whom both—"

I let out such a loud noise of disgust that all eyes swiveled to me, including hers.

"Of course," I said. "Of course you'd hinge the fate of two worlds on getting the best of your ex in a lover's quarrel."

All trace of coquettishness left Queen Dawnrowan as she gazed at me with a sudden, surprising gravity. "You understand nothing of love," she said. "Or of quarrels."

I floundered for a response, found none. She turned to Alvin, something in her movement economically communicating my irrelevance.

"You have heard my terms," she said. "Allow me to choose another king, a commoner of whom the *sidhe* will approve."

"A slaver," Claybriar spat. "You want a king who won't try to free the spirits, who will have no opinion or motive other than pleasing you."

"And you are so superior?" said the queen, "You were just the same, until *that* one touched you." She gestured to me, the limpness of her wrist conveying utmost contempt.

"Don't blame this on her!" Claybriar said, leaning forward so violently that his chair made a noise of protest against the floor. "The reason I started arguing with you was that I *could*! When the commoners swore fealty, they made me a king. Your scepter lost its hold over me, and that *proves* I am your equal."

"You could have had the whole of the Court," said Dawnrowan quietly, "if you had not fought me."

"I had to," he said. "I can't just sit by—"

"What the fuck."

Tjuan, of all people. We turned to stare at him; he'd pulled his phone from his pocket to frown at the screen.

"Are we boring you?" Claybriar asked him in a deceptively casual tone.

A muscle worked in Tjuan's jaw. "It's Naderi," he said, standing and pacing to the far end of the room.

"Please excuse him," I said to Claybriar, and then turned to the queen. "It's his, uh, liege lady. I don't think she understands the gravity of this situation."

Tjuan, on the point of returning the call, turned abruptly. "No," he said. "She understands. She knows this is fate-of-the-world stuff; that's the only reason she let me come. If she's calling me right *now*, something *massive* has just hit the fan."

"Take it, then," said Alvin, "but quietly please." He turned back to Dawnrowan, ingratiating. "I apologize wholeheartedly. And I can understand why you would be reluctant to work with someone who disagrees with you so strongly on a central point of policy."

"*Policy?*" Claybriar said. "Did you just call slavery *policy*? Fuck you. Fuck you both, actually."

"Clay," I said gently, amazed and weirdly relieved that I wasn't the one tanking this meeting. My voice seemed to ground him, and he sat back in his chair, took a deep, shaky breath.

"We understand your point of view on this, Your Majesty," said Alvin to Claybriar. "And I don't disagree, on principle. But we need to take into account what it would actually mean to

Arcadia, to the Project, if we abruptly dissolve centuries' worth of—"

"*What?*" said Tjuan in a tone that made my hands go cold. For a moment I thought he was chiming in on the whole slavery thing, but when I turned to him, I saw he was talking into his phone. Something premonitory gnawed at my gut.

"I did not," he said. Calmly this time, but his eyes had gone as dead as a snake's.

"Tjuan?" I said. He just held up a hand. The gesture was so forceful that everyone at the table fell still; the thread of the meeting dissolved like wet cotton candy.

"Of course he said that," Tjuan said in a low, dangerous voice. "Fucking Tyler. He can't tell black men apart." Uh-oh, I recognized that name. Not a friend of his. "This is bullshit; I've—"

He winced and held the phone away from his ear. I could hear Naderi's shrill transports of rage, but I couldn't make out the words. Astonishingly, Tjuan ended the call and stuffed the phone back in his pocket.

"Tjuan?" I said again.

He ignored me, looking to Caryl. "I need to get back to the Residence."

"Once the meeting is concluded—" she began.

"Now," he said. He almost didn't make it to a chair before his legs gave out; he had to catch himself a little on the back of it.

I got to my feet. "Tjuan."

"I'm fine," he said, and put his elbows on the table, rested his head in his hands.

"Tjuan, you're freaking me out."

He kept his head in his hands. He was *shaking*. I resisted

the urge to go to him, put a hand on him; it wouldn't have calmed him.

"Tjuan, please," I said, feeling as though my lungs had shrunk to half their size. "Talk to me. What's going on? What was Naderi calling about?"

He looked up, eyes empty. "They say I shot a guy."

"What? Tjuan, *what*?"

"They said I robbed a liquor store near USC at noon on Saturday. The news just released a still from the security camera. It's all over the news, the Net. Tyler saw it and he called the cops."

"Bullshit!" I pulled out my phone, started searching. So did everyone else in the room with a phone; Claybriar and Dawnrowan just sat there looking confused and upstaged.

I googled and waited for the maddeningly slow hotel Wi-Fi. "Saturday at noon? That's not possible. You were at the Residence; we had cake with Caryl. And then you went straight to work, and by then it was past one. Tyler has it in for you; he saw what he wanted to see. It'll be obvious once they—"

But then the image came up. It wasn't grainy; it wasn't ambiguous. I'd been living with the guy for three months, and every bone in my body said it was *him*. Same tall, slightly slouching frame. Same cheekbones. Same large-knuckled hand wrapped around the

gun

the gun the gun the gun

"Oh my God," I whispered.

He was looking directly at the camera. Obsidian eyes with down-tilted corners, slightly asymmetrical eyebrows. Looking at the camera as if to say, *Fuck you. I don't care who knows.* Gun still pointed off camera at someone. At someone.

"Oh my God," I said again.

"I need to go home," Tjuan said.

"No," said Caryl. "Tyler identified you."

Tjuan seemed to follow Caryl's train of thought; he put his head in his hands again. I wasn't quite there yet.

"What are you saying?" I asked.

"I'm saying," said Caryl, "that if the police are speaking with Tjuan's employers, they are only a warrant away from showing up at Residence Four."

6

It hit me right about then that as bad as this was, it could have been much, much worse. If not for my freak-out about peeing in Arcadia, I wouldn't have cornered Tjuan, I wouldn't have begged him to come to that first meeting, he wouldn't have insisted on coming to this one, and he'd have been behind enemy lines at Valiant when the security photo hit the news. The cops would be on their way to Valiant right now.

"We need to get Tjuan somewhere safe, as quickly as possible," said Caryl.

Alvin glanced at Dawnrowan, then back at Caryl, frowning. "Caryl, I know this is bad, but—"

"We need to secure his safety before the police have their paperwork in order. This may be our last chance to move him unobserved."

Alvin frowned, scanned the article on his phone. "Says the victim's expected to recover. Wouldn't it be better to cooperate?"

"If I even make it to the station alive," Tjuan said, "I'd be looking at ten, fifteen years."

A moment's silence.

"Go," Alvin said then. "Caryl, take him. I'll stay with the king and queen and try and sort this out."

"I know where we can take him," said Caryl, "but I need someone to walk in with him while I find parking."

"I'll go," I said.

"No," said Tjuan. "I don't need a goddamned chaperone."

"I'm going," I said. He didn't argue further, but he didn't look at me as we all headed out of the hotel to the SUV.

I had no idea what to say to Tjuan; they don't exactly make greeting cards for this sort of thing. I couldn't address the horror of it, so I just kept circling back to the specifics, the facts.

I was used to him calling shotgun, but this time he got in the back. Lay down in the back. My stomach churned, and I got in beside him, nudging his legs. "Sit up," I said. "Let's not get pulled over because someone isn't wearing a seat belt."

After a moment's hesitation he did as I said, but still didn't look at me.

"*Was* it you?" I asked after I'd closed the door.

"Fuck you."

"Tjuan, I'm not being unreasonable, asking this of someone who has been repeatedly possessed by evil spirits. If you did it, would you even remember?"

"You just said I was at the Residence."

"Right. They're sure this happened at noon on Saturday?"

"That's what the news said."

"So what does the law do when a man is in two places at once?"

"They assume the camera and the victim are telling the truth, and the perp and his crazy friends are lying."

My gut churned harder.

Tjuan's phone buzzed. He glanced at it; I saw Naderi's name. He put it away.

"Then how did this happen?" I asked him.

"Not really on my mind right now. Caryl, where are we going?"

"La Brea and Washington," she said. Elliott was still apparently on duty. "Abigail's husband owns and runs a motel near there."

"Who is Abigail?" I asked.

"The older woman at Residence One."

"Creepy lady, white hair? I remember her. She hates me. Has Tourette's or something."

"Severe paranoid schizophrenia combined with Alzheimer's dementia; medications can only do so much for her at this point. She was once one of our finest agents, and her husband, though estranged, still lends us aid on occasion."

There was a soft purring sound, and Caryl slipped her phone from her pocket. I looked over her shoulder, saw it was Naderi again. Like Tjuan, Caryl ignored it.

"Magic," I said, my brain finally snapping into gear. "This is some kind of fucked-up magic. Winterglass and Shiverlash *both* warned us. Belinda made this happen somehow; it's got her stench all over it."

"Let's not leap to conclusions," said Caryl. "Once Tjuan is safe, we can decide how to proceed. Right now I need to focus on watching for police cars."

"Oh Jesus," I said, eyes filling with tears. "What happens if one of them stops us? Are we accessories or something?"

"I told you not to get in the fucking car," said Tjuan. "So shut the fuck up if all you're worried about is your white ass."

I couldn't find enough air; I was breathing like I'd run up a hill. "How is this about me being white?"

"Caryl," said Tjuan, "stop the fucking car so she can get out and call herself an Uber. My temper is not going to hold for this shit right now."

"We're nearly there," said Caryl. "Millie, in the meantime, can you do something for me?"

"Yes, anything! I don't know what to do!"

"I need you to remain absolutely, positively, completely silent unless I specifically ask you to speak."

I sank back against the seat, arms wrapped around myself, my dysphoria pumping my brain full of vicious inner monologue. I shouldn't have gotten into the car; he was right. I was an idiot to think he and I were friends, would ever be friends. We couldn't be. I could never be anything but white. He hated me, everyone hated me, I was useless, what if I just opened the car door and threw myself into traffic—

I clenched my fists to keep from hitting myself in the head like a crazy person with Tjuan sitting right there.

Fuck, Jesus, Millie, get ahold of yourself.

My phone buzzed. Naderi was trying me, now. Some malicious, dysphoric impulse made me show the screen to Tjuan before putting it back in my pocket.

"I need to get out of town altogether," said Tjuan.

"If we leave the perimeter," said Caryl, "Barker can track you. If Millie is correct, and Belinda is targeting you for some reason, we'd be playing directly into her hands."

There was a whole row of motels on Washington between La Brea and Redondo, and none of them looked particularly promising. Sun-faded signs boasted COLOR TV and AIR

CONDITION; the street-facing windows were guarded by an impenetrable fishnet of wrought iron. There were only a few spots where narrow apertures led traffic into motel court-yards; Caryl slowed the SUV near one of them. The parking lot was tiny and full, as all parking lots in central Los Angeles tend to be.

"Millie, go in with Tjuan. Go straight to the office and speak to Gary. Do not act nervous or hurried, but do not linger long enough to let anyone get a good look. I shall try to find a place to park and join you shortly."

It's amazing how hard it is to appear casual and inconspicuous when a man's life might depend on it. I tried to match Tjuan's pace, kept my mouth shut, walked at his side toward the little door with the neon OFFICE sign. The cracked pavement seemed to stretch for a mile and a half; beads of sweat appeared on my forehead despite the chill.

After what felt like a week, we walked through the door of the office, Tjuan first, and approached the old black man doing sudoku behind the desk.

He looked up, all bristling brows and crooked nose.

"Gary?" I said.

"Do I know you?"

"We're . . . friends of Caryl's." It occurred to me that Caryl hadn't told me how much this guy knew. I had no idea what I was allowed to say.

"Carol?" he said. "Carol who?"

"Caryl Vallo."

Gary continued to stare at me blankly. This was not going as well as I'd hoped.

"Arcadia," Tjuan supplied tensely.

Gary stared at Tjuan for three seconds, then made a sharp *ahh* sound, wiry brows climbing toward his hairline.

"Martin's little girl!" Gary said. "Right, right. What's the Project need with me?"

"A room," I said. "For Tjuan here. He needs a place to lie low."

"What did you do, boy?' said Gary to Tjuan.

I looked up at Tjuan and found myself surprised at how hostile his expression was. I'd assumed they'd be pals, which I had the good grace to feel embarrassed about after the fact.

"Tjuan," I said as gently as I could, "we're asking this man for a favor."

"If he assumes I'm guilty he'll be on the phone to the cops the minute we turn our backs."

I looked at Gary, since Tjuan didn't seem inclined to mount a defense. "He didn't do anything," I said. "But I don't know how much I'm allowed to explain. It's all going to get worked out, but we need time, and Tjuan's picture is all over the Internet."

"Jesus," said Gary. "You Arcadians are nothing but trouble, every goddamned time. Drove Abigail crazy."

"I don't think schizophrenia works that way," I said. He gave me a dangerous look, so I floundered for social graces. "Last time I saw her she seemed comfortable. She was gardening."

He waved it away. "Take room two. I'll put it under José Rodriguez."

"Who's that?"

"Nobody, that's the point. I'm saying I've got a Mexican guy in room two and he paid me in cash and that's all I know about it."

"Thank you so much, sir."

Gary stared at me.

I smiled tentatively.

"Mr. Rodriguez paid me in cash, I said."

"Oh!" I reflexively fumbled in my pockets, but I knew there were only about eleven dollars in there. "Tjuan do you—"

"I don't carry cash."

We waited awkwardly in the office for a while. Someone came to check out; Tjuan got really interested in the cheap sailboat painting on the wall while the gaunt, malodorous woman at the desk argued with Gary about the state of the soda machine. I stood with the scarred side of my face toward the wall, but even so, the woman eyed me with great suspicion on her way out, making my stomach flip.

I was too memorable. I was going to lead the cops right here. I felt as though a huge, cold hand were closing around my lungs. I went to Tjuan, touched him lightly on the elbow. He drew away.

"What do you need me to do?" I asked him softly.

"To not ask me shit like that."

I clenched my jaw, turned away. Caryl, finally, entered the office.

"I apologize for the delay," she said. "Gary, I trust they filled you in on the situation?"

"Not really," he said, "but I get the gist. That'll be a thousand dollars. Cash up front."

"What the—" I started.

"I am happy to support a local business owner," said Caryl as she produced a wad of hundred-dollar bills from the pocket of her blazer and began counting them out.

I gaped.

"Just know," Caryl said tranquilly as she handed over ten

of them, "that if my employee is harmed or harassed or even mildly inconvenienced during his stay here, I will sink this building into the foundations of the earth with you inside it."

Gary gave Caryl a once-over, seemed to decide she was sufficiently terrifying. "The boy will have no complaints," he said. "Martin could tell you: I'm a greedy bastard, but I'm a man of my word."

Martin couldn't tell him anything, as he'd been dead for five years, but Caryl didn't seem inclined to correct him on this technicality.

Room two was as far from the street as the rooms in this motel got, and it was clean, at least. The chestnut marbled bedspread was faded from too many washes but had no noticeable stains. The towels felt like sandpaper, but they were blindingly white, and a smell of bleach hung over the bathroom.

"What are you doing in there?" said Tjuan. "Why are you touching my towels?"

"I'm going to bring you some better ones."

"Stop it, all right? Settle down."

"I don't know how else to help."

"Millie," said Caryl in a warning tone. She stood leaning against the front door.

"Just leave me alone," said Tjuan. "Both of you, go back to the Residence. I'll stay here with my door locked. Come back when everyone's stopped panicking."

I squinted at him. "You'll really—you'll be okay here alone?"

"I feel more alone with you here."

The blow felt physical; I couldn't catch my breath for a minute. As soon as I could move, I nodded, turned, and left the room. Caryl was not far behind. I let her walk ahead of me, since she knew where the car was. Her next words took me by surprise.

"It's good to see how much Tjuan has come to trust you," she said.

"Are you out of your mind?" I said. "Did you not hear him in there?"

"I heard him say 'I feel.' Out loud."

That shut me up.

Caryl decided to drop me off at the Residence before returning to the Omni, and frankly I didn't blame her. I wasn't going to be much use. My plan was to head straight up to my room and have a good long cry, but the second I walked in, there was Phil. His beard was looking a little scraggly. He'd been helping orient Alondra to L.A.'s procedures on top of the rest of his work, and the stress had not been kind to him.

"Where's Tjuan?" he asked.

Shit.

"Uh," I said. "He's . . . not coming back for a while."

"How late's he gonna be? The *senior agent* needs to sign off on all these damned I-LA4s."

"Great news," I said. "I think you've just been promoted."

"The fuck?"

"Talk to Caryl," I said. "I'm not touching this one." And with that, I pushed past him to the kitchen, grabbed a Mountain Dew, and went back out to sit on the porch.

"Hey, little spy," I said to the crow as I settled into a rocking chair and opened the can with a *f-chk!*

"Caw," the crow said conversationally, and hopped right up onto the porch.

I drew my arms in toward my body, glad I didn't have anything tender at beak level for him to peck at. "You've crossed a line this time, Creepy. Back in the yard with you."

He went. The damn thing went, and I swear he was glaring at me. I drank my soda and glared back at him until a car arrived.

Sleek and out of place, the black Mercedes purred its way into the cracked driveway. I knew that car. I remembered watching for it, like a dark omen, when I was working as Inaya's assistant at Valiant.

Parisa Naderi had arrived.

7

"Shit, shit, shit," I said. I was already preparing my responses, weaving lies like a little spider.

But I never got to use any of them. The moment Naderi stepped into the yard, the angry stripes of scar tissue on her right cheek lending a truly terrifying aspect to her scowl, Creepy the crow went *apeshit*.

He launched himself into the air as though he had been faking a broken wing for three solid months and began flapping around Naderi's head at such perilous proximity that his wings stirred the grizzled ringlets of her ponytail. She screamed and covered her head with her forearms, possibly having a PTSD flashback to my siren pal's talons ripping her face open.

"Stop that!" I yelled at the bird, but its attack had already begun to subside the moment she started screaming. That's when I realized it wasn't an attack.

All at once I began to suspect that my reaction to the crow was not entirely paranoia. Its agitation, the way it continued to hop back and forth, its eyes more intent on Naderi than they had ever been on me. . . .

"Brand?" said Naderi to the bird, her arms falling limp to her sides.

"*Brand,*" I whispered. Her Echo. "What the actual *fuck*!"

The crow launched itself into the air again, long enough to do a strange aerial happy-dance, but its injury must not have been entirely feigned, because it crashed back down to the ground in a heap.

I watched Naderi's anger drain away like bathwater; what was left looked strangely vulnerable.

"I *knew* he wasn't dead," she said, and sank to her knees on the patchy grass in her A-line skirt and hose.

For a moment it looked as though the crow was going to let her pick him up, but at the last minute he shied away.

"Something's wrong with him," she said, still kneeling. "Why won't he let me touch him?"

"That is the least of my questions," I said, happy to skip the interrogation she'd undoubtedly come here to conduct. "I saw Winterglass kill the hell out of the body Brand was using. That should have killed his real body too. He should be extremely dead."

"I know, I know," Naderi said irritably. "Caryl tried to explain. The bodies are linked or something."

"Well . . ." I tried to think back over the whole messy situation. "They're supposed to be. But this was a rush job; maybe Shock forgot to—" I stopped, my mind racing.

"Who's Shock?"

"Prince Fettershock," I said absently. "The king's son, the kid who made Brand's facade. Maybe he cut some corners, and when the dog exploded—"

"*Too much information, Millie.*"

"Sorry," I said. But my mind was already racing down another track. Shock. Winterglass had been so furious when we'd enlisted Shock to make a facade for a manticore. The boy was important to him.

"Can you get Shock here?" said Naderi. "Can he fix whatever the fuck this is?"

"He might be able to, but . . ." An incredibly talented facade crafter. Someone Winterglass would never abandon, even for Caryl's sake. Someone who could *make fake people.*

"But what?" Naderi demanded.

"I have a sinking feeling," I said, "that he's not on our side anymore."

No matter how much I promised Naderi, over and over, that I'd figure out what was going on, I couldn't seem to convince her to get the hell out of my yard.

"I'm not leaving without Brand," she said.

"Well, he doesn't want to go with you," I said, scanning the street for signs of Caryl's SUV. I'd texted her about Brand and told her that we needed to meet with Tjuan immediately to discuss a theory of mine.

"Why would he be afraid of me?" said Naderi. "That makes no sense!"

"Nothing about this makes any sense!" I exploded. "All I know is that you're chasing him in circles, and if you keep it up, you might scare him somewhere we can't find him. He's been living in this yard for three damn months. If you quit freaking him out, maybe he'll still be here once we figure out how to help."

At that, she hesitated. "You'll call me?" she said. I heard her voice catch on "call," and she was already turning away even before I answered.

"Of course I will."

She just nodded without turning back, got in her car, and slammed the door.

Caryl showed up not long after she'd left. She didn't even get out of her SUV, just waited for me with the engine running. I got in, carrying the towels I'd fetched from the downstairs bathroom while I waited. Caryl was still storing her emotions in the construct; it made for very safe driving.

"How did the meeting end?" I said.

"Much as it began," said Caryl. "Unless we're willing to consider another king, Queen Dawnrowan will have nothing to do with us. Also, apparently Barker has some sort of file on you that 'proves' Claybriar has been tainted by your rebel influence or some such nonsense."

"Well, great. My walking out in the middle probably didn't help. But I'm going to fix this. All of this. I promise." Just as soon as I came up with the tiniest inkling of a plan.

As soon as we got to the motel room, I put the towels beside the sink and tried to dazzle both my coworkers with my deduction.

"I think Shock is working with Belinda, and I think he made a fey look like Tjuan so it could commit that crime."

Caryl met my brilliance with a flat stare, and Tjuan sat silently by the window, glaring across the room at the fluffy blue towels as though they'd personally insulted him.

"I wish I could subscribe to your theory," Caryl finally said, "as it would focus our response, but clearly you did not read the entirety of the news story. The police said the weapon was a blue steel revolver; they named the exact model. We can see it in the bare hand of what you claim is a fey."

"Oh," I said. "Steel. So the facade wouldn't have held?" Shit. I clawed at my hair. "But that weapon could be anything. Maybe the fey cast a spell to make it *look* like steel."

"Camera, Millie. One cannot charm electronics."

Tjuan waved a hand irritably. "Anyway. It's the shooter who vanished," said Tjuan, "not the victim. He's a legit civilian. Article says he's in the hospital, so they pulled an actual damn bullet from him. Cops wouldn't name the gun if they weren't sure."

I sank down onto the motel bed. "What the fuck, then?" I said.

There was a long silence.

"Wait," Tjuan said. His eyes were still empty.

"What is it?"

"Remember the wraith that murdered Tamika? Qualm. Dame Belinda brought it to that meeting."

I tried to think back. "Yeah. And?"

"I think the body had iron shackles on."

Caryl snapped her fingers. "Qualm's facade was possessed, not enchanted. Possession isn't spellwork, so iron doesn't disrupt it. We kept running into that problem."

I got to my feet, excited. "So if a facade of Tjuan were possessed by a wraith? By fucking *Qualm* maybe? Who's operated a human body before and might have a grudge?"

"How many wraiths were in that book that Barker walked away with?" said Caryl.

"Three hundred sixty-four," I said, suddenly feeling less excited.

"Decent army," Tjuan said darkly.

"But she doesn't know their names," I said. "Only Brand knows them."

"She wouldn't need their names," said Caryl. "If she has King Winterglass on her side, he can compel them; they are his subjects. Perhaps more concerning, if the wraiths are no longer bound, anyone who has ever been possessed by them could potentially act as a Gate for them to reenter this world. They'd be bound to that body, but could still do a great deal of damage. We need to make a list of anyone who may be currently possessed."

We both looked at Tjuan.

"No," he said. "Even if you don't think I'd be aware, which I absolutely would, King Winterglass specifically ordered mine not to possess anyone again during his reign. He didn't even put in 'unless I say otherwise.' I was there, I remember. That one's not coming near me again."

"Naderi, though," I said with a sinking feeling. "She might have had one sitting there dormant inside her the whole time I was just talking to her." I frantically tried to remember what all I'd said to her.

Caryl sighed and rubbed at her forehead. "I shall do my best to make a list of potential possession subjects and distribute it to anyone who may encounter them. But to return to the subject of Tjuan's doppelganger, King Winterglass could have commanded any one of those wraiths to possess an unlinked facade. We know it has been done at least once before, with Qualm."

"And his son happens to be a brilliant facade crafter," I added.

"But how's that kid meant to have made a perfect facade of

me?" said Tjuan. "The fey have to get the image from a human mind, right? Nobody in that camp has done much more than glance at me, and the thing on the news looks exactly like me, even to me."

"I may have an idea about that," Caryl said hesitantly. "But it verges on conspiracy theory."

"This is Dame Belinda we're talking about," I said. "She had Vivian kill everyone who knew about your abduction. Please tell us your conspiracy theory."

"Blood magic," said Caryl. "We use blood to sign the contracts, yes?"

"Yeah. I kinda wondered about that."

"DNA, for a human, has a similar effect in arcane processes to a fey's true name. It is binding."

"But it just binds me to the stuff in the contract, right?"

"Yes. But . . ." She looked uncomfortable. "There is blood left over. They take more from you than is needed for one signature."

"Yeah. I remember. What happens to it?"

"We seal it in arcanely prepared vials and send it to London for processing."

"Processing," I said, making air quotes. "What the fuck does that mean?"

"I was told they go into storage somewhere, as a fail-safe. If employees go missing outside the perimeter, the blood can be used to locate them. This much is fact; I have seen it done. This knowledge was leaked, and has led some disgruntled employees to speculate that blood could also be used to summon humans or to compel obedience in any way that a fey's true name can be used."

"I doubt it," said Tjuan. "Belinda would be jerking all our strings to make us dance at this point, not fucking around with facades."

"Without knowing how blood magic works, or doesn't," said Caryl, "I can't speculate. But she does have your blood, and with your genetic material it seems plausible that at the very least a wizard or warlock could 'read' it in order to create a perfect mental image of you that Shock could use in his spell crafting."

"Why Tjuan?" I said. "The fuck's he ever done to her?"

"I was standing right there when we rebelled, Millie."

"So was I! So was Alvin and Caryl!"

"DNA," said Caryl calmly.

"Right," said Tjuan. "Millie's wouldn't show anyone what she looks like now."

"Mine wouldn't recreate the whole of me, either," said Caryl. "Only the part that is human."

"And Alvin's DNA would be female," said Tjuan.

"Holy shit," I said.

Tjuan tried for a slight smile, but it was ghastly. "So I got the short straw."

"What do we do?" I said. "How do we stop this?"

"This is all just speculation," said Caryl. "I'd need to talk to a crafter to see if it is, in fact, even possible to create a facade of someone from his blood, and if so, if it could be tracked and caught. But unfortunately all the facade crafters are attached to one High Court or the other, and the *sidhe* control both Courts."

I blew hair out of my eyes. "I think—I think I could get Shock here."

Tjuan lifted a brow. "Are we not assuming he's the exact one that did this to me?"

"He doesn't know we know. And there's a situation at Residence Four; he screwed up with Brand. If I tell him, if I act like we're friends and like I'm worried he'll get in huge trouble for his mistake, maybe he'll sneak over here to sort it out. And then we can . . . I don't know, hog-tie him and beat the truth out of him?"

"Millie," said Caryl. "He's seventeen."

"If he's old enough to frame my partner for murder," I said, "he's old enough to get punched in the face a few times."

"No punching," said Tjuan firmly. "But we can find some way to get him talking, I bet. How would we even get a message to him, though? His dad's not going to help us here, and it's not like the Crown Prince of the Unseelie High Court carries an iPhone."

"Maaaaybe," I said, pulling out my own phone and sifting through my various junk apps. "Maybe not. He's at a boarding school in Hong Kong, and I don't know what the hell kids use over there." After a moment's searching, I found what I was looking for, turned the screen toward Tjuan. "But he sure loves the hell out of Snapchat."

8

On Wednesday, for the second time that week, I was awakened before sunrise. This time, at least, it was to a knock on my bedroom door, rather than a siren sitting on my bed.

"Dress and come downstairs," said Caryl from the other side of the door. Her voice was fluid and expressive, which meant she'd dismissed Elliott, but she sounded no higher than a 4 on the stress scale. Why so early, then?

I checked Snapchat as I got dressed. I'd sent Shock a "You still use this?" message the night before to test the waters. Now it seemed not only had he not responded, but he'd blocked me. Shit.

I pried Monty off my bed and took him to the upstairs bathroom. I could tell who had been in there last, because the faucet was dripping. Stevie was the only one who either couldn't understand or didn't care that you had to turn it not *quite* all the way to keep it from leaking. Once I'd addressed the faucet, I shut Monty in there with the litter box so he wouldn't bother Caryl. He'd belonged to her mentor, whom Dame Belinda had ordered Vivian to murder five years ago, and so the very sight of the cat could sometimes set Caryl off into storms of sobs.

When I went downstairs, I tried to get a good read on her.

Her gray pantsuit was flawless, but her eyes suggested she'd been up all night. The apparent lack of tension in her voice may have been exhaustion; I had to recalibrate. She'd driven over here in the dark, sleep deprived? I fought back a twinge of unease and settled myself on the smaller of the two couches that faced each other in the large living area.

"I checked the census ward," Caryl said. "The number of fey in the area is exactly as expected."

"What does that mean?" I searched her face, trying to figure out if this was good news, bad news, or what.

"All it means for certain is that our shooter is not a corporeal fey or warlock who breached the perimeter from elsewhere. Which makes sense, as the perimeter alarm was also not triggered."

"Wait, but an incarnated wraith entering from outside would still trigger the alarm, right? Because of the norium in the facade's blood?"

"The facade itself has human blood. The census ward reads the blood of the true form."

I let out an affronted snort. "Uh, Claybriar's facade sure as hell has norium in it. Remember what a big deal it was when he bled all over the tracks at Union Station last summer?"

Caryl grimaced slightly. That event had left a scar in Skyhollow, which she'd seen and told me about, but I hadn't witnessed. "Once the blood leaves the facade," Caryl explained, "it is no longer subject to the enchantment. A trickle down the arm will remain human. . . . The moment a drop falls free, it becomes fey again."

"Ahhh. This goes along with that thing where we don't like to send fey to hospitals."

A firm, resolute knock sounded on the front door.

I watched Caryl shoot straight to 7: Frazzled. The antique clock hanging crookedly on the far wall said eight minutes to seven; the light outside was still wan and purplish.

"The hell?" I said.

"I didn't think they'd come *this* early," said Caryl, climbing quickly toward stress level 8. Not good. At Fractured, her thoughts started to fragment and her motor skills got wobbly.

"What is it?" I said. "Who's here?"

"I came here to try to talk to you before—" She took a couple of slow deep breaths, and her eyes filled with tears.

Another knock. "Police," said a strong voice from outside the door. "We have a search warrant."

Okay, now *I* was at stress level four million or so.

"Elliott?" whimpered Caryl. He must have been standing by, because her expression smoothed immediately. "I shall answer it," she said. "Try to calm yourself."

The cop at the door told Caryl to assemble everyone in one spot, so she sent me to wake the others. In an adrenaline-soaked haze I went from room to room, knocking on doors. I waited to make sure each person actually got up, got dressed, came out. I kept seeing the house through cops' eyes, all the shady stuff I'd stopped noticing. The vicious slashes across the finish of the grand piano. That gun-shaped water stain. The coy edge of an anarchy symbol by Alondra's door where the wallpaper had peeled.

Four cops were in the living room by the time I got back. Two in uniforms, two in ties and dress shirts and blue windbreakers.

"Nothing," said one of the uniforms. The other one spoke

into a radio; I didn't hear what he said, because at the same time one of the suits was asking Caryl to come with him, and my heart was drumming in my ears. Both the suits went with her to the back of the house.

"What's going on?" Phil hissed in my direction as I approached his couch.

I took a moment to consider what, if anything, Phil should be told. "It's probably just—"

"Ma'am," broke in one of the uniforms. "Please wait until the detectives have a chance to talk to everyone. We'll get through this as quick as we can."

Song looked terrified, holding Sterling against her chest. He whined, kicking and trying to get down. Stevie sat on the floor rocking back and forth while Phil spoke to her in a low murmur. Alondra sat still and serious on the opposite couch; I remained standing.

When the suits came back, they beckoned for me. Nothing in Caryl's expression helped me; she simply went to sit calmly next to Phil. I followed the two men to the empty bedroom, the one where a woman had been murdered four months ago. My breath started to come fast; my hands shook.

"You seem rattled," said the taller one. Lean white guy, iron-gray hair.

"I get upset around cops," I said.

"Why's that?" he said in a tone that suggested he already knew I was a hardened criminal.

"Because the last time I talked to any was when I woke up in a hospital after a suicide attempt."

"I'm sorry to hear that," said the other one. Shorter, stocky, Latino. A friendly tenor voice that reminded me of Alvin. Good

Cop, then. Off this conclusion, I gave the taller one a wary once-over.

"Tell me about Tjuan Jamal Miller," said the one I assumed must be Bad Cop.

"I work with him," I said. "And we're roommates. And I know what you think he did, but it's not possible. He was here at lunch Saturday, and then went straight back to work."

"He was here when, exactly?" said Good Cop.

"From around a quarter to eleven until maybe one thirty?"

Bad Cop didn't seem to like my answer. He made a show of writing something down.

"It was her birthday—Caryl's," I babbled, unaccountably panicking at the sight of the pen. "Tjuan got a cake."

"From where?" said Good Cop.

What the hell did that matter? I curtailed my smart-ass instincts.

"Let me think," I said. "My memory's not that great; I have some brain damage." God, I sounded like the worst liar in history, and I wasn't even lying yet. "It was a weird name. I remember thinking it sounded like a disease. But the box is gone; we demolished the cake by the end of the day."

"Was Mr. Miller behaving at all unusually?" said Good Cop.

"Buying a cake was unusual. But it was her birthday, and they've known each other for years, so I guess it's not that unusual." Shut up, Millie. Just shut up.

"Did he seem confused? Distressed?" Good Cop persisted.

"No."

"Does he own any firearms that you know of?" asked Bad Cop.

"No. I've never heard him even talk about guns."

"Have you been watching the news?" Bad Cop said.

"Yeah, that wasn't him."

Bad Cop tipped his head with a weird smile. "What makes you so sure?"

"Because they said it happened while he was here. Also, I know him. He doesn't go around hurting people. Also he barely has time to shower, the way they work him at Valiant."

"Huh." Bad Cop's smile vanished. "I heard he'd been skipping out on work."

Once again he made me feel like he'd caught me in a lie, but I *wasn't lying*. I could feel something rising in me, between rage and panic. "You'll have to ask Caryl about that. He was helping her with some stuff."

"We've spoken to her," said Bad Cop. "I'm asking you."

I felt a rivulet of sweat run down my side. "I don't know what to tell you about that; I'm sorry. You'll really need to talk to her."

"All right," Bad Cop said slowly.

"You say it was a birthday party," said Good Cop. "Anyone take pictures?"

I shook my head. "Tjuan's not really a selfie guy. And it wasn't a big deal; it was mostly just another day. I only remember the time because I kept worrying about how long he was gone from work."

"Why were you worried about that?" Good Cop asked.

"Just, you know. High-pressure job. And it was a big deal that they hired him."

With no warning at all, I started crying.

"The best thing for an innocent man to do," Good Cop said gently, "would be come talk to us."

I should have just agreed, promised to keep an eye out for him, promised to cooperate. But I hesitated, because I was terrible at this.

"Who do you think you're protecting?" said Bad Cop. "My job is to protect people like John LaMantia, who showed up at work one day and got shot by a stranger in cold blood, and now has hospital bills to pay. If you lie to us, if this man gets away and hurts someone else? Kills someone? That's on you. You might as well be holding that gun."

That was about when my dysphoria decided to grab the wheel and swerve this whole conversation into the river.

"Leave me alone!" I blurted. "I've done nothing! Tjuan isn't a criminal, he's a fucking *screenwriter*, and he didn't do anything wrong, and neither did I, and . . . *I don't even have to talk to you!*"

In the long run that was probably the wrong thing to say, but in the short run, it was a magic incantation. They ushered me back into the living room and found someone else to torture. I was shaking and sobbing by that point, and Song's arms were full of Sterling, and so Caryl, to my surprise, sat next to me and held me for a while. I was too dazed to fully appreciate the slow, soothing strokes of gloved hands down my spine.

When the police finally left, she drew away from me and stood to address the assembled household.

"This will not be the last of the interest they take in us," she said. "We must assume they are watching our movements from this point forward."

Wonderful. Because things didn't suck enough already.

• • •

While Caryl told the rest of the household a bunch of scary stuff I already knew, I went upstairs and renewed my attempts to summon Shock.

No more subtlety; I was going to have to go full Internet stalker. As it turned out, not only did the presumed heir of the Unseelie Court have a Snapchat account, he had Instagram, too, as well as Tumblr, DeviantArt, and some stuff I'd never even heard of. You make yourself pretty easy to find when you use the same dumb username everywhere.

His Tumblr account was open to random asks, so I made an account there and sent him a message that got right to the point:

Brand's facade blew up but he is not dead and seems to be stuck in the body of a crow. PLEASE ADVISE ASAP.

Like everyone his age, Shock was plugged in pretty much 24/7 and answered my message almost immediately.

SHIT, he said.

Since that was all, I sent him another ask.

Dude, the crow is hanging out in our front yard. What should we do?

This time the response came even faster.

OMW

On his way? From Hong Kong? There were at least fourteen reasons I had not been expecting that response. High on the list being that he'd just blocked me on Snapchat less than twelve hours ago.

Kids these days.

I looked up flights and things to try to get a vague idea of his soonest ETA. What I did not take into account was that there were apparently "portals" between the High Courts over on the flip side, as well as a "portal" (I still had no idea what those even were) between the Seelie High Court and the nearby estate of Duke Skyhollow. Being royal, Prince Fettershock didn't even have to fill out any paperwork; he could just pop on over whenever he felt like it.

All of this meant that just over two hours later, poor Stevie experienced her second trauma of the day when the crown prince came swaggering through the LA4 Gate in red sneakers and a leather jacket.

9

Stevie was not at all cool with Prince Fettershock's unsched-
uled arrival; it sent her into a fit of moaning and rocking that
even Song couldn't calm. Caryl and I guided Shock to a couch
in the living room, partially to make him comfortable and partially to get him out of Stevie's sight.

"I am *so* sorry," he said, looking up through a navy blue
fringe of bangs. His English, as always, was fast and fluid,
but accented enough that the speed occasionally rendered it
incomprehensible to me.

"She'll be fine," Caryl said.

"I would have given more notice," Shock said, "but I do not
have permission to be here, and so when I saw a chance to
leave, I had to do it right away. I am not supposed to be talking
to you at all."

"Is that why you blocked me?"

He looked sheepish. "I am not angry with you, but Father
is, and you have met him, so nothing more needs to be said
about that."

I was a little bit confused. Winterglass was claiming to be
on Belinda's side because Shock was; now Shock was implying

that he was on Belinda's side because Winterglass was? Who was holding whom hostage, here?

"So about Brand," I said.

"I feel terrible about that," he said.

"You should." Bad Cop seemed like the way to go here, since his obvious shame was the easiest thing to pry a wedge into. "You cut corners with the spell, didn't you."

Shock squirmed. He glanced at Caryl, but she just gazed at him tranquilly under the influence of Elliott.

"With everything that was going on," Shock said, "I thought soon was better than perfect! I put care into the spell where it mattered. I thought that he would be taking a nice tour of Los Angeles, meeting his Echo, that sort of thing. You did not mention that you would be sending him into battle!"

"That wasn't exactly part of the plan," I admitted. "But what's done is done, and now you need to fix it."

"If such a thing even can be fixed!" Shock said, his eyes wide with dismay. "Where is he now?"

My phone made a sudden splash sound in my pocket, making me jump. But it was just a plaintive text from Zach, which I ignored.

"The bird's out in the front yard," I said. "Come have a look."

"Can I come too?"

I turned at the voice and saw Alondra eavesdropping at the entrance to the dining room, framed by the dark molding as though it were a proscenium arch. She wrung her plump hands with picturesque timidity. Goddamn it, I did not have the patience to deal with her right now.

"You live here, don't you?" I said to her. "I'm pretty sure you can go anywhere on the property you please."

"Millie," said Caryl.

"Am I wrong?"

Caryl gave me a flat look, then turned to Alondra and spoke in a velvety, soothing tone that made Shock look up, startled, as though he'd only really just noticed Caryl's existence. "Of course you may come with us," she said. Alondra beamed, winding her dark hair around one hand nervously.

"Get something to feed him," I told Alondra.

"I'm not sure what crows eat."

"Song feeds him cat kibble," I said, "or fruit, or that awful plywood-tasting bread of hers on the top shelf. Take your pick. We'll need someone to keep him calm."

"On it!" Alondra said with the intensity of a waitress who'd just been asked to stand in for a starlet with a broken ankle.

The crow was strolling around the front yard as usual, but he began to hop nervously when so many of us crowded around at once. Alondra brought a plastic container of blueberries, which was fancier than that smart-ass bastard deserved.

"Something is odd," Shock said. "I can see it. Something is definitely off."

Alondra knelt and began cooing to Brand as though she were Snow White and he were a delicate little dove she yearned to befriend.

"What exactly would you say is 'off'?" asked Caryl.

Shock glanced at her and hesitated. "There is a faint Unseelie . . . aura? No, not aura. More like a glimmer. It is mostly around the eyes, but sometimes when the bird moves you can see hints of it. Or, I can. You cannot. Well, perhaps *you* can?" He darted another glance at Caryl. Shy.

His demeanor made sense. Boarding school kid meets cute

girl, half-fey, a couple of years older. But he could stop looking at her like that *any time*, as far as I was concerned.

Caryl stood for a moment with a fixed stare, looking more through the bird than at it. "Ah . . . ," she said, almost seductively. "Now I see."

She had Shock's undivided attention now. He tipped his head so that the blue fringe slipped all the way clear of his eyes.

"If you had to guess what you're looking at . . . ," I prompted.

Shock stopped staring at Caryl and turned to me with guilty alacrity. "It is almost as though my original spellwork . . . rubbed off onto the bird in some way, causing the manticore's consciousness to root itself in the bird's body instead."

"But the dog you made, it . . . exploded. Brand should have been killed instantly, right?"

He fidgeted, wringing his delicate hands. So much like his father's. He'd designed both of their facades, obviously with much more attention to detail than he had Brand's.

"If I had linked the bodies properly, then the other body would also have exploded, and yes, that would have been the end. But that is the hardest part of the spell, and it didn't seem necessary. So Brand's . . . consciousness, or soul, or whatever you prefer to call it . . . it still had *a* body. So it didn't die. But it also couldn't *go* to its body."

"Why not?"

"Because the spellwork was still here, for one thing. But for another, Brand's natural body was in the . . . the in-between space. The void between manifest worlds. The nowhere. That isn't . . . there's no *time* there, no anything. Things can't *live* there. Life is subject to time, and space, and . . . the void has neither. No consciousness is possible there."

Alondra, meanwhile, was squatting on the dead grass, stretching out an arm toward the crow with three plump blueberries in her palm.

"Not like that," I said. "That's a good way to lose a hand." Alondra curled in her fingers with a start.

"Do crows eat meat?" said Shock.

"They're scavengers," I said. "They ate the hell out of Brand."

"Well that's *it*!" Shock said, his tone tinged with annoyance, as though I'd been holding out on some very important information. "This crow ate the dog's ear."

"His . . . ear." I suddenly regretted breakfast.

"That is where I anchored the spellwork," said Shock. "This crow must have found the ear and eaten it. That caused the spellwork to become integrated into its body, and Brand's consciousness just . . . snapped into the properly enchanted body like a rubber band."

"But it's not as though the body were empty," I said. "The crow already had at least a sort of consciousness. What happened to it?"

We all stared at the bird for a moment.

"They are sharing," Shock deduced.

"Yeah," I agreed grimly. "That explains why it still acts like a bird, still shied away when Naderi tried to pick it up. No wonder it's having trouble flying; there's two pilots in there. Jesus. We have to fix this."

I hadn't forgotten why we'd lured Shock here in the first place, but suddenly the detour was starting to seem like a pretty valid destination in and of itself.

"The good news," said Shock with another furtive glance at Caryl, "is that it should not be difficult. I did not fully link the bodies to each other, but the spell still has its basic function, which is that it puts Brand's consciousness in one body here and the other body in Arcadia. If we capture the crow and force it through the Gate, Brand should be returned to his original, unharmed body, and then I can simply unravel the spell completely and start again."

Alondra spoke then, gloomy. "Stranding the poor bird in the in-between space," she said.

I was taken aback that she'd even been listening, much less made that logical leap. It occurred to me that I really didn't know her well at all. I always thought of her as the "new girl," but I wasn't sure how long she'd been with the New York office before she'd had to flee; for all I knew she'd been a senior agent and was an expert in all this crap. That would be just the last straw, really.

I looked at Caryl, but she was studying Shock. I wondered if she'd noticed his shy glances too.

"What would be the most humane way to catch him?" Alondra asked, turning her long-lashed eyes to Shock.

He seemed relatively immune to *her* charms. "Beg pardon," he said, "but what does humane matter if we are about to toss the creature into an interdimensional void? It apparently cannot fly; I say we surround it and grab it. What do you think?" He addressed this last question to Caryl.

"As you wish," she said solemnly. And he flushed to the ears.

Okay, she was *definitely* fucking with him. Which started to piss me off until I realized, no, wait, this was exactly the sort of thing we'd brought him here for. To try to get information out of him. Better honey than vinegar, right? Was that her angle?

Apparently, the part of the crow's brain that really wanted

his real body back couldn't fully cordon itself off from the part that really didn't like the idea of being ganged up on and jumped, so the ensuing scene was pretty entertaining. I was not much help, given my inability to match the bird's agile, erratic changes of direction, but I did a decent job of being a stationary obstacle the others could use to help corner the thing.

As Alondra closed in near enough to grab him, he panicked and tried to fly, which was his worst possible idea. It put him in easy grab range of all three of the others without their having to bend, and it gave them more surface area to catch on to. Shock grabbed one wing, and Caryl nabbed another; they might have pulled him in half like a wishbone if Alondra hadn't darted in to cradle the panicked bird to her bosom.

"Let go!" she cried in an agony of empathy. "I've got him." Sure enough, as soon as Shock and Caryl released him, he went still, no longer struggling in Alondra's hands.

"You're all going to get bird flu or something," I said, and immediately regretted it, as Alondra looked so alarmed I thought she might drop the damn thing and make us start all over.

"Come," said Caryl, dusting a black feather off her own shoulder with a gloved hand. "Let us take him through the Gate."

They didn't let me come with them to Arcadia. Alondra was the one holding the bird, and Caryl and Shock had arcane expertise. My steel made me a liability. Still it gnawed at me, watching Alondra climb the stairs with them (step over step, effortless).

I furtively followed them as far as I could. I found Phil and Stevie at the top of the tower, past the door my mind said wasn't there, up the spiral staircase that made my lower back ache. Stevie was calm, sitting at the desk sorting through paperwork. Phil sprawled on the floor signing things. I ignored the massive semicircle of diamond-veneered graphite that jutted from the center of the floor.

"Need any help?" I asked Phil without enthusiasm. I hadn't expected them both to be there; I'd figured Stevie wouldn't acknowledge my presence and I could wait quietly for their return.

"We've got it," said Phil.

"It looks like a lot," I said, eyeing Stevie's stack. "Maybe you should teach me the basics?"

"Caryl said to train Alondra on that," said Phil.

I felt a stab of paranoia. "I've been here twice as long," I said. "Why wouldn't it be me?"

Phil set his pen on the floor, looked up at me. "You know Alondra's been with the Project three years, right?"

"I . . . didn't know that."

Phil just shook his head and went back to his paperwork, as though he'd been expecting me to say something along those lines.

There was nowhere for me to sit, so I awkwardly went back down the way I'd come. By the time the three travelers got back, I'd unintentionally dozed off on the more comfortable of the two living room couches. I snapped to attention at the sound of feet on the stairs.

"How's Brand?" I asked, rubbing my eyes.

"Still a crow," said Shock. He and Caryl sat on the couch opposite me; Alondra headed for the kitchen, where I could faintly hear Sterling's occasional baby babble. Song must have slipped in there to start lunch while I dozed off.

"Brand has been on this side for three months," Caryl said. "His connection to his fey body is weak, and there is no set formula for how long it takes to recover from that sort of fading. Shock knows this problem well."

Shock straightened as though she'd yanked his strings. "Right," he said. "I only live in Arcadia during school breaks. Over winter break I didn't change back at all."

"Where is Brand now?" I asked.

"At Skyhollow's court, with Claybriar," Shock said.

"How is the duke, that crazy bastard?" I'd met Duke Skyhollow in the summer, when he'd visited Residence One to ask where the hell Claybriar had gone. He talked like refrigerator magnet poetry and looked like a supermodel.

"He's fine," said Caryl. "But Baroness Foxfeather is still living there, so we did not tell anyone other than King Claybriar who the crow actually was."

"Yeah," I said. "Awkward." Foxfeather, Echo to Inaya West of Valiant Studios, had been homeless ever since Brand had lured her out of her estate and destroyed it last fall, eating some of her family and friends for good measure. Foxfeather and Skyhollow were unlikely to feel sympathy for the manticore's current plight.

I looked to Shock, who was of course watching Caryl. "Thanks for coming so quickly," I said to him. "Maybe you can answer a few questions for us while you're here? About facades?"

"I—" Shock fidgeted. He looked on the point of rising from the couch, but then Alondra returned from the kitchen with a loaded tray, setting it down on the coffee table. I smelled tea, and my stomach flipped over for reasons I didn't connect at first.

"Yes, do stay awhile," said Caryl enticingly, gesturing to the tray. "I've had Song make some tea for you. It's an excellent Yunnan black—Dame Belinda herself enjoyed some when last she was here."

Right.

Shock went white as a sheet. "I should not stay long," he said, even as Alondra poured him a cup. "I have to return home before things get complicated."

Caryl leaned forward. Perhaps coincidentally, her silk shirt gaped just a bit, revealing a tantalizing glimpse of youthful décolletage. "We understand," she said. "We're seen as dangerous rebels. But we never intended to cause any harm. All we want is to continue business as usual."

"You want something from me," Shock said to Caryl's chest.

"I just want to understand a bit more about how facades work," she said. "Possibly debunk some old myths."

"I . . . suppose I might be able to help. Depending on the question." He reluctantly reached for the sugar bowl, started dumping cubes into his cup.

Caryl waited for him to raise the cup to his lips, then said, "If a facade crafter had a sample of someone's blood, could he make a facade that looked identical to the donor?"

Shock choked slightly and set the cup down.

"Shock," I said firmly. "What is it?"

He looked at me. At Alondra, at Caryl. Caryl smiled encouragingly.

"That is the *only* way to make a facade," he said gravely.

10

"What?" That had *not* been the revelation I'd been expecting. "No, wait. No. Claybriar's facade; that's not anybody."

"No one living," said Shock. "They likely pulled from old stores."

Alondra let out a cute gasp of astonishment. "Old . . . stores?" she said. "How long do they . . . I mean . . . in a hundred years, is some fey going to be walking around wearing *my* face?"

"Probably, yes. You did give permission when you signed the contract."

I tried to think back. There had been something in there about using my image, but it hadn't seemed all that weird, and the thing had been over forty pages long, so I might have been skimming to get to the weird stuff.

"Are you suggesting," said Caryl skeptically, "that somewhere in London they have been storing huge amounts of blood for decades if not centuries, and this has never been a problem?"

"Not in London," said Shock. "At the White Rose."

"What's that again?" I said.

"The Seelie palace," Alondra said to me. Yes, yes, she'd been here longer than me, knew more than me, was prettier than me—I got it, I got it.

"That would make sense, actually," said Caryl. "Very secure."

"Unseelie have to get blood there too?" I asked Shock. "You have to go to the Seelie palace any time you need to make a facade?"

"Yes," said Shock. "This does not please my father, and it is one reason not many Unseelie fey attempt to travel here."

"But if they stored blood at Nullhorne," mused Caryl, "it would not be as accessible to humans. The Gates in Saint Petersburg were destroyed."

I felt as though little sparks were dancing around the inside of my skull, trying to find something to burn, to flare into ideas.

"Help me understand this," I said to Shock. "You went to the White Rose to get blood to make your own facade? And your father's?"

"I used the same vial for both," he said. "I just made a younger version for myself. But yes."

"How much blood does it take?" I asked.

"It depends on skill. I can make half a dozen facades from one vial."

"Do you ever use the blood for anything else?"

He hesitated. "Besides making facades? No, I don't. That is forbidden."

"I've heard they use blood to track people."

"Human wizards do that. Fey are not permitted to use the blood stores for anything other than facades."

"Because human blood is a sort of intoxicant for fey," said Caryl. "A controlled substance."

"Something like that." Shock was getting fidgety again. "Look, I really should get back. I live inside a perimeter, and I used Gates to get here, so the Project can't track me, but if someone there checks the census ward, they might notice someone missing."

"We'll let you go soon," I said, "I just have a couple more questions."

"How many is a couple? If you really mean two, I will answer them. And then I must go."

So fey of him. He'd hate it if I pointed that out. "Two then." I carefully sorted out the dozens bouncing around in my skull. "Could blood be used to track the facade that was made with it?"

"Yes," he said, shifting his weight. "That is how they find rogue fey."

"Can blood be used for anything else? Besides making facades and tracking people? And settling down flighty fey who don't have Echoes?"

He looked uncomfortable. "A human's blood could be used to compel her to do anything. But only for so long as the blood lasts. That's why they are only allowed to store a tiny vial from each person, in case the stores were to fall into the wrong hands."

"In case," I said wryly.

Shock lowered his eyes. "She doesn't want to do anything bad to you. If you just . . . if you just cooperate with her . . ."

"Shock," said Caryl very slowly. "She already had me abducted as a child so that your father could drink my blood."

He shook his head in denial.

"And," Caryl continued, "we believe she has already framed my senior agent Tjuan for assault with a deadly weapon."

He looked up at her in startled horror. "That— No, that can*not* be true. No."

Clearly news to him. Interesting.

"You seem like a very smart man," Caryl said. "I want you to do some research and think very hard about why we might have taken such a drastic step as to rebel against such a powerful person."

Shock rose from the couch, flustered, almost angry. "I *am* smart," he said. "There's more to—it is very complicated. I know it is easy for you to sit and think me some witless pawn, but I am not a child. I can see when someone is—" He clenched his fists. "I have to go," he said, and headed for the stairs. "I will make a new facade for Brand, because what happened to him was my mistake. But once that is finished, I should not speak with you again."

Caryl made no move to stop him. "I wish you well," she said gently, and his stride halted ever so slightly before he bolted up the stairs two at a time.

Alondra fidgeted. "Should I . . . ?"

"Let him go," Caryl said with a slight smile. "He will be back."

"How could you possibly know that?" I said, unsettled.

"You have your skills, Millie. I have mine."

"My thing is ideas," I said, "and I'm working on one. But we'll need him. Are you sure?"

"I am certain. May I guess your idea?"

"Have at it."

She relaxed against the cushions, draping her arms along the back of the sofa. The look she gave me was frankly seductive, and I felt my pulse accelerate. Alondra looked between us like she wanted popcorn.

"You hope," Caryl said confidently, "to entice Shock to access the White Rose storage and steal Tjuan's blood sample."

"Ha," I said. "So close."

"Do enlighten me, then."

"I hope to entice him to steal them *all*. But first, I'm going to need to run a little errand."

I found an old key and a box cutter, and called Alvin to drive me to the storage place. I needed someone who wasn't too close to me, but also wasn't a dick. My unit was at the back of the complex, sealed by a putty-colored garage door. I took a deep, steadying breath as I unlocked it.

"Are you going to tell me what's in there?" said Alvin. His tawny-brown eyes seemed sympathetic, but I couldn't tell if he was for real.

"Everything," I said. "All the stuff that was in my dorm suite when I jumped. My roommate set it up for me when I was in the hospital, even paid the bill for several months until it was obvious my dad's inheritance would cover it."

"Nice roommate."

"I guess," I said. I hadn't thought of her in a long time. Pale, homely face, jet-black ringlets. She'd always written cute messages for me on the whiteboard. I'd thought I could confide in her what had happened with Professor Scott. I'd been wrong.

"This must be hard," said Alvin.

Tears threatened; I blinked them back. "I knew you'd get it. That's why I asked you."

"That means a lot," he said. Soft, surprised. "I know we haven't always seen eye to eye, but I'm honored."

"You're going to have to stop with all that unless you want me to fall apart before I even get the door open."

"Right. Sorry."

"Can you—will you open it?"

He bent and lifted the door; it rattled and clacked its way up into the recesses of the frame. Inside were dusty stacks of boxes, none labeled.

"This is going to take a week," I said.

"Can I help? Open some things?"

"Ehh . . . God only knows what all was in that room. Contraband? Sex toys?"

"Gotcha," said Alvin, fanning out his hands and backing up a step.

Without much hope, I approached one of the boxes and slit it open. Inside were clothes, packed neatly but strangely: Jeans rolled into tubes, shirts folded asymmetrically. Lacy bras, thigh-high stockings.

My face went hot. I'd worn the stockings to class. A hole in one knee with a trailing nylon scar to either side. I'd had knees then, smooth and tanned. That hole, he'd told me later, drove him crazy.

I rested my forehead on one of the boxes.

"You all right?" Alvin said from outside.

"Fine." I lifted my head.

I tried another box: all dishes except, strangely, a couple of copies of entertainment industry directories. Their proximity sparked my memory, and I felt a surge of hope.

"They're packed by where they were in the suite," I said. "So if I can find something that was *near* what I'm looking for . . ."

Slash, slash, slash. Eight more boxes, none of them what I needed.

Slash. Something caught my eye: a brass-colored braid.

"Oh my God." This time I did start crying.

"Millie, what is it?"

I held up the fragile artifact, tied with a dark blue bow on one end, a red rubber band on the other. "My hair," I said. "From when I was eight."

"Wow," said Alvin.

"It's—my dad kept telling me to cut my hair; I'd cry so hard when my nannies brushed it. They complained. He told me I'd look good with short hair. I didn't even like having long hair, but I dug in my heels so hard for some reason. It was the first, maybe the worst fight we ever got in. The things he said, I—"

I put it down, put my hands over my face. Alvin came into the space; I felt his palm against my arm. I leaned into him, let him hug me.

"It doesn't matter anymore," I finally said, pulling away.

"You can finish the story," Alvin said. "If you want."

I shook my head. "He's dead," I said, slashing another box. "He killed himself too."

"Millie," said Alvin, so sternly I stopped to look at him.

"You said 'too.' You didn't kill yourself. You're still here."

"Right," I said, and looked away. "Sorry."

Three more boxes—slash, slash, slash—before I found the one I was looking for. Bottom drawer of the desk I'd sat at so many times, editing video footage, finishing papers late into the night. After I'd lifted out enough contents to make it light enough, I turned it upside down on the storage room floor.

There it was, a little flash of dark blue in the waterfall of worthless paper. I nabbed it and held it up.

"Your passport?" said Alvin with a little laugh. "I was expecting something, I don't know, a little more epic."

"This is epic," I said, flipping to the ID page to double-check. "Still valid. This means Caryl and I can fly to London and get the Medial Vessel!"

"Wait, what?" Alvin looked like I'd flicked him between the eyes.

"Caryl is great at breaking and entering; I've done it with her like three times. If we take that Bag of Holding thingie, not only do they have to come to us if they want to do Gate stuff, but if Caryl's right about getting Shock on our team, he can take the bag to wherever they store all the blood vials and just clean them the hell out!"

The expression on his face was sheer terror. "Millie, no, no, no. That's insane."

"Hear me out. Their threats are all about resources. They have this, they have that, we have nothing. So just . . . take the damn resources! She's already made this into a war. If we hold the resources, we hold the power, and we can use it for good. For peace. No threats, just forcing people to fucking *behave* themselves."

He spluttered, clenched his fists. "Are you even—? You can't just . . . fucking walk into Mordor! You'd set off a thousand alarms the moment you left the L.A. perimeter!"

I frowned. "There has to be some way of disabling that. For every security system, there's someone who knows how to get around it."

"No," said Alvin. "Just . . . no. This is the opposite of the way we should be thinking right now."

"This doesn't encourage me to be honest with you about my ideas, Alvin."

He ran his hands through his hair in frustration. Exhaled.

"Look, I'm not trying to—can you put aside your authority issues for five seconds and look at this? This is serious."

"Yes! It is! My partner is hiding from the cops! How much more serious does it need to get before we fight back?"

He started to pace. "Millie, please, don't. You're being more of a liability than a help right now. We should be thinking about trying to find some way to reconcile, at least enough for her to—"

"Fuck surrender. That's exactly what that bitch is hoping for."

Alvin stopped short, stood very still. I winced, thinking I'd crossed a line. But when he turned back to me, a little smile was playing around his lips.

"What?" I said suspiciously.

"Maybe that's it," he said. "The sane thing would be to surrender, wouldn't it? So maybe we don't try to *sneak* into London. We throw up our hands, beg mercy, beg for a meeting with her."

"We Trojan-horse it?" I put a hand on my hip, looking sidelong at him. "Excuse me, Mr. Lawful, but did you and I just start planning a heist?"

His expression was wondering, dazed almost. "I think . . . I think maybe we did."

"Well, fuck," I said. "If you and I *both* manage to agree on a plan, it's going to be tighter than a preacher's ass."

"But you have to promise to trust me," Alvin said. "We make a plan, we stick to it—not *one* surprise from you. I do *not* like your surprises, Millie."

I put out my hand, and he clasped it solidly. "You can count on me," I said.

11

Going through international airport security with two prosthetic legs and a steel plate in your head isn't exactly a piece of cake, but it's easier than going through with a turban. All I had to do Friday evening to get past TSA was announce where all my metal was and let them run the wand over me. The worst part of the trip, actually, was sitting in the center seat in economy class on a ten-hour flight. Caryl's claustrophobia meant she had to take the aisle seat, and there was no way I was going to demand the window seat from Alvin when we were actually getting along.

Alvin had gotten us all one-way tickets, since he wasn't entirely sure how long our business would take. It amused me to ponder what the cops might think if they happened to notice the three of us leaving the country with no obvious plans to return.

Actually, we were smuggling fourth and fifth passengers; Elliott and Caveat didn't require tickets. They proved themselves very useful: Elliott kept Caryl calm, while Caveat enveloped us in a subtle auditory bubble that kept the rows ahead and behind from eavesdropping on our conversation.

Over the winter we'd discovered that when spirits were allowed to cast their own spells, they were much, much better at it than humans and *sidhe* were at giving them orders. This, in fact, had been the key to Vivian's seeming brilliance: letting a spirit create its own spellwork opened magic to new levels of fluency and subtlety. It was the difference between ordering someone to dance, body part by body part, versus letting a person follow the music.

It was only after the plane had been at cruising altitude for nearly an hour that the whirlwind of the last forty-eight hours of planning started to sink slowly into reality. I thought back over conversations and suddenly found holes, things I couldn't remember if I'd confirmed. Phantom butterflies flitted around under my rib cage.

I nudged Caryl's arm. "Hey."

"Hm?" She seemed bored, but I knew Elliott was probably containing an ongoing panic attack.

"Did Dawnrowan actually *say* Dame Belinda had a file on me, or did she just say that Dame Belinda said so?"

Caryl stared at me a moment as she sorted out my question. "She said Barker read to her from the file. That something in it apparently proved to her that you were solely responsible for Claybriar's change in attitude. Fey have a hard time understanding that just because something is written down, it isn't necessarily true."

"Claybriar was definitely in the room when Dawnrowan mentioned the file?"

"Yes. When I returned, Alvin and the Seelie monarchs were both still there, and it was shortly after that when the file was mentioned."

I turned to Alvin. "You said L1's files are on the ground floor?"

"Yes," he said.

"Remind me why that matters?" asked Caryl.

"I just keep worrying about how fast we can get this done. Because of Fred."

Fred was the weakest link in our plan, but he was the best we could do. A former agent no longer on active duty, Fred Winstanley had a friendly relationship with Claybriar from way back. He had agreed to take Sunday third shift guarding the Gate so he could let Clay through after the office was closed, ostensibly to peek at Belinda's files. In exchange, Clay had arranged a "date" for Fred with a couple of nymph friends.

"Clay says the L1 Gate room can be locked from the outside," I said. "So he's going to lock Fred in for the duration. Once he gets to the ground floor, he lets us in the street entrance. He'll rifle the files down there while we slip up to the artifact room and steal the Medial Vessel. If Fred ever does tattle about Clay, a few missing papers from my file will explain why he came through the Gate in secret, so there will be no reason to look into it further."

"How important is it that we lock Fred in?" said Alvin uneasily.

"Yeah, that's what's bugging me, too. If he happens to get up and try to leave, suddenly everything looks a lot more suspicious. But if Dame Belinda ever finds out that Caryl or I were there, she's going to put together that we flew to London just to do the break-in, and she's going to start scouring the place from top to bottom to figure out what was so important."

"Would that be so bad, though?" said Alvin. "Isn't the point for all the other national heads to know we have the Vessel and that they have to work with us to get it?"

"Not yet," I said. "Not while Dame Belinda still has her claws on everyone's blood samples. As long as she has the ability to do God knows what to any of us, I want her to feel like she's got the upper hand. We've seen what she's willing to do as a goddamned *warning* shot. So I don't want her trying to escalate things until she's already lost the power to control us. We're fairly sure we've got a couple of weeks at least, right? Before anyone would go looking for the thing and find out it's gone?"

"In my thirty-two years at the Project," said Alvin, "I can count on my fingers the number of times the Medial Vessel has come out of its box. That's not to say Dame Belinda won't suddenly decide to use the Vessel for something besides Gate building."

"I was wondering about that. If the bag can hold *anything* . . ."

"Well, not anything. The mouth of the bag is only big enough to maybe get your fist through. But the blocks the Gates are built of, they're small. It's cool, actually." Alvin's eyes lit up with geeky enthusiasm. "Think Duplos, not cinder blocks. They fit together in a very specific way, and each one has to be identical to its counterpart on the other side. So it's this process of making pairs of identical blocks, putting one in the Vessel, putting one in the pile in Arcadia. Then the two builders work simultaneously."

"I would surmise," interjected Caryl, "that anyone as obsessed with controlling every tiny moving piece as Barker is, will be very, very protective of an artifact that allows perfect control over Project infrastructure."

I shifted in my seat. "And you're sure I won't accidentally destroy this thing?"

"Impossible," said Caryl. "The Vessel's spellwork is inaccessible; that is why it can never be read or duplicated. The charm was placed on the *inside* of the bag."

"And if I put my hand inside . . . ?"

"Your hand would cease to exist in time and space. I do not recommend it."

"If I turn the bag inside out?"

"Time and space would cease to exist altogether, which is why the enchantment makes that impossible."

"Jesus. Then how the fuck do people get things *out* of the bag?"

"When the mouth is stretched wide," said Alvin, "anything that was inside it just . . . barfs out." He looked thoughtful. "We'll have to fill an Olympic-size swimming pool with cotton balls or something when we take the vials out. They're made of glass."

"Wow, that could be a gory mess."

"One step at a time," said Caryl.

"Right. So. We go upstairs, we find the bag, I disable any ward protecting it, and Caveat will copy the ward back over the empty box or whatever."

Caryl frowned. "Leaving her trapped in a ward until we retrieve the vials."

"She'll be doing it herself; no one's binding her!"

"Which means she will either get tired and leave the ward of her own accord, which is bad, or we go to phase two missing one of our spirit allies, which may be worse."

"It's easier to pick holes in a plan than to make one," I said sullenly. "Have you got a better idea?"

"I might," chirped Elliott, suddenly appearing on Caryl's shoulder.

I made an inelegant sound of surprise. "Elliott," I said. "How are you—oh, never mind," I added when I saw Caryl's flushed face, the tears starting to her eyes. He'd handed the poor girl her emotions back the way you'd shove a bag of groceries into someone's arms to tie your shoe.

"I'll make this quick," he said. "But if I follow what you are arguing about, you are both missing something important."

"Out with it," I said, reaching over to stroke Caryl's arm soothingly as she began to hyperventilate and reach for the buckle of her seat belt. Oh boy, we were at a 9 or a 10 here. I pointed to the FASTEN SEAT BELTS sign, which was lit.

"I have to get up," she said. She could still speak, at least, so not at level 10. "I have to—"

"Sit," I said firmly. "Close your eyes and count slowly to thirty. If Elliott isn't finished talking by then, you can get up and fight whichever flight attendant descends on you. Talk fast, Elliott."

"Caveat will not be weaving a spell from scratch," said Elliott. "She will be replacing a ward you have disabled."

"Five . . . six . . . seven . . . ," counted Caryl.

"Yes," I said. "I explode the spellwork; she puts it back the way it was."

"There was a spirit trapped in that ward already," Elliott said. "When you break the spellwork, the spirit cannot transcend dimensions at will and return to Arcadia. It remains trapped in the spot where you released it."

"The stranded fish thing," I said.

"Eighteen . . . nineteen . . . ," droned Caryl, eyes closed.

"If Caveat reverse engineers the spirit's true name from

reading the spellwork on the enslaving ward, she can then command the same spirit back into the same ward."

"She'd enslave one of her own? Why are you speaking for her anyway?"

"She is occupied with muffling the conversation."

"I'll watch what I say," I said, "and no one can hear Caveat if she doesn't want them to. But I need to hear this from her. Also, your time's up."

Caryl, having finished her counting, was reaching for her seat belt. Elliott vanished, and she relaxed.

"Ah," Caryl said. "I am sorry. It seems even on the aisle seat I cannot shake the feeling of being trapped."

"That's because you are trapped," I said. "But if it makes no difference, can we switch seats? Because it would make a difference to me."

She dryly pointed to the FASTEN SEAT BELTS sign, which was still lit. Ah yes, definitely back to normal.

On the shoulder where Elliott hadn't been sitting, Caveat appeared. As usual, she manifested as a pale, slender version of the scorpion-tailed iguana dragon that Elliott favored. But hers lacked life; it was missing all the little tail twitches and weight shifts Elliott used to indicate his feelings.

"Sorry," Caveat said in an incongruously adorable voice. "I'd rather Elliott do the talking." Her diction always surprised me, because I was so used to Elliott's formality.

"Don't be shy," I said to Caveat. "You can talk to me. Besides, Elliott's a little busy right now."

Caveat raised her beady eyes to me, slowly. She probably hadn't quite gotten the hang of feigned body language, but the effect was strangely accurate to her wary attitude.

"That spirit's already lost," Caveat said. "A spirit that's been inside a ward for that long? It . . . dies."

"I thought—" I stopped myself, not wanting other plane travelers to hear me talking about immortal spirits. "I thought you guys didn't do that. The— Vivian's friends. They taunted us about that."

"We don't die in same the way a body dies. But . . . look at it like this. A ward is a spell bound to the earth. For a spirit, that's torture. After a while they just . . . it's hard to describe."

"Take your time," I said.

She sat perfectly still for a few moments. "Imagine," she said, "that you put out your own eyes so you didn't have to see something."

I winced. "Okay."

"Imagine doing that to all your senses. To your brain. Everything that makes you aware. Just . . . erasing every part of you that feels."

I felt like I'd stepped into cold water. "That's what the ones in wards do?"

"Not right away," said Caveat. "But when you visit the old wards, you can see it. Spirits can, I mean. Fey with physical eyes . . . they can only see the spellwork, not the dead fey trapped inside it."

"Oh my God," I said.

Caveat just sat still on Caryl's shoulder for a moment, then said, "While it's a kind of . . . desecration to do this to a dead spirit, to use it this way . . . the spirit won't feel it. The spirit's already lost. If it'll help stop other spirits from being used this way, it's something I'm willing to do."

I looked at her for a moment. "This is why you joined us,"

I said. "Because you know things have to change. You know we're the ones who want to change it."

"That isn't why I joined you," she said, very softly. "But it's why I stay."

We were halfway over the Atlantic when I caught Alvin looking glum, staring out the window. Caryl was reading a book, but reading had been stressful for me ever since my brain injury, and neither Caryl nor Alvin was willing to spring for a headset. So I'd been dozing and mentally rehearsing our plan over and over, and now I had nothing better to do than pester Alvin.

"Hey," I said. "What's on your mind?"

He quickly adjusted his facial expression. "Ah, nothing, really."

I frowned at him. "Alvin. You look seriously bummed out."

He shrugged. "This isn't a great situation, all around, Millie."

"We're going to come out on top," I said. "We can do this."

"On top of what, though?" he said. "No matter what happens, I've got to deal with the fact that my old friend Tracy was so willing to believe I'd lost my mind that he fired everyone who defended me. I've got to deal with the fact that I can't even tell Becky why I'm at the office fourteen hours a day, taking week-long trips out of town, waking up from bad dreams at two a.m. . ."

"Alvin, I'm sorry. I can't even imagine what it's like trying to balance a normal life with all this. I—oh shit, I completely forgot to text my boyfriend back. Welp."

Alvin laughed out loud, which made me laugh too. He sighed then and rubbed at his eyes with one hand. "Yeah. I think she and I are okay. For now. She's a partner in a law firm;

she understands work stress. She thinks I work in some kind of government intelligence, which isn't exactly super wrong. But also . . . you know, if I have to move out of state . . . she's a partner in a law firm."

"Oh."

"Yeah."

I didn't know what to say. He forced a smile. "Hey," he said. "Let's get you a headset, watch a movie."

"Really?" I smiled for real at that.

"Yeah. But I get to pick, and you have to do smart-ass director's commentary."

"Something funny," I said. "Preferably without a heist."

"Or an apocalypse," he said.

"Yeah. We'll get to those movies soon enough."

12

My passport had previously only been used for trips to Mexico and a single jaunt to Vancouver; I had never experienced the joy of traveling more than three time zones in a day. I'd heard of jet lag of course, but I figured it was an exaggerated complaint by people who didn't understand that they'd be sleepy when their body thought it was two a.m.

We'd left around six p.m., and when we arrived, the clocks said it was half past noon on Saturday. By my calculations it was four thirty in the morning, but it shouldn't have been worse than pulling an all-nighter, which I'd done several times in recent memory. We'd get to the hotel in time for me to catch a shower and a few hours' sleep, and then I'd be on my proverbial feet in time for supper at something approaching local time. Right?

Wrong.

As soon as we got off the plane, my entire body rebelled in ways I'd never dreamed possible. I was so disoriented that the customs people had to ask everything three times, and I couldn't seem to remember how to work my prosthetic legs gracefully. I staggered jerky-legged through Heathrow like a zombie.

We'd checked a folding wheelchair with our luggage; Caryl was kind enough to unfold it immediately and push me around, though she was looking a bit undead herself.

Alvin, the bastard, looked fine. "I'm used to this," he said, as if it mattered. Maybe it did; I didn't have enough travel experience to know.

All I remember about my first ride on the Tube is the *clack-clack-rush* of the tunnels by the windows and the way everyone politely gave my wheelchair clearance. I remember staring blearily around me at the busy station when we changed from the Piccadilly to the Central line, musing—as Caryl helped me push my chair through a turnstile—that fey would find it all but impossible to take underground mass transit.

We got off at Marble Arch and made our way around the corner to our hotel, which was just across from Hyde Park. The exterior was overwhelming; my vague impression was of weathered white stone and red brick towering over the three of us as uniformed attendants in top hats—top hats!—assisted those who had arrived via car.

Alvin checked the three of us in; we'd been granted three of the luxury hotel's more modest rooms, all adjoining. Alvin claimed the room between mine and Caryl's, possibly to prevent her knocking on the adjoining door in the middle of the night and crawling into bed with me.

By the time I got into my room after several failed attempts to properly time the insertion and withdrawal of the key card, I was so tired I couldn't remember my name. I had never felt fatigue like this in my life; the closest sensation I could remember was the drugged, brain-damaged fog I'd lived in when first waking up in the hospital a year and a half ago. I stood in my

room doing absolutely nothing for two or three minutes simply because I was overwhelmed by indecision about whether I
should shower.

Finally, I decided to give it a try, since my residual limbs
needed time to dry before I put my prosthetics back on, and I
had nothing to do for several hours. It seemed like a good time
to scrape off the film of miscellaneous travel filth, then catch a
few hours' sleep that would hopefully reboot my brain.

The bathroom completely stymied me, though. Assuming
that I was capable of bipedal movement, Alvin hadn't made
any special accessibility arrangements, which meant the chair
wouldn't fit into the bathroom. My usual habit after an evening
shower was to put on my robe and get into the chair in the privacy of the Residence Four upper bathroom, then wheel myself
back to my room and sleep before putting my legs back on.

It took far too long to occur to me that I had privacy in
the entire hotel room and therefore could just do my three-
legged crawl across the carpet to the bed if need be. It would
feel weird, but at least no one would see me.

The bathtub was nice, noticeably absent the horrific stains
that discouraged me from reclining in the one at home. I soaked
until I caught myself falling asleep and realized that drowning
in a luxury hotel, while high on my list of ways to go, was not
part of the current plan. I gave my face one last scrub and then
pulled the plug, looking forward to collapsing on the huge wide
bed around the corner.

It's amazing the small cultural things we take for granted—
for example, that all American bathtubs are built so that their
bottoms are at exactly the same height as the floor next to
them. While trying to do my usual trick of using my good knee

to vault the rest of me over the side of the tub, I misjudged the distance, causing my body to do an unexpected and violent pivot. After doing unspeakable wrenching things to my crotch on the side of the tub, I landed hard on the tile, half on my elbow, half on the side of my head.

It hurt so badly that all I could do was lie there and groan for a while on the clean white bathmat. Grateful for my solitude, I vowed never to speak of the incident to anyone and crawled my way, painfully now, to the bed.

Ah, it was worth it. I almost wept with relief at the chance to be horizontal under a fluffy comforter, to let my spinning (and now bruised) head sink into a down pillow.

Later, Alvin swore up and down that he knocked repeatedly on my door, then went down to the front desk in alarm to get them to break into the room and make sure I was all right, whereupon they found me sound asleep and snoring under the covers. I can't verify any of this; I only know that when I eventually attained something resembling consciousness, the clock on my bedside table said 11:49 p.m., and there was a note saying KNOCK ON MY DOOR WHEN YOU SEE THIS—A.

I sat on the edge of the bed waiting for the fog to clear, in vain. I felt like a spectral rhinoceros was sitting on me. But my legs were dry, so I put on my prosthetics, a rote exercise by now, lotion on one, powder on the other. I got all the way to the door between our adjoining rooms and had just raised my hand to knock when I realized I was still naked.

Jesus Christ on a unicycle.

I put on a pair of shorts and a T-shirt I'd brought to sleep in, *then* knocked. Then realized I was knocking on my own door, unlocked my side, and knocked on his. Apparently jet lag was everything that sucked about being drunk, without the fun part.

When Alvin came to the door, it was obvious he'd gone to bed already; he was in a pair of elegant striped pajamas, and his hair was all rumpled. Still, he was disgustingly bright-eyed.

"Did I wake you?" I said. "I, uh, saw your note. So. I am knocking. Because . . . note."

"It's fine," he said, strangely garbled. "Just one second, though, let me take out my retainer. I wanted to make sure we're on the same page about tomorrow."

I started giggling as he turned and disappeared into his bathroom.

"I'll just take a seat I guess," I said, and moved to the comfy-looking chair over by the window. His room was a near mirror image of mine, except that there was a second door beside his bed leading to the third adjoining room. I wondered if Caryl was sleeping soundly over there. I wondered what she was wearing. I forced my brain to think about Alvin's retainer instead.

"Okay," he said, sitting cross-legged on the bed. "I won't keep you long; we could both use some rest. Well, I could. I think you've rested enough for three people. But I wanted to confirm that you're good for a meeting tomorrow right after lunch?"

"I can't guarantee I'll be coherent. Are you sure it's a good idea to bring me? Maybe I should just rest in the hotel so I can be ready later that night."

Alvin scratched at his goatee. "The agenda kind of demands that you be there," he said. "It's the only way I could justify bringing you to London."

"What is the agenda exactly?"

"I set it all up with Dame Belinda on the phone; you just have to show up. Then later that night, after everyone but Fred's gone, we go back to get the Vessel."

"How do we get in?"

Alvin gave me a strange look. "Millie, this is the part you and Claybriar arranged."

Christ. He was right. What the hell was wrong with me?

Chill rivulets of panic began to trickle their way through the cracks in my bravado. I caulked them up quickly.

"Right," I said. "Sorry, jet lag. I'll get as much rest as I can before then. I should let you get some shut-eye yourself, so you can lie your face off to Dame Belinda tomorrow."

For a moment he looked like he wanted to say something, but then thought better of it. He gave me a smile, instead, but it had a pained edge. "Good night, Millie," he said.

I smiled back, a little uneasy, then rose and ambled toward the adjoining door. It felt as though gravity worked differently on this side of the pond. I opened his door and then stopped.

"Shit," I said.

"What is it?"

I pressed my hand against the flat wood of the door I'd let close behind me. "There's no knob on this side. And I . . . left my key in there."

"I got a spare from the front desk earlier," he said. "I'll just dash out in the hall and open it for you."

"Thank God," I said, following him out.

When he slid the key into the door and pushed it open, it stopped with a *thunk* after a couple of inches.

"Millie."

"Alvin."

"You put the chain on."

"Did I?"

"I'm looking at it."

"Well," I said. "I don't want to go down to the front desk in shorts, and my pants are all in my room. Can you change and go down for me?"

"To what end, Millie? So they can give me another key that won't work? Just what exactly do you expect them to do?"

We stared at each other in the hall for an excruciatingly long time, because neither of us had any idea.

"Hey, Millie," he said finally.

"Yes, boss?"

"It's possible I've put a bit too much confidence in your planning skills."

13

Alvin was joking, mostly, but the words still hit like a punch to the gut. Everyone had been playing along so nicely with my master-planner routine up to now. I didn't need Alvin implying at this stage of the game that the proverbial emperor had no clothes.

"Well," said Alvin, still examining the small opening in my hotel room door, "we're not getting in this way without a blowtorch. Let's see what the other door looks like."

I followed him back into his room, head throbbing. "I wish Tjuan were here," I said.

"Me too," said Alvin, "because it would mean he wasn't afraid to leave that motel room. But what did you mean?" Alvin peered at the adjoining-room door, then ran his hands along it, looking thoughtful.

"I just mean he'd be able to figure out how to get in."

Alvin turned and gave me an incredulous look. "He's a *screenwriter*, Millie."

"That's not what I—oh Jesus. I just meant he knows how to solve problems. He has this way of seeing through the bullshit, being practical."

Alvin went to his wallet on the desk, pulled out a credit card, and tried to poke it through the crack in the door. "Too stiff," he said.

"Not a thing I'm used to hearing a guy say."

He gave me another incredulous look, then shook his head and turned back to his work.

"It won't bend enough to get where it needs to go," he said. "A piece of paper, maybe?" He moved to the bedside table, ripped off a piece of the hotel stationery, and applied that to the problem. "Damn it. This is too flimsy to push the latch down." He folded it a couple of times, but still no good.

I looked around the room, spotted the DO NOT DISTURB card hanging unused on the back of Alvin's door. I handed it to him.

"Oh, this just might work," he said, and slipped it into the crack in the door, carefully manipulating it to the right angle. Then he grinned and gave the door a little push. "Voilà!" It eased open.

"Ah, thank you," I exhaled, stepping through.

"My first breaking and entering," he said with a grin. "Look what a bad influence you are."

"Or maybe it means we're a good team."

He smiled, but once again I thought I saw something a little strange in it. I was too tired to sort out what I'd said wrong, and he was already wishing me good night, so I let him close the door.

Even through fey glasses the central headquarters of the Arcadia Project was unimpressive for a place that was supposedly the hub of all human inspiration. From our hotel it had been a five-minute straight shot east on the Central line to Tottenham Court Road, then a few blocks' walk to a narrow building in Soho jammed between a hostel and a currency exchange.

The ground floor was painted a steely blue, and what Brits would have called the first through third "storeys" were shit-colored brick with three cut-up, double-hung windows squeezed in to face the street on each floor. Security wasn't tight enough to suggest that the place held anything unusual; those with access to arcane security rarely relied too heavily on the mundane sort. The keep-away ward was visible through my fey glasses; at least I assumed that's what it was: a slightly nauseating weblike mesh of greenish-purple spellwork around the door.

It occurred to me that Elliott could see what I couldn't: the dead spirit inside the spellwork. Caveat was spared for now; she'd stayed behind at the hotel so as not to be spotted. There was no way to bring her along unless she was bound into a construct spell, and rumor had it that Dame Belinda had fey lenses implanted. I was ready to believe anything about Dame Belinda at this point.

The place looked like it was built not long after the Great Fire in the seventeenth century. It didn't have an elevator, so I got to drag the remnants of my left leg all the way up the two narrow flights of stairs that hugged the left side of the building to get to the room where Belinda intended to meet us. The rail was laced with spellwork—most likely a second go-elsewhere ward for mundane visitors—so I couldn't even lean on it. By the time we got to the room, my head was pounding and I was dizzy again. I pretended to clean my fey glasses before putting them in my pocket, to disguise the moment I needed for the hallway to stop spinning.

The decor in the meeting room was mostly black and white, with sleek accents of silver and gray. A silent, broad-shouldered man stood just inside the door, wearing a suit and an extravagant moustache. Dame Belinda Barker did not rise from her chair when we entered; she sat at the far end of a long table that made me think, in my dazed and dreadful state, of a coffin. She should have had one foot in there by now—she'd passed her ninetieth birthday—but her gunmetal eyes burned with purpose and intelligence. Her white hair was flawlessly curled, her blue suit tailored to her withered frame.

"Mr. Lamb," she said to Alvin, with just the slightest emphasis on the "Mr."

"Dame Belinda," said Alvin, light and airy, as he took a seat. Caryl and I followed his lead.

"I did not expect that you would bring them to the meeting," said Belinda.

"I wanted you to see," Alvin said, "that I was sincere. Depending on how things go, their presence might simplify things."

I glanced at Caryl, feeling a twinge of unease. She was storing her emotions, so I couldn't tell if I was being paranoid.

"Would you like me to send for a cup of tea?" Dame Belinda asked Alvin, as though he were the only person in the room. "Coffee?"

"Belinda, I'm here," said Alvin wearily. "I've flown ten hours; I'm on your turf; I've done what you asked. So let's skip the tea and small talk. Can you make Tjuan's problem disappear, or can't you?"

She leaned back, her expression gently disapproving, then

waved a hand in acquiescence. "If we can come to the arrange-ment we discussed," she said, "I can ensure that the right 'man' is brought to justice for the crime."

"I've met your terms," he said, "unless there's more to them than you implied."

"The two of you agree?" Belinda asked, indicating Caryl and me with a gracious open-palmed gesture.

Caryl just looked back at her blankly.

"Uh . . . ," I said. "Did we miss the part with your terms?"

Dame Belinda looked to Alvin with weary resignation. "You've brought them here without telling them?"

"You and I both know they'd never have come."

I opened my mouth, closed it again. Alvin had told me to trust him, so I was going to do that, even though my hands had gone cold.

Dame Belinda turned back to me, the corners of her mouth lifting in something very like a smile. "Millicent Roper," she said. "You have caused me more trouble than the next five people put together, but only because you are every bit as clever and stubborn as I was at your age."

"The last time you flattered me like this," I said, my throat dry, "it didn't end well."

"My dear girl," said Dame Belinda, "do not look so fright-ened. I do not intend to harm you; I intend to train you. I intend to place you firmly in the line of succession here."

I stared at her in shock, then looked to Alvin. He wouldn't meet my eye.

"I . . ." I looked back at her. *Stay calm, Millie. Did you forget part of the plan? Roll with it.* "I don't want to work for you," I said.

"I know you do not *want* to, Miss Roper. But I know that

you want your partner to be safe, and your cooperation is a necessary component of that outcome. For what it's worth, I think you would find the work here challenging and satisfying."

Why the hell hadn't Alvin prepared me for this? I knew my mind couldn't be *that* wobbly. Was I supposed to agree? What was I supposed to say?

Bluff. Stop panicking. Act how you would normally act; that's what Alvin must have planned for.

"Supposing I agree," I said carefully. "What exactly is this office planning to do about finalizing the Third Accord? The *sidhe*? The spirits, and all of that?"

"Interesting," Dame Belinda said. She looked to Alvin. "Did you not tell her any of it?"

"Does it matter?" said Alvin. "They're here."

"And Miss Vallo?" said Dame Belinda. "Is she equally in the dark?"

"Mr. Lamb," said Caryl calmly to Alvin. "Is there something you have failed to mention to us?"

Caryl was confused too? This was not good.

He'd gotten us one-way tickets.

Dame Belinda let out a long-suffering sigh. "I cannot approve of the way this was handled, Mr. Lamb. You told me you had already discussed this with them."

The way he danced around discussions of spirit slavery. Those strange smiles of his when I talked about teamwork.

"Alvin," I said between clenched teeth. "Did you *seriously* fucking surrender? For real? I need you to tell me. I don't know what I'm supposed to do here."

He still wouldn't look at me.

"My apologies, Miss Roper," said Belinda. "Mr. Lamb assured

me that the two of you were sacrificing yourselves to save Mr. Miller voluntarily."

"You actually believed I was willing to work for you?" I was shaking all over now. "What about Caryl? Your last loose end. What exactly did Alvin say *she* was willing to sacrifice?"

"I am not a monster, Miss Roper. Calm yourself. Miss Vallo will be installed as a liaison at the Unseelie Court, as originally planned."

I looked at Caryl, whose gaze was fixed on Alvin. Her voice was low, calm, cold as dry ice as she said, "You disappoint me, Mr. Lamb."

I'd have given anything for an Elliott right now. "Alvin, did you seriously agree to *exile Caryl*?"

Finally, he met my eyes. The misery in them made my stomach drop to my boots. "I'm sorry," he said. "I'm sorry I lied. I had to get you here, so you could see for yourself that this doesn't have to be war. We can work within the system, make changes a little at a time."

"Alvin, are you fucking—" I lost my breath, lost words, like I'd been gut-punched.

Alvin raked a hand through his hair, his guilt tempered by frustration. "Your partner's about to go to jail for a decade," he said, "and you were talking about *escalating*. Enough, Millie. This has to end. There are worse things than being trained for leadership, trust me. And King Winterglass will take good care of Caryl; she'll be fine."

"Assuming Miss Roper integrates herself peacefully into our operations," Dame Belinda qualified.

"And if she doesn't?" said Caryl.

"Then we shall administer the usual consequences to both

of you. In Miss Roper's case, release and memory alteration. For Arcadian citizens, the punishment is death."

"Ah," said Caryl, bitterness palpable even through Elliott's spell. "And conveniently, I shall be an Arcadian citizen."

"Wait—"Alvin started, but I barely heard him.

"Are you kidding me?" I said, my eyes filling with tears. "I do whatever you say, forever, or you kill Caryl?"

"It does sound harsh," said Dame Belinda. "But given that you have already endangered two worlds with your disobedience, this is as merciful an offer as you're likely to get from me."

I looked to Alvin. He was staring at Dame Belinda with an expression of dawning horror.

"That was not the deal," he said slowly. "You said *nothing* about executing Miss Vallo."

"And I shall say nothing about it again, provided Miss Roper uses her many talents in service to the Arcadia Project, rather than against it."

Alvin clenched his fists. "How is it that you keep entirely missing the point?" he said. "I am trying *so fucking hard* to give you the benefit of the doubt here, and it's like you don't *want* me to. Caryl Vallo is an American citizen, and yes, she's screwed up a few times, but all of that is a direct result of a crime that *you* committed against her! You do not get to harm her again. That was *not* the deal. Exile her if you're too ashamed to face her, but you will not harm a hair on her head, ever again. Those are my terms."

"Demand whatever you wish," said Belinda. "Demand a pony and a beachfront home if you like, with the same result. You have lost my trust, Mr. Lamb, and if I were you, I would be scrambling to earn it back."

Alvin rose from his chair so fast it toppled over backward, making everyone but Caryl jump, and making the big guy at the door step forward threateningly. "Caryl's life is not negotiable," he said.

"You deeply misunderstand the situation," said Belinda, "if you believe you are in a position to decide that."

Alvin took a deep, slow breath. When he spoke again, his voice was calmer. "You have until tomorrow to accept my terms, *as I gave them*," he said. "You think we're helpless, but we're not. You can throw every one of us in jail, but you still can't touch the rebellion going on in Arcadia. So I'd suggest you think very carefully about making an enemy of half the US, unless you want to find out exactly what Claybriar and Shiverlash can do Arcadia-side once I tell them there's no further hope of reconciling with the *sidhe*."

"I will consider your words carefully," said Dame Belinda, rising as though the meeting had been amiably adjourned. "And I suggest you return the favor. Take some time to think very carefully about what I have offered you, before you decide to walk away from it for good."

Alvin just stood there, staring her down.

"Daniel," she said brightly. "See them out."

The extravagantly moustached London agent escorted us out of the building with surprising gentleness, given what had just occurred. I was silent as we walked back to the Tottenham Court station; neither Alvin nor Caryl seemed inclined to break that silence. It wasn't until we walked into the lobby of our hotel that Alvin finally spoke.

"Did you notice anything that might be a problem tonight?" he asked.

I turned to him in astonishment.

"Oh," he said softly, eyes going wide. "Oh, Millie, sweetheart."

"Did you just fucking *sweetheart* me?" I said, starting to shake with rage.

"Millie, when you didn't say anything on the train, I thought you'd realized that was how it was supposed to go. I was supposed to get upset, like I hadn't realized the hostage part, and walk out."

The room spun. I drew in several ragged breaths. "You . . . you couldn't have *told* us you were going to do that?"

He looked away awkwardly. "I told Caryl," he said. "It didn't matter if her acting was any good. But I needed to freak you out for real. Belinda's too clever; if she suspected that you were in on something with me, we'd have had no chance."

I went boneless with relief, and then, before I could stop myself, I punched Alvin in the shoulder, hard. Not a love punch.

"Christ, Roper!" His eyes flashed, but then he sighed. "I suppose that's the least I deserve," he said. He stood a moment, searching my face. "You okay?" He put out a hand, tentatively.

I wanted to punch him again. Instead I gave him my hand for a moment, then let go.

"Come on," he said, still watching me carefully. "We've got a heist to get ready for."

14

The three of us gathered in Alvin's room, the doors to our adjoining rooms propped open as a precaution, even though I'd taken care to leave the chain off my door and keep my key with me.

"So," I said. "I spotted a ward on the door and a ward on the stair railing, but if they do anything, I didn't feel it."

"Those were anti-civilian wards," said Caryl. She'd given Elliott a break, so she was at about a 5 or 6, visibly nervous but still focused.

"Anti-civilian?" I echoed. "To keep out non-Project people?"

Caryl nodded. "The London office receives a great number of visitors. They cannot simply incorporate exceptions for each individual, as we do for some of the wards at Residence Four, for example. Though it is slightly more difficult, a ward can be constructed that will *only* take effect in the presence of someone without clearance. Usually we use those wards for Gates, since such a wide variety of Project members need to access them. But it appears the London office makes use of them throughout the building."

"So, wait," I said. "I didn't feel anything from those wards, so does that mean I have clearance? Here?"

"Among other things, the contract you signed in October makes you recognizable as a Project member to anti-civilian wards. That is, essentially, what 'clearance' means."

Just how many spells had I bound to myself by signing that thing? Even if I'd known, I still wouldn't have had much of a choice, but it was distressing to think about. I raked both my hands back through my hair, pushing it away from the little beads of sweat that were suddenly breaking out on my forehead.

"Millie," said Alvin. "Is that a bruise?" He tapped his hairline at the mirroring spot.

I touched my forehead, found a tender, slightly squishy area. "What the—oh, right. That's where I hit my head on the bathroom tile."

I watched Caryl shoot straight to a level 7. "Millicent Roper," she said. "You fell and hit your head, and you did not notify someone immediately?"

"It was just a bump."

"A bump on—on a head that has a steel plate in it from—from prior traumatic brain injury," Caryl said. Level 8, actually, to judge by her stammering and the shaking of her hands.

Alvin rose from his chair to come peer at my bruise, smoothing my hair away from my forehead in a way that made me sleepy.

"Maybe a concussion," he said grimly. "That would explain a lot. Goddamn it. We can't send her in there."

"It's not a concussion!" I said.

"You've been forgetful, groggy . . ."

"I have jet lag!"

"We shouldn't take chances," said Alvin. "You should be trying to keep your blood pressure down."

I pushed him away gently. "In an ideal world, sure. I'd lounge in bed and eat bonbons for a week or two, just in case. But have you forgotten we're on the edge of an apocalypse, here? Dame Belinda might think she can stitch things back together the way they were, but there is no way in hell Queen Shiverlash is going to allow that. All that's keeping her from burning both worlds to the ground is the idea that *I have a plan*."

"Surely," said Alvin, "there's a plan that doesn't involve someone with a concussion trying to pull off a heist."

"We've minimized the risks," I said. "It's not Fort Knox. And we have no way of communicating a change of plans to Claybriar. Plus, I'm already broken in a thousand ways; let's not pretend a bit more damage is going to matter."

"You could *die*," Caryl said, her eyes filling with tears.

"Pull yourself together," I said, more harshly than I'd meant to.

She flinched. "But you could," she said, not looking at me.

"I'll be fine," I said more gently. "But more to the point, this is war. We can't be precious about our soldiers. What about Tjuan? He can't hide forever. Dame Belinda has no reason to call off the dogs, not as long as she holds the cards. And her cards happen to be heavily warded, so unless you have another Ironbones on call, I'm what you have to work with."

The grim silence told me that I'd made my point.

"I will, however, concede that I need sleep," I said. "Wake me before we have to leave."

"Or every two hours," said Alvin dryly, "to make sure you haven't slipped into a coma."

"Don't you dare," I said. "Concussion or no concussion, jet lag is a bitch. If I manage to sleep longer than two hours, you'd better damned well let me."

• • •

The London office closed at eleven p.m., unpopulated but for the lone third-shift Gate guard on the far side of the third floor. By that time Carlisle Street was mostly deserted.

Soho wasn't silent at that hour, but there was a simmering quality to the darkness that night, sporadic drunken forced cheerfulness that seemed ready at any moment to erupt into anger. I wrapped my coat around myself tightly, tried to look unremarkable.

We arrived precisely three minutes late, and Claybriar was waiting on the other side of the door. He let us in so casually that any passerby would have to assume that the business going on at this office at midnight was perfectly legitimate.

All the lights were off inside; I pocketed my fey glasses and gave my eyes a few moments to adjust.

"Fred okay?" I whispered.

"He's sound asleep," said Claybriar, stopping to stroke my hair away from my face with a gloved hand and frown at my bruise.

"Asleep? Awesome! How did you manage that?"

"By tiptoeing quietly and not waking the lazy bastard up."

"He knew you were coming, right?"

"Apparently he wasn't all that excited about it. I still locked him in there, just in case."

"Nice work," I said. He touched his lips to my injured forehead, feather light. I started to melt but steeled myself. Serious business at hand.

"Okay," I said, pulling away, still keeping my voice down. "Alvin said the artifacts are off the same hallway that leads to the Gate, but at the other end. If you could lead us up there, Claybriar, that'd be great. And can you take my coat? It's like an oven in here." At least I hoped that was why I was sweating.

Claybriar relieved Caryl and me of our coats, held them close as though they were in terrible danger. We followed him up the cramped, creaky staircase, which I was no fonder of in the dark than I'd been during the day. I'd thought my nice long nap would fix me up, but my battery drained rapidly from the mental and physical effort of coordinating my steps up the stairs in the dark with two people crowding me and vibrating the floor at every step.

By the time I got to the second landing I was wobbly, and near the top my vision started to gray out at the edges. Before Caryl could move fast enough to steady me, I pitched forward.

I managed to catch myself with a forearm on the railing. But my forearm was bare, and the railing was laced with spellwork.

Or had been, anyway.

I sank down onto the steps, putting my head in my hands.

Claybriar hovered, mostly concerned about my physical well-being, but Caryl had Elliott on emotional duty and instantly grasped the repercussions.

"This is bad," she whispered.

"No shit!" I hissed.

"We have a choice to make, and we must make it quickly. This was an anti-civilian ward; replacing it will be complicated. We dare not take enough time for Caveat to replace it *and* replace the spell protecting the Medial Vessel."

"Abort," I said.

"Not necessarily," Caryl argued gently. "We can either reconstruct the spell on the staircase and hope that no one notices that the Vessel's protections have been disturbed, or we can reconstruct the spell on the Vessel. That will make it clear we destroyed the staircase, but they may assume that it happened while we were here looking through files."

"Is there anyone other than Millie who could have destroyed that spell?" Claybriar said with a gesture toward the railing.

"Aside from the caster?" said Caryl. "No. Unless it were someone else with steel in her bones."

I looked up, dubious. "What if someone hit it with an iron crowbar or something?"

"Inanimate iron and norium simply do not interact," said Caryl. "They repel one another on a molecular level, creating a barrier. Living flesh and blood—they buffer and complicate things. A crowbar could dispel an enchantment on a person. But not a ward."

"So it's a dead giveaway Millie was here," said Claybriar. "We have to fix the staircase."

"I should have had a contingency for this," I said, head still in my hands. "I've fucked this up six ways from Sunday."

"You are burning precious seconds," said Caryl. "Decide, or I shall decide for you."

"Please do," I said. "You're the only one not freaking out. Thanks for that, Elliott."

"I say we focus on hiding the theft of the Vessel. I would rather Barker suspect you were here with Claybriar to look at your file than have her wander into the relic room for something else and immediately spot a ward missing."

"I don't want her targeting Millie," said Claybriar. "Period."

Elliott popped into view, and Caryl drew a shuddering breath as she snapped immediately to stress level 8.

"Apologies for interrupting again," the little dragon chirped.

"Goddamn it, Elliott!" I hissed.

"This is important," he said. "Caryl, if you can hold yourself together, I may be able to help. Caveat could focus on the anti-civilian ward. I may not be able to duplicate the ward protecting the Vessel as Caveat could, but I can cast a spell that will discourage people from investigating it."

"Good enough," I said, exhaling with relief as I levered myself to my feet. "Caryl, can you manage without him?"

"I—I think so," she said in a tremulous whisper.

"Claybriar," I said, "This is too many people, too much noise. Wait down below."

"Fine," he said.

Now it was Caveat's turn to pop into view. "One problem," she said.

I nearly let out an explosive barrage of profanity, only remembering in the nick of time that Caveat was shy. "Yes?" I said between gritted teeth instead.

"The spell on the rail's the same as one of the anti-civ wards at Residence Four," she said, "but I didn't see the name of the spirit before Millie touched it."

"Which means?"

"We'd have to bring in a new spirit."

I let that sink in for a moment. "Enslave one, you mean."

Caveat looked back at me. She still hadn't learned how to make the construct show facial expressions, but I was pretty sure I could guess her thoughts on the matter.

"Wait," said Caryl. She sounded better now, her voice steadier. "Caveat, you have studied the wards in Residence Four, have you not? Perhaps there is a ward we can do without."

Caveat turned her construct's gaze toward Caryl. "You're asking me to free one of the Residence spirits . . . and bind it in a new ward here?"

"Well," I said, "Isn't it already . . ." I couldn't finish.

"Dead," Caveat finished for me. "I'd be taking a dead spirit from its resting place and dragging it across the world."

Caryl wrung her gloved hands. "You're right," she said, tears glimmering on her lashes. "It was a horrible idea—I'm sorry."

Elliott appeared between her and Caveat, as though prepared to physically defend Caryl. "The spirit has already been sacrificed," he said. "At least this way, its sacrifice will mean something."

Caveat and Elliott seemed to stare at each other in silence for a long time, but I had the distinct feeling there was an entire conversation going on that we weren't privy to.

At last Caveat said, "I'll do it, then. Go upstairs. Please make sure this is worth it." With that, she vanished.

15

After the exhausting climb to the third floor, I arrived only to realize that there was nothing there at all—the important business all took place on the lower floors. I turned and bumped into Caryl, who was climbing the stairs behind me. As I tried to push past her, she snaked out a gloved hand to catch my wrist.

Startled, I turned to look at her. The sly half smile I could see on her face in the darkness was just enough to distract me from my intense desire to return downstairs.

"Son of a bitch," I said. "*Another* ward?"

"This one is clearly meant to keep out anyone who does not work in this office."

"I guess I didn't get to check this floor, since the meeting was below." Then I tried to go downstairs again. Once again she grabbed my wrist.

"Have you truly not developed the slightest resistance to psychic spellwork after all this time?" Caryl said. Her amusement seemed to have dialed her stress down to a level 6, maybe even 5. Good that my incompetence could serve a constructive purpose.

"So what now?" I said. "Am I going to have to destroy and recreate *another* spell? Caveat's a little busy."

"Just ignore the ward," Caryl said. "Now that you know it's there."

I gave her what I hoped was a withering look, then sighed and turned to climb the stairs, even though there was nothing up there.

Of course there was. The Gate, and the Medial Vessel, among other things. I had all the intellectual knowledge of the floor's contents, but the parts of me that usually drove my decisions were screaming at me that this entire floor was a dead end, that I had important things to do and limited time.

I forced my legs to do the opposite of what instinct was telling them to do; I continued from the top landing, turned left down the hallway. There were no doors in the hallway, but I kept walking anyway, because the door that I knew should have been there was at the end, on the right.

"Allow me," said Caryl, her eyes taking on a subtle greenish luminescence in the dark as she shifted her perception to the arcane spectrum. I found this strangely, unaccountably hot.

After a moment she reached toward the wall and drew a door out of it as though the wall had been a thin layer of mud, the door lying just beneath its surface.

"*Damn,*" I whispered.

She gave a modest little shrug and preceded me through the dark doorway.

I let my eyes adjust to an even deeper level of darkness. The room had a deceptively dull office-style layout and the same monochromatic color scheme as the rest of the interior, but even with virtually no light I could tell that many of the "every-day" objects were not what they seemed. I recognized the disc-shaped "tablet" that was actually a dish of arcane liquid, used in various scrying procedures. A two-handled coffee mug, on closer inspection, was not quite touching the desk it appeared to rest on. One shelf was lined with small glass vials and flasks whose nefarious purposes I could only imagine. I tried not to touch anything.

Caryl scoped out the room with her eerie, otherworldly gaze, carefully peering in drawers and opening sleek black cabinets above desks. At last, drawing out the bottom file drawer on the far wall, she made a soft sound of discovery.

"Here," she said.

"Found it?" I moved toward her but stopped a few feet away as a precaution.

"The spellwork on this box," she murmured in a tone of sudden dread. "I don't know if it's right to destroy it."

"Uh . . . except that it's the whole reason I'm here?"

"I know," she said. Her voice shook, barely perceptible. "I just—I feel conflicted."

"Ignore it," I said. "Pretend it's a ward." I edged carefully closer, peeking into the drawer she'd opened. All I saw was an old battered cardboard box that had once contained copy paper. It gave off a vague impression of fetid neglect that suggested its current contents were more likely roaches or maggots.

"I hadn't thought of treating emotions as hostile spellwork," said Caryl. "For the most part I—I have been trying to condition myself gradually, calling upon the construct when—"

"Caryl," I said. "Focus. Tell me about the ward on the box. What's freaking you out about it?"

She was tense; her hands clenched and unclenched. I laid a hand on her shoulder, just a ghost of a touch, and she seemed to relax.

"First," she said, "it's a charm, not a ward. But an extraordinary one. From what I can read of the charm's structure, it is designed to exude a sense of unimportance and uncleanliness. More importantly, anyone who pushes past this impression to touch the box must be protected by a certain enchantment, or the charm will trigger a curse of its own. Paralysis, I think."

"Leaving the thief stuck here, red-handed."

"A charm that casts a curse." She looked at me, clearly upset, clearly waiting for me to understand something.

"So do I touch the box or not? Is it going to curse me?"

Caryl exhaled with frustration, stress level rising. "Vivian's metaspell on—on soundstage 13. It was constructed in a similar fashion. Your touch simply dispelled it; you were not cursed. Somatic enchantments have no effect on you."

"So what's the problem?"

"It's a *metaspell*, Millie. One spirit nestled within another, working voluntarily in harmony. This was not cast by a warlock, or a *sidhe*."

Suddenly I understood. "It was cast by a spirit," I said. "Fuck. Still alive." I turned, addressed empty air in a whisper. "Elliott, are the spirits in it alive? Can you confirm?"

Elliott popped into view. "They are," he said. "But they are too dazed to cast any spells in their own defense, so do not let that concern you."

"Why so callous?" I said. "If the spirits are in this spell

voluntarily, and they're alive, then what we're planning to do here is torture and eventually murder them, right? How is that okay?"

"You've met them," said Elliott. "The wraith that possessed Tjuan for months, and the one that possessed Claybriar."

Flashes, as though they were yesterday. Claybriar's hands wrapped around my throat. Tjuan vaulting over the kitchen island toward me, something else's murderous rage in his eyes.

"Here we go then," I said, reaching for the box.

"Wait," said Caryl, grabbing my wrist.

My pulse picked up a notch. "Caryl, I'm going to need you to stop grabbing me all the time."

"Sorry." She withdrew her hand.

"These are two of the wraiths we were going to imprison anyway," I said. "The only reason they're not decorating Valiant Studios or a Residence somewhere is that we let Belinda get away with the book Brand put them in."

"I know." Caryl shifted her weight, wringing her hands. "But I—it's still—now that we know—"

"Elliott," I said. "Can you take away her feelings for a second?"

He neither appeared nor answered me, but the line between her brows and the tremor in her hands disappeared.

"I beg your pardon," she said flatly. "Proceed."

I reached into the open drawer and touched the box. Nothing happened that I could feel: spellwork always died without even a whimper.

"How ya like them apples, assholes?" I said to the empty air. "Remember me? Enjoy whatever spell you're about to be put in."

I lifted off the cardboard cover and saw the most decrepit, discolored, feeble little drawstring cloth sack I'd ever seen in my life. It might have been red once, about a thousand years ago, but now?

"Uh . . . ," I said. "It kinda looks like . . ."

"A waxed scrotum?" supplied Caryl.

"How would you know?"

"You realize," she said dryly, "that I have worked closely with the fey for the past eleven years."

I wasn't going to touch that one. "Okay, you pick it up. I don't want to break it."

"Millie, as we've established, the spellwork is inaccessible."

"If you're wrong?"

"Millie, time is short. Pick up the bag or I'll have Elliott give you hellish waking nightmares."

I grabbed the priceless scrotum from its shabby box, rolled it up, and shoved it into the pocket of my jeans.

"Well," I said. "That was less epic than I'd hoped. What now?"

"Elliott and I will get to work rebinding the wraiths. You are no longer needed."

"You sure know how to make a girl feel special. But I'm not leaving without you."

"I will be fine."

"No, you misunderstand me. I'm not walking the fucking streets of London in the middle of the night by myself."

"Then wait with Claybriar," she said. "I am about to knowingly torture a sentient creature, and so I would rather not have you nearby once Elliott returns my emotions to me."

Ouch.

What could I do but go downstairs? I found Claybriar gazing out the front window, still holding our coats like a damned servant, and something about that rankled.

"Hey, Hurricane," he said softly when he turned and spotted me. "Everything go okay up there?"

"Clockwork," I lied.

"Anything I can do to help? I've already gone through the files, pocketed some papers."

"What was in there that's so damning about me?"

"Just your mental health history, and a timeline of various events, supposedly showing that I started disobeying the Queen's orders immediately after meeting you."

"Correlation doesn't imply causation," I said. "That's weak."

"Not when Dawnrowan already wants someone to blame other than herself."

"Somehow I'm starting to feel less guilty about planning to rob her place. You've been there a lot, right?"

"The White Rose?" He hugged the coats closer, returned to gazing out into the night. "Yeah. You're going to have your work cut out for you."

"Well, it'll be Shock doing the work, if we can get him. He goes there all the time. He has access to the area we need."

"The whole place is watched, though," said Claybriar.

"Watched by who? And how many? Anybody can be distracted. Or bribed." I glanced pointedly upward.

"Not these guards," said Clay. "There's only about half a dozen, but what one sees, they all see; they're mentally linked by an enslaved spirit. It's not dead like the ones in these wards, because it keeps busy; it can see the whole place at once, never sleeps. Anything weird goes down, anywhere, and it flashes the image to all the guards."

"Oh." I scratched at my hair for a second. "Enslaved means spellwork, though." I made a grabby-hands gesture. "What if I sneak in there and free the thing? That seems like a win-win scenario."

"Sneak in?" Claybriar looked at me and let out a soft snort.

"Invisibility spell or something."

"Has no one described the White Rose to you?"

"Uh . . . no, actually."

"It is literally a gigantic rose, made out of stone, standing on its stem. The palace is the flower part. The stem is . . . well, it's a stem. No handholds, no stairs, nothing."

"Uh, how is that architecturally possible?"

"It's not, Millie. It's Arcadia. Upshot is, the only way to get in is from the air."

"You don't have wings."

"They send horses down. Winged horses. They pull a sort of litter."

"This sounds fucking insane."

"Again. Arcadia. My point is, you can't just sneak in there invisible. They have to *let* you in."

"Okay, so we set up a meeting, like we did here. Same Trojan-horse deal."

Claybriar turned his gaze back out the front window. "I can't think of any reason why the—oh *shit*."

"What—"

"Get away from the window. Dame Belinda is approaching from down the street."

I backed away as though the window were on fire. "In the middle of the night? Why?"

"No idea, but she's clearly headed this way, which means you can't leave through the front door." He shoved our coats at me.

"I'll hide upstairs until she's gone," I said, clutching the coats.

"No," said Claybriar urgently. "Use the Gate. I'll let you know when it's safe to come back."

"But Fred—"

"If he wakes up, I'll deal with him. And I'll deal with her. *Go!*"

I fled up the staircase.

16

I hurried upstairs as fast as I could push my titanium legs, extra careful not to touch anything this time. I thought about Fred and came to the slow, sinking conclusion that we were boned.

Caryl was still in the artifact room, admiring Elliott's work on the newly charmed desk drawer.

"Don't get too close," she whispered when I walked in. She moved quickly to meet me. "Anyone who approaches the drawer will now simultaneously forget why he came and remember the second most urgent—"

I handed Caryl her coat. "We have to get out of here," I said, struggling into my own jacket in my idiosyncratic way, compensating for my bad shoulder. "Dame Belinda is coming!"

Caryl drew in a sharp breath; her whole body went stiff with panic. At least an 8; not good. I grabbed her by the arm and steered her down the hall before she could completely flip out, mentally cursing the way the arthritic old building announced our every step. I unlocked the door to the Gate room and pushed a stiff-legged Caryl in ahead of me.

Fred Winstanley was an elderly white man who looked like

he might have been scraped off a street corner somewhere and dressed in a suit from a donation box. Unfortunately, he was also wide awake and on his feet, having heard our approach.

Before he could even quite finish letting out an interrogative squawk, Caryl crossed to him and trapped his head between her shaking hands as though she were about to give him an ardent kiss.

He had just enough time to get confused and a little excited before she began a droning incantation in the Unseelie tongue that made his eyes go as dead and blank as wax.

I slapped my hand over my own mouth to keep from screaming; I wasn't sure what happened if spellwork got interrupted in the middle, and I didn't think this was the prime moment to find out. By the time she was finished, the room reeked like a slaughterhouse. The old man stared at nothing, and Caryl gently eased him back into his chair.

"What the hell did you *do*?" I asked her.

The effort of casting the spell had tired her, easing her back a few steps on the stress scale.

"I removed his memory of seeing us," she said. "He'll be fine, but we don't have long. In less than a minute he'll wake as though from a light doze and have no idea we were here."

"Caryl, you—"

"We have to move," she said, nostrils flaring, fists clenched. "Lecture me on the other side."

She grabbed my arm for about the fourth time that evening. This time I was too off-kilter to deflect a sharp needle of desire.

She dragged me through the Gate, and at that, I did start screaming.

• • •

I could only hope that I was already in the interdimensional void by the time the scream escaped me. Everything in my body and mind seemed to turn inside out like a discarded sock, and then my voice came unstuck from my throat in a place where it didn't belong, violating the moonlit hush of a vast, snowy forest.

It would be an understatement to say that Daystrike was as different from Skyhollow as London was from Los Angeles. It was more as though London and Los Angeles both reflected, faintly, the differences in the soul that lay beneath them.

Here, everything was black and white and silver, still and cold and grand.

We stood in a wild wood whose vaulted canopy of intertwined white branches was dizzyingly far above our heads, clothed in shreds of luminous mist. Here and there, like fragments glimpsed through crocheted lace, I could see a coal-black sky and a huge moon, terrifying in its nearness. The air smelled of cream and peppermint; snow blanketed the forest floor at our feet. As I watched, that strange, fitful mist flowed and flickered among the branches like a visible wind.

They must have built the L1 Gate on the third floor on Earth to mirror a higher altitude of land here; in Arcadia the structure stood atop a modest cairn on the forest floor. On closer examination, the cairn's rocks seemed to be held together with glittering mortar. The Gate was a visual insult, a foreign invader, a massive black half ring with the horror of nothingness inside it, surrounded by wintry sylvan perfection.

I shivered and turned my back on it. Caryl still had her hand around my wrist. She looked at me with those dark colorless eyes of hers and—I blame Arcadia—the small twin flames of anger and desire I'd carried with me from the real world erupted into one raging bonfire. I took her by the shoulders and backed her into a white-barked tree, held her there.

"You enslaved another spirit," I said.

"Just for a little while," she said breathlessly. Her words condensed into white mist in the air. "I'll—I'll undo the spell, once we're safe." Her eyes lowered to my mouth.

My grip on her shoulders relaxed, then somehow became a caress, trailing down her upper arms. She tipped her head back against the tree, closed her eyes. The space between us was unbearable, like ice on bare skin. I melted it away. Kissed her. Her hands were shaking as they found my hair.

I tried to stop kissing her, but it was so cold in that forest, and she was so warm. She made desperately pleased sounds as I coaxed her mouth open, sounds I felt against my tongue and down every nerve.

I was drunk on minty Arcadian air as her gloved fingertips found purchase on the back of my jacket. I bit the side of her throat, just below her ear, and she made a deeper, more animal sound, slipping one hand under my jacket, under the back of my shirt. Through the silk of her glove, I felt the bite of her nails. I shuddered.

"One of us has to come to our senses," I whispered against her throat before lifting my head to kiss her again. She made a noise that I can only assume was a dissenting opinion, judging by how deeply her tongue was in my mouth.

I think the only thing that stopped us was that it was too damned cold to start taking clothes off. I held her against me for a while. She was a shivering mess in my arms, and her frailty filled me with a fierce, overwhelming love that almost split me in half at the sternum. I stupidly told her so, three white-hot syllables misting in the frozen air. She pulled back to look at me.

"I know," she said. She fucking Han Soloed me. But her eyes were stars, her cheeks red roses. So gorgeous. I remembered the first time we were in Skyhollow, how close I'd come to kissing her then.

"Arcadia's messing with us," I said, stroking my fingertips over her flushed cheek. She sank back against the tree, heavy lidded.

"Not really," she said.

"We should stop." I was insistent, even as my hand fit itself gently to the curve of her breast. "I'm not sure what Zach and I are exactly, but I'm pretty sure I shouldn't be doing *this*. We're not thinking straight; this is some . . . passing spirit making us feel things. Like you said the first time we went to Skyhollow. Emotion just . . . flows through the air like water, right? Hits you randomly."

"Not randomly," she said. "Like is drawn to like. The spirits leave you alone unless you draw them." She smiled at me, slow and wicked, then leaned forward as though whispering a Big Secret. *"You already wanted me."*

The taunt irked me, reminded me that I'd been feeling something besides lust when she dragged me through the Gate. I drew away from her, wrapped my arms around myself.

"I shouldn't have let you cast that spell on Fred," I said. "You enslaved another spirit without even thinking about it. Like an addict falling off the wagon."

"Please just kiss me again," she said.

For fuck's sake; I almost did. Only sheer force of will kept my arms folded, my feet planted.

"We need to discuss this," I said. "Have Elliott take your emotions for a second."

From the look of it, I'd dashed her in the face with ice water. "I—cannot," she said.

"Caryl—"

"It was Elliott I put into the spell."

The bottom dropped out of my stomach.

I think even if we'd been on Earth, I'd have been sickened and sad. But here it was suffocating. For the space of five breaths nothing existed except the tragedy of that betrayal. Tears welled in my eyes and flowed freely; there was no consideration of stopping the tide. The air turned grief to ice on my cheeks.

"How long are you going to leave him trapped in that man's mind?" I said.

"I'll recall him by speaking his Unseelie name," she said, "once it's safe to risk Fred's memory returning."

"How could you do that?" I asked, sniveling like a child. "To your best friend? And what if we need him to break into the White Rose? To say nothing of what a goddamned mess you're going to be all the time now."

"Please calm down!" said Caryl, even as she burst into tears herself. "Elliott knows me. He *is* me. He knows why I did what I did, and he knows that I will call him back. In the meantime, he is not in a ward; he's bound to a human who will move and think and keep him amused. If I'd asked, I know he would have consented."

"If you'd asked," I said. "You didn't ask."

Caryl looked at me for barely a second and a half before she broke down into sobs. Neither Elliott nor the laws of terrestrial restraint were going to stop her from facing her guilt now. I held her again, but this time my body felt like it was full of wet sand.

That's when Claybriar showed up. All things considered, it wasn't the most awkward time he might have arrived.

"She's gone," he said. A faun in the wintry wood. He belonged here in a way we decidedly did not. "And I guess Fred must have slept through your exit or something?"

Caryl started bawling again.

"Let's not talk about that right now," I said. "Why was Belinda even there?"

"Fred got up to pee, found himself locked in. He called Belinda and tattled on me, and so she decided to catch me in the act, have a little chat with me."

"I wonder if Alvin rattled her, using you as his parting threat."

"Maybe. I let her 'catch' me with the files, and she and I had a long talk. I gave her back what I'd tried to steal, and I let her think she convinced me to try to bring you 'back to the fold.' As if you've ever been folded into anything."

Caryl stopped crying, at this. "Well done!" she said, and sniffled.

"So she still thinks she can make friends with me," I said. "That's good news. But how'd you manage to make her think you were on board? I mean, you can't lie, and she's awfully sharp."

He shrugged. "I said stuff like, 'What you're saying makes sense,' and 'I've been a complete idiot,' and that was all true.

People who think they're infallible are pretty easy to fool, to be honest."

"You perfect little pumpkin," I said. "So what now?" Behind Claybriar's shoulder, in the distance, I thought I saw a shape moving through the trees. A white stag perhaps, or a horse? But it was gone before I could point it out. "Is it dangerous here?" I thought to ask.

"You're deep, deep in Seelie territory," Claybriar said. "The main danger is that you'll never want to leave."

"I can't say that I do, not with Fred waiting on the other side of the Gate. Caryl already sacrificed Elliott to make the dude think he didn't see us."

"*What?*"

"Oh, *please* let us not start that conversation anew," said Caryl, ruining the mature exasperation of her words with more tears.

"I don't see that we have much choice but to go back through the Gate," said Claybriar.

I turned to Caryl in alarm. "Don't you dare cast any more spells on that man."

"What choice do we have?" she said.

"Lots of choices!"

"Maybe I can distract him," said Claybriar. "I did promise him some nymphs. If he takes them to the receiving area to entertain them, that'll leave the Gate and the front door unwatched for a few, and you can slip out without having to enchant him."

"But he broke the deal."

"That means I don't *have* to pay up. Doesn't mean I can't."

"Fine. Go find your nymphs. Caryl and I will amuse ourselves while we wait."

"Uh-huh," said Claybriar with a grin. "I'll bet you will."

What, could he *smell* it on us? Caryl, currently the poster child for mood swings, burst into nervous giggles.

The look Claybriar gave me before walking away through the trees was equal parts amused and chiding but, strangely, not at all shocked.

17

The moment Claybriar was out of sight, Caryl returned to me, slipping an arm around my back and leaning her head against my shoulder.

"Do you think he minds?" she said. Not even asking if he'd figured out what we were up to in his absence.

"He's uh . . . pretty solidly poly," I said. "I think he just sort of assumes everyone else is too."

"Are you?" Her breath warmed my neck as she spoke.

"No," I said. "I just suck at self-control."

"Is that what this is?" She drew back to look up at me.

I looked down into her face, at her lips all rosy from cold and kisses, and forgot she'd asked me a question. I guess that was my answer. I kissed her again. She melted into it, shivered as I settled a hand on the nape of her neck.

After a moment I drew back, rested my forehead against hers.

"I'm so pleased," she said, her eyes still closed, "that I can even respond appropriately."

"Your pillow talk needs work," I murmured against her temple.

"Find a place with pillows," she said, "and I'll work all you like."

The bestial quality of the lust provoked by those words was perversely what caused me to withdraw. Claybriar had said something to me back in the fall, about the way lust worked for him before his contact with me awakened his higher thought. What I was feeling reminded me too much of that; I felt that my already tenuous self-control was being decimated by the whims of prurient spirits. I was not okay with that.

"I apologize," said Caryl as I withdrew. She sounded a little panicky. "That was too far."

"Everything that happened since we went through that Gate was too far," I said, but when I turned and saw the look on her face I regretted my words. "But it was good," I amended clumsily. "Not smart, and not fair to do without at least having a conversation with Zach about what the fuck he and I are, but . . . very hot. I've wanted to do that for a while. I enjoyed the hell out of it. Thank you."

"Thank you?" she repeated with a blank look. Then she gave a strange, vague laugh, and her gaze wandered off into the trees. I checked her hands; they were shaking. Damn it. "How long do you suppose Claybriar will be?" she said.

"I have no idea how long it takes to round up nymphs."

"That may depend upon whether he intends to do more than round them up."

"Oh, for heaven's sake," I sighed. "Wouldn't put it past the little goat."

I couldn't look at Caryl. I admired the forest, feeling as hazy as it looked. Shock, smugness, guilt, and hilarity mingled in my head. I'd just made out with my boss.

"How would I get to the palace, the White Rose, from here?" I asked.

"Inadvisable, for you," said Caryl. "A long trek through territory covered in fragile spellwork."

"But if I needed to, later?"

"Well, if you're leaving from Los Angeles, I'd advise using the portals." She smoothed her hair where my hands had been. The least of the places they'd been. "The journey from LA4 to Skyhollow's estate should not be difficult, assuming you wear the protective suit we've made for you. Then you'd use the portal there that leads directly to the White Rose."

"Is a portal the same thing as a Gate?"

"No. You will see. Showing you is easier than explaining."

"You've always been awfully light on explanations," I said, daring a glance at her. She was avoiding looking at me, too. "It's amazing I got through the whole ordeal with Vivian, as little as you told me."

"People learn best when the knowledge is about to be put to immediate practical use."

"You know what, Caryl? I think you're actually pretty good at your job."

She glanced at me at that, but then quickly away. "I appreciate the sentiment," she said, "but I do not know if I believe you."

"Nobody ever believes they're any good," I said. "Like my dad. He moved more real estate than anybody in the tristate area, but he was always so driven, like he was trying to prove something to—I don't even know who."

"To you?"

"Pfft. No. Unless I got in trouble, he forgot he had a daughter."

But her words still burned, as though I'd been sprayed with hot glue. *To you?* I took a deep breath, but it didn't help; the minty air made my eyes sting. So I just started crying, as Arcadia demanded. Caryl took a step toward me, but I turned away.

"Speaking of hysteria," I said, dashing at my eyes with the heel of my hand, "how are we going to fly you back home without Elliott? Can Caveat do the same spell?"

Caryl wrung her hands. "She wouldn't. Too intimate."

"You should call Elliott back, Caryl."

She shook her head, tears filling her eyes. "If Fred remembers we were there, he'll notify Dame Belinda immediately. She'll retaliate."

"We've already established she can't make facades of us, and if she could use blood to control us, wouldn't she have just done that to Tjuan instead of going to the trouble of copying him?"

"The vials are small," said Caryl. She held her thumb and finger apart, demonstrating. "Likely she couldn't compel him long enough to have him purchase a handgun and commit a crime. But it wouldn't take long to make you, for example, step in front of a truck."

I shuddered. "Do you think she'd do that?"

"Not without cause. Let us not give her one. Elliott will understand. He and I are of one mind." She was about to wear through her gloves, with all the wringing.

"If you're so in sync, then why didn't you just ask him?"

"I panicked!" Caryl put both hands in her hair, took a few deep, slow breaths. Dropped her hands. "He'll understand. He will."

"Well, we're not getting you on a plane like this."

She paced, clearly trying to think. "I can get to the White Rose from here on foot; it isn't far. I'll go with Claybriar when he returns, follow him to the portal."

"How are you going to explain your presence in Daystrike?"

"I won't. I'll use another ward spirit to cloak myself. It will leave the Residence a bit more vulnerable, but not for long. I'll take the portal to Skyhollow, and then Caveat can replace the ward once I return to Los Angeles. I'll be there before you are."

"Claybriar said people can't sneak into the White Rose."

"They cannot. But the portal to Skyhollow is not inside the palace; it is on the ground nearby. Near the prison."

"The prison?"

"A sort of dungeon. Underground."

"Well I guess you'd really better not get caught, huh?"

"Claybriar will be with me, and we are both very familiar with the area."

"Speak of the horny devil . . ." I tipped my head toward the trees behind her, where Claybriar was returning with a nymph on either arm.

We'd been calling them nymphs, but truth be told, I had no idea what they were. They weren't *sidhe*, because every *sidhe* I'd ever seen had wings. These two were clearly native to Daystrike, all in shades of silver and white, their waist-length hair touched by a hint of the canopy's eerie glow. Their eyes were black and soulless, their lips full; the unsteady moonlight played over their slender bodies like candlelight on silk. They looked enough alike that if I'd closed my eyes for a moment they could have switched places without my knowing.

"Come on," said Claybriar as his hooves crunched through the snow toward us. "Let's get those two into the hands of that lucky old man while they're still eager to meet him."

"Why am I even considering asking what that means?"

"I wouldn't," he said. "Let's just go."

"Caryl's going to head back to the portal with you when you return," I said.

"I'll be borrowing a ward spirit to cloak myself," she clarified.

"Can you make sure she gets home safely?" I asked him.

He studied me a moment, then nodded solemnly. "I promise to see Caryl safely back to Los Angeles." A fey promise. Good. "Don't follow me through the Gate until I say it's clear."

I watched the sway of nymph hips as the two allowed themselves to be led toward the Gate. "This night has been an unmitigated disaster," I said.

"All things considered," said Caryl, "I think we've done a superlative job of mitigating it. Before you go, give me the Vessel."

Only then did I remember, touch my jeans pocket, feel the rolled-up fabric I'd rammed in there. Mess aside, we'd done it. We'd *actually fucking done it.*

I started to withdraw the bag, then hesitated.

"No," I said. "This feels like a bad idea."

"I beg your pardon?"

"I don't want you running off with this thing halfway across Arcadia. It's not that I don't trust you, but—yeah, honestly, right now I don't trust you. My whole plan hinges around this thing."

"Suit yourself," said Caryl. "If you are going to hold on to it, however, I suggest that you do not let it out of your sight."

• • •

I had some explaining to do when I got back to the hotel in the wee hours of Monday without Caryl or Elliott and with a priceless artifact crammed into my pocket, but it wasn't by far the worst loop I'd thrown Alvin for in the last few months, so he just shrugged and sighed and bought us our return flights. He was heading straight back to New Orleans, and Caveat wasn't much of a conversationalist, so essentially I flew home alone.

After eleven hours of fitful sleep I arrived only three hours after I'd left; it was *still* Monday. A fucking endless Monday. Caryl had gotten there before me, as promised; she was at Residence Four, in fact.

Caryl, without Elliott, after what we'd done . . . I was braced for adolescent drama. But to my bewilderment, she seemed to be at no higher than a 4 or so on the stress scale. She didn't demand explanations or clarifications; it was almost as though nothing had happened.

"Brand is still in crow form at Skyhollow estate," she informed me grimly. "But I have been in contact with Shock, who has been furtively working on a new facade for him. He insists it is only to repair his mistake, but I believe his loyalty to Barker may be weakening. I assume you still have the Vessel? Or did you transfer it to Alvin?"

"I think I'm going to hang on to it until Shock is on board. The fewer times it changes hands, the better I'll feel. How's Tjuan been doing? Can we go and check in on him? Maybe bring him a pizza or something?"

"It is too dangerous," she said. "The police may have us under surveillance. But it is good that you are thinking of him, as he has clearly been thinking of you. Come, look at this."

She led me to a cardboard box on the living room couch.

I lifted the lid off the box and pulled out what was now a neoprene shirt, separate from the trousers folded beneath it.

"Tjuan did this?" I said with a disbelieving laugh.

"Indirectly, through Abigail at Residence One," said Caryl. "He had Gary pick up the suit and deliver it to her after work."

"*Abigail?* For real?"

"She was once employed in wardrobe at Paramount, and apparently she still finds that sort of work soothing."

I put the shirt carefully back into the box. "Remind me to go and visit her sometime," I said. "Bring her some cookies or something. Maybe Gary, too, once I'm allowed to go to the motel. Tjuan, I hope to repay with something a lot better than cookies."

Caryl gave me an appalled look, then shook her head as she walked away.

"I meant *freeing* him, Caryl," I said to her back. "Jesus."

Whatever. I was hungry.

After I'd made myself a snack and a terrible cup of black coffee, I tried to find Caryl again, but by then she was occupied with one of Alondra's biweekly meltdowns. Alondra had managed to lose her phone and was sure she was going to be fired for it, have her memory wiped. PTSD from New York, apparently.

At first I tried to just wait it out. It was weird hearing Caryl try to calm someone down when she didn't have Elliott. She was so affronted that Alondra thought she'd fire her over a phone that she made it all about herself, which wasn't exactly soothing. Eventually Song intervened, started doing her Mom Thing at both of them, but by then I'd given up and grabbed the suit to take it up to my room. I wasn't going to have a productive conversation with Caryl anytime soon, it seemed.

When I finally recharged my own phone and started it up, I found a series of subtly plaintive texts from Zach, culminating in this monologue:

Ok it's been a week, guess this is over. Figured you'd have more balls than to just ghost on me, but ok. Consider this tho, I really am sry. I tried to understand, ask urself why I tried. Ask urself if it matters and if not then ok, won't bother you again.

That was more words than I'd ever heard him say all at once even in person. I sat staring at my phone, jet lag layered on top of a possible concussion and the jet lag I hadn't gotten over yet from before. After a minute I texted him back:

Dude sorry i was literally out of the country i am jetlagged as fuck can you give me a day or 2

And then I reached into the pocket of my jeans and took out the ancient fey artifact that was wadded up in there. What the hell was I supposed to do with it? Nowhere felt safe.

I carefully opened it up to peer inside and was instantly sorry. My eyes watered and my ears rang. I smelled copper. When I wiped my nose, I saw a smear of red on the back of my hand.

"Holy *fuck*," I said, and threw the thing across the room. Even as I did so, I felt a little dizzy at the idea that I was actually throwing an infinite interdimensional void, a phaseless nothingness filled with unused facades and God only knew what else. Brand's real body, for one.

Wait. How did this thing work?

I went to pick it up again, rolled it carefully, slipped it back into my jeans pocket. I put a hand over it, considering.

Could we use it to get Brand's body out of the void somehow, or could we only remove things that had been put into the void via the bag to begin with? Because if we could get Brand back now, rather than later, he could take Belinda's wraith army out of commission. Which, among other things, meant that whichever wraith was piloting Tjuan's facade—my money was still on Qualm—couldn't cause any more trouble.

I grabbed my phone, opened Tumblr, sent Shock another ask.

Hey just curious, what if u could somehow shove the crow into the in between void place, would that force the orig body out of there where we could get at it and if so could u redo the enchant?

While I was still typing, my phone made the text-from-Zach splash sound.

I finished the ask and sent it, then felt a clenching in my gut. I just *knew* that since I'd avoided drama with Caryl, karma was now going to explode through the medium of Zach and send me straight into dysphoric meltdown. But all his text said was:

Ok

I went back to Tumblr and obsessively refreshed my messages, tried to psychically *will* Shock to reply, but of course he'd chosen that moment to be busy. So I took the phone to my bed and lay down, resting my aching bones, closing my eyes for a moment.

When I opened them, the sun was coming up; the longest

Monday in the history of the universe was finally over. Ironically, it was now Groundhog Day.

I had to piss like a geriatric racehorse, but first I checked Tumblr.

Like Zach's, Shock's message was one word long.

Yes.

18

Not far from the LA4 Gate, Arcadia side, was a path to Duke Skyhollow's estate. I'd glimpsed it before when Caryl first sneaked me into fairyland to negotiate with our manticore friend, back when he was terrorizing Skyhollow out of rage at his lost chance to meet his Echo.

The path looked like a heat mirage over the golden sand, long and serpentine and leading to what appeared to be distant haze-cloaked towers against the apricot sky on the horizon.

I hadn't bothered trying on my suit for this Tuesday afternoon visit, because if it protected the path's spellwork from me, it stood to reason it would also protect me from the spellwork. That meant with the suit on I wouldn't be able to keep up with Caryl and Claybriar and without it I'd destroy the path, so I had to stay behind. I did put on some latex gloves, out of respect for Claybriar.

I wasn't willing to let anyone else take the Medial Vessel out of my sight, so the two of them had to go and bring Brand back to where I waited near the LA4 Gate. They needed me not only because I was keeping an iron grip on the Vessel, but because if Brand decided to start cursing people the minute he popped out of there I could whip off my gloves and fix everything with my iron touch.

I also happened to be the only person Brand was 100 percent unwilling to eat.

When Caryl and Claybriar returned from their trip to the estate, Claybriar was carrying the crow in a dainty wooden cage. The bird looked neither happy nor healthy. Claybriar looked strangely smug. Caryl was in her element, having been brought in on all the geeky details by Shock via text message, so her stress level was fairly low.

"He lets me handle him sometimes," said Claybriar, standing there in the bright sun in the full shirtless glory of his native form. "So I'm probably the best person to do the actual, uh . . ." He mimed cramming something into a bag.

"What exactly is going to happen?" I asked Caryl. "I mean, how's the manticore going to come out of that thing?"

"He will not be emerging from the bag," said Caryl. "The destruction of the crow, as with the destruction of the dog, will leave Brand's consciousness trapped at the site of the 'death.' Meanwhile, once the spellwork enters the intermediate space, it will trigger its original function and rotate the alternate form into place at the site of last sensory input."

"What I'm getting at," I said, "is where exactly is this gigantic lion-scorpion guy going to appear? On top of whoever's holding the bag?"

"At the last place from which the crow perceived the world, so . . ." Caryl acquired a sudden look of dismay. "Yes, in a manner of speaking. At the opening of the bag."

"I feel like this isn't going to end well."

Caryl cleared her throat, fidgeted with her gloves. "Well!

Let us simply do our best to stand clear of the opening, shall we?"

That wasn't the only problem, we realized, now that the bag and the bird were in the same place. In comparison to each other, the opening of the bag was slightly smaller, and the crow slightly larger, than we had quite anticipated. Claybriar reached into the cage and grabbed the bird around its middle, and I held the bag's mouth open wide, but we could tell just by looking that he wasn't going to fit.

One of Claybriar's ears twitched. "This is a problem," he said. The crow just stared into space listlessly, feet dangling.

"Perhaps," said Caryl, "we should cut the bird into pieces."

The bag fell out of my hands, and Claybriar made a plaintive sound.

"Are you kidding me?" Clay said as I bent carefully to retrieve the bag from the sand. He cradled the bird against his fuzzy chest, which was too much indignity for it to handle even in its current state of depression. It struggled feebly. "I've been taking care of this stupid thing for a week, and you think I'm going to watch you mutilate it?"

Caryl let out a stormy exhale and fixed Claybriar with an exasperated look. "We are preparing to consign it to an eternity of timeless nothingness!" she snapped. "What difference does it make if we mutilate it first?"

"It's moot anyway," I said, "because I seem to have forgotten my hacksaw."

"I will use a spell," Caryl said.

"Hell no!"

"I mean I shall *ask* a spirit, as the commoners do. We have the luxury of a few moments for me to attempt this, do we not?

I have been very curious about it, and I even have Claybriar here to guide me."

Claybriar looked startled. The bird was really starting to fight him now, so he put it back into the cage. "It's, uh, kind of an easier thing to do than to explain," he said. "You've never done it?"

"No, but I am a quick study."

He considered. "I'm told it's a bit like praying."

"I have never done that, either."

"Ah." Claybriar scratched at a horn. "Well, just hold in your mind the image of what you want. And, uh . . . cast your mind out into the infinite . . . uh . . ." He gestured expansively.

"Clay," I said, "you are the leader of a revolution. You really need to get better at explaining shit."

"It's my first time, all right?" He folded his arms. "Just think about reaching outward. Casting, like you're fishing."

"I have never—"

"Done that either, right. But you know what I mean; don't be difficult. The point is to remain open, to put your idea for a spell out there, like bait. Keep holding it, even if it's tiring, and wait for a spirit to come to you and say 'Let's do this.' Or they might negotiate a bit, or clarify, but it's all—without words. It feels like it's all in your mind. Then either they're in or they're out. If they agree, you'll know it when you feel it. Like a sudden burst of energy that's yours to shape."

Caryl sat on the spongy sand, cross-legged, as though meditating. She closed her eyes.

"This feels ridiculous," she said after a moment.

"Now you have to start over," said Claybriar. "You can't be thinking about anything else, including how ridiculous you feel."

"Focus is difficult for me without—" A flicker of distress passed over her face, and then irritated determination. "I shall try."

She sat for a very long time. It was extremely boring.

I looked over at Claybriar, met his eyes, lifted an eyebrow. He shrugged and walked over to me, careful not to disturb Caryl.

"Caryl told me about your suit," he murmured, taking my hand.

"Yeah?"

He leaned in then, to whisper about a quarter inch from my ear, and traced a little circle on my gloved palm with his thumb. "It would take some creativity, but I think I could show you a good time in that thing."

I smacked him on the arm, and he grinned.

"It worked!" Caryl said, childlike. I gave a guilty start and stepped away from Claybriar. Caryl was oblivious; her eyes sparkled with wonder, and her cheeks had gone pink. "A spirit came to me!"

"Cool!" I said, surprised into sincerity.

"Apparently, it enjoys severing things! It wants to know how many pieces."

"You make the loveliest friends, Caryl," I said.

Caryl closed her eyes again, to all appearances communing with the spirit. I had no way of eavesdropping, and things went on for so long I started to wonder if negotiations weren't going well. Meanwhile Clay removed the crow from the cage again, holding it carefully.

"Easy there, fella," said Claybriar. "Try not to—"

The bird fell from his hands into eight cauterized segments. They pattered to the sand in a heap.

I let out a strange, hysterical laugh, and then my stomach gave a lurch. I backed away from the remains, wiping at my damp forehead.

"You all right?" Claybriar asked. He wasn't looking so hot either.

"Just put the pieces in the bag," I said.

"I shall do it," said Caryl, seeming more pleased than disturbed by the carnage.

She had only gotten six pieces in when suddenly there was a sickening wrench in the immediate atmosphere, an indescribable torsion of reality. My ears popped, and then I think I might have had a slight consciousness brownout, because next thing I knew, Claybriar was helping hold me upright despite the obvious pain it caused him to touch me. As soon as I felt steady again I pulled away.

The manticore lay on the sand, his terrifying ruby red eyes as fixed and lifeless as billiard balls.

"Oh God," I moaned. "Is he dead?"

Claybriar pointed to the creature's shaggy red rib cage, which slowly rose and fell.

"Brand," I said gently. I stepped closer to his horrible face, so close to human, but big enough to serve tea for two on. Hesitantly I touched his brownish-red mane with my gloved hand.

Words emerged slowly from the manticore's too-wide, ear-to-ear mouth, in a distant echo of his usual panic-inducing brassy rumble.

"Don't . . . ever . . . pet . . . me."

"You're alive!" I said. I laughed, tearing up a little. "You're all right!"

"By what . . . fucked-up . . . definition . . ." He let out a sudden barrage of coughs like two trains crashing into each other, and a venomous spine shot off his jointed tail, narrowly missing Claybriar.

"Fuck!" said Claybriar, standing rigid.

Brand shuddered and lay still again.

I hovered over him. "You don't look so good," I said. "You need something to drink? Someone to eat?"

"Millie," said Claybriar sternly. But the corners of Brand's mouth twitched upward, and it filled me with glee.

Brand tried to get up. I was reminded of his first efforts to work the dog body Shock had made him back in the fall. His huge bat wings unfurled halfway, flailed and then furled again. His feet slid out from under him, and he face-planted in the sand.

"Take it easy," said Claybriar.

"The wings are still in my head," Brand droned without even lifting his face. "Four sets, two I can feel that aren't there, two I can't feel that are. But backward now. Vivian . . . Vivian . . . find me a naughty unicorn! I could eat sand. Does Parisa still want me? She'll feed me . . . I'm a good doggie. I'm a good doggie . . ." He trailed off into an incoherent groan.

Caryl began to look fretful, wringing her hands and worrying at her lower lip. "I do not think he is in any condition to help us," she said.

"We should feed him," I said.

"You're kidding, right?" said Claybriar. "He eats *live fey*."

"Well," I said, "surely there are some fey that are slightly more disposable? Fey cows, fey zebras? I saw something that looked like a deer or a horse, back in Daystrike."

"Whatever you saw," said Claybriar, "it was just as intelligent as you or me. No matter what the *sidhe* tell you, we don't have animals here. Everything has a soul. Plays games, feels love and despair, makes art."

"Okay, but they all die, eventually, right? Some of them eat each other?"

"If it's part of a Hunt, then it's a game. There's honor in it: The stronger party gets to live and the other to die, and all that. But he is in no condition to Hunt; we'd just be kidnapping some poor creature and feeding it to him."

"Is there a quick way to find someone willing? Someone dying of a wasting disease or something?"

"The Seelie don't get diseases, and the Unseelie don't die from them."

"Condemned prisoners? The White Rose has a prison. Does Skyhollow?"

"It does." Claybriar looked thoughtful for a moment and then suddenly straightened. "Oh."

"What?"

"I may have an idea."

"What? What is it?"

"It may be nothing. But it also could be a big deal. I don't want to get anyone's hopes up. Just wait here, and make sure that Brand doesn't go anywhere."

I looked down at the manticore, who had just begun to snore gently. "I don't think that will be a problem," I said.

19

When Claybriar returned, he brought company: a stunning *sidhe* woman leading a lean, shaggy canine by a chain. I was so distracted by something unidentifiably *wrong* about the animal that it took me a moment to recognize my former boss Inaya's Echo. Vicki Plume, a.k.a. Foxfeather, the homeless baroness.

She was homeless, incidentally, because Brand had destroyed her estate. What the hell was Claybriar thinking?

Once the trio stepped off the enchanted path, I hurried to meet them halfway, as though I could prevent them from seeing the giant red lion-beast that was sprawled on the sand next to Caryl.

"What is this?" I said uneasily to Claybriar.

"Millie, this is Baroness Foxf—"

"I know who it is. Why is she *here*? And what's with the dog?"

Only when I glanced at the pointy-eared beast from closer range—a coyote, monstrous and lanky, its back at my hip level—did I notice what had disturbed me about it from a distance. It had no eyes. The glittering chain around its neck looked to be made from diamonds. Its tongue lolled, dripping; ribs showed through the golden fur. But it had no *eyes*.

"Hello again, Ironbones," said Foxfeather. *She* had eyes: lavender novas. Her hair was an undulating stream of opal silk, and diaphanous wings caught and scattered the sunlight where they lay folded against her back. She reached a four-fingered hand toward me in greeting, and I took it gently with my glove.

"Sorry for being rude," I said. "But given the situation, I thought Claybriar was supposed to be keeping certain things *secret* from you."

"He was right to tell," she said, a little pouty. "Despite what the manticore did to me, his Echo and my Echo are partners. So I have decided to redeem him. And redeem *this* wretch here." She jerked the eyeless coyote's chain. It let out a choking sound, then a menacing snarl.

"What exactly did it do?"

"It betrayed me. It was my vassal, the one who cast my estate's wards. It knew the Words of Power."

"She means he knew the spirits' names," said Claybriar. "He's a trickster with spirit-sight."

"And spirit-sight means . . . ?" I prompted.

"He sees the same way the spirits do. Well, not exactly; he has a limited field of 'vision.' But to see a spirit lets you figure out its name. This asshole befriends them and then enslaves them for the *sidhe*." He looked down at the beast with such contempt I thought for a minute he was going to actually spit on it.

"That is no crime," said Foxfeather. "The beast's crime is that it joined forces with the manticore to betray me. The manticore made me believe it was safe to leave my estate, and once I was gone, the trickster canceled all the protective wards that it had cast!"

Sidhe estates were closely tied to their owners; their wards could not be destroyed, even by the original spell casters, so long as their owners were inside them. That was why Vivian had spent decades hatching a plan to spill fey blood at all the corresponding spots in our world simultaneously. That would have bypassed the problem by dumping all the noble estates—wards, owners, and all—directly into the void.

I looked between the creepy, blank-faced coyote and Brand, conspirators to destroy Foxfeather's little barony. "You've brought these two pals back together why?"

"Justice," said Foxfeather. She beamed at Claybriar. "The king gave my ex-vassal a choice. A poetic end—devoured by the monster he allowed to devour his friends—or he could rot in Skyhollow's prison forever."

"Fey are big on poetic ends," explained Claybriar. "Religious thing, sort of. Or as close as we get to it."

I turned back to Foxfeather. "So Wile E. here wants some sort of religious absolution. How does this square things with you and Brand?"

Foxfeather smiled. "The manticore has been well punished, according to King Claybriar. Now he will be redeemed in a different way. He will swear fealty to the Seelie Court."

"Ohhh boy," I said. "Yeah, I think Brand's probably going to pass on that."

Claybriar looked up at me entreatingly. "Millie," he said. "Shiverlash nearly got Brand to murder Caryl. If he's going to be working with us, he needs a kinder person holding his leash."

"I'm not arguing the logic," I said. "Just saying he's not going to do it."

"I can persuade him," said Foxfeather.

"You'll . . . persuade the guy who destroyed your estate."

"Trust me," she said with a smile. Something about her reminded me so much of her Echo Inaya in that moment that I was willing to believe she was capable of anything.

"Worth a try," I said.

The four of us approached Brand and Caryl. Caryl knelt in the sand a little too close to those jaws for my liking; Brand lay with his eyes half-closed. When Foxfeather approached, though, Brand made a futile effort to sit up.

"Shit," he said.

"Hello, friend," said Foxfeather. "I brought you something to eat."

"Really, I couldn't," Brand said. "Couldn't eat another bite. Your aunt was *incredibly* filling."

"Cut it out, Brand," I said.

"You know," Caryl observed, eyeing the listless manticore, "your Echo would be displeased to see you mistreating Foxfeather. Foxfeather's Echo is Inaya West: Parisa's partner and best friend."

"The manticore and I were friends too," said Foxfeather softly. "Once he let me climb on his back and ride all over Skyhollow."

"Pfft," said Brand. "I just like to make *sidhe* trash straddle me."

"He was lonely," Foxfeather insisted. "And I wasn't afraid. We had fun together, until I found my Echo. Then he got *so jealous*."

Brand snarled, making Foxfeather jump. "Fuck off," he said. "Or I'll eat you, too."

"I know you're hungry," Foxfeather said, unruffled, leading the coyote closer. "To show that I forgive you, I offer you a choice. You may—"

Brand, showing a sudden strength I could never have antic-ipated, lunged forward over the sand, mouth stretched wide, and engulfed the coyote in one swift *hrrrrrlllllp*.

I shrieked, slapped a hand over my mouth. Foxfeather leaped back, dropping her end of the diamond chain, which Brand drowsily slurped into his mouth like a spaghetti noodle.

Foxfeather burst into tears, turned, and clung to King Claybriar.

"Welp," he said.

"Yep," I agreed.

Brand squeezed his eyes shut, swallowed hard. I heard muffled crunching, as though the muscles of the manticore's throat were so impossibly powerful that they pulverized the coyote's bones into a fine paste on the way down.

"Holy mother of garbage disposals," I said.

"I feel sick," said Caryl. I went over to rub her shoulders.

Brand, still in the process of doing whatever it was he did to render an entire live wriggling carnivore digestible, did not answer. After a moment he collapsed back onto his side with a groan.

"Well, now what?" I said to Foxfeather. Claybriar was strok-ing her hair. I suddenly realized he'd probably slept with her, too, and tried not to get too distracted picturing it.

"Not fair!" Foxfeather exploded at Brand, still clinging to Claybriar as she stamped her foot.

"Unseelie," Brand reminded her.

"Commoner," she riposted.

Clay stopped stroking Foxfeather at that; she almost fell over as he approached Brand.

"Hey, buddy," he said. "Feeling better?"

"Not your buddy," Brand said, tail giving a peevish twitch.

Caryl sighed. "I suppose I knew better than to expect gratitude."

"All right, coyote breath," I said, going to stand in Brand's eyeline. "Caryl and Claybriar and I have just *literally* given you your life back. So I suggest you start showing us a little respect."

"Or what?" said Brand, glaring back at me. "Obviously you need me, so don't pretend you did this because you're so very *fond*. Let's get to what you want, and what you think you can offer."

"Besides giving you back your body?"

"I didn't ask for that. So I don't owe you shit."

I had a feeling that even though he wasn't willing to eat me, it probably wasn't a good idea for me to punch him repeatedly in the eyeball.

"Well," I said instead, "we can give you a new facade, which means you can come back to our world, see your Echo."

He was quiet for a minute.

"Can't she come here?" he finally said.

We could, technically, arrange for Parisa Naderi to visit Arcadia now that she had a confirmed Echo. But he didn't know that.

"Nope," I said.

Claybriar opened his mouth, then closed it. Smart boy.

"So what is it you need from me?" Brand said.

"We need you to bind all those wraiths again," I said. "They got out of your book."

"I'll have to see Parisa first," said Brand. "After what I just went through, I don't remember the names. Barely remember hers."

I narrowed my eyes at him. "If you weren't fey," I said, "I would be a hundred percent sure you're bullshitting me right now."

"And if I weren't fey," he said, "I absolutely would be. So jealous you guys get to do that." He let out a deep sigh.

"So if we put you in contact with your Echo, do you *promise* you'll bind all those wraiths again? Same ones you bound before?"

"I promise," said Brand.

Caryl rose from the sand to stand next to me, so that we both loomed over him. "Say the entire sentence," she said.

"Fine!" Brand repeated my phrasing of the promise more or less word for word, though he inserted a few colorful adjectives and adverbs.

Foxfeather hung back watching, nibbling adorably at her lower lip. "I don't know what to tell the duke," she said nervously. "Does this mean the manticore is on our side now? Or not?"

"He is," I said, at the same time Brand said, "I'm not."

"Damn it, Brand!" I said to him in frustration. Then I looked back to Foxfeather. "Read my mind a second," I said. "I know you *sidhe* can do that, right?"

Her eyes went as wide as though I'd suggested she put her hand in my jeans. But she said, "All right."

I looked at her and thought, as hard as I could, *You tell the duke I'm still going to make Throebrand swear allegiance to the Seelie Court. I have his Echo; I can make him do anything I want. The manticore is not going to be any more trouble to you.*

"All right, all right!" said Foxfeather, folding her arms in a way that showed off some intriguing, opalescent cleavage. "You don't have to *shout*."

• • •

Shock had the facade ready. The kid was a pro, and possibly motivated by a combination of shame at his previous failure and an infatuation with a certain someone. Even only being able to work on the body under the radar, it had taken him just five days. Finding time to slip away and meet us was hard, though; he had to work around not only the watchful eyes of mundane authorities, but also those in Arcadia monitoring the three portals he needed to use to get here.

Finally, he messaged Caryl that he could meet us on Wednesday after eight a.m. our time, which was after eleven p.m. in Hong Kong. That was an easier time for him to slip away from school using only the tiniest traces of magic to divert attention, and as for his dad, he could tell him that he'd heard a rumor the manticore was active again. He had. I'd told him.

When he showed up early on Wednesday morning, he surprised us by whipping the lid off a large hatbox and saying, "Ta-da!! Your manticore's new ride."

Caryl and I peered into the box. It was a crow. Not the same type Brand had occupied before, but a big handsome thing with a bold white breast.

"Shock," I said. "Do you *want* to get eaten?"

The princeling shook his head, grinning. "This is best," he said. "Brand has months of experience operating a body like this. This one is an African pied crow; they are legal to own as pets in your country. His Echo can walk around with the bird on her shoulder, looking incredibly cool. He should be pleased!"

He should have been, but he wasn't. When the three of

us arrived in Arcadia to meet him and Claybriar, he took one look at the bird, dug his claws into the sand, and let out a jangling, brassy roar that made me wish I'd been born without ears.

When Brand started yelling in English, it was actually an improvement.

"I WILL EAT YOU! ALL THREE OF YOU, AND SPIT OUT THE IRON IN THAT MONSTER'S BONES!"

"Relax, sir, please," said Shock, and then began to murmur a few words in the Unseelie tongue.

Brand interrupted him with a powerful swipe of one paw, sending the poor kid sprawling back across the sand. The hatbox fell; the lid rolled one way and the box another. The crow just lay limply on the sand like something freshly dead.

Caryl stood for half a second before getting a sort of *oh!* look and racing over to kneel next to Shock.

I moved to retrieve the facade, picking up the disturbingly warm, lifeless thing and dusting the sand from its feathers.

"This is your revenge," snarled Brand, narrowing his eyes and coming to loom over me in a way that made me very aware of my intestines. I bluffed; Caryl had said something about never letting predators see fear.

"You think I'm going to be any nicer to you than I have to be, after the way you've treated us?" I said, clutching the crow to my chest. "I was operating under the assumption that you and I were friends. But you made it clear we're not, so you don't get a damned thing more than we've agreed on."

Brand actually hesitated. His uncertainty spurred me on.

"We said you'd get to see Naderi again, and I'll keep my word, because you know I want the names of those wraiths.

But if you ever want to see her after that, you'd better get used to rules, and playing nice, and the Accord—once we get a third one nailed down—because fey who break the rules don't get fired, they get executed. And I am not going to watch Naderi go through your death a second time. Prove to me that you know how to be helpful, if you ever want to see a Project contract."

Brand looked at me silently for a moment with the hatred of two worlds all concentrated in his baleful stare. Then he lowered his eyes to my feet.

"Tell me what you want me to do," he growled.

"Three things," I said. "Do three things for me, and once you've done those, I will start putting the wheels in motion to get you a contract made up. The first," I said, holding up the crow, "is that I want you to agree to have this facade bound to you by a consenting spirit."

"Wait," said Shock. "I thought I was going to cast an enchantment."

"You are," I told him, passing him the bird. "Enchantments are spirits, Shock. Caryl and Claybriar will explain. It's the same spell you've always cast—you're just going to *ask* first."

Shock looked uneasy; I turned back to Brand. "You going to play ball?"

"Fine," he said. "What's the second thing?"

"The second thing is that you're going to gather an army of commoners willing to destroy the White Rose."

"*What?*" said everyone more or less at once. Brand sounded slightly more delighted than the others, though.

But then he shook his head irritably. "I doubt we could lure the queen out," he said, tail lashing. "*Although*—if we had *two* like you, one at each of the standing stones, you could unravel the lofting wards and send the whole thing crashing down, wards and—"

"Brand!" I interrupted in alarm. "I am not actually planning an act of terrorism here! I just need you to find a bunch of commoners who'd be *willing*. As many as you can. And make sure the rumors get out."

"Gotcha," he said, looking visibly disappointed. "Third thing?"

"I want you to swear fealty to Claybriar."

"WHAT?"

"Don't you start roaring again. Remember when Shiverlash took control of you last fall? Remember what she made you do?"

Caryl silently rolled up her sleeve, showed him the ugly scars on her forearm. His tail lashed again.

"There's only one way to release a monarch's hold on you," I said, "as I learned last fall with Blesskin. You've gotta swear fealty to the other Court. Once all the dust has settled, you're welcome to go back to the Unseelie Court, if they'll have you."

He began to pace, his great shoulders rolling, his face contorted with feckless rage. "Why would they? They won't. I'll be stuck serving the Creampuff Court for eternity." He growled, deep and menacing, and let me see his three rows of razor-sharp teeth.

My stomach had just started to tie itself in knots when he suddenly fell onto the sand, prostrating himself before Claybriar. I had never seen the four-legged version of the pose before; it was actually a bit comical, with his front paws outstretched and his hindquarters in the air. But this didn't seem like the best time for a giggle.

Claybriar scratched at a horn, nonplussed. "Well," he said. "I accept your service. Welcome to the Seelie Court."

"Now," I said as Brand heaved himself to his feet. "Claybriar, Caryl, please walk Shock through the process of binding Brand to his facade the Good Guys' way. I'm going to go catch a couple hours' more sleep."

20

After a two-hour nap in my room I was actually feeling pretty great, until I caught Caryl and Shock making out on the living room couch.

Whatever sound of betrayed horror I made must have been pretty loud, as it distracted them all the way from the top of the staircase.

"For fuck's sake, Caryl!" I snapped as the two sprang apart. "I know Elliott's gone, but could you try to act like a regional manager for five seconds?" I'd meant to sound contemptuous, but my hands, my voice, my everything was shaking.

"I—I should get back to school before people start to wake up," said Shock, red-faced.

He passed me, bolting up the stairs two at a time, as I carefully descended, leaning on the rail. He didn't even look at me. I should have reassured him, since we were supposed to be talking him over to our side, but I was not in a leadership frame of mind. I just stared at Caryl, who met my gaze defiantly.

"Calm yourself," she said. She looked way less rattled than I was, and that only upset me more. "You said you and I shouldn't . . . I didn't think it was cheating."

"It isn't!" I snapped, moving to stand near the other couch. "But you seriously think I'm going to just—"

"I am not attracted to that boy in the slightest," she said earnestly.

"That's *worse*!" I said. "That you would even think it's better shows how far off the rails you've gone."

"Sometimes leadership requires morally ambiguous choices."

"That wasn't leadership! And it's not ambiguous! He's underage, and he's got a crush on you, and you're just—what *are* you even doing?"

"Recruiting," she said.

"Oh Jesus," I groaned. I sank onto the couch across from her and put my head in my hands.

When she spoke again, her voice was softer. "I wouldn't have done it if I thought it would upset you. You seemed so casual about what happened with us. But you know it's you I want."

I looked up at her. "Caryl. How can you do this to him? This is straight-up supervillain stuff. Do you even care whether or not we're the good guys? Why are you even fighting on this side of the war?"

"To put an end to Dame Belinda's tyranny. But one cannot always achieve an end through spotless means."

"But to play with a kid's heart like that . . . on purpose."

"I tried everything else I could think of," she said. "After telling him what Belinda did to me, what she did to Tjuan, after showing him that the spirits were real . . . he was so *close*, but he was still hesitant enough that I couldn't trust him. Now? Now he'll do anything for me."

"This is so fucking twisted, Caryl. I mean, don't you and his *dad* have kind of a thing?"

Caryl made a face. "King Winterglass thinks of me as a daughter. And my feelings for him are . . . complicated, but not sexual."

I shuddered. "Are you planning to sleep with Shock?"

She made another face. "No. I . . . don't think I like men that way at all, actually."

"So you were really just . . . recruiting. What about me? What were you recruiting me for?"

Her eyes showed a flash of hurt at that. "Millie. I've wanted you since before I met you. You *know* that. How many times do I need to tell you that I love you?"

I winced, stood up. "It's been a few too many, actually. This isn't love. I don't know what this is. Did you at least manage to link the fucking facade?"

She blinked, disoriented by my sudden change of subject. "Yes," she said. "Brand is ready to come here whenever Naderi is ready to meet him."

"Then let's deal with that," I said. "Because I cannot deal with this. Not even a little."

Caryl, more familiar with the workings of law enforcement than I was, thought it was a bad idea for us to drive to Valiant to meet with Naderi. If the cops were watching our house, they might have someone check out where we were going and wonder what business we could possibly have with Tjuan's employer. If she came to see us, though, if anything, it would look like she was conducting a little investigation of her own.

She came over that evening after work, and when I heard her knock on the Residence door, I braced myself for a blistering tirade about the week's worth of dodged calls. So when she greeted me with a lopsided, scarred grin and immediately gave me a hug, alarm bells went off like crazy.

My dysphoria had flared up again after Shock and Caryl's make-out session, and so I knew better than to trust anything I was feeling. Still, the wave of intense distrust that hit me now was beyond the pale. I physically recoiled from Naderi, but she barely noticed. She breezed in past me in her fuzzy leopard jacket and red blouse, looking like her usual badass self, but that *smile*—it was all wrong.

It's a facade, I thought instantly. *A copy. Belinda knows, and she sent a fake Naderi to do something horrible to us.*

Caryl didn't seem to notice anything amiss; she greeted Naderi with a gloved handshake and an answering smile. "Please, have a seat," she said. "I will return with Brand."

I glared at Naderi as she moved to sit on the nearest couch. "You seem awfully happy," I said, "for someone whose supervising producer is in the news for shooting a guy."

"All publicity is good publicity," she said, "and to be honest I never liked Miller. You, meanwhile, are awfully hostile for someone who just supposedly went to a lot of trouble to get my Echo back." There was no real bite in her words.

"Brand was suffering," I said. "It was the right thing to do. I didn't do it to curry favor with you. You've been making Tjuan's life miserable, and now, the second he gets accused of something, you turn on him."

"You know where he is, don't you?" she said. Still calm. She'd nearly ripped my head off for worse before.

"What, are you wearing a fucking wire?" I said. "What is your deal? Why are you acting so weird?"

"*I'm* acting weird?" said Naderi. "You're the one who started in with the third degree the second I—" She broke off, sitting up straight and looking toward the stairs. I turned to look too; Caryl was descending the staircase with the bird on her shoulder. Brand took one look at Naderi and spread his wings, getting ready to launch himself into the air.

Suddenly I panicked, rising to my feet. "Don't," I said. "Don't let Brand near her. It's not her!"

To my surprise, Caryl actually halted on the staircase and grabbed the bird, holding him in place.

"Hey!" Brand squawked. He lunged as though to take a big bite of Caryl's fingers but pulled up short at the last minute. "Let me go!"

"Millie," said Caryl, holding the struggling bird. "What is this about?"

"It's not Naderi," I said. "This isn't how she acts."

"What," said Naderi, "you think I'm possessed again or something?"

"Oh God!" I said. "Or that! She could have been possessed *this whole time!*"

"We've already discussed that," said Caryl from the staircase, her irritation showing, "which is why we have limited the information we share with her until the wraiths are recovered. Recovering the wraiths is, in fact, what we are trying to do here, Millie."

"But what if it isn't Naderi at all, if it's a facade? Then touching Brand won't do anything!"

"Millie, you need to calm down!" said Caryl, flushed with frustration herself. "Look at her! She has the same scars that Shiverlash gave her in the fall! And if there were a wraith possessing her, it would not allow her to reunite with Brand, because then Brand would remember its name!"

Caryl and I both turned to look at Naderi.

"Whatever," said Naderi. "I don't understand half this shit, but come on, if it wasn't me, wouldn't Brand just . . . *know*?"

"It's her!" Brand squawked. "Also, Caryl, you are squeezing me way too hard."

Caryl relaxed her grip, smoothed Brand's feathers. "Well then," she said. "If Brand touches her and gets his memory back, we know it's not a facade. And if she is possessed, she won't be for long."

"Fine," I said.

Brand winged his way across the room to light on Naderi's shoulder. Her indrawn breath, the light in her eyes, was unmistakable.

"Brand," she whispered, reaching up a hand to stroke his white breast.

"Hi, beautiful," he squawked.

Naderi gave a wobbly laugh. "I look like shit. But it's good to see you again, my friend." She found what was obviously just the right place to scratch on Brand's neck, given the way he tipped his head until he nearly fell off her shoulder.

Once he'd righted himself, he gave me a piercing birdy glare. "It's her, trash-wit."

"Okay," I said. I felt disoriented, shamed, a little dizzy.

"This is a fucking large bird," said Naderi gruffly. Tears glimmered on her lashes. "I'm going to need a masseuse on call if he plans to spend all day up there."

"Unfortunately," said Caryl, looking a little misty eyed herself as she descended the stairs, "we will have to take him back from you, at least for a while. He needs to recapture the escaped wraiths, and he also needs to help us with an important project we are working on."

"It's going to be great," said Brand. "Millie's asked me to go around Arcadia telling the—"

That was how long it took me to get there and clamp his beak shut. "Brand," I said. "No telling anyone, until it's done." I released his beak, tentatively.

"Not even my *Echo*?" he said.

"Especially not your Echo, since she could be, you know, *possessed*? Remember that bit?"

"Oh, right." He ruffled his feathers. "Well, don't worry, Parisa, if there's any nasty thing hitching a ride inside you I'm gonna rip it right out of there and find it a better place to hang out. Like maybe that siren's feathery crotch."

"Do *not* annoy Shiverlash!" I said. "I've barely got her pacified."

"You be good, Brand," said Naderi. "You hear me? Don't you go getting grounded or something, just when I've gotten you back. You go with them for now. I'll wait for you."

"*What?*" I said. "No, no, this just isn't right. I know you. You'd be fighting us. You'd refuse to give him back. What is your *deal*?"

"Honestly?" she said. "I don't know. I've been in an amazing mood all day. Just . . . done with all the anger, the stress . . . life's too short. Yelling at everyone doesn't get things done any faster, anyway."

"Oh *my*," said Caryl suddenly, and put a hand to her mouth.

"What?" I said. "Caryl, what is it?"

"The oath of fealty," she said. "Brand is channeling an entirely different form of arcane energy now. His connection to her is . . . making her *happy*."

"Oh Jesus," I said, and burst into nervous laughter.

"I'm not Seelie!" Brand croaked indignantly. "I'm still a manticore, you assholes! I'm not Seelie! I'm not!"

"Okay, big guy," I said, scratching at his new favorite spot. "Settle down."

He did not, I noticed, tell me not to pet him.

I probably wouldn't have slept very well Wednesday night even if King Winterglass hadn't walked into my room in the wee hours. I screamed, of course.

"Do not be alarmed," he said in his most silken voice. He stood silhouetted in the doorway; the dim light that burned every night in the hallway highlighted the slender perfection of his facade. "I am not here to harm you."

"Well, I doubt this is a booty call," I said, scooting nervously toward my headboard.

"My son told me everything," he said.

My gut sank. "Everything meaning . . . what exactly?"

He crossed the darkened room toward me. I pulled the covers up to my chest even though I had on a T-shirt.

"He told me," he said, coming to sit on the edge of the bed near where his nemesis Shiverlash had sat not long ago, "that you were going to use him to break into the vault at the White Rose and steal their vials of human essence."

"What?" My hands dropped into my lap, taking the sheets with them. "No, seriously, *what*? Oh boy. Caryl and I are going to have *such* a talk."

"My son also told me that he will no longer take orders from Dame Belinda, nor 'enslave' spirits."

"Okay, so why are we talking right now? Why aren't you

just . . . making me gouge out my own eyes, or something?"

His head dropped slightly for a moment. It looked eerily like shame, though I'd never have thought the Unseelie King was capable of such a feeling.

"I need something from that vault," he said.

"Uh, okay. Blood, I'm guessing?"

"My Echo's blood."

"There's a vial of *Fyodor Dostoyevsky's blood* at the Seelie palace?"

"The vault contains not only the blood of living Project members, but of every human who has signed an Arcadia Project contract since the Renaissance."

"Holy shit."

"My son believes he can find this vial for me. I want your promise that you will return it to me."

"Why?"

Winterglass lifted his head to gaze out one of the large windows in my octagonal room, out into the night. He seemed to love gazing out of windows into the night.

"It is . . . difficult to explain," he said. "Arcanely, on a deep level, it *is* my Echo. It is all I have left of him. It eats away at me that they have it, could destroy it on a whim. It is *mine* by right."

"And if I got it for you?"

"You and Caryl have already freed my son. If you can free my Echo as well, then I will join your side in this war."

"That's a promise? A bona fide fey promise?"

"Yes. I promise that if you safely deliver to me that vial of my Echo's blood, I will swear allegiance to this new Arcadia Project that Alvin Lamb is attempting to create."

"That . . . that would win us the war," I said. I felt like a lottery winner, but then something occurred to me, and I gave him a slanted smile. "Either way," I said, "you come out on the winning side."

"That is correct," he said, returning my smile, eyes as distant as ever. "So make no mistake: you also have my promise that if my son leaves the White Rose without that vial, I shall inform Dawnrowan of your plan, and I shall join her in the hunt for you."

21

I was so manic after Winterglass left that I couldn't sleep. I didn't care about Caryl and Shock; I wasn't worried about the police; all I had room for in my head was that my idea was going to *win this war*. I was going to save the world.

Best of all, with Winterglass on our side, we'd have someone who could command Qualm, just as we'd seen him command wraiths last fall. He could make Qualm walk that Tjuan copy right into a police station with the murder weapon in hand. In theory Shiverlash could do the same, but she seemed unlikely to willingly send a spirit to prison, even though we knew it had murdered Tamika Durand.

With Tjuan out of commission, Phil was now the agent in charge of the LA4 Gate, so as soon as he was awake Thursday morning, I asked him to get a message to Claybriar. I needed my expert on the White Rose to put together the missing pieces.

I also sent a message to Shock, trying to make up for our last awkward encounter by thanking him for so effectively bringing his father into the loop. I let him know we'd be in touch as soon as I knew exactly what we needed him to do, and when.

Claybriar showed up in the afternoon, and I sent a text to Caryl so that we could have a strategy session in my room. I wasn't entirely sure yet how many people I wanted to bring in on this, so I started with the ones I knew were necessary. I invited Caveat to eavesdrop as well, but if she heard the invitation, she didn't say anything.

I started by summarizing the development with Winterglass. Caryl turned my desk chair to face the center of the room as she listened; Claybriar sprawled across my bed like we were gossiping at a slumber party. As usual, I elected to stand.

"So. We now have the Medial Vessel," I said, patting the pocket of the sweatpants I'd put it in that morning. "By the way, Caryl, does this thing have any weird One Ring kind of properties? Could it be messing with my mind?"

"Not at all," said Caryl. "Why?"

"Every time I try to put it down I freak out. Last night I slept with it tucked into my pillowcase."

"That is called anxiety, Millie."

"Gotcha. Sometimes I can't tell the difference between sorcery and insanity. Moving on. We have the Vessel, and we have Shock."

"You are quite welcome," said Caryl.

I ignored that. "And thanks to Brand's rumormongering, I've also set in motion a way to get me inside the palace to help Shock by disabling that guardian spirit."

"Bad news," said Claybriar. "I checked when I went back, and it looks like the spirit is actually bound inside the *prison*. That's a completely separate structure—"

"Under the ground, right? Caryl mentioned that before.

Shit!" I scratched at my hair irritably. "I don't suppose they give tours of the dungeon to curious visitors?"

"Nope," said Claybriar. "There's a guard who will turn away anyone but the queen or the other guards. I mean, you could get yourself *thrown* in there, but they'd lock you in the cage, and you wouldn't be able to reach the part where the spirit is bound."

"The cage? There's just one?"

"Mostly they don't use cells," said Claybriar. "Prisoners are held by spellwork. But you they'd have to put in the actual cage, since spellwork wouldn't hold you. They have one down there, a big wooden thing, for those rare cases when—" He broke off suddenly, and I followed his gaze.

Caryl had gone dead white.

"Oh shit," I said. "Caryl, sweetheart, put your head between your knees or something." I moved to her to ease her into position. "Clay, maybe we shouldn't talk about . . . wooden cages underneath palaces right now?" I rubbed her back.

"No . . . ," Caryl murmured faintly, head still down. "I'm all right. Also . . . if I could get into the prison, with Caveat cloaking me, I might be able to release you."

"Without triggering your PTSD?"

"I will . . . be better prepared at that time."

"It's not an unreasonable idea," said Clay. "There's only the one guard down there, and that guard would have a key to the, uh, to your situation."

Caryl sat up, some of her color coming back as she engaged with the problem. "The easiest thing might be for you to convince the guard to open your door for some reason, and the moment it is unlocked, Caveat could remove herself from the cloaking spell and paralyze the guard. But . . ." She frowned. "At that point the guardian spirit wouldn't be freed yet, and it would be able to see me."

"Wait," I said. "Spirits can see each other. Wouldn't the guardian spirit see Caveat there cloaking you anyway, and alert the guards way before that?"

"Nah," said Claybriar. "Remember last fall at Cera? Even the spirit possessing that woman couldn't tell that Tjuan and Winterglass were there cloaked."

"A good cloaking spell cloaks its own spellwork," said Caryl, "and Caveat should have no trouble with that."

"You listening, Caveat?" I said to thin air. "You on board?"

She popped into view. "Yep," she said, and then immediately vanished.

"Okay," I said. "So, I get out of the cell, I touch the guardian spirit, and only *then* should Shock start stuffing vials into the bag."

"Problem," said Claybriar. "I know the queen. If you've just gotten yourself thrown in prison, she'll be panicky. Checking in with the spirit constantly, even if it doesn't alert her. So the second she goes 'blind,' she's going to know something's up."

"Unless we give her something else to worry about," I said. "Could you pick a fight with her or something? When you're around, she doesn't pay attention to anything else."

He looked uncomfortable for a moment, then nodded slowly. "Yeah, actually. I could do that. But then how do we get the message to Shock that it's safe to start stuffing vials into the bag?"

That one stumped me. We all sat in silence for a moment. Then Caryl spoke up, quietly. "Elliott."

I gave her a dubious look. "Isn't he a little busy keeping Fred from telling Dame Belinda we were at L1?"

"There are ways we could reduce the risk, if I timed Elliott's withdrawal just right. And if we had him, he could serve a similar function to the captive guardian, but voluntarily. He could convey images and messages between members of our team, because in Arcadia he can be anywhere he wishes simultaneously."

"Why not use Caveat?"

"She'll be needed for the other spells, and also, she does not like to be intimate with humans."

"You sure he'll be up for it?"

"Yes. He wants victory here as badly as any of us, if not more so."

I nodded, satisfied. "In that case, we have the beginnings of a solid plan. But I want contingencies covered this time. I want a catchall cover-your-ass exit strategy if things go pear-shaped, and I do have a vague idea about that. Brand said something about standing stones keeping the palace in the air?"

"Right," said Claybriar. "An ancient spell that even you couldn't undo, and don't take that as a challenge."

"I don't want to undo it," I said. "I just may want them to *think* I will. Use it as a gun to hold to their heads to cover our escape if necessary."

"They'll all know you can't do it," said Claybriar. "One doesn't exactly hinge a palace's integrity on a spell like that unless there's a rock-solid way of keeping it from coming apart."

"Which is?"

"The spirits inside the two standing stones in the forest are aware; they're volunteers who have pledged to protect the

White Rose for eternity. What keeps them sane, I think, is their relationship to each other. They're half a mile apart or something, with the White Rose between them, but they're in constant communication. If one of them were freed, the other would simply recast the spell, rebind its partner."

"If I were fast enough," I said, "could I take out one and then the other?"

"No. Like I said, they're half a mile apart. So unless we could get another Ironbones, this isn't a threat you could believably make."

"And if we had another Ironbones," I said glumly, "I wouldn't dare make the threat. Too much chance we actually *would* touch the damn things at the same time by accident. Well, fine. I'll think of something while we put all the other pieces in place."

"Let us not pull Elliott back from London," said Caryl, "until we have those pieces. I shall confer with Shock on the fastest way to load so many vials into the bag. Perhaps there is a spell that can help."

"Claybriar, you plan your distraction," I said. "I'll work on how to get us the hell out of there safely."

As soon as Claybriar returned to Arcadia and Caryl returned to her apartment, I started shaking like a kite in a strong wind. When we'd been talking, it had felt like directing a film again: My job was to project confidence like a visible light, changing the color of everything in the room. But now the reality of it was hitting hard: I had just volunteered to somehow get myself tossed into prison.

Ironic, given I was doing it to keep my partner *out* of one.

What counted as a prison-worthy crime in Arcadia? I'd have to look into it. Would they give me a choice, like that poor coyote, between execution and rotting in a cell for eternity?

My head was starting to hurt; a snack would help. I went down to the kitchen, only to find Alondra there stirring some coffee into her mug of cream.

"Hi," she said shyly. She looked as though she'd been crying. I was really not in the market for a fresh batch of drama at the moment.

"Hey," I said. "Just grabbing a banana."

"Can we— Do you have a minute to talk?"

"I really, really don't right now. Sorry."

Her complexion turned as pallid as the pitiful excuse for coffee in her mug, and her lower lip trembled. I braced myself for hysteria, but she didn't make a sound. She just left the mug there and walked slowly from the room.

Well, shit.

"Alondra," I called out after her. She was already climbing the stairs and didn't respond. I went after her, but I was slow going up, and by the time I got to her door—which had once been my partner Teo's—I could hear her sobbing.

For fuck's sake.

No, no; I reminded myself that this was no more stupid than my own Borderline freak-outs. I'd cried myself into an incontinent stupor in an alley last summer; who was I to judge? I knew this intellectually; I could feel the exact place inside me where compassion was supposed to bloom, but there were tumbleweeds blowing through it.

I tried one of my DBT tricks: opposite action to emotion. When I knew I was feeling the wrong thing, I just acted as though

I felt its opposite, hoped my actions would get the right feeling going. What would I do if I genuinely wanted her to feel better?

I knocked on her door. "I'm sorry, Alondra," I said.

"It's fine," she said from inside. But she didn't come out.

Crap. She had BPD too, so a half-assed apology wasn't going to cut it if she thought I was the bad guy. I'd have to subvert her devaluation of me by doing something genuinely nice. *Ugh.*

I didn't know what she liked, besides opera and show tunes and cake, and I was fresh out of all those. So I just looked around a little while for her still-lost phone. I looked in any kitchen cabinets she might have absentmindedly placed it in, checked behind the toilets, under living room couch cushions, and even, as difficult as it was to get down there, under the couches themselves. With her laundry habit in mind, I checked between the dryer and the wall, and—miracle of miracles— there the goddamned thing was.

I felt a burst of elation. It was like I could do no wrong today! I grabbed a broom from the kitchen and nudged the thing out where I could reach it.

When I grabbed it, its screen lit up, and even before I had finished marveling at its battery life, I spotted a missed call from a 212 number.

212. Wasn't that Manhattan, where the Project's New York office was located? Why would they be calling her now?

Paranoia started to gnaw at me again. Or was it paranoia? She had really seemed upset about losing her phone. Panicky, even. No matter how often Caryl told her she wasn't fired.

I poked and swiped at the screen, tried to get in to see more, but the phone was password and fingerprint protected. Of course it was.

But whoever it was in New York might try to call back. And if they did, anyone who could get to the phone in time could pick it up.

I pocketed the phone and took it upstairs to charge it. Wouldn't it be *extra* nice of me, after all, if I returned it to Alondra with a full battery?

22

Thursday afternoon I got word that Brand had locked down all but the Vessel-guarding wraith into another book, pending eventual distribution into more permanent spells. We'd have to sort through which wraiths had done what during the rebellion before we decided their "sentences," but there wasn't going to be time for that in the foreseeable future. All that mattered for the moment was that they were no longer wild cards in the war.

I made a date to meet Shock in Arcadia early Friday morning; coordinating with him was much easier now that his dad was covering for him. I set the meeting in Arcadia to reduce the chance of Caryl stumbling in on us and distracting him, and I decided to use the opportunity to test out my new suit. It was heavier than regular clothes, I still couldn't get the shirt off by myself, and I was going to have to figure out a better way to keep the pants from riding down aside from yanking them up every couple of minutes, but all in all it was a fine piece of work. Once I got my surgical gloves on, I felt ready for anything.

Shock and I found a place to settle, a pair of warm, flat rocks not far from the LA4 Gate. I was actually more comfortable standing, but I wanted to *look* comfortable to my guest.

"I've got another question for you about facades," I said once we'd exchanged apologies and small talk. "Do you have to make them exactly from the DNA blueprint, or can you vary them?"

He made a wobbly, equivocating gesture with one hand. "We always make some choices," he said. "How the hair is cut and so on. But each choice adds time, and so we keep them as close as possible to the way they 'grow' naturally."

"But once a facade is grown? Can you alter it? Could Belinda, for example, make one of me, and then put scars and iron into it so it would match?"

He shook his head, wincing a little. "You cannot make a wound heal in a certain way. No two scars would be the same. Besides, every cut you made on the facade would cut the fey linked to it as well."

"If it was just a facade, though, not linked?"

"Then the wounds would not heal at all, unless you had a Seelie spell caster nearby to do it right away. And then the wounds would not leave scars. The Seelie Court's healing magic is based upon the body not 'remembering' that it was injured at all."

"Okay, well suppose you had a facade, and Claybriar sitting right next to you to help you. Could you cut it open and put iron in its bones?"

Shock looked flat-out horrified. "I—why would I want to do that?"

"I'm trying to figure out a way to make Dawnrowan and her guards *think* we have a second Ironbones, in case we need to make a threat to get away safely. And I had an idea of maybe using a facade to create that illusion."

"So you want me to make another facade for you, and then

try— I have no idea how long this would take. I have never tried to . . . alter a facade this extensively before."

"If it helps, you can shave off the time it would take to make it. I want you to use one you've already made, one that's currently lying empty somewhere, now that Brand has locked the wraiths down."

I'd thought Shock had already gone as pale as he could go, but apparently I was wrong.

"Don't try to tell me you don't have a way to track that thing down," I said. "You can do whatever experiments on it you want. And then when we're done with it, we can put Qualm into it and send it to jail. It was Qualm, wasn't it? That was the wraith you put into it?"

"You knew," he said softly. "You knew all along." He raised his eyes to give me a pleading look. "Yes, I made that facade, put Qualm into it. Dame Belinda said she needed it to gather information. A spy, I thought. I didn't know what she actually used it for until I met with you that day about Brand. I promise, I would never have—"

"I know, Shock. Otherwise I'd be hammering you full of iron nails right now. Let's focus on the matter at hand. Can you do this? Will you?"

"I—I do know where the facade is," he said. "The spirit brought it back to Arcadia, through the NY2 Gate."

"Wait, how did it get all the way to New York?"

"Buses," Shock said. "During off hours. It was cloaked, and it is quite easy to take public transportation when no one can perceive you."

"Can you get it? Stick some iron in there, have Claybriar patch it up afterward?"

"I—I could try. Just—please don't tell Caryl it was me, all right?"

"She already knew, Shock. That's why we invited you here in the first place."

He stared at me a moment, then rose to his feet, pacing. "She knew, and she—" The words "kissed me" seemed to hover in the air unspoken. "—forgave me," he finished instead.

"Caryl is complicated," I said diplomatically. "But you see why we need you to make this work. Not just to get the vials, but to access this facade. We can use it to make them think Tjuan has iron bones like me. So you get caught, trying to get the vials out of there? The real Tjuan and I can threaten the standing stones until they let you out safe."

"The st—wow." Shock's eyes flew wide beneath his blue fringe. He laughed. "Well, that would certainly get their attention. You'd do that, to save me?"

"Of course I would," I said. "But don't get teary eyed about it. You understand, don't you, that the entire fate of this war depends on getting those vials back to Los Angeles? Even if the rest of us don't make it, you have to get that bag back here."

He turned to me, solemn, and gave a slight bow. "I understand," he said. "This is about more than my father's mourning. I will not fail you."

"That leads me to another thing. You're going to need your wings for this."

"No, it's fine," he said nervously. "I go up there all the time like this. They have horses that—"

"To leave, Shock. Remember, I'm planning as though things might go pear-shaped at some point. You grab the vial your dad wants first, then living employees, then everything else. If you get caught somewhere in the middle of it all, you may have to just make a run for it. No waiting for a ride."

"Ah. Ah, I see." He started to gnaw at his fingernails. I wondered if somewhere in the void his natural form was slowly filing down its claws.

"How do you change back into your fey form?" I said. "How long is it going to take for you to recreate that link?"

Slowly his face took on that wine-red stain I'd seen when I caught him kissing Caryl.

"Shock, what is it?"

He sighed. "Okay, here is the secret. I made my own facade; I customized it. I control when I change. I did not want to be forced back into my normal form even when I came to Arcadia. I hate it."

"You're saying you could change back anytime?"

"Yes."

"Show me."

His head snapped up; his small dark eyes went wide. "Miss Roper, no. I do not like for humans to see me that way. This is how I want you to see me. This is how I look, even in my own mind. This is who I am."

I felt a pang of sympathy for the kid. "I'm not asking you to *claim* the body," I said. "I'm not saying it's *you*. I'm asking you to *use* it, when it helps you. I need to see how it works. It's a tool to use in our heist, that's all."

Shock let out a long, slow exhale. "All right," he said. "Okay. I will—I will show you."

I'd forgotten, until I saw him, that he was Vivian's grandson. It was like a slap of cold water to the face; I sucked in a sharp breath. Bat wings, pale praying-mantis arms, bleeding wounds for eyes.

I rose from my seat on the tawny rock and staggered back, breathless nightmare screams escaping my throat. Almost immediately I lost control of my limbs and fell down hard on my ass, half catching myself on one forearm in the mercifully spongy sand.

Next thing I knew, Shock was kneeling beside me in human form, and for a moment I saw his father in him, in the graceful way he reached for me, confident in his ability to comfort. He put his arms around me as I had seen Winterglass do to Caryl, but there was restraint here, both from politeness and from his efforts to avoid touching any part of me the suit left exposed.

"It's all right," he said. "It's only me. It's me."

He held me for a moment, and I might have objected to being comforted by a seventeen-year-old if it weren't for the fact that I was shaking uncontrollably. When he spoke again, his voice was bitter.

"I am so sorry," he said. "I truly hate myself sometimes."

"No," I said. "No, it isn't you. I mean sure, you look scary, but I've gotten used to scary, and I trust you. It's just . . . you look like her. Like your grandmother."

He pulled back, looked at me gravely. "Feverwax," he said. "The mad countess."

"I knew her as Vivian Chandler. I'm the one who—who murdered her. She looked just like that."

"Oh," he breathed. "I should have warned you."

"No way you could have known."

He carefully arranged his hair. "Father always said I looked like my mother. The princess-consort, Slakeshadow. I suppose she took after her mother too. I am truly sorry."

I got to my feet carefully; he let me lean on his arm. "This is good, though," I said. "It means you can access the form when the time comes, escape by air if you need to."

Shock made sure I was steady on my feet before drawing away from me. "I wish you had not seen me that way," he said. "You—you won't tell Caryl that I look like the countess, will you? She and my mother are the reason Caryl got abducted."

Something twisted a little inside my chest. "That's Dame Belinda's doing," I said. "She is the one who ordered it. If you care about Caryl, you are definitely on the right side of this war now."

"I thought helping London was the right thing," he said. "I didn't know. Dame Belinda made you all sound so dangerous, evil, insane. All I knew was that you had asked me to make a facade for a monster. It sounded plausible."

"You're a good kid," I said, giving his shoulder a brief squeeze with my gloved hand. "Belinda's always been good at making people believe she's on the side of virtue. Alvin fell for it; I fell for it at first; even your dad fell for it. Don't feel bad. Thanks to you, your dad is going to be on our side soon. With the whole Unseelie Court behind us, Belinda will have to surrender."

"The whole Unseelie Court?" A bit of his father's disdain entered his tone. "Do you see Queen Shiverlash settling in with my father in wedded bliss?"

I thought of the way she'd laughed the first time Winterglass had addressed her. The utter contempt with which she'd shoved him to the soundstage floor.

"Sure," I said, grinning to hide the gnawing uncertainty in my gut. "We're all going to be one big happy family."

23

The key to setting up a meeting at the White Rose without drawing suspicion was to make it look like it was all Queen Dawnrowan's idea. My experiences working with actors on a film set had prepared me well for this sort of subliminal inception, and I'd already gotten started.

Thanks to Brand's indiscriminate recruiting, rumors were already trickling out that the dread manticore Throebrand was waiting for the queen to exit the palace so that he and his hidden commoner army could destroy the wards protecting the White Rose. Foxfeather was especially helpful in spreading these rumors, as she had a nightmarish tale of her own to tell, and we sort of hadn't bothered to inform her that it was all a ruse. The fewer fey we had to count on to tell truth "creatively" the better.

On Friday morning after my meeting with Shock, I approached Phil to get the proper paperwork sorted out to employ the usual local courier to the queen. I needed to talk to Tjuan, too, but Caryl had made me pretty paranoid about getting in touch with him, so I got Song to lend me one of the spare prepaid phones she kept in her room, activated it, took it up to my room, and used it to call Gary's motel.

"Have you got a mobile phone?" I asked Gary once we'd established that I was the girl Abigail had made the suit for.

"Yeah, why?"

"I need you to give it to the guy in room two for a few and tell him to call this number."

Gary didn't seem too pleased by the arrangement, but he said he'd do it. So I ended the call and set the phone aside on the desk, using my own to text Alvin while I waited.

Going to need 2 more suits, will send measurements soon, get this rolling ASAP tho

He texted me back in a few minutes: *Do I even want to ask?*
Will fill u in later

The prepaid phone buzzed, and I snatched it up like the desk was on fire.

"Tjuan?"

"Yeah."

I leaned my head into my hand, closed my eyes. "You all right?"

"I'm here. What is it?"

"We're going to need your help with a heist."

"Millie."

"No, no, it's safe for you. It's in Arcadia. It's going to be me and Shock and Caryl and Caveat and possibly Elliott if we can get him back from where he got stranded in the last heist."

"Alvin told me about that. You got the Medial Vessel." I couldn't tell if he sounded impressed, or if I just wanted to hear it so badly I was imagining it.

"Sure as fuck did." I put my hand over my pocket. *My precious.* "Anyway, Shock's going to bring us that facade they used to frame you; Brand already yanked Qualm out of it. We're going to fill it full of iron, make the queen and the guards think you're an Ironbones too, to help with an emergency exit strategy. It's complicated. But when we're done . . . Winterglass is going to put Qualm back in it and send the thing to a police station."

There was a brief silence. I could almost see Tjuan's flat expression as he processed this. "A John Doe that happens to look just like me," he said. "Nice. Especially if you can plant the gun on it."

"So, you in?"

"What will I have to do?"

"Not much, actually. You'll be pretty safe; you're just going to be part of the exit strategy if things go sour. Otherwise it's going to be fake you doing the hard part, piloted by Elliott. But I wanted to make sure, before I nail all this down, that you're okay with this, because the copy of you is going to get into trouble again. Just, in Arcadia this time."

"You gonna clear my name in Arcadia when it's over too?"

"Well, we are actually going to be committing a crime this time. But if it goes well, there will be no one left in power who'll care about punishing us for it."

"If it doesn't go well?"

"Well, we're all fucked six ways from Sunday if this doesn't work, regardless. Our reputations are going to be the least of our problems."

A long silence as he thought it over. "Beats the shit out of sitting here eating Triscuits for the rest of my life," he said.

"That's the spirit. Now I need just one more thing. We've gotta make you a suit like mine. Two of 'em, exactly the same. So let's make sure they fit."

He talked me through what he could remember of his measurements, shoe and shirt sizes, et cetera, and then I reluctantly ended the call so that I could send the info to Alvin and then check in on the situation with the courier.

By afternoon our courier was cleared to go. The tiny butterfly-winged blue pixie Glitterbell was our go-to because she was fast as hell and had an Echo—a painter living ironically in Echo Park—that made her good at remembering orders. The letter I sent with her claimed that I was reconsidering Dawnrowan's demands and was willing to hear her out regarding potential candidates for Seelie King, if she'd come back to Los Angeles for a few hours.

Then I waited. The only break in the excruciating suspense was an annoying text from Zach.

Just dump me already, i hate this shit

I was strongly tempted to just reply *ok* and have done with it. But then I remembered my opposite-to-emotion thing. What would I do if I were a person with a heart and soul who actually cared about the feelings of the guy she'd been regularly fucking since October? Once I'd looked at it from that perspective, I texted him an apology.

Sorry it's been crazy at work and i'm kind of falling apart, i just have not had the brain space to deal with this rn

Millie he texted back. Dot dot dot underneath, my name hanging there over it like a sentence unto itself. Those dots lingered forever. I stared at them in astonishment, wondering if he was writing a novel or if he just couldn't figure out how to make words anymore. Turned out it was a bit of both.

The thing is I think we haven't even really given this thing a fair try and i get why, we just fell into it because we were next door and it was easy, and so it's easier not to think about it i guess. But im just going to put this out there that i actually miss you, that i am curious so much about you, i know you tried to kill yourself, its all over google, also that you were a filmmaker? And you seem like you dont have a lot of friends and i worry that one day you'll just be dead and i wont even know why or if there was something i could have done. Sorry if this is too much but what have i got to lose at this point, i care about you is all im saying

I sat there reading it and wanting to be stirred, wanting to feel some abrupt outpouring of affection. I didn't, but something ached in the vicinity of my breastbone. It was probably pity, but it was at least *human*, something I was feeling for a person who wasn't a scary warlock or the king of the fairies. It was a close enough feeling to normality that I wanted to cup my hands around it and blow on it gently and coax the ember into a flame.

I care about you too, I lied. *But I still need a little time. I will let you know when, ok?*

He replied with his signature *ok*, and I congratulated myself on putting out at least one of the fires currently licking away at the edges of my life.

But the rest of the evening was a misery. I ended up using the prepaid phone to call Tjuan back and tell him the whole story of the London trip in excruciating detail until he literally begged me to leave him alone and let him watch a movie. Then I called Gary and demanded a full list of what Tjuan had been eating, then made a few suggestions for Gary's next trip to the store, until he, too, told me to bug off. And then I was pretty much out of minutes, so I tucked the Vessel into my pillowcase and tried to sleep.

• • •

On Saturday morning Glitterbell finally came back with a letter, likely dictated by Dawnrowan to one of her Echo-enhanced servants. I knew for a fact she couldn't muster up a word of English without drinking blood and using a translator.

You must think me mad, the letter began. *I do not wish to believe that you are collaborating with the manticore Throebrand to destroy my palace, but it is well known that you are friendly with the beast, and the timing of your invitation is suspicious. I am afraid that I will have to decline the meeting.*

I had expected this, and so I had the response already written to give to Glitterbell.

Your Majesty, I know nothing about an attack on your palace. I asked Brand, and he denies even being involved in, much less leading, such a conspiracy. As we all know, he can't lie. I suspect these rumors are Dame Belinda's clever attempt to keep you from allying with me. She needs to keep you penned up in your palace until the war is over so you don't have a chance to see our side of things.

Making such a specific and persuasive argument was a risk, but I was banking on either her or her advisors being smart enough to see the obvious hole. Sure enough, after spending the rest of the day in my room working out the remaining details of the plan, I received a lengthy, emotionally charged reply first thing Sunday morning.

I have no way of knowing whether I can trust the content of this letter. Brand cannot lie, but you can.

If you truly had my interests at heart, you would understand. The White Rose is not just my home. It is my people's collective memory, our long history and transcendent vision made real. After what you did to the Bone Harp, imagine my lack of surprise that you are unconcerned about the risk to the palace, should I, its right-ful resident, leave while it is threatened. And do not feign ignorance of the way protective wards work, when Baroness Foxfeather, a ref-ugee of Throebrand's last trickery, is still living in Skyhollow.

If you were truly sincere in your desire to parley with me, you would be willing to come here. Despite your unusual handicap I have it on good authority that you have visited Arcadia before. I see no reason why I should come to Los Angeles, unless my leaving the palace is in fact at the heart of your intention.

I refrained from doing an air-punching victory dance when I got this letter; it wouldn't have been classy.

Instead I calmly wrote her back and let her know that while it was difficult for me to dress properly to protect spellwork in Arcadia, peace was important enough to me that I would meet on her terms. She had only to name the time and place, and I would come. I would bring Caryl, my partner Tjuan, and, of course, Claybriar.

Slam dunk. Her reply came so swiftly it seemed she must have bent time itself; it was in my hands just after lunch on Sunday.

I was not aware that Claybriar also intended to be present at this meeting. Please come as soon as your limitations make possible.

So that was it. All we had to do was get that facade finished, get Elliott into it, and go pick up the real Tjuan. And then we were going to either win the war, or I was going to end up rot-ting in a Seelie prison for eternity. Or dead.

I suddenly remembered Zach's text: *i worry that one day you'll just be dead and i wont even know why*

Nobody deserved that. I texted him a coffee shop for us to meet at and took a cab there.

• • •

"I have a weird job," I said once we'd gotten drinks and a decent table. "And I can't tell you about it."

Zach considered me with his heavy-lidded green eyes. "I thought you worked in entertainment."

"I did," I said. "I quit, and I work somewhere else now. It's dangerous, so yes, there's a slim possibility I might die."

He leaned onto his elbows, lowered his voice. "Are you, like . . . CIA or something?"

"I literally can't tell you, Zach. Do you still want to do this with me?" Half of me was hoping he'd break up with me so that I didn't have to be the asshole here. But there was another, weird, rebellious half of me that panicked at the idea that I might never again just sit and have coffee with a well-adjusted human being who didn't know about Arcadia. Even as we sat there on the edge of a breakup, his aura of normality soothed me in a way few things had lately.

Also, he was pretty good at getting me off. There was that.

He leaned back again, picked up his coffee, and took a long sip, thinking it over. "It's possible you're bullshitting me," he said without rancor. "But if so, you get points for creativity."

"I wish I were bullshitting you," I said. "I'm about to go on another trip, and this one . . . if it goes well, then I'll be around for a long time, and everything's going to be great. If not, you might not see me again."

"Oh come on, that sounds—" He turned to me with a peevish look, but then his expression fell. "Hey," he said. "Look at your face. You're really scared, aren't you? Why do I feel like this isn't bullshit?"

"It isn't," I said.

"Fuck." He reached out to give my forearm a little squeeze. "Shit, I'm sorry."

I looked away. "So, yeah. Maybe we should hold off on any big Relationship Decisions until I get back, huh?"

"That's fair," he said. "Okay."

I saw it in my head as *ok*

that's fair

ok

Shouldn't it be the other way around? Shouldn't I be reading his text messages and hearing his voice in them?

We sat there, drinking our coffee, and I tried not to look at the clock.

24

On Monday morning in Arcadia, the sky was a bright tangerine, its western reaches violet tinged and spangled with pink and blue stars. The sun hung low and silver in the east. I sat on a warm rock and waited until Shock stepped off the enchanted path to Skyhollow, dragging behind him a long wooden cart.

"I am so sorry this took forever," he said as he approached. In the cart was something covered with a silken sheet.

"It's been what, three days?" I said, feigning calm. "Four maybe? Hardly forever."

He drew the cart to a stop near me and turned toward it. "Mostly it was the research," he said. "What sort of screws and pins were best, how surgeons clamp off arteries, and so on. I played sick at school today so that I could finish, but with Claybriar's help the actual operation took less than an hour."

"Show me," I said, pushing myself to my feet and approaching the cart.

He whipped off the sheet with a flourish, and my heart stuttered.

Gray T-shirt, jeans, asymmetrical eyebrows. My partner lay on the cart with his dead eyes staring up at the sky.

Second partner.

The first, I'd found with his dead eyes staring up at the sky. His blood had been spread beneath him like a cloak. I'd come back to find him lying on his back, eyes staring up. Just the shell of him, vacant. He'd died, alone, while I was looking the other way.

"Millie?" I heard Shock say from what sounded like a great distance. "Are you all right?"

I stepped forward, laid a hand on the facade's chest.

It was warm.

No heartbeat, still as dirt, but *warm*. It tripped me into a merciful uncanny valley. This was no *person*. Too still, too warm. The things didn't go together. Touching it broke the illusion.

I tried to breathe, to get air back into my lungs, but that just started the tears going.

"Oh no," Shock said. "What did I do?"

"It's fine," I said. "Only . . . it looks so much like him."

"We want that, right?"

"Yes. Absolutely. It just . . . it made me realize how worried I am for him." I wiped my eyes, smiled for Shock, made the muscles of my face do the thing my heart couldn't even remember the meaning of right now. It wasn't the kid's fault he'd triggered my PTSD about the same night twice in a row.

"Your friend will be fine," said Shock.

"Absolutely," I said. "The suits are supposed to come this afternoon, so all that's left to do is call back Elliott and hope he's still speaking to us."

We had to wait until around dinnertime, even though it was risky for Shock, so we could be sure that old Fred would be sound asleep in London. According to Caryl, if the memory was returned while he was sleeping, there was a chance he'd mistake it for a dream. Worst case scenario, he at least wouldn't have his attention called to it the minute it returned and might not think of it unless something triggered it later.

While everyone in Residence Four knew by now that I'd stolen the Medial Vessel and was leading an expedition to steal blood vials from the palace, Caryl and I had decided that the details of the plan were best shared only with those who needed the information in order to take part. So it was Shock alone who dragged the Tjuan facade through the Gate, staggering backward with his arms locked around its chest.

"Whew!" he said, laying it out carefully on the floor for Caryl's inspection. She didn't seem disturbed by it at all, possibly because she'd had more experience with the empty Qualm facade and its disposal a few months back. Also possibly because she was already a stammering nervous wreck about the prospect of calling Elliott back.

Shock seemed to sense her distress, and he gave her a reassuring caress on the shoulder. The expression on her face reminded me of my own every time Zach touched me.

"So what happens," I said, "if the Gate guard tattles immediately?"

"As we are picking up Tjuan first thing tomorrow morning," said Caryl, "I suspect that even if the worst occurs, we will be to Arcadia and back before Barker has a chance to put the pieces together."

"All right," I said. "Are you ready?"

Caryl took a deep breath, then nodded. She spoke the three warped, guttural syllables of Elliott's Unseelie name, which dissolved the spell she had bound him into and summoned him, in theory, to her immediate vicinity.

For a moment nothing seemed to happen; then, to my profound startlement, Monty the cat waltzed into the room and addressed us in a rather creaky English accent. His mouth didn't move, but the voice clearly came from that direction, and the cat's eyes were fixed on Caryl.

"I thought perhaps you planned to leave me there forever," said Monty.

"Elliott!" I said.

Caryl's knees wobbled. Straight to a level 8. "I—I would never! Are you—are you possessing Martin's cat?"

"No," said Elliott.

"Uh, guys?" said Shock awkwardly. "I do not see anything."

"It is an illusion," said Elliott, apparently only to Caryl and me. "But I find I have suddenly acquired a distaste for my old form."

Caryl wrapped her arms around herself, then stumbled toward the desk chair. Shock helped her into it, confused and concerned.

The cat was silent. His shredded ear twitched once.

"You're . . . upset," Caryl managed, her eyes filling.

"You speak as though I were a child," said Elliott. The voice he used now was of an old man. Fred, maybe? "As though I held a grudge over something small. You enslaved me and abandoned me in a foreign land. I do not think you understand how thoroughly you have broken the bond between us."

"Caryl, what's the matter?" said Shock. "Why can't I see anything?"

"Shh shh shh," I said, pulling Shock gently by the arm toward me. I wanted to put an arm around his shoulders, but

I was only protected by surgical gloves at the moment, so instead I patted his shoulder.

"I am not your pet," said Elliott. "I was drawn into your service against my will and had no ability to reason or remember until you gave it to me. I served you because you needed me, and because you were innocent of the suffering you caused me. But you are no longer innocent. With full knowledge, you trapped one sentient being in the mind of another, used me as though I were a cork to keep something in a bottle."

"What—" Caryl's voice was choked and strange. "What can I do to—to earn your forgiveness?"

"Nothing," said Elliott, and then turned toward Shock.

"Ah!" Shock said. "Now I see it. It's . . . a cat?"

"Greetings, stranger," said Elliott.

"I'm Shock," he said. "It's good to meet you, Elliott. I'm here to help."

Elliott looked thoughtful for a moment, or as thoughtful as a one-eared cat can look. "I suppose you can still call me that," he said. "It is as good a name as any."

Caryl rose and, as carefully as though the floor were strewn with eggshells, crossed the room toward the stairs.

"Should I go after her?" Shock said softly as she descended.

I shook my head. Caryl was about to go into full-on level 10 meltdown, if I knew the signs, and she didn't usually like for people to be around for that. I clenched my jaw and turned back toward Elliott.

"What now?" I said to him. "We needed your help, and now we're up a creek because Caryl did something awful in a moment's panic? You weren't carrying her emotions, and you know better than anyone how messed up that can make her."

"Do not try to convince me to forgive," said Elliott. "I am not human, nor Seelie, and I do not share your weaknesses. I also do not wish to discuss Caryl's transgressions further in front of a stranger. I have, however, pledged myself to the cause of the new Arcadia Project, because I wish to see the end of coercive magic such as the sort that was just used upon me."

I exhaled slowly. "So you'll still help us?"

"That depends upon what you wish for me to do."

"I need you to pilot this facade," I said, gesturing toward it. "And take it to a meeting at the White Rose with me."

"To what end?"

"So that we can pretend to assault the queen, get ourselves tossed in prison. Once we're in the cell, you leave the body and serve as our eyes and ears all over the palace. Voluntarily, though."

"This will enable you to steal the vials of blood from the vault?"

"That's my job," said Shock proudly. "You're going to be the one to tell me when it's safe, when Millie has freed the guardian spirit."

"He also made the facade you'll be using, and he's going to help you get into it."

"There is a trick to it, you see," Shock explained, all teenage enthusiasm. "Because there is no emotional thread for you to follow into the body, you must allow a spell caster such as myself to create one. Using a complicated bit of spellwork, I shall project my own consciousness temporarily into the facade and open a pathway for you."

"Wait," I said. "Shock, are you saying that fey spell casters can *possess* other bodies?"

"Not just any spell caster," he said smugly. "And it is not done lightly. While I transmit my consciousness into this new body, I am abandoning my real body—both of them. They are temporarily and quite literally dead. So I can only do it for mere moments, or my real bodies would expire permanently, thus ending the enchantment, thus removing my consciousness from any body whatsoever, which is, as far as we know, the permanent end of any living being, barring some form of heaven or hell or afterlife."

"Shock!" I grabbed his arm, not even thinking about whether I was gloved or not, which I fortunately was. "No, no. That can't be safe. I don't even know CPR if this goes wrong."

"I have done this before, remember?" he said. "I helped Qualm into this very body. There is no need to resuscitate me afterward; so long as I return to my body within a few moments, vital processes begin again on their own. There is no damage; I carry on as though nothing happened."

"Shock, if I knew you'd be risking your life for this, I would never have asked it of you."

"That is why I did not tell you. We are all risking our lives, are we not? And I understand the way humans feel about death; it is a predator that stalks you all your lives, and so you fear it. For fey it is different. Our deaths are always either by betrayal or by choice, to make room for others. We see our lives as stories which, at the moment most fitting, must end. I do not think this will be my end, but if it is, it makes a very cool story."

Elliott spoke up in that dry, old-British-man voice. "What is your stake in this fight?" he asked. "Altruism is very Seelie."

"The *sidhe* were all Seelie once," Shock said. "Either we

resign ourselves to that part of our history or we go mad. I do not fight my impulses toward love and beauty the way my father does. But enough of that. Do you agree to this, Elliott? Caryl has taught me your Word of P—your name, but I am only casting spells now with full consent."

"I consent," said Elliott. And the cat vanished.

"Very well." Shock moved to the center of the room and began a low, guttural chant. Immediately the air in the small, close tower room filled with the rotting-garbage smell of Unseelie magic. He lowered himself to the floor, still chanting, closing his eyes and lying back with his hands crossed over his chest.

A coffin pose? Really? This kid had inherited his father's flair for theater. I bit my nails, waiting on tenterhooks.

I saw the moment when he died. Saw his breath sigh out of him after the last word of the incantation, saw his body make an impossible, indescribable transition: once host to a bright, talkative soul, now a piece of biological garbage. I knelt by him, took his hand from his chest, held it. It felt much too cool through the latex of my glove.

His skin was waxy, *dead*. This was no empty facade, but the fresh corpse of a teenager. Suddenly I couldn't breathe.

Everyone was going to die. This plan was going to kill us all. Everyone I loved, bones in the dirt, like Teo, like Gloria, like Vivian's dust and the dust of her facade somewhere in the in-between, its animating spark ripped away forever by my iron hands.

But then Shock's hand gripped mine tight, and he sat up.

And so did Tjuan.

Not Tjuan. Elliott.

"We've done it," Shock said breathlessly.

Elliott looked at his new, long-fingered hands, moved his face around seemingly at random.

"It will take a while," said Elliott in Tjuan's voice, a little hoarsely, "for me to become accustomed to operating this body."

"You have until tomorrow morning," I said. Then I reached into my pocket, pulled out the Medial Vessel. I pressed it into Shock's hands.

"Is this—?"

"It is," I said. "If I had any doubt left that you were with us a hundred percent, it's gone now. Keep this safe, and don't give it back to me until there's enough blood in it to save us all."

25

"You just ran a red light, Caryl."

It was the first thing I'd said to her since we'd gotten into the car on that awful Tuesday morning, because she didn't seem inclined to talk, and I had enough on my mind to keep me busy. But some things can't really pass without comment.

"It is customary in Los Angeles to make left turns during yellow lights," said Caryl, "due to the inexplicable shortage of left turn arrows at intersections." No stammering, but her face was flushed, her hands unsteady. About a 7. Not great for driving.

"That light was decidedly red, Caryl. Just because the guy in front of you has time to go, that doesn't mean you necessarily do. And, not for nothing, maybe the day we're going to pick up a wanted fugitive is not the greatest day to attract the attention of the authorities."

"I'm sorry!" she snapped. Then added bitterly: "At least marry me before you start harping on my driving."

The blood rushed to my face, and I leaned my head against the passenger-side window. There was absolutely no safe reply to that.

"Did you mean what you said, in Arcadia?"

Oh brother.

"I said a lot of things, Caryl."

"Don't pretend to be stupid. You said you loved me."

"Please, Caryl, just focus on driving. I'm really nervous about today."

"As am I. And I need to know, before we risk our lives together, exactly what I am to you."

My temper exploded in one white-hot burst, and I slammed my fist so hard into the dashboard it made her jump.

"No!" I said. "You do not!"

"Millie—"

"No! You're my boss—which makes this harassment, by the way—but you are not the boss of my goddamned *thoughts*. What happened, happened. Regret it or feel smug about it or whatever you want, but you do not get to own my feelings about it. Those are *mine*."

To that she had no reply. We drove in silence until we got to the motel. She pulled into one of the parking spaces in the narrow lot, but kept the car running.

"He should be expecting you," she said, her voice trembling. God, she was going to get us killed on the way back. I should have said something, anything, to calm her.

I nodded, unable to speak, and got out of the car.

The weather was strangely beautiful, one of those audaciously sunny days you sometimes get in February here, a fake spring. Even the cracked parking lot, strewn at the corners with Dorito bags and cigarette boxes and sheets of unused coupons, couldn't take the glory away from that sky. I kept my eyes turned up as I walked, breathing in the calming blue, imagining it filling my entire body.

I knocked on the door to room 2. It took way too long for him to answer, and my palms were getting sweaty by the time the door opened. But then there he was. The real Tjuan, alive and warm and smelling of shaving cream—this I knew because I hugged him.

"God I've missed you," I said.

"Quit it," he said, peeling me off. "Let's go. You can have shotgun."

I grinned at him, but said nothing, so "shotgun" was the last word spoken before we got into the car. It seemed to hang there, too loud in the still air. I could still hear it in my head—*shotgun*—as Caryl began to back the SUV out of the parking space.

Looking out the passenger-side window into that blue, blue day, with Tjuan's most recent word echoing, I saw the patrol car come lurching up the badly paved drive and stop at an angle, blocking our exit.

Time, at this point, came unhinged from itself. Ticked by one agonizing frame at a time, or skipped chunks entirely, or played back in loops.

The last coherent thought I had was, *Don't panic.* When this was, in fact, a damned good reason to panic.

I'd been spending weeks flipping out at every tiny thing—a weird smile, an unknown number that was probably just Alondra's boyfriend or girlfriend, the creak of the house settling—and now I was in a car with a fugitive, hemmed in by cops, and I felt a strange, numbing calm.

"GET OUT OF THE VEHICLE WITH YOUR HANDS UP."

I looked at Tjuan. I noticed the shape of his skull under his skin. Those gorgeous cheekbones. His eyes were flat, dead as the facade's, as he opened the car door and let in a slab of yellow sun. I stared at his back as he got out, hands in the air.

The police were still shouting orders. The words ran together now, but I knew what I was supposed to do. I opened the car door and got out, hands raised. Lights flashed. The sky was so blue.

The car was also a barricade. Two uniforms were behind it, pointing guns at us. There was a gun pointed directly at me.

The gun came closer. A woman, dark and fierce, grabbing me and pushing me to my knees. I fell forward. I don't know if she pushed me, or if I fell. My face was against warm concrete, and I felt handcuffs cinch tight against my wrists.

I stayed silent; I had that right. Why wasn't she telling me? Weren't they supposed to tell me that?

Her hands were rough, but I felt them hesitate when they started patting down the legs of my jeans.

"You've got prosthetic legs?" she said.

"Yes," I managed to say. "Double amputee. I . . . can't get up without my arms."

She just left me lying there, on my face in the parking lot. I turned my head to the side, tried to see what was happening. They were putting Tjuan in the back of the car that had blocked us in. His shadow was sharp on the pavement. Somehow there were already two more cop cars.

Two completely different armed men walked up to me, hoisted me to my feet, bruising my arms. Walked me past the car they'd put Tjuan in. One of them put his hand on my head, shoved me into the back of a different car. It was dark in there, after all that sun.

Being in the car made me feel safer. Distanced from all the noise and chaos outside. At least one more new car had pulled up. But I was a passenger now, waiting to take a ride somewhere. My mind stubbornly edited out the handcuffs.

More blaring of orders. "GET OUT OF THE VEHICLE OR WE WILL SEND IN THE DOGS."

There were dogs? But they had Tjuan already.

Caryl. They were sending dogs after Caryl. I thought of Brand savaging her forearm, the hot red spray of her blood.

Whatever was happening out there took long enough that I was finished crying before the two men got into the front of the car and started to drive me away.

"I've never been arrested before." My voice sounded friendly. Insane under the circumstances.

"Then let me give you some advice," said the uniform in the driver's seat. "Whatever you're told to do, just do it. Don't get clever. We've seen everything. Tell the truth and cooperate and this will all go faster."

"Yes, sir," I said.

"Yes, sir," echoed the uniform on the passenger side, and then laughed. I didn't understand the joke.

"Am I going to jail?" I asked as politely as I could.

"Oh, absolutely, ma'am," said the one on the passenger side, just as politely.

I didn't say anything else after that.

At the station they put me in a little room with Tjuan. I don't know what they were doing while we waited. He looked so hollow.

"You didn't do anything," I said to him. "You didn't shoot that guy, so they can't possibly prove that you did."

He didn't say anything. He just sat there, staring empty eyed at the wall.

"They can't prove you did something you didn't do!" I insisted. Tears in my eyes now.

"Please stop talking," he said. And once he'd said that, almost immediately they came to get me. I wondered if the last thing I would ever hear him say was *please stop talking*. It was fitting. It was so Tjuan.

Was he still going to *be* Tjuan, after this? No, I couldn't think that far. Couldn't look past this frame, this moment. That way lay madness.

Now they said the whole thing: right to remain silent, anything I said could be used against me, all that. I was dimly aware that the Project probably had lawyers on retainer for crap like this, but I didn't have any phone numbers on me, and I wasn't thinking straight anyway. I was also that stupid girl who thinks that because she's innocent, she doesn't need a lawyer.

"Where were you taking him?" asked the older white woman they'd sent to interrogate me. I didn't remember seeing her before. "What was the plan?"

"We were just going to take him back to the house. We thought it was safe."

"You thought that the man with the gunshot wound would just forget the whole thing, and the police would decide it was all okay and we'd just let the shooter go?"

"Tjuan didn't shoot anyone."

"Who is it you think did it? Does he have a twin brother?"

"He must. That's all I can say. I was with him when the news said this happened. Noon on January twenty-third, right? I was sitting in the kitchen eating cake with him."

"But you have no proof of this."

"I didn't know I was going to need it."

"You lied to the officer who came to question you at the house. That's obstruction of justice. Do you understand how serious that is?"

"No! I never lied!" I blurted it out without thinking. A Borderline thing. I was so convinced of my injured innocence that the facts got fuzzy in my head.

"You said you didn't know where Mr. Miller was."

I had no response to that. My skin felt cold all over.

"Who was driving that car?"

They hadn't gotten Caryl, then. No one would be ripping off her gloves, pressing her bare hands into ink, putting her in the system. How convenient, to be able to make yourself invisible. Who had she enslaved to save herself, to walk away while a cop shoved my face into the pavement?

"I'm going to remain silent now," I said. Should have said that at the start.

It was all slow, so fucking *slow*.

They took my name and social security number. They took my fingerprints. They took my picture. They took my phone. They even took off my prosthetics, searched them, gave them back. I couldn't get the seals right again, so I shuffled around like a kid in her dad's shoes, trying to keep them from falling off. I had to sign a little paper saying that was all I'd had on me. My fingertips were black from the ink, and the pen felt weird in my hand, too thin.

It took so long that by the time they transported me to the jail in Lynwood it was pitch-black outside, I had that fuzzy late-night feeling in my head, and a bail bondsman was already waiting there to get me out.

I have never loved someone quite the way I loved that short, beefy black man with the pushed-in pug-dog face. I nearly fell over from gratitude. I found religion. I made a thousand silent promises of future perfection.

"What about my friend?" I asked him. "What about Tjuan?"

"Nothing I can do." His voice wasn't as kind as his face. "His bail was set at a million, and no bondsman in their right mind would take a flight risk like that, even if someone could afford it."

"What?" I stared at him. "So he's still in jail right now? I can't just leave him in jail."

"You have two choices, ma'am: leave here with me, or stay the night."

26

Phil drove me home in what had been Teo's car. He was silent until we'd gotten a good distance away from the jail, and then he said, "We need to get Tjuan out of there."

I tried to think despite a pounding headache. "Maybe we can. Elliott is in a facade of Tjuan at the moment."

"I know."

"We could send him to the police station. Shock may know where the weapon ended up. We could put the gun right in the facade's pocket."

"And send Elliott to jail?" said Phil.

"I don't know, he could fake a heart attack or something, leave the facade once it was in there. Except . . . the body wouldn't die. It would just . . . sit there, warm, without a heartbeat."

"Are we caring about that?" said Phil. "Are we caring about the Code of Silence more than we are about Tjuan?"

"I don't know. I don't know." I massaged my head. "I've had kind of a day."

"Sorry," said Phil. "You and Caryl figure it out."

"Caryl? She's all right?"

"She's the one who called me, Millie. And the bail bondsman."

Of course.

Another idea hit me. "Qualm. We have Qualm now. Shock can put Qualm into the facade!"

"And then Qualm will snap the kid's neck. Great idea."

"Oh. Right."

We couldn't actually make Qualm *do* anything. Only Winterglass could do that, and he wouldn't do shit for me until I got him that vial.

We were silent after that on the long drive back to the North University Park district in the dead of night. When Phil let me back into the house, the clock on the wall in the living room said seven after three. The house was quiet.

"Where's Elliott?" I whispered to Phil.

"In Arcadia," he said. Good. I wasn't sure I could stand to see him right now, walking around in my partner's skin.

Phil's room was downstairs, so I left him, heading straight to the upstairs bathroom to shower. I sat on my little plastic stool and let the water pound me, wanting it to scour off every skin cell that touched anything in that place.

I couldn't wash off my record, though. Charged with obstruction of justice, arraignment set for mid-March. Even if Tjuan got cleared of all charges, I had broken the law, and that made me a criminal.

Maybe that should have made it easier for me to calmly pull off a heist, but without Tjuan I had no contingency plan, no exit strategy. If this had been a movie, I'd have gone ahead, called it additional motivation to do things right. But this was Caryl and Claybriar and Shock, people who had been (mostly) good to me, people whose lives I couldn't just throw away.

I dried off, put on a T-shirt and shorts to sleep in, and wheeled myself back down the hall to my room, trying to make my exhausted brain think past the missing piece in my perfectly balanced plan.

I still had one "Tjuan"; I still had an Ironbones to use as a threat to the second standing stone. But Elliott couldn't be in two places at once, and I didn't want even the slightest risk that a real Ironbones might touch the stone at the same time I did. The whole point was that it had to be the real Tjuan making the final threat.

It didn't work now. But I had to make it work, or Tjuan was going to spend the next decade behind bars, and Dame Belinda was probably going to find ways to get the rest of us too.

At some point I stopped pretending that I was trying to patch up my plan and just sat on my bed crying.

"Get some sleep," said a tiny voice nearby.

I started and turned to find Caveat in her winged iguana form.

"Were you watching me in the shower, too?"

"Sorry. Caryl asked me to. Was worried you might harm yourself."

Despite everything, I suddenly felt so fucking *proud* of Caryl that, even without Elliott, she'd thought to save herself, to call the bail bondsman, to have a spirit watch out for me. She was being a *goddamned regional manager*. At twenty. She'd grown up in a *cage* and she was handling this better than I was.

"You need to sleep," Caveat repeated, "or you'll be no help to anyone. Caryl has contacted Queen Dawnrowan to let her know what happened and why the meeting is delayed. But we still need to follow through."

"Is that you talking, or Caryl sending a message through you?"

The little spirit was silent for a moment, and I felt the weight of her hesitation.

"Caveat," I said, "what is it?"

"Have you ever wondered," she said, "why I can speak to you at all? Why Elliott was able to recruit me?"

"To be honest, I've had other things on my mind. But you do make me curious."

"I'm not like the other spirits."

"You're . . . more like Elliott," I said. "Like the wraiths. You—you've been exposed to human thought."

"Not by choice," she said. "I've been watching this city for a long time, longer than you've been alive. Spirits can see through the barrier, you know. We just can't cross it at will."

"That's . . . creepy."

"I crossed it once by accident. It happens sometimes."

"Right," I said, arranging myself more comfortably on the bed. "Traumatic or intensely emotional events. That's what causes hauntings, apparently, and certain miracles. We learned about that last fall, and we've been working on getting it added to the Project handbook. So you're saying some kind of trauma pulled you over?"

"A fast-food place. A gunman came in, opened fire on the crowd."

"Holy shit."

"I'm what you might call . . . a spirit of extreme caution. I merged with a small boy as he decided to be very still, to hide. He watched seven other people die."

"Oh my God," I said. Even as tired as I was, I knew. I *knew* immediately. "Tjuan."

"Yes," she said.

"And you just . . . stayed with him."

"At first I didn't know how to leave. And then I felt for the boy. I cast a spell to make him forget what he saw, not realizing that the spell trapped me here. That I wouldn't get called back, when the other spirits were, because I was bound."

"So what happened? When he got sick, was that you?"

"I . . . made an error in judgment. I'd come to care for him over the years. He was bright, and he found success, but there were people who resented his presence. I tried to use just a little influence on him, make him cautious, because he had such a run of good luck that he became too trusting. He didn't see the contempt his coworkers had for him. Somehow, between the stress at work and my attempts to communicate with him, he started to sense me. He turned on me. It was . . . bad, for both of us."

"That's when he got committed."

"They medicated him, but of course that didn't do anything to me. Only the electricity they eventually channeled into his brain disrupted our link. But it also gave him back that terrible memory I'd kept from him."

I felt like I'd been punched in the stomach. The whole time I'd known him, he'd been carrying that around. "What happened to you?"

"I stayed trapped in that room, watching the doctors perform procedures on one person after another, until the next convergence, when the Bone Harp was played to draw me back to Arcadia. From that point on, I stopped watching this world."

I sat for a moment, massaging my forehead, trying to take

it all in. "And then Elliott came to Arcadia, telling stories of what happened in the fall."

"I recognized a name in those stories."

"Oh, Caveat. Does Tjuan know?"

"No."

"Does Caryl? Does Elliott?"

"You're the first person I've told."

"Why me?"

"Because you're the one with the plan. You're his only hope. I came here because I wanted to make sure he was all right, to find some way to help him."

"And now—"

"And now it's my responsibility, more than any, to help save him. I'm the one who brought him to this place, who made him into a man who trusts and is trusted by no one."

"I trust him. I'd trust him with my life."

Caveat took the trouble to project a respectful inclination of her head. Her usual stillness made the gesture all the more striking. "And so for you," she said, "and for him, I need to see this thing through, this plan you've made for the White Rose. Even if it means sharing another human's mind. I'll do whatever you want. Please, don't give up."

She brought her forelegs together in what looked like entreaty. Her eyes fixed on mine.

"I . . . kind of want to hug you," I said.

"Not necessary," said Caveat.

"I can see it now," I said dryly. "The resemblance between you."

"Sleep now."

"Caveat?"

"Yes?"

"You need to tell him."

Caveat was silent for a long time. Then she said, "If you manage to save him, I will."

I did manage to sleep a little, but in just a couple of hours I heard an unfamiliar *boop-boop-boop* in the drawer of my night-stand. Instantly I knew that it was Alondra's phone.

I rolled over at the speed of sound, pounced on the drawer, grabbed the phone, and hit the button to answer the call. I didn't speak. I just sat there listening.

"Hello?" said a male voice on the other end.

I said nothing. I was still waking up, still trying to figure out what I should do. If this was Alondra's boyfriend, I was going to feel like a heel.

"It's Tracy," the voice said. "You okay?"

A man named Tracy. The Eastern regional manager was a man named Tracy.

My mind raced. I tried to find something approaching Alondra's high, breathy voice. "Was sleeping. What's up?" It was crisper, more curt than she would have been, but I didn't want to risk saying more.

"You haven't been reporting in, and I was worried, that's all."

My skin went clammy. It took me a minute to find English sentences, much less my fake Alondra voice.

"Can't talk right now," I said.

"What's wrong? Are you in danger?"

"No privacy. Let's talk later."

"Okay. Be sure to let me know if you feel threatened in any way."

"Of course. Bye for now."

I ended the call and stared at the phone. Then I picked up mine and used it to call Caryl.

"Millie," she answered. There were tears in her voice, and my heart lurched despite everything.

"Yes, it's me," I said, pushing past it. "Someone named Tracy just called Alondra's phone from New York and asked why she hadn't been reporting in."

There was a long silence. When she spoke again she sounded as though she were trying to squeeze the words out through as little air as possible.

"I'll be there first thing in the morning," she said.

27

I slept longer than I'd meant to. By the time I got my prosthetics and my clothes on and went down to the kitchen, Alondra was in there eating a cinnamon-raisin bagel. I wasn't sure how long it would be until Caryl arrived, so I tried for small talk.

"How are you?" I asked her as I made coffee.

"The doctor didn't find anything," she said as though I could somehow possibly be aware of the context of this statement. "But I know my own body. I don't know why nothing's showing up in the tests."

"I'm sorry to hear that," I said.

"I'm living on borrowed time anyway," she said. "If I hadn't run away that night, if I hadn't been mad at my mother? I'd be dead too. I should just be grateful."

There was not enough coffee in the world for this conversation.

"My parents are dead too," I said after an awkward silence. Trying for sympathy, but I guess it came out more like *suck it up, join the club*, to judge by the way she looked at me.

"How did yours die?" she said, obviously braced for some sort of angst competition.

"My mom got something rare when I was a baby, some kind of cancer. My dad killed himself several years ago."

Alondra considered this. "At least mine didn't suffer. Carbon monoxide from a generator after a big storm. I thought they were asleep at first." She didn't exactly seem lost in the memory; her eyes were defiant on mine. *Beat that.*

I looked at her for a moment, felt such a rush of hatred that my coffee almost came back up.

"I'm fine, by the way," I said. "But Tjuan isn't. He's in jail."

"*What?*"

"Tjuan and I got arrested yesterday," I said. "We spent the entire day at the police station because of what Dame Belinda did to him, while you were racking up medical bills over nothing. He never came back last night. Thanks for noticing."

As proof of a just and merciful universe, at that exact moment I heard the unmistakable (to me, at least) sound of Caryl's key fumbling in the stubborn lock on the front door. I left my coffee sitting on the island and went to the front room.

When Caryl saw me, she made a beeline for me, eyes kindling with relief and a kind of desperation, but just as she reached my threshold she hesitated. My heart, like that poor crow, fell quietly into pieces.

"I'm sorry," she said. "If they'd taken me—"

"I know," I said.

"I—I tried to get Tjuan out—I explained everything to Naderi—she was willing to pay the bail—"

"It's okay, Caryl. You did good."

I knew if I held her I'd be doomed, but I couldn't not hold her, not when she broke down into sobs right there in the living room. I wrapped my arms around her and let her rest her head on my shoulder, eyes turned in toward my neck. Her sobs slowly calmed, and I ached in every possible way, without Arcadia as an excuse. There was no one else in the room, so when I drew back, I kissed her: once, twice, firmly, as though sealing something inside her.

She reached up to lay a hand against the scarred side of my face, looked at me for a long moment with those dark chameleon eyes of hers. Then she drew away, seeming calmer. "Where is she?" she murmured. I didn't have to ask who she meant.

"She's in the kitchen," I said, almost a whisper. "Caryl . . . she was here, the very first time I mentioned that I wanted to steal all the blood samples from the White Rose. Dame Belinda has to know by now. We almost walked right into a trap."

Caryl frowned, looking uncertain. "Why would Barker let us leave the London office?" she whispered. "If she knew before we got there, why did she just let us walk out?"

"She wants to catch us in the act, I'll bet. She's known this whole time. God, what if Shock is spying for her too? And Winterglass?"

"Millie, don't let yourself—"

"Caryl?" Alondra's voice, from the dining room, where she stood watching us. She looked pale, afraid. "What's going on?"

By way of answer, I reached into my pocket and held up her phone.

Her expression went very, very blank. "You found it," she said, approaching me. Wary.

"I stole it," I said bluntly, too pissed to bring up the fact that I'd been trying to be nice to start with. "I saw a New York number calling you, and I had an attack of what I thought was paranoia, but apparently wasn't."

Alondra stared at me, openmouthed. "What are you talking about?" she said. "I still have friends back in New York; I didn't break off contact with *every*—"

"Like your friend Tracy?" I said. "Why don't you give him a call back?" I tossed the phone at her.

She fumbled it, and it fell to the floor.

"He's awfully worried about you," I said, "and wonders why you haven't been reporting in."

Alondra sank to her knees like a grieving princess, grabbed at the fallen phone, and checked it for damage without looking at me.

"Alondra," said Caryl quietly. "How much does Dame Belinda know about our plans?"

Alondra looked up, eyes wide and hurt. "No!" she said. "It isn't like that at all!"

"Don't you dare call me a liar!" I snapped at her. "You think you have Caryl wrapped around your little finger? She'll never take your word over mine. Not that she has to. I could call Tracy back right now, pretend to be you, just like I did this morning."

A spark of real anger lit Alondra's eyes then, and she rose to her feet. Short, heavy, and yet her every movement was so perfectly balanced, so regal, it made me all too aware of how hard it was for me to just pass for having all my body parts.

"You must not have talked to him long," Alondra said, "if you think I'd spy for that insane old bat."

Her sudden confidence made me angrier, and a little panicky. The world seemed to tilt under my feet; I could no longer tell the difference between insight and paranoia.

Alondra smiled at my hesitation. She knew Caryl would flip to her side now; she'd played the innocent damsel too well.

This was what always happened. Someone noble and pretty always came in, made me look like the twisted mess I was, turned me inside out so everyone could see my sickness. Made sure that no one, not even my closest friends, would take my side.

Gloria trying to snipe my first case out from under me, pretending concern when it was really Teo she was trying to protect. From me.

Professor Scott, his feigned bewilderment. *I knew she had formed a sort of attachment to me, but I never dreamed she would invent a story like this.*

Seventh grade, chalk letters in the study hall saying MILLIE LIKES GIRLS. My seat filled by someone else at the lunch table, leaving me to go sit alone by the teachers.

Over and over, carefully making connections in a new place, only to put one foot wrong and watch them all turn their backs.

"Just listen to me!" I said to Caryl. "Just believe me for once!"

Caryl looked bewildered. "Millie, I've never done anything but—"

"This woman is poison!" I said. "I knew it from the minute she showed up here, batting her lashes and playing the victim and making me look like a monster every time we were in the same room. Belinda sent her here *specifically* to discredit me."

Caryl continued to stare at me, wide eyed. "Well, I'll agree that you certainly do not appear at your best any time Alondra is in the room."

"You can't fall for this bullshit!" I said. "You can't! Not you!"

I could hear myself spiraling out of control, but I didn't care anymore. It felt good, like that psycho Disney princess on the mountaintop burying her whole family in snow. "Stop treating me like I'm crazy!" I said crazily. "I wasn't making up the wraiths, I figured out that Vivian was trying to build a Gate on stage 13—"

"And both times, I listened to you," said Caryl sharply. "But just because you're right some of the time—"

"All of the time! Alondra is Belinda's puppet; she's here to gaslight me—"

"Stop it!" Alondra interrupted in the firmest voice I'd yet heard from her. When I turned to her, I saw that her face was flushed, her lips unsteady. "You're freaking out!" she said. "I'm not saying you aren't brilliant. Maybe you are. But this time you're wrong, and you are *losing it*. I know what losing it looks like, okay? You're doing it."

"Shut up," I snarled.

"Millie," said Caryl in a quelling tone. Then she turned to Alondra. "If she is wrong, then explain yourself."

Alondra took a deep breath, made a steadying motion with both hands. "Tracy sent me and my friends to New Orleans on purpose, yes," she said. "But because the three of us really believed in what you were doing! And he respected us! We were supposed to tell Tracy what we thought of the people there. Tell him if we thought you were legit, if it was better for New York to join with you than with her. Obviously we couldn't let Dame Belinda suspect that we were waffling, right? So we had to make it look like Tracy cut us off."

The world tilted the other way; all the blood drained from my face. "And what did you tell them?"

"I hadn't made up my mind, last time we talked," she said. "But I think I have now."

"Alondra," said Caryl firmly.

"No," Alondra said. She breathed on the screen of her phone, dusted it off with her sleeve, a casual motion at odds with the tears brimming in her eyes. "You stole from me. You pretended to be me. All this after treating me like garbage since the very first day I got here. Looking for reasons to hate me. New York wanted to know who the villains are in this story. Well . . . if the shoe fits!"

"Alondra," Caryl said again, more firmly.

"No." Alondra stuffed her phone into her pocket. "I've had enough." She flounced to the front door, opened it, slammed it behind her.

I felt as though I were screaming, standing there like that melty-faced guy in the painting, but the room was quiet.

"Go after her!" said Caryl, grabbing my arm. "Stop her! She has a key to Teo's car! God knows where she'll go!"

"Me?" I said. "You want *me* to go after her?"

"I am not the one who drove her away!"

We both heard the engine start in the driveway. "Well," I said, "I'm not catching her now." I turned back to Caryl, and what I saw in her eyes was not panic, but cold Unseelie fury. I did not have a number to assign to the thing I was looking at right now.

"We could have had New York," she said.

My voice came out weak. "I'm sorry."

"There is no way to measure how much this might have helped us."

"I said I'm sorry! What do you want me to do, fall on a

sword?" Horribly, for a flash of a second, I wanted her to say yes. I just wanted to be finished with it all: the pressure on me, my upcoming court date, the slow slide as I watched myself fail bigger and harder and messier.

"No," Caryl said without the faintest hint of sympathy or tenderness. "I want you to fix this."

28

Sometimes when dysphoria reaches a certain point there's really nothing to do but shock yourself out of it. It's why self-harm is such a common thing with Borderlines; the intensity of physical pain wipes out everything else. But there are ways to get that kind of sensation without damaging yourself. For example, filling a big bowl of ice cubes and water and sticking your face in it for thirty seconds.

All mammals have something called a "dive reflex," a thing that activates your parasympathetic nervous system when icy water touches the skin under your eyes. It works especially well if you're bent over. Your heart rate slows, and the shock of it pretty much reboots your brain. It's best used as a last resort, though, because it sucks out loud. It's better than dysphoria, but not better than a whole lot else.

I drew back from the bowl on the kitchen island and grabbed at the towel I'd placed nearby, mopping down my face as best I could. I had exactly the wrong haircut for this little exercise; the front layers were drenched. As soon as I'd addressed the worst of the dripping, I went back out to the living room to join Caryl on the couch, the one that faced the door rather than the stairs. I wanted to keep an eye on the windows, on the off chance Alondra came slinking back.

"Better?" Caryl said.

"I'm fine," I said, raking back my hair. Rivulets of water had run down under the collar of my T-shirt, making dark splotches on my chest.

"I've spoken to Tracy," Caryl said, lifting her eyes from my shirt with obvious effort. "Alondra got to him first, but he said that she is having a dysphoric episode and was making very little sense. He and I managed to have a reasonably productive conversation, and he says that her previous reports had begun to cast us in a decent light. Well, except for you."

"Of course."

"I also left a message for Alvin alerting him to the presence of two spies in his ranks."

"Did Tracy say if any of them have been feeding info to Dame Belinda?"

"He says absolutely not. Apparently he gave strict orders otherwise. He was, unfortunately, not willing to speak with me for very long. But he says his policy is hands off in the conflict right now; he is gathering information and waiting to see how it plays out."

"And how *is* it going to play out now?"

"Our plan is still sound," said Caryl, "even without Tjuan. We only need the iron-laced facade of him to make it work."

I shook my head. "No," I said. "It's an unacceptable risk. Going without real Tjuan means either we abandon the exit strategy and count on everything to go like clockwork—which I am *not* willing to do after the mess in London—or we use a version of the exit strategy that could potentially be a massacre. If

I accidentally touch a stone at the same time Ironbones Tjuan does, the White Rose comes crashing down *with everyone inside it*. Just . . . absolutely not."

"Perhaps Shock could make another facade entirely."

I paused, thought it over. "We could bring Phil in, maybe. Have him do Tjuan's part. Do we have enough time?"

"There is no way to know how long it will take before someone in London spots the missing Vessel and begins to put things together, but Dawnrowan at least is willing to put off the meeting in light of our recent complications. I imagine Shock could put together another facade within a few days. But we cannot use Phil; he is without exaggeration the only glue holding Residence Four operations together at the moment."

Caryl's phone buzzed; she pulled it out of her pocket to look at it.

"Stevie's definitely out," I said. "Alvin might be up for it, but a facade of him would have boobs, so that's not going to work."

"Perhaps this is what you could use to win Alondra back," said Caryl. She turned her phone toward me. "Tracy just sent me her location."

"Wait. You'd trust *Alondra* with this?"

"Why not? She left New York because she felt strongly that Dame Belinda was in the wrong. She was clever enough to pull off a fairly complicated bit of espionage without arousing either my or Alvin's suspicions. She is an experienced agent, and clearly wants to help."

I raked a hand through my hair again, looked down at myself. "I can try to go talk to her, but let me at least change my shirt and dry my hair first."

I rose and headed for the stairs, but before I could even start the ascent toward my room, I stopped in my tracks. Standing at the head of the staircase was a tall Greek beauty with eyes like clouded jade, head cocked at a bizarre angle.

I bit down on the cliché: *How long have you been standing there?* "Caryl," I said. She turned, saw what I was seeing, went pale. She leaned forward against the back of the couch, clutching it with both hands as though for support.

Had Shiverlash deliberately concealed herself, or were we just that oblivious?

Caveat made herself visible, appearing on Shiverlash's shoulder.

"The queen orders me to translate again," Caveat said. Her voice and manner were flat; I couldn't tell if that was her usual unwillingness to transmit emotion, or if that in and of itself indicated her feelings.

"Of course," I said. "Your Majesty, by all means, tell us what we might do for you today."

"Give it to me," Shiverlash said in her cool alto voice.

"Give what to you?" I said in my most agreeable tone.

"The facade with iron bones. If you no longer need it, give it to me."

So she'd been standing there a while, then.

Caryl and I looked at each other, and I didn't need to do a *sidhe* mind-reading trick to know that she and I were seeing the same horrific image: Shiverlash commanding an Elliott-piloted Tjuan lookalike to march around Arcadia indiscriminately destroying every spell in sight.

I looked back at Queen Shiverlash.

"I . . . can't really do that," I said tentatively. "It's a likeness of a real, living person who is in enough trouble as it is right now. Also, Elliott took it to Arcadia, and he hasn't come back; he was waiting for us to call him."

"You know the spirit's true name, do you not? Call him now. If he can take me to this empty facade, then I will have no further need of you."

"Please, Your Majesty," I said. "I know you're impatient to free the spirits, but I'm *this close* to getting Winterglass on my side, having the entire Unseelie Court."

"I feel I have heard this tale before."

"For real now!" I said. "He has made me a *promise*. We have a *plan*. And we might still need that facade for it; I don't know. But we're going to go to the White Rose, steal something for King Winterglass. Once he has it, he's on our side. Once he's on our side, Dame Belinda has to surrender. Once she surrenders, Alvin's in charge, and we figure out the best way to free the spirits."

Queen Shiverlash directed her facade's gaze toward me, stared at me for a long time without speaking.

"It was a real promise," I said. "Once I finish this, Winterglass *has* to be the ally of the new Arcadia Project. Even if we decide to do things he doesn't like. He's tied his hands."

The siren tipped her head, considering. Then she said, "This is the third time you have delayed me. You were warned. You have three days to make good on this 'plan' of yours. After that, I will find the iron facade, and I will take it." At that she strode down the hall toward the stairs to the Gate, her movements both graceful and grotesque, and decidedly inhuman.

"Three days?" said Caryl in a panic once Caveat had confirmed the queen's exit through the Gate. "I doubt we could even get a new facade made in three days, much less bring the plan to completion."

"We don't have to," I said. "All we have to do is make sure Elliott is locked down in some kind of spell before three days is up."

"What?"

I went to sit with Caryl again, grabbed her hand, gave it a reassuring squeeze. "The threat she made is empty. If she'd bothered to catch up on current events, to learn how facades and possession work, she would never have even made that threat."

"But I understand facades and possession," said Caryl, lacing her fingers between mine, "and I still do not follow."

"Because you're upset," I said. "Stick your head in some ice cubes and think it through. She can't just tell any old spirit to possess the facade. Shock had to set that up very carefully. Only Qualm and Elliott can even get in there. If they're both locked down in spells, she can't use them. Even if she uses her song to call every free spirit in both worlds to her side, the ones locked down in spells still can't come to her."

"A fair point," said Caryl, brightening.

I nodded, then released her hand and stood. "Let's get this show on the road," I said, heading toward the stairs. "You driving?"

"I shouldn't right now."

I didn't need to ask what she meant; I appreciated her self-preservation. "Then call me a cab; I'll go get ready to play nice with Alondra."

Alondra hadn't gone far. Teo's car was parked in the lot of an Indian-Mexican fusion diner just a few minutes from the

Residence, and the cab let me out in front at about a half hour before noon. I paid my fare and got out, approached cautiously for fear my quarry might bolt; I didn't want to find out if my fake legs could outrun her short ones. Through the glass of the narrow cafe's front door I could just make out the dark tumble of her hair; she was at a table for two against the orange wall.

I pushed open the door as quietly as I could and made my way over to her, plopping myself down into the chair across from her. She was about halfway through a plate of chicken tikka tacos. My stomach rumbled.

When she saw me, her pretty face twisted. "What," she said, "did you just search every restaurant for the fat girl, one at a time?"

"Yeah," I said. "That makes *way* more sense than Tracy being worried about you and telling us where to find you."

She looked away, folded her arms. Tacos just sitting there.

"Are you going to finish those?" I asked. "I've had nothing but coffee all morning."

"Get your own," she said, pulling the plate closer, but still not touching the food on it.

"Look," I said. "I'm sorry about this morning. I've been in a constant dysphoric loop for a couple of months now. You do know what dysphoria is, right?"

"I've done DBT too," she said, still not looking at me. "Three times. Tracy made me."

"Well, so I'm seeing everything through this filter. Everything's ominous; everything's doom. It doesn't help that a lot of things *are* doom."

"So what's your point?"

"My point is, it's shitty that you were spying on us, but I don't really think you're trying to destroy me."

"Wish I could say the same."

I deserved that, and I knew it. I leaned back, combed my fingers through my hair. "Look," I said. "Before I stole your phone, what did you think of us rebels?"

Alondra sighed. "I don't know. Caryl without Elliott worries me. She's like . . . half child, half demon. Alvin's always been level-headed, though; I really like him. Had a huge crush on him when we first met, actually. So when Dame Belinda said he'd gone crazy and lied about her, I was just like . . . nope."

"So you trust Alvin, and Alvin trusts us. He let me plan a heist, Alondra. Would he do that if I were a bad guy?"

"I don't think you're a bad guy," she said with a sigh. "I really wanted to like you, honestly. Caryl made you sound *so cool*. She said even before you came to the Arcadia Project and started saving the world all the time, you were making movies and stuff, you were nominated for awards."

I tried to look modest. "Just the one award."

"Still, that's amazing. *I* wanted to be friends. But I could tell you hated my guts from the first day."

I sighed. "I'm not great at friendship," I said. "Haven't ever been, really. Can't promise I ever will be. But I can try to do better at treating you like a coworker at least, all right?"

"You . . . want me to stay?" she said, her dark eyes disbelieving. "Even after . . . what I did?"

"You were trying to serve the Project in your own way," I said. "You believe Dame Belinda needs to go, right? And where do you stand on the spirits?"

"I like Caveat," she said. "She's one of the few people in Residence Four who actually listens to me. So yes, I'd love to figure out a way we can work with them, instead of just using them. And . . . I want to help Tjuan get out of jail, even though he's barely ever even spoken to me."

"That's just the way he is," I said. "He's slow to warm up. But for what it's worth, he never lets me talk shit about you."

Alondra started to smile, then turned it to a frown halfway through. "Wait, why were you talking shit about me?"

"Because I'm an asshole, Alondra, and because I'm jealous of you."

"Jealous? The skinny badass is jealous of me?"

"Do you seriously want to trade bodies? Because I'd be willing to give it a whirl."

She laughed uneasily. "So you really want me back?"

"Honestly, because we lost Tjuan, we may need you for the White Rose heist."

Her hands flew to her chest. "Are you *serious*?" She looked at me like I'd just cast her in *Hamilton*. I decided it might not be the best idea to tell her that we'd just basically run out of people.

"You've shown us you can be clever, and careful," I said. "You've taken risks. I think you can play the role he was going to play. We could make this work. But this means we'll have to make a facade that looks like you, put Elliott in it. Is that going to creep you out?"

"Honestly?" she said. "Yeah! Big time! But I don't care—do it!"

"If you're sure," I said.

"Ohmygod, ohmygod, ohmygod," she said, fanning herself with both hands. "You will *not* be sorry."

"Well, we might very well be, but it probably won't be your fault."

"Seriously." She reached out, grabbed my hand. "I won't let you down. Thank you so much."

"Don't thank me till it's over," I said, resisting the urge to pull my hand away. "Now finish your damn tacos before I do, and give me a ride home."

29

Of course, as soon as we got Alondra back to the Residence, she started panicking about everything. First she bawled like a baby about getting her blood drawn. Then I realized I'd underestimated how much bigger around she was than Tjuan; we couldn't get the top of the suit zipped when we tried it on.

"Alondra," I said, standing in front of her and holding her by the shoulders as Song continued gently trying to bring the two edges of the neoprene together in back. "Breathe. We have a seamstress at Residence One. She can—"

"This is my fault!" she snarled. "I'm a fucking *pig*." I'd never seen rage from her before; apparently it was all kept in-house. She was shaking, her pretty face blotched red. "You should just start hacking pieces off of me to make it fit."

"Snap out of it," I barked, straightening like a drill instructor, grabbing my own wrist at the small of my back to keep from throttling her. "If I'm not allowed to have a breakdown right now, neither are you. Take a fucking breath, Serrano."

I must have sounded very commanding, because she actually inhaled deeply, then exhaled.

"I'm sorry," she said. "I'm sorry!"

"And don't fucking apologize. Did you go to DBT or didn't you?" I glanced irritably over her shoulder. "Song, quit it. It's not going to fit. Tjuan is built like Gumby. We need to get Abigail on this."

"I'll make some calls," said Song.

"I'm delaying everything," moaned Alondra as Song began easing the sleeves back off, starting at the shoulders. Trying to pry Alondra away from self-pity was like trying to pry Monty off his cushioned window seat.

"No, you're not," I said. "The bottleneck here is getting that facade; that's going to take days. We're just trying the suit on so we can get to work on adjustments while we wait."

"I can't believe I'm already disappointing you."

"To be frank, Serrano, you are behaving pretty much exactly as I expected."

It landed like I'd slapped her.

"Song, comfort her," I said, and headed for the stairs. Caryl had gone to Arcadia looking for Elliott, to warn him about Shiverlash, and she was due back any time now. I couldn't quite bring myself to climb that spiral staircase, but I listened for a moment in the part of the hallway that I knew was next to the invisible door. Not a sound from above.

I went into my room, but left the door open behind me in case Caryl needed comforting when she got back. She hadn't spoken to Elliott since his devastating rebuke nearly two days ago, so I wasn't sure it would go well.

I took a seat at my desk and pulled out the sketches I'd been making. They weren't recognizable as anything, weren't labeled, not just because I was afraid they'd fall into the wrong hands, but because I wasn't trying to make storyboards here, just putting my mental process into some more tangible form. The visual artist's version of thinking out loud.

I traced back over the arrows I'd drawn, jotted down some numbers meant to represent approximate time frames. The asterisk meant Elliott; the dollar sign was Claybriar; the White Rose prison was a big triangle for some reason. No one had to understand but me. I was rehearsing it the only way I could, pencil moving over the paper as I visualized who would be where, and when, and how things could go wrong. Every time I thought of a new way we could screw up, I started again, adjusted the plan.

I don't know exactly how long I sat there doing that, but it was dark outside when my phone rang. A generic ring; no one I was expecting. I glanced at the caller ID.

London, England.

The Clash merrily thumped its way into my subconscious in time with my accelerating heart.

I probably should have let the call go to voice mail, but some self-destructive impulse made me answer it.

"Good evening," said Dame Belinda, although it wasn't evening there. So thoughtful, that mental math. What a considerate lady.

"If it isn't my number one fan," I said.

"I trust you're well? Recovered from your travels?"

I had no idea if she knew Tjuan and I had been arrested yesterday. If not, I didn't want to give her the satisfaction. "What can you possibly want at this hour?" I said.

"Ah, is that how we're to behave? Very well, then. I am calling to inform you that your clever little plan has been betrayed."

Shit. Shit. All the shit in the world.

I lost the feeling in my hands; I tried to work out who could possibly have leaked. Shock? Winterglass? Dawnrowan? Tracy? *Shiverlash*? Too many moving pieces.

"I'm sure I don't know what you mean," I said in my best fake British accent. I flattered myself that the ensuing hiccup in the conversation meant I'd affronted her terribly.

"Mr. Winstanley remembered," she said then. "The man Miss Vallo violated. Did you know that was his name?"

"I did," I said, leaning my head on my desk. I took deep, slow breaths. Bad, but not as bad as I'd feared.

"Once I realized that you and Miss Vallo had been upstairs that night, I of course had my people do a *thorough* search. How strange, when I had to send someone to check for the Medial Vessel *three times*. Very clever."

"That's me," I said weakly. "Clever."

"We take good care of our Gates, Miss Roper," Dame Belinda continued into my silence. "The time it will take for that artifact's absence to be a handicap is much longer than it will take for us to thoroughly destroy your resistance. You are inconveniencing us at best."

"And yet you're calling me at what, four in the morning? Are you always up before the cock's crow to let people in Los Angeles know how little they matter?"

My blood started to flow again; I could feel it throbbing in my fingertips. She still had no idea. If she even knew we were meeting with Dawnrowan, she'd have taunted me with it by now.

"I am calling you because I realize I must be missing something in your grand scheme. I know you are intelligent enough to realize that my patience is wearing thin, and that what I have done to your partner I can do to any number of others in your organization."

"Can you, though?" I said. "Have you checked on your pet wraiths lately?"

A silence.

"Yeah, you might want to look into that," I said. "That one that was guarding the empty box? That's your last wraith, and now that I know I don't need it in London anymore, I'm going to take it away too. So just how exactly are you going to pilot this army of facades you're planning to ruin our lives with?"

Another brief silence.

"So it's true, then," she said. "The manticore has somehow returned."

"Would you be shocked to hear that the Medial Vessel was involved in his recovery?"

"Ah," she said. I could hear the pieces sliding into place in her mind. "I would not be shocked to hear that, no. It raises many questions, but it answers others to my satisfaction."

"Are we finished here then?"

"No, because you are still in possession of stolen property, and I would like it returned."

"Or?"

"Miss Roper, I still have the entirety of the Arcadia Project at my disposal. Do not force me to become *creative*."

"Or, maybe *you* shouldn't force *us* to tell the rest of the world we have the Vessel. What will they think, when they find out they have to play nice with Los Angeles if they want their Gates repaired? Maybe if you want to keep your control over all those other hundred and ninety-seven countries, you should *leave ours the fuck alone for a bit*."

The longest silence yet.

"This is a stalemate, not a victory," said Dame Belinda. "And keep in mind that the more you narrow my civilized options, the less you will like the options I am forced to pursue."

I ended the call. As much as I hated to let her have the last word, it was important to let her keep that smugness, to let her think she had all the time in the world to crush us under her heel.

Despite what I'd said to Alondra, it actually took nearly a week for Abigail to finish the alterations to the suits and to have them delivered back to the Residence. I spent the entire third day after the Unseelie Queen's ultimatum biting my nails and popping Tums like candy, but we didn't hear so much as a peep from Her Majesty, and Elliott was still safely bound up in spellwork. Shiverlash's silence was somehow more unsettling than having her show up in a towering rage, but we were not in a position to investigate and potentially poke a sleeping dragon.

By the time we got the suits Monday afternoon, the day after Valentine's Day, Shock's facade was ready.

He'd done his best, but the facade's skin was a shade and a half lighter than Alondra's, and Alondra was noticeably plumper. The facade's hair was a little shorter too, and Alondra refused to cut hers to match. We found a way they could both wear it up that disguised the difference in length, dressed them both identically, and hoped we'd be assisted by the fact that they would never be seen standing next to each other.

Elliott—who was now on polite speaking terms with Caryl and keeping himself constantly spellbound to avoid a summons by Shiverlash—had gotten pretty good at piloting a

human body. He still took some time to study Alondra's movements and mannerisms once Shock had helped him into his
new ride. Back and forth the two gals walked in the upstairs
hall; Alondra giggled at the way he mirrored her.

"Have you been to Arcadia before?" I asked her as I watched.

"Once," she said, fingertips gingerly touching her freshly
dressed hair. "A few years ago, when we thought we might have
found my Echo."

"I'm guessing it wasn't?"

"No."

"I'm sorry."

She shrugged and gave me a sad half smile. Yet another
reminder that all this time I'd spent resenting her voice and
her face and her superior trauma, I'd been ignoring all of the
reasons she had to envy me.

This particular reason, Claybriar, wasn't long in joining us
once all the rest of the pieces were in place Monday afternoon.
I finished suiting up, shouldered a lightweight backpack with
a collapsible toilet (thanks, Tjuan), travel first aid and sewing
kits, emergency food, prosthetic supplies, et cetera, and the
whole team headed through the Gate into Arcadia.

30

When I finally set foot on the enchanted path to Duke Skyhollow's estate under a blushing peach sky on the afternoon of February 15, I received a *mostly* pleasant surprise.

The road's enchantment was meant to work by advancing each bipedal traveler a thousand steps for every step taken. We'd assumed I'd be immune to it, as I was to every other somatic enchantment, but that my boots would insulate the path enough that I at least wouldn't destroy it. What we didn't bargain for was that the enchantment worked perfectly well on my *boots*, and that apparently my boots had no intention of leaving my body behind.

First step I took, my body got yanked almost half a mile.

On Earth, the physics would have killed me, but here in Arcadia those kinds of laws were more relaxed. All the same, since my body wasn't fully enveloped by the spell, the effect was alarming and sickening; I ended up leaning on my knees and moaning, forehead drenched in sweat.

"That was . . . unexpected," said Caryl, appearing beside me belatedly once she took her own first step along the road. Despite the warm climate, she wore a long brown coat, dressing for Daystrike rather than Skyhollow. From her serene demeanor, and the similar attitudes of Elliott and Claybriar when they appeared nearby, I quickly figured out that I was not experiencing the enchantment quite as intended.

"Rest here for a moment," said Caryl. "Look around at the landscape, reorient yourself. It will take your mind a little while to accept what is happening, and then your body will stop rebelling."

After the first dozen steps or so, one at a time, gazing miserably at the scenery in between, my consciousness began to adjust to the idea. After a dozen more, I was left with nothing but a mild dizziness.

If all of us walked in step, we were able to stay next to each other on the road. Sometimes one of us would fall out of rhythm, and then there'd be confusion as we tried to figure out who was ahead and who was behind. Some small figure would wave pitifully from far behind or ahead on the glittering path, and we'd take a step in whatever direction was necessary.

The view was worth stopping to look at now and then. The wind picked up little eddies of sand; they glittered as they swirled over the tops of the dunes. Great arches and columns of red and golden rock were scattered over the landscape like ancient ruins, but they looked as though they'd been sculpted by weather and not by deliberate hands. There were signs of wildlife, too, but living creatures were harder to spot at the pace we were moving.

About halfway to the estate, I spotted something marring the horizon to my right. I stopped and turned toward it, letting out an involuntary sound of dismay.

I felt as though I had a bruise on my eye, a hole in my mind.

The inside of a Gate was the closest thing I could compare the sight to, but even that was more bearable because of the way it was bound, controlled, by the inner circumference of the arch. This blot of darkness was smeared across a patch of sand, its edges unclean. The whole thing was about the size of a decent duck pond, at least so far as I could judge from this distance.

"What the hell is that?" I said.

"Union Station," said Caryl. "Or its equivalent. That is the hole that Viscount Rivenholt tore in Arcadia when he shed Claybriar's blood last June."

"That can't be right," I said.

"Have you lost your sense of direction?"

I shook my head. "Never had one to start with. But I mean I saw the bloodstains on the tracks myself. You could have covered the whole thing with a bath mat."

"It is only by luck," said Caryl, "or perhaps careful aim, that the damage was not greater. Where norium touched the earth in our reality, it acted as though a plug were pulled in this one, and Arcadia drained away toward the other dimension. Luckily, the iron in the train tracks took the power away from the metamorphosis on that side, and greatly reduced the damage on this side."

"Is it . . . spreading?"

"No, that is done now. But nor will it heal. That part of this reality is lost forever."

I stared at it, or near it; it was hard to look at directly. "So that—that mess over there—that's what Vivian wanted to replace every *sidhe* estate with."

Caryl nodded, her expression grave. "That many holes in reality might well have caused this entire realm to collapse into the void, like a house eaten through by termites. She was not what one would call a conservative planner."

I shuddered but felt a surge of pride at what I'd managed to help undo. And I hadn't even had a very good plan then, or any idea of what I was doing. Surely this time my chances were better.

"Okay," I said. "Rest stop's over. Let's get to the estate."

Duke Skyhollow's estate was a magnificent oasis, a startling patch of rain forest in the midst of the desert. What appeared from a distance to be towers and spires were not built of stone but somehow *grown* from astounding, impossibly huge living trees whose tapering tops soared above the main canopy. The entire oasis was shrouded in an apricot-colored haze that smelled of Christmas oranges stuffed with cloves. The haze hung so heavily that I expected it to choke me as we approached, but instead I found myself refreshed, invigorated, and many times *lighter*.

This change in the function of gravity wasn't exactly beneficial to someone who'd only recently relearned to walk. Caryl and Claybriar took turns steadying me as I careened back and forth, pushing too hard off the ground and making unintentional leaps. I soon learned the reason for this bizarre ward on the property; all guests were expected to scale the trees like little monkeys to get inside.

Even without much in the way of gravity, I was a piss-poor climber. Claybriar stayed beneath me so that he could ease me back on course when I slipped, and with his help it became strangely fun. Eventually we reached a great window in one of the tree-towers and climbed through it into what passed for the duke's entrance hall. There were saplings inside the hall:

trees planted inside a tree, growing toward a magical source of golden light that dangled from the top of the hollowed space. On the far side was a path that led through the greater tree's branches to other hollowed-out trees, all shaded by green leaves and wreathed in orange fog.

The duke awaited us in the entrance hall. As he strode toward us, the picture of willowy grace, I recognized him from that day at Residence One last summer. I was pierced by a pang of nostalgia for a more innocent time. He had a green mask-marking across his liquid silver eyes, four fingers on each hand, and a mouth that made you feel kissed just to look at. His pale green wings were nearly invisible, narrow and folded limply against his back.

"Allies, I greeting yours!" he intoned as he approached.

"Fantastic," I muttered. "His English has gotten even worse."

"He is very proud of it," Caryl whispered to me. "It's quite astonishing, for a fey without an Echo. Don't be rude."

"Please to remember thy names to?" the duke said.

"I am Marchioness Caryl Vallo," Caryl said smoothly, as though he'd made a lick of sense. "With me are the Baronesses Millicent Roper and Alondra Serrano."

Caryl gestured to me and to Elliott. The real Alondra was . . . somewhere in the room, I assumed, cloaked by Caveat. Caryl could see her; I could not. It would have made more sense to cloak Elliott and let Alondra introduce herself to all the fey, but Elliott's facade, like me, was impossible to physically enchant. Elliott was, however, casting a subtle look-elsewhere spell outward from inside her at all times, not only to protect her from close examination, but to keep himself safely locked down inside spellwork.

"And of course," Caryl continued, "you are familiar with His Majesty, King Claybriar, Champion of Queen Dawnrowan, Beloved of the Beast Folk."

"Beast Folk?" I said, wrinkling my nose. Caryl made a curt shushing gesture, even as the Beloved of the Beast Folk let out his own annoyed grunt.

Duke Skyhollow stepped forward and greeted Claybriar, his supple body draping itself against the faun's in a familiar embrace. Clay bent his head and kissed the half-swooning *sidhe* full on the mouth, a shameless display of kingly dominance, which I found intensely, embarrassingly arousing. Caryl gaped; Elliott averted his gaze. I could only imagine what Alondra was doing.

When they were finished kissing (this seemed to take way longer than necessary), Skyhollow gave us a bright smile and then started in on a bit of a tour. It was a nice gesture, but I couldn't understand a word he said. He threw "beauteous" in there a lot; everything he gestured to was beauteous, apparently. Beauteous hall, beauteous trees, beauteous table.

"We thank you for your hospitality," Caryl said when it became obvious that the tour had no clear conclusion in mind. "We are on our way to meet with Her Majesty, hoping to either reconcile her with King Claybriar or else find a more appropriate ruler to honor the Third Accord."

"Excellous!" Duke Skyhollow said. "Many luck to your meet."

"We came here in hopes of using your portal to shorten our travel time," said Caryl.

Duke Skyhollow stared at her blankly.

"I'm going to tell him he can use me to translate," Claybriar cut in gently. "Let's see if I can manage this without insulting him."

For a moment Claybriar and Skyhollow gazed at each other. I was envisioning a slow circular pan and some seventies-style porn music about the time Skyhollow finally seemed to experience a lightbulb moment and turn back to Caryl.

"Of course!" the duke said. "But I could never let His Majesty pass through without paying my respects. You will all stay to dine with us and avail yourselves of our comfortable accommodations."

Judging by where his eyes went at the word "accommodations," he was planning to accommodate himself comfortably on Claybriar's lap.

What could we do? As one of the few *sidhe* who was considered an ally of both Queen Dawnrowan and King Claybriar, he was too important to piss off, particularly given that he controlled the territory on the flip side of our Gate.

So we stayed the night, and we whored out my Echo. The duke's vassals showed us all to our own separate chambers, but the rooms were all just a *little* too close to each other for comfort.

My weird round little tree-bubble of a chamber had a window open to the purple deepness of the night, a window that was also, incidentally, convenient for emptying a portable toilet out of (sorry to anyone below). I'd brought my powder and lotion, so I felt safe removing my prosthetic legs for the night and doing my routine check for bumps and scratches. After I lay down in the dark, I listened to Claybriar and the duke making sounds like I'd never heard.

There's no ignoring the sounds of sex under any circumstances, and this was no anonymous couple in a motel. I could *picture* both of those guys. Knew what one of them kissed like. Every groan, every gasp, felt like someone had lit a fuse leading straight to my crotch. I wasn't jealous in the possessive sense—Clay and I had long since established that sex was a sort of constant pastime of his, with whomever—but intensely jealous in the sense that I wanted to be *in* there with them, getting some of whatever the hell was going on.

It went on for much longer than I thought anyone could physically endure, long enough for me to relieve the horrible, awkward, urgent tension twice myself before the racket finally died down. I lay there shaken and shocked in the silence, but also so boneless from exhaustion that before I could ruminate too much on the complexities of the situation, I was already asleep like the dead.

31

In the morning I carefully re-donned my prosthetic legs and set the valve on my hydraulic knee to give minimum resistance. It would make walking a little wobbly, but I figured that was an acceptable trade-off for the ability to effectively sprint when things started to get dangerous. After I'd pulled up my neoprene pants and clipped them to my shirt, there would be no more easy adjustments.

Once I was suited up, we all joined Skyhollow for breakfast in the estate's central dining hall. Located atop the tallest tree in the compound, it was open to the sky, which at this time of day was the color of dried apricots, shading to umber in the west. We were high enough that we could see past the verdant tangle of the estate to the barren sand all around it. A brilliantly green sun, just visible on the desert horizon, washed that side of the great upended bowl in a glaze of lime.

Arcadia was beginning to genuinely unnerve me.

Claybriar and Skyhollow sat together in much the way you'd expect lovers to do. Claybriar at least tried for reserve, but Skyhollow's eyes barely left him. He fed him spoonfuls of honey, whispered occasionally in his velvety pointed ear.

Baroness Foxfeather came to join us at our table, fresh as dew on grass, but she was resolutely pretending not to notice anything inappropriate going on at the duke's end of the table as she attended to our needs. A few of the other courtiers looked vaguely disgusted, but they were a mix of *sidhe* and other fey I wasn't as familiar with, so I wasn't quite sure which guy they thought wasn't good enough for the other.

Whoever did the cooking at Skyhollow Estate had clearly made an effort to cater to human dietary needs; we were served something almost but not quite resembling bread along with crystalline glasses of white liquid I couldn't bring myself to drink. I'd been well schooled that every animal in Arcadia was sentient, no matter how bovine it might seem.

Furthermore, I really didn't want to have to empty my portable toilet any more than necessary.

It was hard to light a fire under Skyhollow and his people, to give them a sense of our urgency. Some of them might have lived through war, but they would have no real way of remembering it. Threatening them with its potential devastation would be as useful as threatening a dog with heavy taxes.

So I gritted my teeth, watching the sun turn silvery pale as it climbed toward its apex. At last King Claybriar himself lost patience and gently ordered Skyhollow to let us through the portal.

"You wound me with your haste," said the duke. "But I shall do as my king commands, in this as in all things." His eyes were half promise, half plea, regarding the commands of the king he hoped to satisfy at a later date.

The portal, apparently, was at ground level. After peeing one last time to be on the safe side (I didn't foresee much chance for a potty break during the heist), I packed all my things back into my backpack. Now I got to experience the dizzying nightmare of climbing *down* the outside of the main tree, which somehow felt more precarious than climbing up. Again, Claybriar was invaluable, hands steadying me now under an arm, now under a thigh, now at the small of my back. I tried not to think too hard about where those hands had recently been.

I'd expected something similar to a Gate, despite the fact that Caryl had already told me more than once that they weren't the same. But the "portal," as it turned out, was less of a structure and more of a mental transition, a weakness in reality that had developed between two locations bearing a strong emotional and causal connection. One area of the estate grounds, shaded by drooping salmon-colored blooms, bore a concave wooden wall that had been plastered over and painted with a mural of the White Rose. We were to stand at just the right spot by the wall and simply *imagine* ourselves at the actual location until reality melted to match our perception.

In theory this could be done anywhere in Arcadia, if one had a strong enough mind, but a portal was a place that had been specifically weakened time and time again until anyone could do it with barely a thought. That said, using a portal to an unvisited spot was difficult for anyone, doubly so for a first-time portal traveler, and quadruply so for me in particular that morning. True belief was a necessary part of the process, and my sense of reality was so off-kilter that I could hardly wrap my mind around what I was experiencing, much less something a picture was merely *suggesting*.

"Remember," Caryl said to seemingly thin air at her left side—Alondra, I could only assume. "Wait by the portal on the

White Rose side while we go into the palace. But if you get too cold, you can come back here—*briefly*—to warm up."

"Got it," whispered a portion of thin air that seemed to be virtually *vibrating* with anticipation.

Caryl went through with Elliott and, apparently, Alondra, as I didn't hear any dramatic whimpers of dismay at being left behind. Caryl and Elliott's success was marked by their simply vanishing, as though I'd been imagining them and the hallucination had dissipated.

Claybriar stayed with me, even though he could likely have used the portal in his sleep by now.

"Make the scene more real in your mind," he said. "See the snow in the picture, and let that call up the feeling of it on your skin. You were in Daystrike before. Remember how the air smelled and felt in the forest. You weren't far from the White Rose."

As he spoke, as I remembered, I started to feel the wind— not just imagine it but actually *feel* it. My skin prickled, from cold and from the uncanny, but then I lost the thread of it. Trying to do this while my senses were flooded with the weirdness of Skyhollow Estate was like trying to reach orgasm with a circus calliope playing loopy music in the background.

The futile effort made me remember something I hadn't thought of in years: those times when my dad had been in a foul mood and I'd hidden in my room, trying to *will* myself elsewhere. In particular, I'd developed a fixation with the movie *Mulan*. How many times, at age nine or ten, had I squeezed my eyes shut, just *knowing* with all my heart that if I imagined a yard strewn with cherry blossoms, made it *real* enough, I would open my eyes and find myself there?

As a child with eyes closed I could make it so real that I was *there*, and each time I'd leave them closed longer, trying to get my new reality to "stick." But every time I opened my eyes, the fantasy dissolved into the drab reality of my room, leaving me bitter and empty.

Now, in Arcadia, I felt like that child again, betrayed by the useless promise of my imagination. I clenched my fists in frustration.

Claybriar pulled me close, his palm gently circling my shoulder blades. I closed my eyes again, hard.

"It's all right," he said. "Don't overthink it. Just hold on to me so I can take you with me. It's going to be cold there. Remember Daystrike? It's just like that, except it's daytime now, so the sky will be a very pale green. It's windier, too, because there's a big clearing the air can sweep through."

I *felt* it. It was *real* this time; it actually tugged at my hair. I shivered and opened my eyes. Saw bright snow and pale green sky and sucked in a lungful of frozen air in shock, coughed it back out as my lungs rejected the cold.

"Claybriar!" I said, still hugging him. "You took me with you!"

He looked down at me, clearly not having fully expected that I'd still be there. The surprised warmth in his eyes, his wondering smile, made me no longer care what the hell he'd done to the duke last night.

"It wasn't me," he said softly. "It was you, believing in me."

The portal deposited us near enough to the base of the White Rose that I had to crane my neck to see the towering, dizzying whole of it. It was exactly as Claybriar had described it: an architectural and gravitational impossibility.

The "stem" that erupted from the snow-blanketed meadow was untouched by the local winter. It looked to be made of jade or a similar vividly green stone, and from this distance there was no sign that the whole thing hadn't been carved from one unimaginably enormous piece. There would have been more than enough room inside the stem for a generous spiral staircase, making the column's entire organically undulating length traversable by terrestrial creatures, but even if there had been such a thing, it would have taken a healthy person a full day to climb. For me it would have been a living hell.

There was no door, no window, no indication that the stem was hollow or was meant to be anything other than support for the tremendous palace that unfurled atop it, rebelliously massive against the mint-green sky. Haloed by a white-gold sun were four stories of concentric architecture cleverly disguised as gilt edged, creamy petals.

The visual spectacle of the Seelie palace was so overwhelming that it flowed into my other senses, crashing through me like an orchestral chord and a rush of warm water. It occurred to me that I would at some point have to return to a place of graffiti tags and discarded Raisinet boxes, sneakers dangling by knotted laces from telephone wires. The injustice of it brought tears to my eyes.

"Say what you will about the *sidhe*," Claybriar murmured, "but my people don't have anything even close to this. No one does."

Caryl and Elliott were waiting for us at the portal, which on this side was marked by a freestanding mural of the Skyhollow oasis. Around us the snowy meadow was dotted with concentric rings of other murals, hundreds of them. Caryl, perhaps seeing my tears, moved silently to stand closer to me.

Before I'd quite finished crying, four pairs of harnessed winged horses, varying in color but each a matched set, wheeled down from the great pointed jade sepals of the palace toward us. Hanging between each pair was a strange contraption of rope and leather, made stiff with a wooden frame and lined all on the inside with fur. The structures made great important *thunks* on the ground, spraying snow, just before the horses alighted on either side of them.

As Claybriar left my side to climb into one of the contraptions, I got a better look. It was a kind of basket with a single seat inside and a smooth wooden bar to hold on to for security, like a damned amusement park ride, as the animals launched themselves into the air. Off and away Claybriar went, as though he'd done this hundreds of times, which he probably had.

"I don't know what the fuck made me think I'd be okay with *this*," I said in a thin little voice as I stared at the pair of palomino pegasi who were watching me with sentient purpose, their impractical flaxen manes dragging in the snow.

"Go on," said Caryl. "It's perfectly safe. Close your eyes if it helps."

It didn't. I squeezed them shut the second I climbed in, but I could *feel* all that empty air underneath the swaying basket, feel every shudder of my steeds' wings vibrating through the ropes. The air was cold and thin, and even though I had been careful to empty my bladder before this, I still somehow came pretty close to peeing myself.

But then we landed, far above the world, with the thump of wood and leather and the clatter of hooves. Carefully I opened my eyes, only to be nearly blinded by sunlight on white stone. Claybriar and Caryl helped guide me past a tall, steel-blue guard with yellow wings. She saluted His Majesty as we passed through a triangular doorway, and I had just enough time to register a sort of vague surprise at her show of deference before she was out of sight. Once we'd passed through, the winter's chill abated immediately, and I found myself in the high, white heart of the Seelie Court.

32

There's a phenomenon known as Stendhal Syndrome, which some people say doesn't exist. Plenty of doctors in Florence could attest to it, though, given the number of tourists who come to them after face-planting at the Uffizi Gallery. There is only so much beauty the human soul can take before it tries to rip itself right out of your cruel joke of a body and ascend.

That's what it felt like to me, anyway, as I found myself in a luminous vaulted paradise, surrounded by an embarrassment of angels. These were not marble statues on display in alcoves, but slender, winged *sidhe* going about their unfathomable business, glistening like diamond and fire opal and mother-of-pearl. The milky stone floor seemed to pitch under me like the deck of a ship. Thanks to the slight weight of the backpack, plus having set my knee at sprinting resistance, I couldn't compensate too well for my inner ear malfunction. I'd probably have fallen if not for my attentive Echo and the strong arm he looped around my waist.

"This is my first time here without Elliott," breathed Caryl from nearby. "I can only imagine how I would feel if I had never seen it at all."

"You've been here before?" I said into Claybriar's chest. Or at least that's what I intended to say. I think what I actually said was "Beef bore?"

"All the national heads and regional managers come once a year to pay respects," Caryl said. Then, after a moment: "Take your time."

"I'm fine," I said. Words now, at least, but my voice sounded like it was coming from across the room. "Let's get this over with."

"You aren't fine," said Claybriar. "I'm supporting your entire weight right now."

"Are not," I said.

Claybriar let go of me, just for a quarter of a second, to prove his point. It was as though there were nothing between my ass and the floor but two lengths of ribbon. He caught me before I could collapse, then straightened me gently.

"Give yourself a minute," he said.

"I'm not sure a minute will help," I said. "A blindfold, maybe." But even as I said it, I knew it wouldn't do much good. It wasn't just the infinite shades of near white that exploded like a rainbow against my retinas; it was the harmonic echo of footsteps against the stone and the antique scent in the air, powdery and musky sweet. Now, too, the warmth and the woodland smell of my Echo's body against me added a visceral source of dizziness to the spiritual elation that was already turning my limbs to Jell-O.

Claybriar and Elliott helped me to a bench at one side of the hall so that I could sit for a moment. Caryl hung back, her eyes alight with childlike wonder as they roamed the high arching expanse of the ceiling. As Elliott drew away, crossing my line of sight, I momentarily confused him for Alondra before remembering that the real one was supposedly still freezing her ass off down by the portal.

I leaned over and put my head between my knees, feeling the weight of my backpack shift uncomfortably toward my neck. "It's a pretty close race," I said, "but I think I functioned slightly better with a concussion."

Claybriar patted my arm. "Deep breaths."

I had been so overcome by my first impression that it wasn't until I tentatively raised myself to lean my backpack against the wall that I realized everyone was staring at me.

We often say "everyone is staring" to mean "a few people have given me lingering glances," but in this case, literally every single fey in my eyeline was gazing at me, and only me, relentlessly, even those who were walking past on their way somewhere else. It was like the reverse of the painting whose eyes follow you around the room, only several times creepier.

"Have they never seen a human before?" I whispered.

"It's the iron," said Claybriar.

I blinked. "I remember when I first met Winterglass, he said it 'sang' or something. But no one's looking at Ell—at Alondra."

"All of her iron is covered by her suit," said Caryl. "It muffles it."

My gloved fingers reflexively found the seamlike scar on the left side of my head. "Ah."

"On Earth," Caryl said, "you are part of the general white noise of metals and electricity. And some fey are less sensitive to it when occupying human facades. But here, you are rather disruptive, it seems. We ought to have made you a hat."

"How bad is it for them? Is everyone going to instantly hate me?"

"It is difficult to describe to someone without arcane senses," said Caryl. "But if we are to continue the auditory metaphor, think of it as a feedback whine from a microphone."

"Yeah, that's super attractive," I said. I glanced at the nearest passing *sidhe*, whose forehead bore two delicate, shell-pink horns. As she breezed by, glaring, I said, "Sorry." She started and averted her eyes.

"Your color's better now," said Claybriar. "Think you can stand?"

I tested my arms, lifting myself a half inch by the heels of my hands. "Yeah, things seem to be in working order," I said. "Elliott, you still remember the word to listen for?"

"Champion," he said in Alondra's sweet, lilting voice.

"So," I said. "We're doing this?"

"We're doing this," said Clay.

"The queen's audience chamber is on the top floor," Caryl said, and helped me to my feet.

There was one main flight of stairs that cut all the way up through four floors, broad as a church at the bottom and slowly tapering. At each floor the landing branched off into hallways edged with gold and white balustrades at the near side, overlooking the grand foyer. At the apex of the staircase stood an arched set of double doors. The doors were flanked by a pair of icy-pale guards, alike enough to be brothers, with broad feathery wings the color of an overcast sky.

"Shit," Claybriar murmured. "*These* guys."

"You know them?" I whispered back.

"Greyfall on the right has an Echo; he can speak. Silverwind won't understand you. They're both ornery as hell."

Real, actual *sidhe* guards. This was the part where my

plan stopped being a plan and became an actual performance. Underneath the latex of my surgical gloves I felt my palms start to sweat.

"Try to say as little as possible," I murmured back to Claybriar.

"What?" he said in a tone that suggested he might be getting a little too used to being king.

"The less you say, the less the truth can fuck us up," I said. Though even he didn't know exactly what I planned to do in the meeting. I'd taken a page from Alvin's book here. If you want people to seem appalled, sometimes you have to actually appall them.

I wouldn't have thought the guards could stand any taller, but they did as the four of us approached. Like the other *sidhe*, they glared at me as though I stank, but they were professionals and gave Caryl and Claybriar a thorough once-over as well. Elliott was the only one they didn't examine minutely; he wasn't invisible to them—he just projected an aura of drab insignificance. Because he didn't have to speak aloud to cast a spell, they had no way of knowing they were being enchanted.

"I am Baroness Millicent Roper of Los Angeles," I said, addressing the guards. "Her Majesty is expecting me, and my companions."

The guards exchanged a look, in the way *sidhe* tended to do when in silent communication. Then Greyfall said, "Come with me, then." I'm not sure why it surprised me that his English was London-accented; it would make sense that his Echo would be local.

As he turned away to push on one of the doors, I saw that he had a long tail, like a lemur's, ringed in gray. The huge door eased open, soundless.

"I'd prefer that you remain outside," I said to him. "What we plan to discuss is for the queen's ears only."

"As you wish," said Greyfall with a condescending smile, holding the door open for us. *Let the ignorant human think herself unwatched*, his expression said.

Good. I wanted him to think I was ignorant. Because it was the only thing that would explain why I thought I could get away with what I was about to do.

The audience chamber, being at the pointed apex of the rose, had a high peaked ceiling, every inch of which was covered with paintings that would have made Michelangelo gnash his teeth with jealousy. Hell, maybe his Echo had made them. On the dais at the center of the room, flanked at a distance by two *sidhe* ladies-in-waiting, was an antlered throne carved either from bone or pale wood. I couldn't tell from my current distance, nor did I look long, because next to the pale throne reclined an enormous lead-gray gryphon, and sprawled upon the throne itself, one leg thrown comfortably over the arm, was the white-winged Queen of the Seelie High Court.

She was not wearing her human facade, and Claybriar had to catch me again to keep me from crashing to my knees.

Draped in sheer, snowy silks and glowing as though lit from within, the golden, voluptuous, diamond-eyed queen beckoned us forward with one of her four arms. Two of the other arms were stroking the gryphon, who watched me through fierce, slitted yellow eyes. The remaining arm was holding the scepter. Although her golden face and breasts were as smooth as a human's, her lower half and the distal ends of her arms were covered with honey-colored, satiny fur. The soft, multi-textured hourglass of her body was the quintessence of sensual opulence; I wanted to dissolve into it and disappear.

Her attention was all for Claybriar, but he refused to speak; he only cast his eyes down to the rose-marbled floor.

Caryl leaned over to whisper to me. "You will have to make the blood sacrifice." I didn't even remember what she was talking about, and yet I docilely extended my arm to one of the *sidhe* maidservants as she approached me with a half-filled cup of what looked like white wine. She pierced my wrist with a thumb claw, which my vague mind did register as unsanitary, but no sooner had three drops of my blood bloomed like red roses in the goblet's depths than the servant murmured a few words in the Seelie tongue. There was a sudden scent like crushed leaves, and my wound closed without a trace. I watched the servant's dragonfly wings as she moved away to the queen's side.

Dawnrowan took the cup and drained it avidly to the dregs, each swallow rippling along the perfect curve of her throat. I glanced at Claybriar, but his eyes were still on the floor.

"So," the queen said, a low, coaxing sound like the cry of a mourning dove. She handed the cup back to her maidservant. "You arrive."

"Thank you for receiving us, Queen Dawnrowan," I said. "You know me, and you've met Marchioness Caryl Vallo and, of course, Claybriar." I left off the title, to appease her. "With us is Baroness Alondra Serrano, here searching for her Echo."

She barely glanced at "Alondra," instead watching the servant return to her place near the dais. She dismissed both servants with a gesture, then turned her glittering gaze to me as they headed for the double doors through which we'd entered.

"You are willing to reconsider my offer," she said to me. "Why?"

"King Winterglass refuses to negotiate with us," I said, rattling off my prepared speech even as I stared uneasily at the gryphon. Having a giant, unpredictable monster in the room had really not figured into my plan. "Without a complete fey court on our side," I went on, "we have no way of removing Dame Belinda from power. We are ready to do whatever it takes to earn the allegiance of your entire Court."

She inclined her head graciously. "Then please allow me to introduce you to Arrowmorn, future King of the Seelie."

The great double doors boomed closed, and I turned toward them, but it had only been the servants leaving. Belatedly I realized what Dawnrowan had meant and turned back to her in astonishment. She helpfully gestured with her scepter toward the massive beast reclining at her side.

I stared at the gryphon. He blinked at me.

"You want to replace Claybriar with—him." I'd stopped myself just short of saying *with that*.

"Regal, isn't he?" Dawnrowan gave his head a scratch. "Unusual, perhaps, but the Third Accord hinges upon my sharing my rule with a commoner, so it may as well be one who can *fly*."

"Right," I said, trying to remember that I was supposed to be amenable to this. At least until I could figure out how the hell to get that thing out of the room. "Can he—can Arrowmorn understand us? Can he speak?"

"He does not have the use of words," said Dawnrowan, "but I can translate for him."

"How convenient," broke in Claybriar bitterly. "A king who can't give any orders except through you."

"Claybriar, what did I say?" I hissed at him.

But Queen Dawnrowan had already turned to Claybriar, magnificent in her outrage. "On your knees, faun!" she cried, pointing her scepter at him.

Claybriar, still standing, made a great show of looking down at himself, then back up. "Whoops," he said. "Looks like I'm still king for the moment."

Queen Dawnrowan rose from her throne, eyes flashing, and the gryphon rose too. Oh Jesus he was big. He spread his wings menacingly; the shadow of them was like a lake of ink on the dais.

"Ob-obviously," Caryl interrupted, stepping forward, "we will need to give the commoners time t-to shift their support to the proper candidate."

"*Proper?*" said Claybriar, his face going red. "You expect me to stand here and— No. You know what? No." He turned to me. "I thought I could do this, but I can't listen to my own friends talk about me this way. Fuck this."

I grabbed him by the arm. He turned to me, his gaze full of dark wrath, but his fingers were gentle as they tried to pry my hand loose.

"Calm down!" I barked at him.

He stood still, eyes startled.

I turned to Queen Dawnrowan, tried to look exasperated. "Look," I said, "we're never going to have a civilized discussion about the future so long as these two . . . *men* are in here posturing at each other. So let's send them out and let those of us who are calmer finish working out the details."

Of course the queen was the least calm of anyone, but she didn't want to admit that, and probably liked that I didn't seem to notice.

"Arrowmorn, Claybriar, wait outside with the guards," she said. They both moved to obey, the gryphon because he had no choice, and Claybriar, I could only assume, because he trusted me. He did give me a hell of a puppy-dog look over his shoulder, though.

It was a risk. I had counted on his being there in the room to help me if things got too dangerous, but things were ten times as dangerous with a giant eagle-monster in the room, so this was as good an arrangement as I was going to get.

Once the doors had closed solidly behind the two men, I turned back to Dawnrowan, who was seated again on her throne, though without her previous air of insouciance.

"Their kind are not made for diplomacy," she said with a weary sigh.

Apparently my kind wasn't either, to judge by the sudden urge I had to put a fist through the back of her head. I gritted my teeth and smiled. "He was a better *champion* than he is a king, huh?" I said.

"Millie," Elliott said, interrupting me on cue in Alondra's timid voice just as Dawnrowan had begun to look affronted. "I'm so sorry to intrude, but I think . . . I think it might be *her*."

"What?" I said, feigning surprise inexpertly. I didn't worry about it too much with Dawnrowan; she'd never shown the faintest sign of reading my cues. "Might be who? You don't mean the queen?"

Elliott nodded, giving me a doe-eyed look. Boy, he'd really been practicing Alondra's moves, hadn't he?

"Well—wow," I said. "Forgive me, Your Majesty, but . . . as I said before, this is Baroness Alondra Serrano, from New York. We brought her with us because we had reason to believe that her Echo was someone powerful here in Daystrike. Would you be so kind as to indulge her? Let her see if it might be you?"

"Me?" Suddenly all of Dawnrowan's offense and irritation melted away, leaving only a childlike wonder. "You believe *I* might be her Echo?"

Well, I thought. *Now we know what to get the girl who has everything.*

"If Your Majesty will permit me," Elliott said with becoming shyness, "I could take your hand, and I would know." As he spoke, he shifted the spell he'd been casting to make the queen pay him no mind and made her oblivious to me, instead.

Elliott and I approached the queen at the same time. The guardian spirit must already have found this alarming and flashed it to the guards, because I saw the doors begin to swing open. Elliott quickened the facade's pace, pulling off his glove. The queen's eyes flew wide as the song of iron hit her from *both* sides, and then Elliott seized her bare wrist. Between the pain and the enchantment, she hardly even noticed as I snatched the scepter from her hand and ran.

33

This daring theft looked a little bit stupider than I'd hoped it would, as I was now running directly *toward* two guards and a huge, angry gryphon. *Please, Caryl and Elliott, be fast,* I prayed.

I heard Caryl reciting the grim words of an Unseelie curse. Fake, since it was actually Elliott silently weaving the spell, but who in that room besides our team would know the difference?

Elliott had thoroughly prepared me for the psychic enchantment he intended to cast on me, but all the same I didn't have to feign horror when the scepter in my hand turned into a writhing, hissing snake. I *hurled* that thing at the floor and let out a yell, coming to such a sudden stop that I overbalanced slightly and had to career *into* Silverwind just to keep from falling down.

The large *sidhe* grabbed me roughly, turning me and pinning my arms, my backpack crushing against his chest. He must have been briefed on the meaning of my suit, because he was careful not to touch anything uncovered. If I'd really wanted to fight, I could have just head-butted him in the throat, but I'd done more than enough already.

Meanwhile Greyfall stooped to carefully retrieve the royal

scepter from the floor. He was a Seelie fey, but since he was male, the scepter didn't give him any particular powers during the brief time it took him to reach the shell-shocked queen. He knelt to present it to her, and she seized it eagerly with two of her four hands.

"What were you thinking?" Caryl cried at fake Alondra as loudly as she was able in her low, hoarse voice. Her acting wasn't great, but she was stressed out and scared enough that she did at least sound genuinely shaky.

"Millie said she could get past the guards!" Elliott/Alondra whined in protest. "I was only following her orders!"

"You assaulted the *queen*!" Caryl persisted. Just in case for some reason the guards hadn't seen that bit.

"Come with us quietly," said Greyfall, approaching Elliott, "and we will not harm you."

"She has iron in her!" the queen cried breathlessly. "Just like the other! Be cautious."

"Don't you *dare* attempt to fight the guards," said Caryl in a genuinely threatening tone, "or I shall execute you *myself*. Your Majesty, please forgive me. If I had known the baronesses had *lost their minds*, I would never have brought them into your presence."

"Your assistance in apprehending them is appreciated, Your Ladyship," said the queen. At least that part of the plan had worked, I reassured myself in an attempt to keep from panicking as Silverwind manhandled me out the doors and down the long staircase. The low resistance on my prosthetic knee made it extremely difficult for me to manage the steps; more than once I almost lurched out of Silverwind's grasp before he adjusted his grip to better support me.

"Where are you taking us?" I said to Greyfall once he caught up, dragging Elliott. "Will there be a trial? What's happening?" This wasn't how I'd really behaved when under arrest, but they had no way of knowing that, and the experience was too recent for me to comfortably mine it for verisimilitude.

"Marchioness Vallo will continue discussions with the queen," said Greyfall with admirable restraint as he muscled Elliott down the long hallway and back out into the sunlight, onto the sepals that jutted out into the cold, minty sky. "You will remain in prison below until your fates are decided."

The steel-blue guard I'd noticed on the way in stepped into our path. "Was King Claybriar involved in this?" she demanded of me.

Another *sidhe* calling my Echo "King," here in the heart of the High Court? Dawnrowan seemed to have an exaggerated view of his unpopularity.

"No," I said quickly. "He didn't even know what I planned to—"

"Silence!" Greyfall snapped at me, interrupting. Then he turned to the blue guard. "Don't bother talking to her, Whisperdrift. She'll just lie anyway. Wait for the trial. Then we'll see how innocent your 'king' really is."

Whisperdrift stepped aside, her expression troubled. I didn't have much time to ponder the situation. The guards dragged us out onto the edge of one of the sepals and, instead of loading us into a horse-drawn contraption, simply locked their arms around us and leaped off the edge.

I screamed. Everything in my body clenched; I curled phantom toes against the nothingness beneath. The guards' broad wings caught at the air like parachutes. We were most definitely falling—I don't think they could have gained altitude while holding us if they'd tried—but there was enough strength in their wings to help us drift toward the snow at a safe speed and land with something less than bone-shattering force.

"Oh my God, oh my God," I said in a quaking voice as silent Silverwind steadied me; I'd gone all wobbly again. The guards waited for my legs to regain the power of movement, and then they pushed us ahead of them toward a sort of double storm-cellar door built into a snowy hump of earth near the base of the palace. The doors looked to be carved from the same green stone as the stem.

The guards let go of us for the moment—where would we go? An array of portals was spread out around us in concentric rings, but we'd never be able to get to any of them before they stopped us, and they knew it. One guard each took a door and heaved them apart; then they shoved Elliott and me onto a stone stairway that angled steeply down into the darkness.

We went ahead, abreast, the guards holding us by the arms from behind. Silverwind had noticed my trouble on the stairs from the audience chamber and steadied me with surprising care. Behind us, Greyfall murmured the words of a spell, raising the scent of greenery and setting both the guards' forms to glowing softly in the darkness. Below, there was no light source at all, but the guards' luminescence now suggested the prison's dimensions. It appeared to be a high-ceilinged cavern, roomy enough that it could have comfortably seated the patrons of an opera, had the room been furnished for it.

As we descended, a half dozen prisoners became faintly visible scattered throughout, sitting motionless on the cavern floor without even looking up at the approaching light. Some sort of enchantment must have held them all immobile. In the dimness I couldn't tell what types of fey they were, only that they varied in size and shape, and none appeared to be *sidhe*.

Our cell, our cage, looked to be made of twisting, smooth-sanded tree limbs, entwined until there was barely enough space for an arm to poke through in the widest of the gaps. A gumdrop-shaped doorway had been cut from the frame of the cage and replaced with a slab of solid oak.

Not far from the cage were a table, chair, and cot; from the cot rose an autumn-hued male *sidhe* with elegant branching antlers who had apparently been sitting there in pitch blackness until our arrival. He reached into a bag at his belt as his path converged with ours, and from it he withdrew a simple wooden key. He approached the cage, turned the key in a wooden lock, and swung the door wide. Greyfall and Silverwind took my backpack and shoved us into the cage. Before I'd even quite regained my balance, the great oaken door was swinging shut again, and the key turned and clicked in the heavy lock.

Without another word, the two brother-guards turned and ascended the prison staircase, taking their light with them as they went. In the deepening gloom, I peered through a gap in the cage at the antlered guard, who was putting the key back into his bag with one hand and carrying my backpack away with the other.

"Hey," I said. "Is there any way you could turn on a light down here?"

Either he didn't speak English or he was ignoring me, because he simply dropped my backpack on the table and then lay back on his cot, closing his eyes. His manner, his absolute stillness, was so like the prisoners' that I wondered if he, too, were under an enchantment.

The door closed with a soft *boom* behind the departing guards, leaving the cavern in absolute darkness.

"Well, this is scary," I said to Elliott. "Now I'm not sure I want you to . . . fall asleep." The guard probably couldn't understand me, but I wasn't going to take any chances by talking about our plan.

"Why not?" said Elliott. So like Alondra's voice in the darkness, though not at all her tone.

"I'll be alone down here if you do. I can't see a thing; it's creepy."

"If I don't . . . sleep, then I won't be any good to you."

"I know," I said, my belly knotting. "Get some rest."

I helped Elliott arrange his facade into a sort of fetal position at the back of the cage, and then he abandoned it. In a flash the entire cavern was revealed to me, and I cringed, glancing toward the guard, looking for a light source.

I am showing it to you, said what sounded like Elliott's Alondra voice. *In your mind. The guard cannot see it, nor hear me.*

Elliott made himself appear on fake Alondra's inert shoulder, in the form of a crow—not white-breasted like Brand, but as black as the ones in L.A.

Are you ready to let me fully into your mind? he asked me.

I nodded, not sure if he could hear my thoughts until I'd given him permission, and not wanting to speak aloud to a cell mate who was supposedly asleep.

Just relax your mind, said Elliott. *I am not going to possess you; I am simply going to accustom myself to the energy of your thoughts so that I can pick up on them and transmit them to others.*

I nodded again impatiently and tried my best to relax.

Whatever he was doing in there, it felt unnerving, like a couple of daddy longlegs skittering around all over my brain.

How long is this going to take? I thought at him experimentally.

It is already done, he said. *You can communicate with images, or by imagining speech, whichever is easier.*

Go see what Claybriar and Dawnrowan are doing, and show me. Find Shock, and tell him that now would be a good time to come to the White Rose.

Elliott made the crow appear to fly away—a nice touch, unnecessary but grounding for me. Once the illusion was gone, I was alone in the cell, and darkness descended again as Elliott turned his focus to other things. I tried not to panic.

Before the darkness could completely claw away at my sanity, Elliott started to transmit what he was seeing, and that filled my mind just as thoroughly as though I were seeing it myself, making the darkness fade away.

At first it was a tentative trickle of images, but when he seemed sure of the connection, it became way too much. The entirety of the White Rose exploded into my head: every part of it, every person in it, the thoughts and feelings of hundreds of other people, mingled in one cacophony of sensation.

Elliott, stop, I said to him in my head. *I'm only human; my mind can't take all this.*

It stopped, all at once, and I was in the dark again.

Show me how you need it to be, Elliott's voice said in my suddenly quiet mind.

I wasn't sure what to do for a moment, how to explain, but then I tried to picture it cinematically: the movement of a camera, tracking one person, then cutting to another, showing only their outsides, not what was going on inside their heads.

Anyone who needs to talk to me, I told him, *can just speak out loud, and you can relay my messages back to them.*

I understand completely, said Elliott. *I shall present things to you as you require.*

34

EXT. WHITE ROSE - DAY - CLOSE ANGLE - SHOCK

As he lands awkwardly on one of the palace sepals in his mantislike native form. He steadies himself, then folds his wings and approaches the female sidhe *guard WHISPERDRIFT.*

Whisperdrift is smooth skinned, the color of blue steel, with wings like yellow sails. She inclines her head to the prince, but barely.

WHISPERDRIFT

Your Highness. Her Majesty is currently indisposed.

SHOCK

It's fine. Just returning some samples to the vault.

Shock holds up a black drawstring purse; the CLINK of glass vials can be heard inside. The guard nods again and steps aside to let Shock pass.

INT. WHITE ROSE - DAY

Shock proceeds down the long, high-ceilinged hallway. SEELIE COURTIERS bend their paths to give him a wide berth but otherwise ignore him.

CUT TO:

INT. WHITE ROSE AUDIENCE CHAMBER - DAY

DAWNROWAN, CLAYBRIAR, and CARYL are in heated conversation. Claybriar has one arm around Dawnrowan's shoulders as she leans against him, trembling visibly.

CARYL

Is there nothing I can say to convince you to at least let me speak with them before I go? If we can at least discover their reasoning . . .

DAWNROWAN

You speak of reason, when I can still feel the chill of that poisoned touch? You are human after all.

CARYL

I am sorry. I am not accustomed to using my
emotions to evaluate situations. Perhaps
the best thing for me to do is report this to
Alvin as soon as possible.

DAWNROWAN

Yes. Go.

CLAYBRIAR

(softly)
May I stay with you, my lady?

Dawnrowan looks up at him and for a moment seems incapable of speech. Caryl looks between the two of them and then bows, making her exit. Dawnrowan does not seem to notice her departure.

DAWNROWAN

I thought you no longer cared for me. May
I . . . will you let me into your mind?

Claybriar reaches out, tentatively, his fingertips finding the delicate bones of her face.

CLAYBRIAR

I don't think that would be a good idea right now.

DAWNROWAN

Why not, my love?

Dawnrowan lays her hand over his where it rests on her cheek. The scene seems to stutter slightly, flicker. The voice of MILLIE intrudes.

MILLIE (V.O.)

Hey, Elliott, can I see what Shock is up to?

ELLIOTT (V.O.)

Of course.

INT. WHITE ROSE VAULT - DAY

The vault is dimly lit, but white stone, glass, crystal, and mirrors make a little light go a long way. The place is a maze of delicate shelves and ladders, and the shelves hold hundreds of thousands of tiny vials of red liquid.

Shock, back in human form, takes his time searching among

the shelves. He holds the bag of vials in his hand.

ELLIOTT (V.O.)

Shock, Millie is--

Shock starts, nearly dropping the bag.

ELLIOTT (V.O.) (cont'd)

Apologies. It's Elliott. I've linked with Millie now, and she is using me to keep track of what is happening. The guardian spirit is still active, so raise no suspicion.

Shock hesitates, looking as though he wants to respond, but finally he just carries on pretending to look for something.

MILLIE (V.O.)

Can he hear me, too?

ELLIOTT (V.O.)

If you wish.

MILLIE (V.O.)

Make it so.

ELLIOTT (V.O.)

Shock, Millie wishes to address you.

MILLIE (V.O.)

Hey, kiddo. You're doing great. Do you know where to find Dostoyevsky's vial?

SHOCK

I know this place like the back of my hand.

MILLIE (V.O.)

Well, play dumb for a bit; act like you can't find where to put the vials you brought until Caryl gets down here to free me so I can disable the guardian. I'll let you know when it's safe to start loading up the Vessel.
(beat)
Okay, now I need to find Caryl.

CUT TO:

EXT. WHITE ROSE - DAY - TRACKING SHOT - ON CARYL

Caryl white-knuckles the wooden bar at the edge of her litter as the two rose-winged horses harnessed to either side bank and spiral their way toward the ground.

They land with a jolt, and Caryl carefully eases herself to the ground. She begins to walk through the snow with purpose.

PULL BACK to reveal that she is walking directly toward the storm doors of the prison.

> **MILLIE (V.O.)**
>
> Wait, that's not right. What is she doing? Why is she coming here in broad daylight? Goddamn it, do I have to do everything myself?

> **CARYL**
>
> (aloud)
> I would think you would trust me by now.

> **MILLIE (V.O.)**
>
> Elliott, she wasn't supposed to hear that.

> **ELLIOTT (V.O.)**
>
> You keep changing the rules!

> **MILLIE (V.O.)**
>
> Just use some goddamned common sense, okay? I'm a little overwhelmed.

Caryl approaches the prison doors, pauses. She glances up at the White Rose contemplatively as she murmurs under her breath, lips barely moving.

> **CARYL**
>
> I'm leaving tracks.

Caryl sighs, as though in resignation, and then begins to head back toward the portal, dragging her feet a little.

PAN DOWN to the trail of disturbed snow.

> **MILLIE (V.O.)**
>
> But the tracks go right to the prison. Isn't that a dead giveaway?

> **CARYL**
>
> The dead giveaway would be fresh tracks approaching one by one from nowhere. Remember, every inch of these grounds is observed at all times.

Caryl arrives at the portal to Skyhollow. She stands before it, closes her eyes, and, in a moment, vanishes.

Suddenly the scene shifts. Everything is in the same spot, but nothing looks the same.

EXT. WHITE ROSE - DAY - SPELLSIGHT

The mundane elements of the scene dim almost to non-existence. What was once an innocuous mural now writhes with intricate lacy golden spellwork.

Two human-shaped masses of seething, purple-green webbing move slowly away from it, single file, tiptoeing as they carefully walk in the tracks Caryl has already left in the snow.

> **MILLIE (V.O.)**
>
> Elliott, don't. That's gonna give me a migraine. I trust that they're there.

> **ELLIOTT (V.O.)**
>
> As you say.

EXT. WHITE ROSE - DAY - NORMAL

We continue to slowly PAN along the tracks in the snow, toward the prison. There is little if any change in them.

> **MILLIE (V.O.)**
>
> Okay, I get it now. Give me the audience chamber.

CUT TO:

INT. WHITE ROSE AUDIENCE CHAMBER - DAY

It's empty but for a single maidservant sweeping the floor.

MILLIE (V.O.)

Where the fuck's Claybriar?

CUT TO:

INT. QUEEN'S CHAMBER - DAY

An opulent canopy bed dominates the large space. At one side is a bay window with a cushioned seat; Dawnrowan and Claybriar sit upon it, knees almost touching.

Near them is a small tea table with two chairs; someone has laid out bowls full of berries and honey and cups of golden liquid, but they sit untouched.

CLAYBRIAR

You think that's a compliment, but it isn't.

DAWNROWAN

I don't understand you.

CLAYBRIAR

You seldom do.

MILLIE (V.O.)

Hey, Claybriar. Sorry to distract you from your lovers' quarrel, but it's time for you to do your distraction. Still have a plan, I hope?

DAWNROWAN

You know, my love, that no matter--

Claybriar lets out a roar and leaps to his feet, picking up one of the chairs at the tea table and hurling it across the room. It splinters against the wall.

MILLIE (V.O.)

Well, that's one way to do it, I guess.

DAWNROWAN

(frightened)
Claybriar!

CLAYBRIAR

I never even wanted to be king!

INT. WHITE ROSE EAST HALLWAY - CONTINUOUS

GREYFALL makes a beeline for the nearest staircase.

INT. WHITE ROSE WEST HALLWAY - CONTINUOUS

With perfect symmetry, SILVERWIND does the same, leaping up the stairs two and three at a time, wing assisted.

> **MILLIE (V.O.)**
>
> Caryl, now.

EXT. WHITE ROSE PRISON - CONTINUOUS

One of the storm doors eases open, just enough for a human to slip through.

INT. WHITE ROSE PRISON - CONTINUOUS

A shaft of wintry sunlight pierces the darkness.

At his post, the lone ANTLERED GUARD stirs from what looks like slumber, gazes toward the light with a faintly curious expression.

The shaft of light narrows, disappears. The guard watches for a moment longer, then closes his eyes again.

INT. QUEEN'S CHAMBER - CONTINUOUS

Claybriar dashes a bowl against the floor, shattering it amid a sticky pool of honey and porcelain shards.

Silverwind and Greyfall burst into the room. Silverwind waves a hand, and a blinding light explodes in front of Claybriar's eyes. He groans and slaps his hands over his face, halting his assault on the crockery.

CLAYBRIAR

I'm still your king, you nitwit! OW!

The guards look to Dawnrowan in confusion. She stares at them for a moment, then bursts into sobs. Greyfall flies immediately to embrace her, and Silverwind grabs Claybriar roughly by the arm.

A GOLDEN GUARD and a LAVENDER GUARD arrive and immediately begin to attend to the mess on the floor.

INT. WHITE ROSE PRISON - OAKEN CELL - DAY

Millie stands with her back to the wall of her cell, staring blankly into space. Her hand instinctively flies up to cover the scarred side of her face as she--

MILLIE (V.O.)

Elliott, don't! That's too fucking weird.

QUICK PAN TO THE ANTLERED GUARD.

ELLIOTT (V.O.)

This is your cue, however.

MILLIE (V.O.)

On it.

Off camera we hear a shrill, prolonged SCREAM.

The guard leaps up from his seat and heads toward the oaken cell.

The camera carefully PANS BETWEEN the guard and the inert FACADE OF ALONDRA curled up on the other side of the cell, without catching Millie in between.

MILLIE (OFF-SCREEN)

She's dead! She's dead! Oh my God, she's dead!

The guard doesn't seem to understand Millie's words.

MILLIE (OFF-SCREEN) (cont'd)

Do you not speak English? I'm locked in here with a dead woman! Help!

GUARD POV

CLOSE ON Millie's pointing finger, then PAN TO the body again.

MILLIE (OFF-SCREEN) (cont'd)

(gibberish)
Chimmaray jabean slawfish! Nib framenob halloo!

BACK TO SCENE

The guard pulls the wooden key from the pouch at his belt, then seems to hesitate.

MILLIE (OFF-SCREEN) (cont'd)

Come on, come on . . .

The guard puts the key back into his pouch and starts to move away from the cell door.

MILLIE (OFF-SCREEN) (cont'd)

What are you doing? She needs help! Get in here!

The guard moves around behind Millie, pulls a long cord

from the other side of his belt, snags one of Millie's wrists through a gap in the cage, and ties her to one of its tangled limbs.

Then he walks to the cell door and inserts the wooden key into the lock. The moment the latch clicks free, he freezes, face going blank, at the exact moment CARYL and ALONDRA appear behind him to ease his fall to the floor.

Alondra looks nervous but excited; Caryl is on the verge of a panic attack.

CARYL

Alondra go--go untie--

ALONDRA

Yes, ma'am! Goodness, it's so much warmer in here than out there.

MILLIE

Yeah, it's a real picnic. Just a second; let me check on my boys.

CUT TO:

INT. WHITE ROSE VAULT - DAY

Shock removes a vial from his bag and replaces it on the shelf, looking restless.

INT. QUEEN'S CHAMBER - DAY

Claybriar sits on the window seat. Dawnrowan stands beside him, a hand resting between his horns, seemingly in communion with the guards. Just as they seem on the verge of relaxing, Claybriar leaps to his feet and grabs the remaining chair, threatening a guard with it.

INT. WHITE ROSE PRISON - DAY

Alondra manages to get the cord off Millie's wrist. Millie stares off into space, unseeing.

MILLIE

Shit. We need to hurry and disable that guardian before Clay gets himself killed or something.

Caryl rushes to her side, trying to help her out of the cage but mostly hindering in her panicked rush.

ALONDRA

He's the king, right? So no Seelie can harm him, even the guards.

MILLIE

Let's not test that, okay? Where's the spell-work? Elliott, I'm going to need my own eyes back for a minute.

MILLIE'S POV

Caryl moves to the place where the guard had been sitting and gestures to the wall nearby.

CARYL

Just put your hand here. Caveat has it memorized and ready to replace. Please, please, let's get out of here.

Millie grabs her backpack off the nearby table and shoulders it, then reaches out and touches the wall.

MILLIE

Did it work?

                                        CUT TO:

INT. QUEEN'S CHAMBER - DAY

Dawnrowan's head snaps up suddenly. She looks at the

four guards. As one, they hightail it from the room, leaving
Dawnrowan and Claybriar alone.

MILLIE (V.O.)

Oh shit. They felt the spell go down. Here
they come.

35

INT. WHITE ROSE PRISON - DAY

Millie and Caryl stand frozen near the guard station. Alondra paces near the cage, wringing her hands. Millie is fully visible now, and this does not seem to distress her; she has the unfocused gaze of someone watching something far away.

CARYL

(panicking)
No one panic.

MILLIE

How long before the guards get here, do you think?

CUT TO:

EXT. WHITE ROSE - DAY - EASTERN SEPAL

The door from the interior bursts open, and four guards pour out of it, heading for the edge.

ELLIOTT (V.O.)

Dawnrowan suspected you immediately and transferred the thought to them.

In orderly pairs, the guards leap from the edge, wings unfurling.

MILLIE (V.O.)

Fantastic. Get me Shock.

INT. WHITE ROSE VAULT - DAY

Shock is pacing back and forth along a row of shelves. His human facade is sweating slightly.

MILLIE (V.O.)

Guardian's down.

SHOCK

Oh thank God.

MILLIE (V.O.)

Thank who?

SHOCK

Figure of speech.

He immediately makes a beeline for the back of the vault.

MILLIE (V.O.)

Shock, you're going to have to hurry. I underestimated how alert Dawnrowan would be to my fucking with the guardian spirit.

SHOCK

How much time do I have?

CUT TO:

INT. WHITE ROSE PRISON - DAY - MILLIE POV

Caryl has propped open one of the storm doors, letting a shaft of light in to illuminate the stairs. We move toward them and up as Millie speaks.

MILLIE

Basically I need to go for the Hail Mary exit strategy approximately nowish. The good news is that I'm about to freak the guards out so much they won't think to pay attention to what you're doing in there.

SHOCK (V.O.)

But there is bad news.

We move to the top of the stairs and out into the blinding whiteness of

EXT. WHITE ROSE - DAY – MILLIE'S POV

CAMERA ADJUSTS slowly to the brightness.

MILLIE

Of course there is. The bad news is that I can't just stand there with my hand on the stone indefinitely. Once they agree to let me escape, I have to actually, you know, escape.

Alondra emerges from the prison, blinking and squinting.

SHOCK (V.O.)

And then someone will surely remember I was in the vault, and think to check on me.

MILLIE

Yup. Alondra, Caryl told you where your stone is?

Alondra points east across the clearing.

ALONDRA

In the woods, over that way.

PAN UP to see the descending silhouettes of four guards against the pale green sky, still small, but circling closer.

MILLIE

Go.

ALONDRA

Millie, will you be able to--

MILLIE

Go!

Alondra takes off at a sprint.

MILLIE

And now it's my turn, I guess.

PAN DOWN, a CLOSE shot as Millie gives her left knee a pat under her neoprene suit.

MILLIE

All right. Time to stress-test my hardware.

PAN TOWARD the western woods. It's a long way across the clearing.

The camera begins to move forward. Accelerates, shakes as Millie breaks into a run.

BRIEF, SHAKY PAN over Millie's shoulder and up. The guards have spotted Millie, and all four have changed trajectory toward her.

MILLIE

The fuck? Not one of them goes for Alondra?
She's going to take this personally.

We hear Millie's BREATH as she sprints unevenly across the snow.

CARYL (V.O.)

I'm coming out of the prison. I have to stop them somehow.

MILLIE

No! You're visible! You're supposed to be gone already!

The camera WAVERS as Millie stumbles slightly.

CARYL (V.O.)

I don't know what else to do. You're a sitting duck out there in the clearing.

MILLIE

It's fine. I'm almost there.

She isn't. There is a shrill WHISTLING sound, and then a flaming arrow THWACKS into the snow about two feet in front of her.

MILLIE

Fuck this! Caryl, save me!

The camera lurches forward even faster.

CARYL (V.O.)

I--I believe I can buy you some time, but it means letting the prison guard go. I need Caveat.

ALONDRA (V.O.)

It's okay, Caryl. I used that cord to tie him up while you were opening the door.

MILLIE

Well look who turned out to be fucking useful!

CARYL (V.O.)

I am impressed, Serrano. Millie, do not slow down, whatever you see.

MILLIE

(out of breath)
Well that's . . . not at all . . . ominous.

CARYL (V.O)

Are you all right, love?

Millie stumbles again. When she speaks, her voice is choked.

> **MILLIE**
>
> Fine . . . just . . . definitely . . . not . . . used
> to . . . running . . . in snow . . .

The world begins to grow dark.

PAN UP to see an apocalyptic-looking purple haze boiling out of nowhere to block the sun.

The guards panic, forgetting Millie for the moment; two of them crash into each other and nearly spiral to their deaths.

CAMERA moves forward again, approaching the woods.

> **MILLIE**
>
> Jesus Christ, Caryl.

> **CARYL (V.O.)**
>
> I learned that from King Winterglass.

The STANDING STONE is now in sight, a rough obelisk with delicate runes etched into it.

Millie makes a beeline toward it. Her hand reaches out.

> **MILLIE**
>
> I'm here, guys. I'm here!

The moment she touches it we

CUT TO:

EXT. EASTERN STONE

Alondra is bent over with her hands on her thighs, catching her breath.

> **ALONDRA**
>
> Me too. I'm here.

> **MILLIE (V.O.)**
>
> Strike a pose, in case any of the guards fly over that way.

Alondra grins and moves closer to the stone, holding her palm out toward it.

> **ALONDRA**
>
> Like this?

MILLIE (V.O.)

Perfect.

CARYL (V.O.)

The guards are still in a state of confusion
for the moment.

MILLIE (V.O.)

Elliott, show me Dawnrowan. What's she
doing? Is she watching? We need to deliver
her the ultimatum directly.

INT. QUEEN'S CHAMBER - DAY

Queen Dawnrowan sits in the window seat, watching Clay-
briar with tragic eyes as he paces back and forth before her.

DAWNROWAN

Do not say that. Why would you say such
a thing?

MILLIE (V.O.)

(sotto voce)
Maybe let him finish dumping her first.

CLAYBRIAR

You know what I am. I don't know why the
spirits were so cruel as to make a *sidhe* love
a man who can't love the way *sidhe* love.

*Dawnrowan rises, moves to him, but stops just short of
touching him.*

DAWNROWAN

And what way can you love me? Let me
inside your mind. I have no skill at talking
in this way.

CLAYBRIAR

I told you, I can't do that!

He tries for anger, but it suddenly twists into despair.

*He falls on his knees before her, curling his hands into her
skirt, hiding his face. She lays a hand on his head, then
slowly kneels so that she is at his level. She gently turns his
face so that he must meet her eyes.*

DAWNROWAN

Then so be it. Whatever limits you place on

love, I must accept. For me, there will only
ever be you.

*He looks at her, lost. She closes the distance between them,
cradling his face in her hands as she--*

MILLIE (V.O.)

Show me Shock.

INT. WHITE ROSE VAULT - DAY

Shock is loading vials into the Medial Vessel by the handful.

MILLIE (V.O.)

Shock, did you get your dad's vial?

SHOCK

Yep, got it first thing. Almost done with the
US employees now, and then I'm going to
start on Canada.

MILLIE (V.O.)

Nice work.

Shock continues to load vials.

It's really not that interesting.

ELLIOTT (V.O.)

Millie?

MILLIE (V.O.)

Yeah, yeah, I know. Fine.

INT. QUEEN'S CHAMBER - DAY

All four of Dawnrowan's arms are wrapped around Claybriar as they share a kiss worthy of epic ballad status.

MILLIE (V.O.)

(sotto voce)
Oh, fuck me.

ELLIOTT (V.O.)

It looks as though you may need to wait in line.

Sure enough, Claybriar's hands have already expertly located the fastenings to Dawnrowan's diaphanous garments. They melt away to the floor.

MILLIE (V.O.)

The fuck is up with his timing? I need to be delivering an ultimatum.

ELLIOTT (V.O.)

He doesn't know that. Last he heard was "distract her."

Dawnrowan begins to emit some deeply erotic sounds as Claybriar kisses his way down her throat.

MILLIE (V.O.)

Well, she's not the only one distracted.

Claybriar lifts Dawnrowan into his arms and carries her toward the bed, laying her down on it.

MILLIE (V.O.)

Caryl, why are you so quiet? Where are the guards?

CARYL (V.O.)

(a little breathless)
Pursuing me, for the time being.

Dawnrowan looks up into Claybriar's eyes, the very picture of adoration.

DAWNROWAN

Speak to me. Out loud. As humans do. Tell me you desire me.

CLAYBRIAR

I want you. I want you so much.

He lowers himself onto her, greedily tasting her skin.

ELLIOTT (V.O.)

Millie?

CLAYBRIAR

You beautiful little slut.

He grabs a handful of Dawnrowan's hair, forcing her head back. She gasps.

ELLIOTT (V.O.)

Millie, I need to show you--

MILLIE (V.O.)

Is Caryl in trouble?

ELLIOTT (V.O.)

She's fine. Leading the guards on a merry chase.

MILLIE (V.O.)

Then hush.

ELLIOTT (V.O.)

Millie, I can see where your hand is. And we're about to have a problem.

MILLIE (V.O.)

Ugh, fine. Show me.

INT. WHITE ROSE HALLWAY - DAY

The guard WHISPERDRIFT moves toward the door at the end of the hall with purpose.

ELLIOTT (V.O.)

She's heading toward the vault.

> **MILLIE (V.O.)**
>
> Shock!

INT. WHITE ROSE VAULT - CONTINUOUS

Shock is still merrily loading vials into the bag.

> **MILLIE (V.O.)**
>
> Shock, you're about to have company. Take
> what you've managed to steal and go. Meet
> me at the western standing stone.

*Shock stuffs the Medial Vessel into the pocket of his jacket,
then suddenly changes back to his mantislike fey form.*

> **MILLIE (V.O.)**
>
> Nice. Now get out of there.

> **SHOCK**
>
> No need to tell me twice.

He heads toward the door.

> **MILLIE (V.O.)**
>
> Shock?

SHOCK

Yes?

MILLIE (V.O.)

Do I want to think too hard about where the Medial Vessel is right now?

SHOCK

I would advise against it.

INT. WHITE ROSE HALLWAY - CONTINUOUS

Shock emerges from the vault and nearly collides with Whisperdrift.

WHISPERDRIFT

Your Highness.

SHOCK

Hello.

WHISPERDRIFT

You are still here?

SHOCK

I had . . . I had some trouble. . . .

MILLIE (V.O.)

Shit, he can't lie.

CARYL (V.O.)

Shock, wipe her. Make her forget she saw you.

WHISPERDRIFT

You had trouble?

SHOCK

I . . .

ELLIOTT (V.O.)

Caryl, you will have to release Caveat; I am a bit occupied.

CARYL (V.O.)

Caveat is currently the only thing keeping the guards from finding me. Shock, do what you must.

ELLIOTT (V.O.)

(direly)
Shock, do not enslave another spirit. Find
another way.

WHISPERDRIFT

Your Highness, I am afraid I'm going to
need you to come with me. A . . . situation
is unfolding.

*Shock starts to back away from the guard, who advances
on him.*

CARYL (V.O.)

Shock, you can't let them take the Vessel
from you, or all of this is for nothing! Cast
the spell!

ELLIOTT (V.O.)

No, Your Highness. Not until she releases
Caveat.

CARYL (V.O.)

(panicking)
I can't! Shock, just wipe her! Now!

Shock, also panicking, murmurs a few words in the Unseelie tongue. Whisperdrift stops, looking zombie eyed.

Shock hesitates, then walks past.

There is a long, awful silence in which there is nothing but Shock's FOOTSTEPS echoing through the stone hallway. Then:

ELLIOTT (V.O.)

Farewell.

I found myself alone in a snowy forest, leaning with one hand braced on the standing stone.

"Elliott?" I said, disoriented by the still emptiness. My voice sounded small as it disappeared into the forest.

I looked around through the trees, tried to make out what was going on in the clearing. The purple haze was gone from the sky; Caryl must have only needed it to get the guards' attention.

What had Caveat been doing to protect her? What was so important that it had been worth what Caryl had done?

"Elliott?" I said. "If you're there, please talk to me. This wasn't my fault. Don't just leave me."

Nothing. A wind hissed through the trees and kicked up little flurries of snow.

I was on my own.

36

The forest was sparse here, and I could still see the Rose itself, towering high above the tops of the skeletal trees. My first impulse was to rush back toward the clearing, to reestablish connection somehow with the people I'd lost. I backtracked nearly to the edge of the woods before common sense told me that this was a terrible idea.

Shock expected me to be at the western standing stone, and he was the guy with the bag. I had no way to update him about my location. I wasn't sure how I was going to deliver my ultimatum, but that didn't bear thinking about. As counterintuitive as it felt, I had no choice but to turn back, disappear into the forest, stand by the stone, and wait for someone to find me.

Someone did find me mere moments later, but, unfortunately, it was Greyfall. Against snow and white trees, the pale cloudy silver of his wings was an ominous shadow.

"Don't take another step closer," I said, and put my hand on the stone.

He stopped as though he'd hit a wall, his surprised exhale misting in the air.

"The Ironbones you took to prison," I said. "She's waiting by the other stone. I have a guardian spirit at my command, just as you once did, and if you don't do exactly what I tell you to do, the spirit will signal her to touch that stone as well."

For a moment Greyfall didn't speak. His jaw worked; I could almost sense the glittery fey blood throbbing in his temple veins. When he finally spoke, his voice was like the crust of ice over old snow.

"What is it that you want?"

Right. Demands. I'd need to make them complicated, to give Shock time to find me. I tried to channel my inner Hans Gruber.

"Glad I have your attention," I said. "I have six demands. And until you've met all six, I am not withdrawing from this stone."

Greyfall's eyes literally clouded over, as though he were about to manifest twin tornadoes from his eye sockets. "What *are* your demands?" he said.

"Number one: withdraw all guards from the eastern standing stone immediately." It really wouldn't do, after all, if Alondra pulled off a glove and any of them happened to notice that her iron wasn't "singing."

"How am I to give this order?" said Greyfall. "The spell allowing us to communicate has failed, leaving us blind and deaf to one another."

Since I couldn't tell him how much I sympathized, I said, "I apologize for that, but it was necessary. You'll just have to do it the old-fashioned way and find them yourself."

"So it *was* you."

"Of course it was me," I said. "Surely you know my reputation by now." I drummed my ungloved fingers on the stone in a way I hoped looked nonchalant, and I was rewarded by a visible cringe. "I destroyed the Bone Harp," I said. "I destroyed the security systems in London, and I just destroyed the one here, too. Do you really want to find out what else I'm willing to destroy? Go deliver my first demand, and when you come back, we can move on to the second."

Greyfall gave me an icy stare, then began to back slowly away. "I will return swiftly," he said, and then launched himself into the air.

"Okay, Shock," I murmured low, like a prayer. "Now's your cue."

The snowy woods remained cold and silent. My hand was going numb, so I tucked it between my thighs. I cursed myself for not bringing a coat like Caryl, but I had never intended to be standing outside in the snow this long.

"Shock?" I said louder. "If you were hiding from that guard, now's the time to show yourself."

Silence. I was revisited by the almost irresistible urge to leave my post, to go looking for him. But of course the second I did that, he'd manage to make it to the stone.

I closed my eyes, wrapped my arms around myself, and invented a long list of demands I hoped I would not have to use. The quiet chill of the woods began to seep into my bones. I sympathized with wild fey's lack of memory; I was starting to forget what warmth and safety felt like.

When I heard wings beating the air, I looked up, heart accelerating, but it was only Greyfall.

"All guards have withdrawn from the eastern stone," he said briskly as he landed, "and the remainder have been notified not to proceed there. What is your next demand?"

I'd had time, while he was gone, to think of something actually useful. Just as I'd coerced a promise out of Greyfall, I would coerce Dawnrowan to let me escape, or even coerce her into an alliance. In theory there was little she *wouldn't* promise to keep the White Rose safe. But only if I could get her close enough to have a conversation.

"I need you to convince the queen to come here and speak with me," I said. "Let her know that at this point ignoring my demands endangers the palace far more than leaving it for a few moments."

Greyfall let out a frustrated sigh. "How do I even know, if I meet all of your demands, that you will keep your part of the bargain? You are not the first human I have met."

It occurred to me to wonder, since this wasn't his first expression of mistrust in humans, just exactly how much of an asshole his Echo was.

"Look," I said. "Do you think I *want* to destroy the White Rose? If that were Plan A, it would be done already. How could it possibly benefit me? My Echo is entitled to a throne there! I resorted to trying to steal Her Majesty's scepter, to threatening the palace, because it's the only way to scare her enough to *listen* to me. I won't do this unless she gives me no other choice."

Greyfall seemed to measure me with his eyes, as though he had some sort of arcane lie detector installed. "Very well," he said finally. "I will continue to meet any reasonable demands, but I expect you to keep your word and retreat from the stone once I have delivered everything you ask. If not, remember that the penalty for harming the queen or her property is death."

As the blood drained from my extremities, I suddenly

became even more aware of the numbing cold in my fingers where they touched the stone. Where the hell was Shock?

"And if I do manage to get out of this without destroying the palace?" I said. "What happens to me then?"

"It depends upon the mercy of Her Majesty," said the guard. "There will still be a trial, during which we will attempt to ascertain your reasons for—"

The distant sound of screams distracted him. Me too, to be honest.

It's adrenaline, they say, that dilates a moment, lets you watch in slow motion as a car swerves suddenly toward your bike. The instinct is probably meant to make you react faster, give you time to avert your doom. But the problem is that your body is still subject to the laws of time, and sometimes there is nothing you can do but watch.

I can only guess that the *sidhe* inside the palace must have felt the lofting enchantments drop, sensed it in a way I couldn't. That extra sense probably saved their lives.

Before I even wrapped my brain around what was happening, what shouldn't and couldn't be happening, there were already *sidhe* streaming from the windows and doors of the palace, a mass exodus silhouetted like a flock of crows against the green sky.

"What . . . ," I murmured. "Why are they—"

Greyfall launched himself into the air, forgetting me completely.

Then I saw it. First the great blossom began to list atop its stem as though wilting. All of the *sidhe* had wings and were making their escape.

But Claybriar was still in there.

That's when the time dilation kicked in. An eternity passed in my mind, but it couldn't have been more than ten seconds, the whole thing.

I began to stumble toward the clearing, as though there were anything I could do to stop it, but my limbs were trapped in slow motion along with my perception as the whole magnificent column began to tilt eastward and away.

How? Why?

I glanced back at the standing stone. The runes, the delicate designs, had turned as black as dried blood.

I forced myself to charge forward through the snow, too late, too late. Each step took a day, a week. I fought the constraints of time as though it were icy water.

Seven steps, I think, maybe six, before the tower reached about a thirty-degree angle and began to fall in earnest. So fast. Even adrenaline couldn't make it seem anything but instant.

The sound was unimaginable: the rushing of air against that mass of stone, the cracking and rumbling as it came apart. When it hit the ground, the noise was like the end of the world as vast petals were pulverized, trees were shattered, and everyone in a mile radius was flung like rice on a hot pan.

I lost all control over my body as the tremor hit; I fell facefirst into the snow, eastward like the tower itself. The seal on my right shin loosened slightly as I fell, but there was no way to adjust it; I just had to find my way upright again amid pain and the sound of screaming. I stumbled through the snow toward the portal with my skin chafing at every step.

Caryl was there at the Skyhollow portal in her long brown coat, her face nearly the same green as the sky.

"How is this happening?" I screamed at her.

"I don't know!" she said. "I don't know!" She put both hands to her head, clutching at her hair. I went to her, embraced her. She was trembling.

A *sidhe* courtier staggered by, vacant eyed, golden blood dripping from one wing and hissing in the snow. She was close enough to have thrown a rock at us, but neither she nor anyone else was paying any attention to me at all.

Caryl pulled back to look up at me with wide, frightened eyes. "Do you—do you have the—" She couldn't seem to find the word.

"I don't," I said. Mesmerized, I stared at the wounded courtier as she staggered away across the clearing.

I was the author of all this destruction, and no one was even looking at me. I moved my gaze to the vast, rubble-strewn emptiness where once the White Rose had stood. With a shudder, I forced myself to look back at Caryl, tried to think past the sound of screams and sobs.

"Where is Claybriar?" I said, feeling my throat close around his name. It felt colder out here now than when we'd arrived. "Have you seen him?"

"I haven't," she said. She was stroking my arm now, her eyes fixed on my face with concern. "Nor Alondra, nor Shock. I've been here waiting for you since the guards broke off their pursuit of me."

"Alondra," I said. "The tower fell eastward." My teeth started chattering. Everyone was dead. I'd killed everyone.

"I'll stay and look for them both," said Caryl, taking hold of my arms.

"No," I said. "I have to find Claybriar."

"You have to get *out* of here!" Caryl said, giving me a little shake. "Once they stop panicking, you're the one they'll be looking for!"

"You're not safe here either," I said.

"You always underestimate me. I will find Claybriar. I will find Alondra. I will find Shock, and send him to Skyhollow after you with the vials. But you must go now. If they find you, there will be nothing left that any of us can do to help you."

"But Claybriar couldn't have—"

She threw her arms around me fiercely. "I will find him. Be safe. This is not our last meeting."

At that, she took off across the snow, the swirl of her coat in the icy wind making me think of Winterglass. I watched her for a moment, then turned my gaze back to the rubble, searching for some sign of my Echo. Surely he'd have been smart enough to grab one of those horses, that damned gryphon, *something* with wings. If he were dead, I'd feel it, wouldn't I?

I couldn't think about it. Not unless I wanted to run straight into the rubble, straight into the guards.

I turned to the mural of Skyhollow. Tried to imagine myself there, somewhere warm. But I didn't want to be there, and the magic knew it.

Maybe he's already there, I told myself. *Maybe before the palace even fell, he fled the queen's bedchamber. Maybe he ran to the arms of his less complicated lover, and I'll find him there, warm and safe in the orange haze.*

It was that thought that carried me through.

37

The oasis of Skyhollow Estate was warm and beautiful and oblivious. The change in temperature and ambiance was so extreme that it set me to shuddering all over. I hugged myself, standing for a moment as I fought a wave of nausea and dizziness.

There were some little fey gamboling about on the forest floor; they seemed to recognize me, or at least find me pleasing in some way. A pair of them, one greenish and one brownish, came chittering up to me and reached for my gloved hands. I let them lead me, one skipping along on either side of me, to a little bench that was half-hidden by a partial tunnel of branches and climbing vines. Since it had a good view of the portal, I took a seat.

Beneath the tangled foliage the air was dim and green, and I found myself slowly hypnotized by the faint rustle of plant life and the weird distant calls of fey birds. I slipped off my backpack and set it on the ground near my feet, rolling my shoulders in relief. The snow, the screams, the bleeding wing—it was all just a bad dream.

Everything in Arcadia *was* a kind of dream, wasn't it? I pondered this as I stood up and unhooked my shirt from my trousers, pulled them down, and scrunched them at the ankles of my boots so I could remove my already wobbly BK prosthesis. I remembered how shy I'd felt about undressing in Arcadia and absently wondered why. I grabbed the bottle of Dry-Lite from my bag and slathered some on my shin so I could redo the seal. Nothing here was real in the way that my world was; it was all just a projection of group consciousness, right?

Then why was that fey bleeding? Why had everyone agreed to accept that my screwup had destroyed the Seelie palace? If they all wished hard enough, could they bring it back?

Deep in my heart, I knew that wasn't how it worked. But as I finished readjusting my shin socket, keeping an eye on the portal, I let my mind rest in a pleasant daydream.

"Put your damned pants on!" said a deep rumbling voice behind me.

"Jesus Christ!" I said, startling so violently I hit my head on a branch.

"Ugh," said Brand. "Bad enough the fey around here just fuck each other left and right all over the forest, I have to look at *your* ugly wreck of a body now?"

I turned to look at the tea-table-size face of a grinning manticore. "You don't *have* to look," I said. "You're just a pervert."

"Seriously, what's the deal?" he said. "Why are you dropping trou right now of all moments? Shouldn't we be hightailing it out of here at hurricane speed with Dangerous Contraband? Isn't that my part in this shenanigan?"

"There were some complications," I said, carefully replacing my trousers and hooking them to my shirt again. "Best not to go into it."

"Got the loot, at least?"

"No, that's part of the complication. I have to wait here for Shock to deliver it."

"You trust that little runt?"

"That little runt got your body back," I said defensively, hefting my backpack again. "Worst-case scenario he takes them to his dad instead, and either way Belinda is screwed." I blinked as I realized something else. "I mean, really screwed. Every vial he didn't manage to take just got pulverized. Oh, shit, I *really* hope he got the right ones."

"When you say there were complications," Brand said dryly, "it sounds like you mean everything fell completely to shit."

"Can we not talk about that?"

"Well, what am I supposed to do? I thought I was going to be in and out of here before Skyhollow spotted me. He's still not a fan."

"Yeah, you should probably start thinking about patching up that relationship, given that you kind of live in his territory and swore fealty to his king."

Brand let out a frustrated growl, his wings rustling slightly.

"Uh, Brand?"

"What."

"There at the edge of your wings, is that—?"

"Shut up."

"Are you growing *feathers*?"

"Shut the fuck up . . . pig face."

"Pig face? Oh, Brand."

"Millie!" From the other direction, a high clear cry that brought me to my feet. Alondra was running toward me from the portal. The real Alondra, to judge by the length of her hair, which had come loose from its careful twist.

I rose from the bench, moved as quickly as I could to meet her. She threw her arms around me, almost knocking me over, which would have really pissed me off as I'd just gotten my leg straightened out. Couldn't deny I was kind of glad to see her, though. I patted her awkwardly on the shoulder.

"I thought maybe you'd been squished," I said.

She just sobbed for a minute, and I dutifully stroked her hair, which smelled a little like green apples.

"I was already running," she said hoarsely, "before it started to fall."

"Did you happen to see Claybriar?"

"Yes!" she said, pulling back to gaze up at me, her wet long-lashed eyes full of something like awe.

"What happened?"

"Dawnrowan saved him!" she said. "I saw them falling! She wasn't strong enough to fly holding him, but her arms were around him and her wings were just—" She demonstrated, flapping her arms wildly. "They fell, really slow, and I ran, think-ing, I don't know, that I'd catch them? But she hit the ground before I got there, turned so he landed on her. She broke her leg! I didn't even know she had bones! Claybriar fixed it."

"Jesus. What about him, is he all right?"

"Not a scratch, from what I could tell! But I was afraid the guards would spot me, so I just . . . I ran!"

"Caryl? Shock? Where are they?"

"I'm not sure."

"How did this even happen? I don't understand."

Alondra sobered immediately. She stepped away, her eyes dark and full of fear. "Tjuan showed up," she said.

"What the hell?"

"No, not Tjuan. I'm sorry. The facade. It pushed me down and out of the way and then touched the stone."

"Oh my God . . . Elliott? *Why?*"

"I don't know that it was Elliott! He didn't say anything!"

I rocked back and forth, hugging myself. "Could it have been Qualm? But no, he's locked in the book. And nobody else had a link to that body."

"Why would Elliott do that, though?" Alondra said.

"Well, he—he was angry," I said. "But I didn't think he'd gone full-on fucking *dark side*. We'll sort it out later. Let's just get you out of here safely."

Alondra wrung her hands. "Are you sure? I can wait here with you. . . ."

"No. You go with Brand back to—"

But as I turned, I saw that Brand was gone.

"Welp, there goes my ride. What the hell?"

Brand must have seen what I only noticed a moment later, Duke Skyhollow approaching with several members of his retinue.

I shared a panicked look with Alondra, but when I looked back at Skyhollow, he had spotted us and was clearly *delighted*. Right, they didn't have CNN in Arcadia. Nimbly the duke picked his way through the foliage with occasional assistance from his servants, and once he stood before us, he gave me a sweeping bow.

"Rewelcome," he said. "Is the Claybriar-king accompany?"

I looked at Alondra again.

"You'd better tell him," she said. "It's not like he won't find out anyway, and you may as well get some honesty points."

I felt my weird breakfast bread threatening to make a

reappearance, but I steeled myself and turned to face the duke.

"Something terrible has happened," I said. "The White Rose has fallen."

"Fallen?" Skyhollow echoed, uncomprehending.

"The queen was injured, but she's fine now. Claybriar is fine. The Seelie Court seems to have mostly come out all right. But the building itself is . . . it's gone. A rogue Unseelie spirit destroyed it."

"Destroyed?" Skyhollow echoed. He still seemed to have no idea what I was talking about.

I looked at Alondra. She just shrugged at me as if to say, *I don't know this guy from Adam.* I looked back to Skyhollow.

"I can . . . show you?" I said. I tapped my skull with one forefinger. "If you want to . . . look in my head."

"Aye!" said Skyhollow. "I look. No use, your wordings."

I closed my eyes, forced myself to see it again, tried to seal off the horror I'd felt, the guilt, everything but the visual. The listing of the blossom, then the great stem tilting, tilting, and then crashing to the earth.

When I heard Duke Skyhollow suck in his breath, I opened my eyes. He looked faint.

"Someone help him," I said to his retinue. I don't know if anyone understood me, but someone did move in time to catch him as his knees buckled.

He was deadweight, though; there was nothing to do but lower him to the forest floor. I had my gloves on, so I knelt beside him and took his hand.

"Alondra," I said quietly. "Take the road back to the Gate. Get yourself safe. I'll stay with the duke while I wait for Shock."

Alondra nodded, looking teary again, and I watched for a

moment as her rounded form slipped away through the under-growth, eventually disappearing into the tangled green.

Then I looked down at Duke Skyhollow. He stared up at the forest canopy, his green mask-marking standing out sharply against his sudden pallor. Tears like mercury pooled in his alien eyes, and he returned the pressure of my hand only weakly.

"I'm so sorry," I said. "I'm so sorry this happened."

He grew paler and paler; his breathing became shallow; his gaze was unfocused. He really did not look well. I looked up at his courtiers, hoping one of them could tell me what to do, but they were slowly backing away from him with expressions of horror, as though he were a stranger bleeding out on the forest floor.

Was he bleeding? I checked him over briefly but could see no wound to explain why he was looking more and more like a corpse every moment.

Then I remembered what Claybriar and Shock had said, about fey "choosing their endings." Could they do that? Just *decide* to die? Check out of existence the way you would a motel? If so, that looked a hell of a lot like what was happening here.

"Your Grace!" I said sharply, seizing his jaw in one hand to turn his face toward me. His gaze still didn't focus. "Snap out of it! The king and the queen are both still alive! What would they think of you, if you just lie down and die right now? Who would even rule Skyhollow after you? This is a *terrible* ending!"

His eyes focused on my face now, at least, but even at his best, the duke had never been all that great at understanding me. This was definitely not his best. I couldn't tell if any of my words were actually getting through; he continued to lie there, pale and limp. I leaned over him, gave him a little shake.

"Please," I said. "I can't carry the weight of this, too. *Please.*" Tears of frustration stung my eyes; one slipped free down my cheek.

His eyes found focus, tracked the tear's path. Slowly he lifted an arm, reached his hand toward me, caught the tear; it slipped over the backs of his fingers. His curiosity was as tyrannical as a child's; he brought his hand to his lips for a taste.

The expression on his face sent one of the little commoners nearby into a fit of chittering giggles.

"Bitter, right?" I said. "And salty. I could have told you that."

Strangely, his color looked better, as though his curiosity had reminded him that he was alive, but he still made no move to get up. It gave me an idea, though. I pulled off my backpack, rooted through it until I found the little travel sewing kit at the bottom. I used one of the needles to prick my middle finger, pried his mouth open as though I were giving medicine to a baby, and gave my finger a squeeze directly into it.

"Sorry," I said. "I know it's gross, but I need you to understand me."

He shuddered and made an even worse version of the previous face. Then he drew in an audible breath, and his eyes widened.

"Ah!" he said, a sort of pained rapture coming over his face. "All my long memory, laid out before me, all the words of your tongue remembered, and the way of laying them in a line. I could tell the tale of my life from beginning to end."

"As much as I'd love that," I said, "it's more important to me that you *get up* and stop acting like you're about to die."

He turned his head and met my eyes, more grave than I'd ever seen him. "We are all dead," he said. "The *sidhe* are finished."

38

I knelt on the forest floor there in the oasis of Skyhollow, next to the supine body of its lord, and felt my heart crack like glacial ice.

"What do you mean?" I said. "What do you mean the *sidhe* are finished? Are they all just going to . . . lie down and die? Because of a *building*?"

"Some may," said the duke. He rolled to one side, weakly propped himself on an elbow, and looked at me with an intensity that I found reassuring after his blank stare of before. "But most will not. Most will continue living, and their sorrow will fade. The memory of fey is short. But each time they return to where the White Rose once stood, and find only its ruin, they will become more certain that this is the way it has always been."

"They'll forget," I said. "Even something like that, they can just . . . forget?" I felt so cold that I was surprised my breath didn't form a cloud in the air.

"The price of immortality," he said. "Some few fey, those with Echoes, will remember. But most, in the time it takes for the moon to make a full cycle, will consider that site a mysterious ruin, a ruin whose very physical presence diminishes from month to month, year to year, as its significance fades in the collective consciousness and reality shapes itself to match."

"So the *sidhe* . . ."

"Will no longer be the fey who built and reigned from the White Rose. Our history, our identity, existed only so long as it was shaped in that stone."

I couldn't wrap my head around it. Why would Elliott do this? No matter how angry he was, why would he try to erase a people's collective identity so thoroughly? That level of vengeance was more along the lines of—

Goddamn it.

"Shiverlash," I said aloud.

"I beg your pardon?" said the duke.

"Nothing," I said. "Look, you need to get up. We won't let the memory of the White Rose die, I promise. You have my *promise*. I was there, and I'll remember, for one."

He was looking much more himself now, so I pushed myself to my feet, then reached to help him. Several of his retinue rushed forward to lend their hands as well.

"What good is the memory of a human?" he said as he carefully regained his feet. "It is longer than ours, yes, but it dies with you."

"*Sidhe* can pass images and memories to each other," I said. "There were guards there who knew every tile of that place, who had Echoes. If all of you work together, pass those memories from person to person, you can remember it forever. And you should," I said with a sudden vehemence. "You should remember *all* of it. Not just the way the *sidhe* remember it, but my memory of it too, and Caveat's, and Elliott's. The dead spirits in the bones of it. The rage that led someone to destroy it.

Because if you don't remember *all* of it, you'll just build it the same way, and doom it all over again."

The duke's hand was still wrapped around my forearm, but his eyes sparked anger at this. "You would blame *us* for this atrocity?"

"Oh, I blame the one who did it. Believe me. There are going to be . . . *conversations*. But if you don't acknowledge why someone *thought* it was okay, you'll never fix the problem. And Arcadia has problems, Your Grace. *Serious* problems that are only just—"

"Millie!"

I heard the pounding of sneakers on the forest floor, saw Shock running toward us from the direction of the portal. He held the Medial Vessel in one hand as though he were trying to choke it to death.

"Oh thank God," I said, moving to meet him.

"The guards know I'm with you!" he said, panting, as he all but crashed into me. "Take this and get out of here, now!"

I snatched the bag from him, stuffing it down the side of my trousers, against my hip.

"What is happening?" said Duke Skyhollow, looking slightly affronted.

"I'm so sorry," I said. "I have to go."

"You are in danger?"

"I . . . took something from the palace. Good thing, too, or it would have been destroyed. Anyway, I need it to stop Dame Belinda, but there's no time to explain; I think the guards will be after me shortly. I'm sorry."

"Worry not," said Skyhollow. "You have given me a new purpose, renewed my life. For this, you have my protection. Return home safely, and I shall delay the guards when they arrive."

"I owe you one," I said. "Seriously. Take care of yourself, and think about what I said." I moved to give him a quick, probably painful kiss on the cheek, and then turned to Shock as the duke headed off toward the portal.

"Is Caryl all right?"

"A couple of guards caught her, took her to the prison. I was on my way to help when I ran into Father."

"Your *dad* is there?"

"I was surprised too! I could not just give him one vial, and I did not trust him with the rest—he was very angry. I ran. I hope I made the right call."

"And Caryl?"

"That is why my father was there! He knew, somehow, that she had been caught. He was going to save her."

I let out a long breath of relief. If Winterglass was good for one thing, it was saving Caryl.

"Get somewhere safe, kiddo," I said. "You've done your part. You're free."

Shock nodded and took off running.

"Fly, you fool!" I yelled after him in my best Ian McKellen, which wasn't very good. Not sure if he got the reference, but he did see my larger point. He shifted into his natural form, taking to the air.

I, however, did not have the luxury of wings. It was difficult to find my way back to the road, not only because the foliage made traveling in straight lines impossible, but because I kept getting distracted by extraordinary views and obscenely cavorting fey. Despite delays, I eventually found my way to a spot where I could see the road through the trees ahead.

That was when vines erupted from the ground and wrapped

themselves around my ankles, twined their way up my legs, engulfed my torso and arms. I couldn't move. I thrashed in place, but the vines held fast, thick as my wrist.

"What now?" I said aloud, addressing my remark to the forest canopy.

"Lies," said Duke Skyhollow's voice quietly behind me. "I always forget that humans cannot help but lie, even to their allies."

"What? What did I lie about?" I tried to twist around to see him, but the vines had snared me too tightly.

I heard his footsteps approaching. Not just his, either. When he finally came around to stand where I could see him, he was flanked by two of the palace guards: Greyfall and the steel-blue woman, Whisperdrift.

"According to Her Majesty's guards," said the duke, "you are the one who destroyed the tower."

"Not true!" I said.

"You would accuse the *sidhe* of untruth?" Skyhollow scoffed.

"They're not lying," I said. "They're just mistaken. They can say it if they *believe* it to be true."

The guards fixed me with the same cold stare as Skyhollow. I knew they could both understand me; that must have been why these two, in particular, had come.

I struggled against my restraints. "Look, I didn't mean to destroy the palace," I said.

"But you did destroy it," said Skyhollow. He looked heartbroken. "All those pretty words about preserving its memory, from the one who made the effort necessary."

"It took two people," I said. "I thought I was alone. I thought there was no *way* the other stone would really be endangered."

"You told me you would do it," said Greyfall, "if I did not meet your demands."

"I was bluffing!" I said. "I never really meant to do it; in fact, I took great pains to make sure I *wouldn't*!"

Greyfall shrugged. "Either you were lying then, or you are lying now, and I tire of trying to sort through human deception. You will come with us and stand trial."

I thought of the Vessel, tucked against my hip, so *close* to the road, so *close* to the Gate. If the guards took it from me, they'd return it to its "rightful" owner. Dame Belinda would have my blood right there in her hands, after being told that I had destroyed the center of the Arcadia Project's power. I did not want to find out what she'd use blood magic to do once she decided to stop pulling her punches.

"Skyhollow," said Whisperdrift, in a gentler tone than Greyfall had used. "Please release the baroness into our—"

Before she could finish, a bone-rattling roar slashed through the hazy air, shredding the *sidhe's* calm. Batlike wings spread, Brand dropped out of the sky like the judgment of God. He shot a venomous tail spine right into Greyfall's eye before knocking Skyhollow to the ground.

Whisperdrift rushed to Greyfall's aid, yanking the gold-slicked spine from the eye socket of the screaming fey and dropping it to the ground. She murmured a quick spell, and Greyfall's eye looked as though it had never been pierced.

"Catch that beast!" cried Skyhollow from the ground. Brand responded by seizing Skyhollow with all four paws and beating his wings frantically, lifting the man from the ground and carrying him away. Low and slow they flew, smashing and tearing their way through the tangled growth.

Of course the two guards pursued. I had suddenly slipped way down the priority list, being immobilized and all. But I wasn't going to waste the opportunity. Carefully I curled down the fingers of one hand, inched the latex of my surgical glove up over my palm. Slowly, twisting and tugging and pinching, I scooted the glove up and over the fattest part of my hand, then used my thumb to push it the rest of the way off until it dropped to the ground.

I circled my wrist, nearly dislocated the damn thing trying to stretch my bare fingers down to touch the nearest edge of the vine that held me. Urgency lent me mobility, and when the edge of my littlest finger barely brushed the vine that was cuffing me, the whole structure fell apart, dumping me onto the forest floor. I grabbed my glove and slipped it back on, then levered myself to my feet and started stumbling toward the road.

I nearly ran into Brand as he came plummeting back down through the branches and landed heavily in my path.

"Get on," he said.

"Where are the guards?"

"Helping Skyhollow," he said. "I might have shredded his wings and dropped him into a sinkhole."

Brand crouched, and I heaved myself onto his back. "This is not going to increase your stock with the Seelie Court, you know," I said. "Also, Skyhollow isn't a bad guy. I do not approve of—GAH!"

Brand, ignoring me as usual, started running through the trees before I had even fully settled myself on his back. Conversation was impossible as I attempted to right myself, and then away we went.

39

The road that led from Skyhollow Estate was made for creatures that walked on two legs; the ward simply didn't acknowledge Brand's presence, making it pointless for him to use it. Instead, he cut through the rocky, semiarid wilderness to the right side of the road, where his physics-bending strides would put him at an advantage over two-legged pursuers.

"We should have practiced this," I grunted as we raced along, fast enough to make me squint against the warm dry wind. It was hard to stay seated properly without the full length of my leg muscles to squeeze against his back; mostly I just gripped his mane tight and held on for dear life.

Unfortunately, Brand had chosen the side of the road with most of the rock formations, and after a few minutes' exultant gallop we found ourselves navigating a sort of maze. This side of the landscape had been on my left as I'd made my way to the estate before the heist, and I was almost positive it hadn't been quite such a labyrinth at the time.

"Damn it," said Brand just as I was about to ask him if he'd noticed the same thing. "He's fucking with the landscape."

"What do you mean? Who is? What's happening?"

"Duke Skyhollow has a certain amount of influence over his land. He doesn't want us to escape, and so the land is responding to that."

Brand darted back and forth, trying desperately to find a view between the multiplying rock formations. It was like a dream; they never changed while we were watching, but then we'd turn to find more behind us than had been there before.

"At this rate we'll never find our way back to L.A.," I said, readjusting my grip on his mane in an effort to keep my seat through his wild changes of direction. "We're fucked."

He paused for a moment, giving me some relief. "Maybe if we cross to the other side of the road I can help us out a little," Brand said, "but it's not going to be pretty."

"What do you mean?"

"We'll have to plan our escape route so that it passes by that abyss. Spirits won't go near it; the closer we are to it the less likely that weird magic will spring up to stop us."

"Is the abyss dangerous?"

"Not unless we jump in, but it's fucking creepy."

It was also on the other side of the road, which meant we had to find our way back across. We could no longer see the road over the maze of rocks, but Brand was able to estimate the direction we were moving by keeping his eyes on the slant of the shadows.

"So long as we keep heading this way," he said, "we'll eventually get back to the road. We were mostly traveling parallel to it, so it shouldn't take long."

Of course, the nature of a maze is that it makes it impossible to keep going in one direction, and without a bird's-eye view, you can't tell which turning is going to eventually point you the way you want.

"Why are we even bothering with this?" I said in sudden frustration. "Can't you *fly*?"

"That's bad for two reasons," said Brand. "One, you'd fall right the fuck off if I did that. Two, as much of a pain in the ass as these rocks are, they're also hiding us from the royal guards, who are still after us—don't doubt it for a second. Skyhollow's people too now, I'll bet. The minute I launch myself into the air, they'll make a beeline for us. They've got wings too; my only advantage is on the ground."

"Not much advantage at the moment," I said.

"Just be patient," said Brand. "I've had contact with my Echo recently, so my mind is razor sharp. I'm tracking our position even as the rocks lead us off course. Pretty sure I know exactly where we are. Just have to find an opening."

Putting my trust in a manticore was not a thing I'd ever anticipated needing to do, but there we were. As Brand paused again to consider his options at yet another blocked pathway, I leaned forward to give him a scratch behind the ear with my gloved hand.

"What have I said about petting me?"

"You're Seelie now. You need to get used to cuddles."

"I will fucking throw you off and eat you."

He broke into a sudden lope, nearly unseating me. I held on tight as he made an unnecessarily complicated figure-eight pattern around a line of rock columns.

"You can stop punishing me any time now," I said.

"I'm not sure I can. And hey, look there."

Sure enough, the shimmering heat mirage of the road's enchantment loomed before us, closer all that time than I'd dared to hope. Brand galloped across it to the other side, which was less littered with rocks but had a profusion of scrubby plant life and a few scattered, twisted trees.

"Do you know where the abyss is located?" I asked him. "I can't remember exactly where it was along the path."

"I can feel it," he said. "It's like reality has a bad headache. I just follow the throb."

"Super sorry about that, by the way. Claybriar was only at that train station to get pummeled because of me." Then I stopped, reconsidered. "But you were helping Vivian at the time, so fuck you, apology retracted."

When Brand loped through the undergrowth, it writhed as though it were trying to catch at his limbs. He hissed in pain.

"Fucking Skyhollow!" he growled, trying to weave around the thickest plant growth and find bare patches of spongy Arcadian sand. Its golden expanse shimmered in the late-afternoon light.

I could measure our progress toward the abyss by the way the plants began to thin out and the sand to lose its luster. At last I spotted darkness on the horizon.

"I think that's close enough," said Brand. "Do you see anyone pursuing us?"

I glanced over my shoulder, which almost made me slip sideways, but I steadied myself as I turned forward again, feeling a surge of hope. "I think we lost them," I said.

"Not slowing down," said Brand, "just in case."

"Do you know how to find the Gate from here?"

"I think so," he said. "But I'll admit I wasn't really paying close attention the last couple of times I got dragged through it."

"When we get there," I said, "just drop me off. I need you to stay on this side, help Caryl and the others if they need it."

Brand was still moving fast enough that the abyss quickly shifted its way along the horizon and out of our sight. I was happy to have it behind us.

More rocks appeared as we began to get close to the Gate; I knew the Gate was located atop a large formation that I'd easily be able to recognize. It had been invisible to me before I'd signed the Project contract, but thanks to Caryl's little lecture about anti-civilian wards, now I understood why it wasn't anymore. Ah, Caryl. I hoped Winterglass was keeping her safe.

As we rounded a jagged wall of vermilion rock, Shiverlash appeared in our path so abruptly that Brand's paws threw up a spray of sand and I slid halfway off his back. He had to crouch so that I could ease myself gently the rest of the way onto the ground.

Leaning against Brand's side, I stared at the Beast Queen of the Unseelie Court in the full glory of her eyeless natural form.

"What fresh, roaring trash fire is this?" I said.

The queen's greasy black wings were folded, her talons braced in the sand as she turned her melted-wax face toward us. Despite her wings, there was no mistaking her for *sidhe*; she was half again as tall, and her proportions were all wrong, more avian than human. It occurred to me suddenly that Foxfeather's doomed coyote friend had also lacked eyes. Something tried to knit itself together in my memory about that, but my brain refused to cooperate.

Shiverlash opened her jawless mouth, a vertical oval, and a stream of guttural Unseelie words poured out.

"Nice try," said Brand. "I'm not your pet anymore. I've sworn fealty to the Seelie King." For the first time, he seemed pretty smug about that.

Shiverlash hesitated, clearly not understanding his words, but having no trouble noticing that her command had not compelled him. After a moment's pause, Caveat appeared on her shoulder, projecting a weary not-again vibe that was straight out of Tjuan's playbook.

"Caveat? Where the hell did you come from?" I asked her. "Weren't you with Caryl?"

"The queen summoned me," she said. "To translate. Again."

"But *how* did she summon you? Did you tell her your name?"

"She can *see* it," said Caveat. "Anytime I come to her. And I've come to her a lot."

Spirit-sight. That's what I'd been trying to remember about that coyote. Reading the names of any spirit that came to him.

"Shit, Caveat," I said. "This is not good."

"It doesn't bother me," said Caveat. "To you she's a monster; to me she's just the queen. She has the right to give me orders, and she's never asked me to do anything I objected to. Can we get back to the topic at hand?"

"Yes, of course, sorry."

A voice emerged from the queen's direction, though her mouth didn't move. Her face was turned toward Brand. "Why do you resist?" she said.

Brand snorted. "It's not rocket science, Birdbrain. Did you think, after what you did to my Echo, and what you made me do to my allies, that I wouldn't jump at the first chance to defect to the sparkly side?"

For a moment Shiverlash stood in silence, seemingly unable to process the enormity of the betrayal.

"Caveat," I said quietly. "Did Shiverlash order Elliott to destroy the White Rose? Do you know?"

"Are you serious?" said Caveat blandly. After a moment's delay, she remembered to project her astonishment. "Did you think even for a *minute* that he did it on his own? Just because he won't take abuse indefinitely, you assume he's evil?"

"Whoa, whoa . . ."

"The queen didn't know his name. So she had to wait until he—"

Caveat froze like a bad Skype connection as her queen's command overrode her communication. The disembodied voice of Shiverlash spoke again, instead.

"Your 'Elliott' is my subject," she said, "just as this one is. But his name was not imprinted into my memory. I could not call him until he released himself from bondage, and then he was drawn, as all spirits are, to my song."

"With all due respect, Your Majesty," I said, "what the fuck? Don't you have enough hell to raise in your own lands?"

"I do not have access to the 'portals' that King Winterglass uses, and so for the time being I am stranded here while I devise another means of return. Meanwhile, you provided an opportunity that I could not, in good conscience, let slip away."

"Did you seriously just use the word 'conscience' to describe that decision?"

"Even by Seelie standards," said Shiverlash, "that was among the most nonviolent actions I might have taken. We are at war. But I should not be surprised by your lack of appreciation for my restraint. From our very first encounter, you have treated me and my cause with profound disrespect. But as a creature of honor I could not help but attempt to find common ground with the one who freed me from my own enslavement."

Of course. Of course she'd want to see that place crumble

to the ground, and not just because it would devastate the *sidhe*. When Shiverlash had been trapped in the form of a harp, the White Rose had been the site of her imprisonment—and regular use—for hundreds, maybe thousands of years. That situation had been due to her own ridiculous act of spite, but still. I was disappointed in myself for not having spotted her hand in this immediately.

"What did you do to Elliott? Is he all right?"

"Why should I wish to harm my subject?" said Shiverlash. "Once he had executed my command, he chose to abandon the body and destroy his link to it. His actions not only prevented my repeating the command, but showed me the extent of his objection. I released him from my service and will not call him again. My intent was not to harm him."

"Cry me a river."

"I do not understand why you act as though we are adversaries," said Shiverlash. "We both wish freedom for every being in Arcadia."

"Yeah, yeah, and we're both great at destroying shit, but that doesn't make us alike. I'm just a clumsy idiot; you do it on purpose. I refuse to set one Arcadian race free by destroying another, and that's what you want. Don't lie to me—oh that's right, you can't."

"There comes a time when a people are too corrupt to be saved," she said. "Do you not, even in your own world, kill those who kill? Take the lives of those who are too dangerous to live?"

"Honey, the vast majority of the people you want to exterminate are about as dangerous as inbred kittens. Most of them don't even realize spirits are people. It isn't their fault they've been lied to for longer than they have memory."

"You delude yourself," said Shiverlash, "but I am not here to debate a child who has lived barely the length of a lightning-strike. I still have need of you, now that there is no honorable way to access another creature of iron."

I let out an exasperated sigh. "You don't just get to 'access' me," I said, "but, unfortunately, I also still have need of you if there's going to be any hope of a united High Court against Dame Belinda. There has to be some way we can find a compromise."

"There will be no united Unseelie High Court while Winterglass lives."

"I beg to differ," I said, holding up the bag. "I got what he asked for. But you're going to have to let me go so I can deliver it to him. Once that's done, he's on my side. Bound to my side, in fact. So he has to listen if I start talking about freeing the spirits."

"Forget about Winterglass," she said. "He is easily destroyed."

"Well, he just saved my best friend, and also I happen to need him. For something you'd never help me with." Namely, sending a spirit to prison in Tjuan's place.

"Ask, and we shall see."

"If I even tell you what it is, you'll rip me to pieces. Not risking it."

"It disappoints me," said Shiverlash, "that you still fail to see the inevitable. Two worlds are arrayed against us, and we have only each other to rely upon."

"If we're really such great pals," I said, "then let me go. Let me get what I need from Winterglass, and then I'll come back and help you build a better Arcadia. I know my promises are worthless to you, but I'll give one anyway."

Shiverlash was silent for a long moment. Then she simply

spread her wings—God, they seemed to swallow the whole sky—and launched herself into the air, leaving Caveat behind. The little construct still hovered in the air in the same spot, at the queen's shoulder height.

"Hey," I said to her gently. "Do you think you'll be able to keep an eye on the queen? Will you be able to get free to report to me if she tries any more fuckery?"

"I'll do my best," she said, and then she vanished.

Brand crouched down. I pulled myself up by his mane, resettled myself on his back. "Let's go," I said. "We have to be close by now."

Sure enough, he'd not loped another five minutes before I saw the tall rock formation with the winding path up the side. I could even dimly spot the black semicircle of the Gate at the top of it.

"There," I said.

"Right!" said Brand. "That's the fake drop-off that hides your Gate, right? I hate that ward."

A vast wave of relief swept my worries away; even if Brand were to disintegrate underneath me, I'd still be able to hobble the rest of the way on my own.

Brand loped toward the Gate, but as we approached, five White Rose guards and a half dozen of Skyhollow's retinue emerged from where they'd been crouched behind scrub, waiting for us.

"Not good," said Brand.

"They knew where we were headed," I said. "They didn't even bother following; just took the road. Slowed us down so they'd have time to cut us off."

"I can take them," said Brand.

"All of them? At once?"

"Enough that you can get away. It's just a few steps past them."

The guards began to advance toward us. Some had staves, but no bows, no sharp blades. They were still trying to take me alive.

"Wait," I said to Brand. "They aren't armed to kill; you are. I'm not turning this into a massacre when they're just doing their jobs."

"Fucking cream puff."

I tried to think, fast. We didn't have a lot in the way of nondeadly resources. "How close do you think they'd dare get to that abyss?" I said.

"Seelie are cowards. They'll scream and run like gazelles at the sight of it."

"And you? Are you afraid?"

"Terrified. Difference is, I'm still Unseelie enough at heart to enjoy it."

"All right then," I said. "It's time to play a little game of chicken."

40

Brand began to back up, his eyes on the wall of *sidhe* guards advancing on us.

"Explain," he said to me.

"First we need to bait them. Can't let them know we're leading them somewhere; it needs to look like we're panicking."

"That doesn't seem too hard."

"Also you need a plausible reason to run slow enough that they think they can catch us. Can you fake an injury?"

"I can do better than that!"

And without warning, the stupid manticore charged directly at the guards.

They had all moved close together, instinctively trying to shield one another, so Brand just plowed through them like bowling pins. There weren't enough of them to stand up against an all-out cavalry charge, but their mental unity worked in their favor; one of the *sidhe* at the edge of their row managed to keep his feet. He quickly brought his staff into play, striking Brand in the rear leg as he charged by.

Brand let out a brassy roar of real pain, making me cry out as well, since I was too busy clinging to his mane to shield my ears against the noise. He wheeled around, knocked two guards to the side with one forepaw, while I hung on desperately, still screaming. For a moment Brand looked as though he were gearing up for a second charge; the guards arranged themselves as though to prepare for it. At the last minute, Brand bolted to one side instead, the change in momentum nearly unseating me.

He was hobbling three-legged now, one hind leg dragging in the sand, but even so, the guards were barely able to keep him in sight as he lurched away.

"Are you okay?" I said. "Did they hurt you for real?"

"That fucker cracked my fucking thigh bone," he moaned. "Charmed staff. The pain . . . bothers me more than I thought it would. I'm not used to even caring about it."

"Don't go all feathery on me now, Brand," I said. "I need you at maximum badass."

"If they catch us," said Brand miserably, "you know they'll have no problem killing me to get to you."

"Not going to let you die on my watch again," I said. "If only because Naderi would tie me to the back of a truck and drag me down the 10. If they catch us, you just dump me and fly away. It's me they want, so I doubt they'll chase you."

"You're sure they won't kill you?" he said. He was panting as he ran; he hadn't done that before. I felt a twinge of genuine concern.

"I haven't had a trial," I said. "Pissed off as they are, they're Seelie. They don't just murder people. Worst-case scenario, I'm decorating the duke's dining hall in a nice suit of vines, or back in that cage under what used to be the White Rose, until they decide what to do with me."

"Which, let's face it, will probably be to execute you."

"Are you caring about that now?" I said. "I can't keep track."

The *sidhe* guards fanned out in such a way that they actually helped us, herding us directly toward the abyss we were hoping to lead them to. They must have thought they were corralling us against an impassable obstacle, forcing us to surrender, which was fine by me.

As we got close enough to the abyss for even me to feel the bone-deep dissonance of its presence, Brand began to falter a little.

"How's the leg?" I asked him.

"Not the problem," he said. "This may not be such a good idea, Millie. They're still following. Just how close do you expect me to get to this thing? And what makes you think they won't be willing to get even closer?"

"Trust me," I said.

"I really hate it when you people say that. Especially you, with your track record of getting me killed and whatnot."

As we got closer to the void, further approach became almost unbearable. The nearer we got, the less there was to look at besides void, and the more my stomach churned and my ears rang. Brand slowed, hesitated, and finally stopped.

"I can't go any closer," he said. "If this isn't close enough, you're just going to have to carry on without me."

"All right, then," I said, and started to carefully slide off his back.

"You're insane," he said.

"Sweet-talker." I ignored the tremor in my voice and the faint taste of copper on my tongue, giving him a slap on the shoulder before I checked the Vessel's position against my hip and then started walking right up to the edge of that thing.

The guards made it as far as Brand's stopping place, at which point he promptly launched himself into the air. A couple of them went after him, but the rest must have seen it as the diversion it was, because they stayed, fanning out to block my escape routes.

I pulled out the Vessel from where my pants had been pressing it against my hip and held it up so they could all see. I searched and found Greyfall in the group, addressed him since I knew he could understand me.

"Do you recognize this?" I said.

All the guards' eyes went glassy and unfocused for a moment, in a way that suggested to me that they were communicating among themselves.

"That's the Medial Vessel," said Greyfall, hesitating for the first time. "For building Gates." His tone held a hint of reverence, and as I looked around at the faces of the other guards, I saw that they, too, knew exactly what I held.

"You know how this goes," I said. "You've been threatened by me very recently. So this is the part where I tell you that if you don't turn around and go straight back to Skyhollow, I am going to toss the Medial Vessel into the void."

"As you point out," said Greyfall, "I *have* been threatened by you very recently. And what I learned from that is that you'll probably destroy the Vessel anyway, even if I give you what you want."

"Please don't do this," said another voice. Whisperdrift, the steel-blue woman with the yellow wings. She advanced to stand at Greyfall's side. "Just come with us," she said. "I know that you're King Claybriar's Echo. He is a good man; try to be worthy of him. Do the right thing here. Face justice."

"I can't," I said. "This is about more than me at this point. Dame Belinda—our queen, you'd call her—she is *not* a good woman. She's a tyrant. If I let you take me, you'll take the Vessel back to her. And if she has it, very bad things are going to happen. Old bad things will continue happening, and she'll think up some new bad things to keep anyone from rebelling again. We're *this* close to completely remaking the Arcadia Project without her."

"It is not your place to depose your queen," said Greyfall in disgust. "This is exactly what happens when even one commoner gets lifted above his station. The next thing you know, you have collapsing palaces, war, mayhem."

"What else are the commoners supposed to do, exactly?" I said. "What other powers, besides mayhem, have you allowed them? The Project hardly ever lets them through the Gates to look for their Echoes."

"It's too dangerous," said Whisperdrift, looking fretful. "They won't follow the rules that keep everyone safe."

I recognized Belinda's rhetoric, as I'd heard it filtered through Alvin last fall. Even the *sidhe* themselves apparently embraced Belinda's line of bullshit as though it were religion. It all seemed so futile; she'd had decades to indoctrinate everyone. I felt anger eating away at my composure.

"That's all *lies*," I said. "A faun and a manticore did just fine, once they had Echoes to ground them. The *sidhe* get let through in droves just to *look* for their Echoes, so why do you act like it's some kind of natural superiority that allows you to—"

"Silence!" Greyfall began resolutely to approach. "Enough of this," he said.

I could tell by the wide darkness of his eyes, by the lashing of his tail, that he was as terrified of the void as I was. I was lucky enough to have my back to it, so I had to respect his bravery.

"Give me the Vessel," he said, "and your cooperation will be weighed in your favor at your trial. Do not make this more contentious than it needs to be."

"Wait!" I said, reaching behind me over the void and letting the Vessel dangle. That brought him up short. "Please just listen to me," I said. "I'll go face my trial. I will. But you have to let me take the Vessel somewhere safe first. Safe from Dame Belinda. I can't exactly explain why, but giving this to her will give her the power to harm a huge number of humans, most of them innocent. And it will make everything I've done all month, *everything that has been lost, absolutely meaningless!*"

"Even if I cared about that," said Greyfall, "which I do not, your promises are worthless."

"Here's a promise you can take to the bank," I said, trembling with fury. "If you take a single step closer to me, any of you, and I mean a *single* step, I promise I will toss this bag into the void."

He continued to approach, and I realized that, only partially through my own fault, I had created a man I could no longer bluff. For a moment I whited out in complete panic.

I need to stress that it was only for a moment, and that what I ultimately did was a calculated decision, a split-second weighing of pros and cons. Most of the pros and cons, anyway. There was one I'll admit I didn't consider at that precise juncture.

I *didn't* do the thing panic yelled at me to do, which was to take a step backward. Just to let myself fall. To get out of the corner I'd painted myself into the only way I could, by ceasing to exist entirely. That thought pulled at me like a black hole, but apparently I'd not yet reached the event horizon, because I veered away from that decision, savagely cut off all access to my emotions, and looked at the facts.

Radical acceptance: I could not stop myself from being captured. I would go to an Arcadian prison. They might execute me; they might not. But the world would go on either way. It could either go Belinda's way, or it could go my way. My way mattered. My way mattered more than *me*, more than anything.

More than this priceless artifact.

I couldn't get the vials to L.A.—in fact it was possible I myself would never see L.A. again—but I could keep them from Belinda.

With what I hope was a very dramatic sweep of my arm, I hurled the Vessel into the void.

The guards all cried out at once, and their outrage overcame their fear. They charged toward me, void be damned, and I let them come, raising my hands in a gesture of surrender.

All at once, everything was all right.

It happened very suddenly. All my problems vanished. I couldn't even really remember where I'd come up with the whole idea of "problems" to begin with. Life was a beautiful song.

So beautiful.

The guards all seemed to agree. They stopped and stood there, enjoying the song with me. We all understood now that there was nothing to fight, never had been. Nothing much to do at all but relax and listen to the perfect, nihilistic sound of our own utter surrender.

There was a lot of wind then, which was fine. There were huge talons wrapping around both of my arms, which was also fine. The song continued, so that meant that everything was fine, even the ground falling away, way down below me, moving away, my feet dangling over it. Maybe especially that. I was flying! What could possibly be wrong with that?

41

When the music stopped, I found myself sprawled on the sand behind a wall of rock, staring at Shiverlash and Caveat.

It took a moment for the fog of the siren song to dissipate, for the sluggish processes of my cognition to work themselves back up to normal speed. Shiverlash just sat waiting, watching me.

"Am I losing my mind," I said to Caveat, "or did the Beast Queen just rescue me?"

"I told her you were in trouble," said Caveat. "I asked for her help. But she sure sat there watching for an awfully long time before she pitched in."

"I'm not saying I'm not grateful," I said to Shiverlash, assuming Caveat would translate for me. "But it would have been awesome if you could have performed your heroic rescue *before* I lost the Vessel."

The queen's cool voice washed over me from the general direction of her unmoving face. "Have you not noticed, human, the great pains I have taken to avoid revealing myself to the Seelie?" she said. "I am stranded behind enemy lines, and I do not yet have the gathered strength to defend myself against a unified counterattack. So long as there was any hope of your escaping on your own, there was no reason for me to expose myself."

"But now you have," I said. "And those guards are going to start looking for both of us any minute. So why don't you give me a lift back to the Gate, and we can both have a nice cup of tea at Residence Four, safe from Seelie justice."

"I do not trust your 'Project' not to hand us both back over to the *sidhe*. From what I can see, the interests of the *sidhe* and the interests of the 'Project' are one and the same."

I sighed and pinched the bridge of my nose. I wanted to argue, but aside from Alvin and his allies, she was right. And I wasn't sure how much longer Alvin was going to be able to protect me. We still had absolutely nothing to entice the other nations to hear us out. No fey court, no Medial Vessel, no blood samples.

"You have another problem," said Shiverlash.

"Yes," I said irritably, "I have a shitload of them. I'm sure you don't mean my court date, or the fact that I really need to piss, but that only leaves about a hundred others. How the fuck do you even keep *track* of my problems, anyway? How is it you keep scheming and counter-scheming? You're supposed to be a wild fey; you should be forgetting I even *exist* by the end of the week. Do you have an Echo I don't know about?"

"Does Winterglass?"

I stared at her. "Are you saying you had your own little baby human in a cage at some point?"

"Nothing so crude and desperate. But where do you think your Queen Belinda acquired the idea? She was well familiar with my legend, and one of the few truths that survived was that certain humans sacrificed their unwanted offspring to me. I was exposed to infant blood in great quantity and diversity."

"Wow," I said. "You know, I really love our little chats, but I think I'll take my chances going home."

"There is the problem you have still not addressed."

"Which is?"

"That bag you carried. You said it was what Winterglass required of you, in order for him to ally with you."

"Yeah, I know," I said. "That's fucked now—I get it."

"But there was a personal favor, as well, that you required of him. Was there not? Something you dared not ask of me?"

Oh shit.

That was the one thing I'd not thought through sufficiently at the edge of the abyss. Without Dostoevsky's blood, Winterglass had no reason to do me even the one small favor of ordering Qualm to go to jail in Tjuan's facade. Even his loyalty to Caryl only seemed to extend to keeping her safe; he'd refused her any number of lesser favors already. Which meant that by tossing away those vials, I'd cut off Belinda's nose, but sliced up my partner's face pretty good in the process.

"Perhaps I can be of use in this matter, after all?" Shiverlash said.

She wasn't offering to be nice, I knew damned well. She was still trying to find some way to put me in her debt. I could take the deal—assuming she'd even agree to it—and then just not hold up my end, but this weird fantasy Shiverlash had of us being allies in the revolution was the only thing that had kept her from tearing me limb from limb by now. If I went back on a promise to her, even that thin thread would snap.

"I'm afraid to tell you what I need," I admitted. "Either you'll use it to bind me to you, or you'll refuse and use that knowledge to screw me in some all new way."

"We all take risks," said Shiverlash. "I just took a tremendous risk in revealing my presence here to the Seelie Court."

"Passive-aggressive really isn't your color," I said. "But fine. I'd need you to imprison a spirit."

Shiverlash tipped her head. "I can see why you assumed I would refuse. I will at least let you explain further. Why must I be the one to cast this spell?"

"It isn't a spell. It would be an actual prison that you would order this spirit to go to. It's the wraith, Qualm, who murdered an Arcadia Project employee last fall. You'd order him into the facade you used to destroy the Rose, order him to stay there for, oh, let's say, twenty years. You'd order him to retrieve the weapon he used to commit the crime, then order him to walk into a police station in Los Angeles. They'd take care of the rest."

"This spirit you speak of was serving Countess Feverwax, and Countess Feverwax was attempting to do my will. Why should I punish my own ally?"

"Because the woman he killed was innocent. She wasn't even a spell caster; she'd never harmed a spirit in her life. In my world, if you kill an innocent woman, you go to jail. Qualm was in my world when he committed that crime, and when he shot another innocent human a few weeks back. Honor demands that he be punished for those crimes."

Shiverlash seemed to think this over. "If you can give me what I need, then I will give you what you desire."

"So what is it you want of me in return? I'm guessing not a pedicure."

"Instead of facing this trial by the Seelie High Court, you

will return with me to my lands and assist me in freeing the spirits there."

"That will put me directly at war with Winterglass."

"In the end, as I think you have always known, you will be at war either with Winterglass, or with me. You have lost all chance of using the usurper for your own purposes. And he will be far easier to vanquish, as conflicted and weak as he is."

"I don't choose my enemies based on who's easiest to kill. And I haven't heard great stories about your homeland."

"You will be under my protection. No one there would dare harm you. I will see to it that you are treated with respect and that you have all you desire."

"How long would I have to stay?"

"Until the war is won. Until all the spirits are freed."

"Just in Unseelie lands? Or are you going to keep running around kicking Seelie sand castles too?"

"Destruction of the White Rose was not about freeing spirits," said Shiverlash, "but about destroying their slave masters, the *sidhe*. In truth the Seelie spirits are not my subjects, and so I will leave them enslaved at the Seelie estates if it secures your agreement. You should be ashamed, however, for bargaining their freedom away."

I cradled my head in my hands, leaning my elbows on my knees. "I hate the way you twist my mind all around. I can't tell which end is up after talking to you for five minutes."

"Yes, complexity can be bothersome."

I ran over and over it in my head, trying to think of another way. I couldn't ask one of our friendly spirits to walk the facade to jail. They couldn't just bail afterward, because then the empty facade would shatter the Code of Silence and open up an investigation into the arcane at a moment when the Arcadia Project was already on the verge of imploding. And even if we decided that didn't matter at all, to let the Code of Silence crash and burn, the spirit would still have to stay inside the facade until "John Doe" was officially convicted; otherwise they could still come after Tjuan. And conviction could take forever; we'd be punishing a spirit simply for being useful, which is exactly the kind of thing we were supposed to not be doing anymore.

Furthermore, unless we used Elliott, whose status as our ally was iffy at this point, we'd have to get Shock to cast another of those dangerous linking spells, and I'd literally just told him he was done helping us. Once he found out what had happened to the bag he had risked his life for, I wasn't sure I could count on him, either. The likelihood of striking another deal with Winterglass *himself* at this point was nil. In fact, the chance of his murdering me the next time he saw me was higher than the chance of his ever trusting me with something that mattered to him again.

Here I had someone offering, someone willing. And all she wanted was for me to help her do what I kept saying I wanted to do anyway. I kept *saying* I wanted to free the spirits, as long as it wasn't too inconvenient for me. Well, fuck that.

"I can't think of another way to get Tjuan out of there," I admitted. "Can you, Caveat?"

Caveat didn't choose to project any particular emotion, but something about the quality of her hesitation suggested that the question had surprised, even startled her. "I should stay out of this," she said. "I can't really do two parts of a conversation."

I sighed. "If this were just up to me, I'd take the deal and run. A life sentence in Unseelie hell is probably better than I deserve at this point. And who knows, maybe the place would suit me. The thing is, though, I can't just do this unilaterally. I'm making a decision for my partner, too, about the fate of the guy who put him in there, about the way he gets freed."

Shiverlash rustled her wings impatiently. "If you wish to confer with your 'partner,' I suggest you do it quickly. No doubt Dawnrowan's lackeys search for us even as we speak."

"I can't just 'confer' with Tjuan," I said. "He's in jail, on Earth. And I'm awaiting a trial date there myself—yes, a completely *separate* trial in another world; I'm a well-traveled criminal."

"You have guards looking for you on Earth as well?" said Shiverlash. I couldn't tell if she was appalled or impressed.

"Well, I'm out on bail. But if I walk back in there—which I am not at *all* keen on doing—and ask to talk to Tjuan, everyone and their cousin is going to be listening in. I can't be talking to him about Unseelie queens and spirits. Getting off on insanity sounds great in the movies, but I've been in a psych hospital, and no thanks."

"Well, then," said Shiverlash. "It sounds as though you must make this decision yourself."

"No," I said firmly. "No. This is his life. I'll have to . . . I don't know. Maybe I could get Alvin to go in my place. Maybe they could come up with some kind of code . . . I need to think."

Caveat spoke up then, quietly. "I have a thought."

I looked at her with interest. "You know him better than anyone," I said. "Do you think he'd go for this?"

"I don't," she said. "But . . . you don't have to take my word for it."

"Why not?"

"I possessed him before," she said bluntly. "I can go back to him anytime I want."

During the ensuing silence, a whisper of a breeze made its way around the rock wall that sheltered us. I heard a sound that made me think of wings stirring air, and I remembered the guards that were looking for us. My stomach knotted, and I glanced up. Seeing nothing untoward, I turned my attention back to Caveat.

"I know you could go to him," I said, "but I can't ask you to do that. That would be . . . traumatic for both of you."

"I think at this point," Caveat said, "it would be like bombing rubble. You said I should come clean with him. Maybe this is fate telling me now's the time."

"And you'll tell him what Shiverlash proposed to me? See how he feels? How will you get back to us?"

"The queen knows my name."

"Right. So she can call you back. After how long?"

"I'm not restrained by distance," said Caveat, "so just as long as it would take to introduce myself and explain. Then I can go back and forth, and you can converse with him, in a sense."

"Caveat . . . are you sure?"

But she was already gone.

42

Just about the time I was wondering if I should ask Shiverlash to hypnotize me again to spare me the misery of several minutes alone in her nonverbal company, the manticore landed heavily on the sand between us.

"I knew it," I said, still sitting on the sand with my legs asprawl. "I knew I heard wings earlier. Glad it was you and not the guards."

"Oh, I saw a couple of them snooping around," he said. "But I cast a cloaking ward around this spot and they fluttered right on past. When I saw Caveat vanish, I was a little worried about you being alone with Birdbrain."

"Brand," I said. "Did you *ask* the spirit to cast a cloaking spell, or did you enslave it?"

"Hey. You wanted me to find more permanent homes for the wraiths in the book, right? Well, now one of them is making a nice little hidey hole for fugitives in Skyhollow."

"But isn't cloaking an Unseelie spell, anyway?"

"I haven't instantly forgotten everything I knew how to do," Brand said. "It feels different now, though. Weird. Like I swallowed a human or something."

"Awesome analogy. By the way, is it just the way the light looks here when the sun's about to go down, or are you a little more . . . uh . . ."

Brand bristled. "A little more what?" he said in an ominous tone.

"Uh, nothing," I said. "Definitely wasn't going to say 'pink.'"

"Not allowed to shed human blood in Arcadia, so I'd have to swallow you whole, and we've talked about how much that would hurt. So what have you been talking about with Birdbrain? Couldn't hear from where I was perched."

"We're trying to come to some kind of agreement, to get Tjuan out of jail." I glanced at her. If she could tell we were discussing her, it didn't show in her body language or in her awful scarecrow face. "I may end up going back with her to Unseelie lands and trying to free the spirits."

"I like that idea," said Brand. "Mostly because you'd be miserable, but also because then maybe it'd be safe for Birdbrain to take me back, and I could shed these fucking feathers. Should I go ahead and swear fealty to her now, you think? While I'm here?"

"That would be spectacularly stupid," I said. "Wait until the deal is done, at least."

"Where did that little spirit of yours fuck off to? Carrot or Cadillac or whatever."

"She'll be back in a minute. She's going to talk with Tjuan about our potential agreement, and then Shiverlash is going to call her back. I wonder if I've given them enough time yet. I don't want to interrupt, but what if they're both just sitting there in awkward silence?"

Brand settled onto his haunches, wrapping his spined

scorpion tail around himself like a contented cat and tucking his wings against his back. "So I've saved your life like eight times now. Do I get a Project contract yet?"

"In case you hadn't noticed, I seem to be having trouble getting to our files."

"Well, I can't wait to tell Naderi everything. This has been kind of fun. Haven't worked with anyone since Vivian, and that wasn't exactly a picnic."

"Glad to hear I'm a better boss than a vampiric supervillain."

I glanced at Shiverlash and found her blank face turned steadily toward Brand in a way that gave me the screaming creeps.

"Hey," I said to her. "Go ahead and call Caveat." I pointed vaguely in the direction Caveat had last appeared, since the siren probably couldn't understand me.

Shiverlash inclined her head slightly and then whispered a chilling four syllables that I could only assume was Caveat's name.

When Tjuan appeared, I nearly fell over.

It wasn't him, of course. Caveat was just copying the image of him she'd seen. He was sitting on the edge of a cot, a gray wall behind him, a gray expression on his face as he stared in my approximate vicinity. The edges of the wall blurred out as they met reality, making a bleak halo around his image.

"So Caveat's the one who fucked up my brain," he said without preamble. I searched his face for any sign of emotion, though I should have known better. To all appearances he was reacting to this revelation as though we'd just told him the soup of the day. "She won't tell me what you want, though," he went on. "Said you needed to explain it yourself."

"Tjuan," I said. "God, it's good to see you. Are you all right?"

No sooner had I asked the question than Tjuan vanished. Oh, right. He wasn't actually there. Anything I asked him, Caveat had to jump back into his head to deliver.

"This is going to get awkward," I said to Brand. "It's everything that's annoying about voice calls combined with everything that's annoying about texting."

"When should I poke Birdbrain to call the spirit back?"

"I don't know," I said. "Just kind of . . . double the amount of time it takes me to say everything, to give him a chance to respond."

Brand mumbled something to Shiverlash, and "Tjuan" reappeared.

"Let's not get into that," he said. Which, honestly, I should have predicted. "Tell me what it is you need to tell me."

"Fine," I said to his image.

Rather than freezing the image when he was finished talking, Caveat showed a seamless loop of him sitting idle; he continued to breathe, to blink, in impassive silence. It made his presence seem more immediate, less like talking to a recording.

"God, this is so weird," I said. "I—I miss you. Shiverlash is going to help, though. And before you give me that look I know you're going to give me, she's a mixed bag, and it's not all pure evil, I swear. She did just destroy the White Rose, but . . . we'll talk about that later. Anyway, I've pissed off Winterglass, probably irrevocably, so Shiverlash is the only one left I can talk into commanding Qualm to show up at the police station with the gun. In return she wants me to help her free the spirits in her lands. She said she'd leave Seelie lands alone now. But if I go with her, she'll send your facade to the police station with the weapon in its hand. She'll command Qualm to stay passive inside there for years; as a fey his only choices will be to tell the truth—that he did shoot that guy—or stay silent. Either way, they can't keep you in prison when they'd now have zero evidence to hold you there. Right? This is the only way to get you out."

I stopped for long enough that Caveat could assume I was finished, and Tjuan's image disappeared. This time, when he did, I started to cry.

"Don't do that," said Brand. "Seriously, I am not equipped to deal with that shit."

"You and me both," I said. I dashed furiously at my cheeks. "I gotta pull myself together before he comes back. If Caveat is projecting what she sees . . . Tjuan's got enough to deal with right now without my stupid feelings." I scrubbed at my face vigorously. "How's that?"

Brand leaned over to peer closely at my face. "Just looks like your normal level of ugly to me."

"Thanks, Feathers. Tell Shiverlash to call Caveat back."

When Tjuan reappeared, he finally had an expression on his face, and it was a dire one.

"Are you out of your goddamned mind?" he said.

"Ah, there's my partner," I murmured to Brand. But Tjuan was still talking.

"Don't get me wrong. I can see that you thought this through, and I don't have a better plan. But this is not okay. You talk about going to Unseelie lands to 'free the spirits,' but you realize what that means, right? Those lands are full of *sidhe* and their estates. Whatever Shiverlash just did to destroy the White Rose—you better believe we're having a conversation about that later—she's going to do that to every *sidhe* in her lands, including the ones who have Echoes here, and she's going to kill them. You remember that's her deal, right? Death to all the *sidhe*? She has literally *said* that, about eight times, Millie."

That seemed to be the end of his rant. He sat there staring through me, arrested in an endless loop of expectation.

"You know I wouldn't allow her to do that," I said. "I'll find some way to undo the protection on their estates without— She can't order me directly, so she'll have to—"

It all sounded stupid. He was right. There was no way to end spirit enslavement on Shiverlash's timetable without essentially destroying the Arcadia Project, and, with it, human innovation and progress. This was not a decision I got to make on my own, or even with my partner's help.

"What choice do I have?" I finally blurted at his passive image. "Leave you in prison for ten years? Twenty? I don't even know. I can't, Tjuan. I *can't*. I literally cannot live with it if I know there's something I could have done to prevent it."

I let that sit there for a moment, then decided there was nothing I could add. I tipped my head toward Brand.

When Tjuan returned, he looked downright livid.

"Fuck your guilt," he said. "Cry me a goddamned river. You expect me to just run off, free as a bird, knowing I owe it to the genocide of an entire fucking race? The *sidhe* won't have their estates, they'll be outnumbered, and they won't even be able to fight back with magic, because Shiverlash can silence them. Remember that? The whole reason that her own fucking husband turned on her a thousand years ago? Because she was too fucking powerful and was going to exterminate the *sidhe*. And you want to give her an iron weapon, and say you're doing it for me? Fuck that. I'll rot in here first. Take back your goddamned spirit and leave me alone."

He folded his arms and sat back with finality. Caveat shifted back into her accustomed visual illusion, taking her place on Shiverlash's shoulder.

"I'm sorry," she said. "He told me to go, and I won't force myself on him."

"Is he mad at you?" I said. "He knows what happened to him isn't your fault, right?"

"He doesn't want to see me again," said Caveat. "I have to respect that."

I knew that had to hurt. But I didn't know what to say to her; she was possibly the only being in existence whose emotions I understood even less than I understood my partner's.

"Don't translate this next bit," Brand said to Caveat. "Here's the thing, Millie. Shiverlash didn't understand a word of what you and Tjuan just said. So you can just lie to her and tell her you're going to go through with it."

I shook my head slowly. "No," I said. "Lying to fey feels like punching someone who's tied to a chair. I'll do it to some asshole I don't expect to deal with again, but we're running a little short on friendly fey monarchs."

Brand let out a frustrated growl. "This does not end with you and Shiverlash holding hands," he said. "The sooner you start treating her like the opponent she is, the sooner you start winning this game."

"Elliott," said Caveat.

Brand and I both turned to her in confusion, but she wasn't looking at us.

"If you have something to say to Millie," she went on, "you

should say it so that she can hear you. I'm not your translator."

"Wait," I said. "Elliott's here?"

"Spirits have no *here* in Arcadia," Caveat reminded me. "But he has been attempting to address me since I returned from speaking with Tjuan."

I pushed myself to my feet, feeling vulnerable and strange. "What does he want?"

Caveat just sat still, staring off blankly.

"Elliott," I said to thin air, turning myself around slowly. "Go ahead and show yourself. It's not like I can do anything to hurt you, and if Shiverlash were going to, I guess she would have by now."

After a moment Elliott appeared, perched warily on Brand's back in his original winged-iguana form. The sight of it tugged at something in me, something on the wobbly border between affection and grief.

"There you are," I said.

He looked at me impassively. "Only you are hearing this," he said. "Not Brand, not the queen."

"I understand," I said.

"King Winterglass, Shock, and Caryl just finished destroying the Alondra facade, and now they are searching for you. If you like, I can let them know your location."

If Caryl and Shock were with Winterglass, surely he wouldn't murder me, right? He must be feeling at least a *little* bit kindly toward our side, toward me, if they were all searching for me *together*. And thinking of him gave me an idea of how to put off refusing Shiverlash until I was back on my turf and she couldn't summon any spirits to attack me.

"All right," I said to Elliott. "Do it."

43

"Your Majesty," I said to Queen Shiverlash with Caveat translating. "I've not yet managed to reach an agreement with Tjuan, but I'm afraid that will have to wait. I've just received word that King Winterglass knows our location. He is on his way here, and he is not alone."

"Do you think he means to attack?" she said, her oil-black wings rustling.

"I'm not sure which of us he's after. We'd best split up. Can you get away from here unseen? A personal cloaking spell doesn't work on me, so I'm safest if I stay put."

"He will not detect me," said Shiverlash, and immediately launched herself into the air.

"Well," I said, turning to Brand. "That was surprisingly easy." Then I noticed his murderous expression. "Uh-oh."

"So he's coming *here*, is he?"

"Brand," I said firmly. "I know he sort of . . . exploded you. But to be fair, you were trying to kill Caryl. Please don't attack him."

He bristled, looming over me. "Give me one damned good reason."

"Because you want to see Naderi, ever again?" I said, holding my hands palm out and backing away. "Also, he could kill you?"

"Or I could kill him!"

"And if you do, who the fuck gets his scepter?"

"Me!" said Brand with a grin. "I'd be a great king!"

"Even if that were anywhere in the same zip code as true, you're Seelie now. You can't use that scepter."

He sat down heavily on the sand, exhaled in frustration. "Shock, then! He's all right."

"Shock doesn't want to be king, never has, and, P.S., *don't attack Winterglass*. Because it's rude to attack someone who comes in peace, because you'd probably just get exploded again, and honestly mostly because I fucking said so, and I'm in charge of whether you get to see your Echo again."

"I promise I won't attack Winterglass," said Brand. "But let the record show that I'm killing him *in my mind*."

It took about an hour for them to reach us, and when they did, I hardly had time to process the horror that was King Winterglass in his native form before Caryl ran to me and threw her arms around me, kissed me squarely on the mouth.

Okay, so we were doing this. Publicly. All right.

I kissed her back if for no other reason than to spare her public humiliation, one hand on the back of her head, the other arm wrapped firmly around her. But I kept my eyes open, checking out Shock. He was watching us with a slightly sad smile that suggested he and she had already had a Conversation about this.

Winterglass, I couldn't read at all. Flaming-eyed owl skulls are not really known for their subtle ranges of expression.

When I finished kissing Caryl, I kept my arm around her and looked to Winterglass.

"I'll have you know," I said to him, "you just got me out of a very awkward conversation with Shiverlash."

"Where is the Vessel?" he asked. Oh, wow. I had never heard his natural voice before, and it was at least *eight* kinds of Nope. I was so disturbed by the warped, nightmarish rattle of it that it took me a minute to realize what an alarming question that was.

"Oh," I said. "I, uh . . . it's gone."

"Gone where?" said Caryl, pulling away from me and leaping straight to about a level 8.

"Gone . . . from existence. I got cornered at the abyss and it sort of . . . fell into the void."

Caryl crumpled to the sand. Winterglass stood for a moment like an extremely creepy statue, then began to advance on me.

Brand stepped between us, bristling. Winterglass came to an abrupt halt; even when Brand had been Unseelie he'd shrugged off royal commands, since the manticore was older than the scepter itself. Winterglass had learned the hard way not to fuck with Brand, and he didn't know I'd made him promise not to attack.

For a long moment Winterglass said nothing at all. And I'd have lost a ton of money if I'd wagered on what his next words would be.

"Thank you," he said.

"I— What?"

"You have freed me entirely from the Arcadia Project's control," he said. "There is now nothing left in either world that could convince me to make even the smallest agreement with any human again."

"Father . . . ," Shock began. But Winterglass put up a hand, and he fell silent.

"I won't try to stop my son or any of my other subjects from cooperating with you. But I have my own troubles to attend to, namely the Beast Queen that you unleashed."

"The Arcadia Project could help you with that," I said.

"Oh?" His native form didn't have eyebrows, so he had to redouble the sarcasm in his nightmarish voice. "You will send armies of humans to stop the teeming masses of Unseelie commoners who salivate waiting to rip my people limb from limb?"

"Probably not that, no."

"Then there is nothing you can do to help me in the struggle I must wage, and your demands will only serve to distract me. Whatever Third Accord your Project hopes to make, you will have to make it without me."

I looked to Shock, to Caryl. Caryl was sitting on the sand, chewing one of her knuckles, tears in her eyes. Shock stood looking at his sneakers, resigned. Neither of them had anything much to say.

"I'll give you this advice for free, then," I said. "Shiverlash will stop at nothing to see the spirits freed. The best thing you could do for yourself would be to start befriending commoners rather than doubling down on exterminating them. Talk to your son there. Actually listen to him. He can help you kick the spirit-slavery habit."

Winterglass turned his skull toward Shock. The kid kept his eyes on his shoes.

"There are just too many commoners," I said. "Every enemy you make is a new body for the siren's army, and since she can cancel magic, it's going to be bodies against bodies."

"Why are you telling me how to fight the only ally you have left in the Unseelie Court?"

"Because I would rather that ally have been you. I love Caryl, and she loves you, and so I wanted to love you too. I still haven't given up hope that one day you might look past your fear of change and see us as worthy allies."

Caryl moved to him, touched his skeletal arm with gloved fingers. So she was skittish about closed spaces, but had no trouble cuddling skeletons. Okeydokey.

"You can't really be leaving the Arcadia Project," she said in a tone of hurt disbelief.

He raised one bony hand to cup her cheek. "If you had any sense," he said with surprising tenderness for a nightmarish demon lord, "you would too. Dame Belinda will not be gentle with you when this is all over. Come with me now, and I will keep you safe."

"I cannot abandon the Arcadia Project!" she said, her eyes overflowing with tears. "It is necessary for human progress. For fey progress as well! The White Rose could not have been built without it, nor your palace at Nullhorne. Without it we would all be wild creatures scrabbling for survival, never dreaming of anything more. Everything you attribute to the *sidhe*, as part of their innate superiority? It's because of their relationship with us!"

"I don't believe that," said Winterglass. "The *sidhe* have always been the best of either world. And Shiverlash is trying to destroy that. If you came with me, you could destroy her, you could *rule* there."

"I don't *care* what happens to the Unseelie Court!" Caryl blurted with such vehemence that Winterglass stepped back. "I wish I had never seen the place!"

Winterglass stood for so long that I thought maybe he

really had turned into a statue this time. A monument to an Unseelie King, dead of a broken heart.

"I'm sorry," Caryl said. "I shouldn't be unkind to you. It wasn't your fault."

He reached out to touch her hair once, briefly, then let his hand fall.

"If you must go home," he said at last, "then I will ensure that you get there safely."

"No," said Caryl resolutely, though her voice still shook a little. "I know what that means—it means you'll enslave another spirit to hide us. I will never allow that to be done in my presence again. For any reason. Deciding there were exceptions to that rule lost me my best friend."

"You haven't lost me," said Elliott. I started. He was on *my* shoulder now. Not really, of course. He had no *here* in Arcadia. But that was what he chose to project.

Caryl put both hands to her mouth, starting to sob in earnest. "Elliott . . . ," she said brokenly. "I thought Unseelie couldn't forgive."

"You are Unseelie," he countered logically. "Did you not forgive me for leaving you, for making myself vulnerable to Shiverlash?"

"I am part human," Caryl said.

"Then so am I, perhaps. Let me be the spell that will see you safely home." He showed himself fluttering over to land on her shoulder, wrapping his tail around her neck, just like old times.

"Hey," I said. My voice was hoarse for some reason. "Can Brand and I come too? The Seelie guards are still looking for us."

"Can you make a spell that will hide all of us?" Caryl said to Elliott. "Even with her iron?"

"Hmm," said Elliott. "An interesting challenge."

After a few experiments, he determined that if he used Brand as the base for the spell, he could weave an enchantment that radiated outward for twenty feet or so, creating a null space that most would feel subtly compelled to look away from.

Caryl mounted Brand behind me, wrapping her arms around my waist and leaning her head against my shoulder. Shock kissed her hand farewell.

"Though you will never fully return the admiration I hold for you," he said, "I hope that you and I shall remain friends. I hold no true power in the Unseelie High Court, but I will do what I can to assist the Arcadia Project with what talents I do possess."

"Wait for me at Nullhorne," Winterglass said to his son. "I wish to make certain that Caryl arrives safely home."

The king flew alongside us as Brand sprinted homeward, despite the fact that his wings were all air and bone and would never have worked in a world that made any sense. When we reached the base of the rock formation that held the L4 Gate, Brand crouched down so that Caryl and I could dismount.

"Brand should come with us to the Residence for a little while," I said, "just until we can get some sort of pardon for what he did to Duke Skyhollow."

"Very well," said Caryl.

"Baroness Roper," said King Winterglass, startling me with the respectful address. "Will you remain with me a moment, to speak privately?"

I turned to Caryl and Brand. "Go on," I said. "Pretty sure he won't eat me."

Winterglass waited until they had disappeared through the Gate, then turned to address me.

"You seem to care for Miss Vallo," he said, "in the human fashion. If Caryl insists on staying with the Arcadia Project, I place the onus on you to make certain that she is safe."

I blew my hair from my face in frustration. "How?" I said. "How am I supposed to protect anyone? I've fucked up everything. I have no more monarchs on my side than I started with, and I'm probably going to lose Shiverlash. Sure, I took some resources away from Belinda, including you, but she still has two hundred countries' worth of people she can send at us in various ways. We're fucking doomed."

"Not if you take the Seelie Court from her too."

"Well, yeah. But there's no way to do that."

"Submit yourself to their trial," he said. "Thus far you have only tried to strong-arm Dawnrowan into submission; that is not how the Seelie mind works. If you want her to ally with you, you must play the noble hero."

"Dude, seriously. I'm an antihero at best."

"If you want Dawnrowan on your side, you must set aside your conception of yourself. You must *act* as a hero would act, and hope that the truth follows in the footsteps of the lie."

Wait. That sounded suspiciously like . . . opposite-to-emotion action. Did King Winterglass of the Unseelie Court just paraphrase my *therapist* to me?

"Free advice," he said quietly. "In exchange for yours."

I sighed, raked back my hair. "But I can't take your advice," I said, "any more than I expect you to take mine. There are too many ways I could screw up the trial, end up in prison or dead."

Winterglass gave a graceful shrug of his spiky shoulders.

"I just want to go home," I said quietly.

"As do I," said Winterglass. "That advice was my last gift to you. Having offered it, I take my leave."

"Wait. Can't you help me free Tjuan? Please? If you don't help me," I bluffed desperately, "I have to go back to Shiverlash. And what she wants in exchange . . . she wants to use me as a weapon against the *sidhe*. To destroy their estates."

"I do not think you will do that," he said. "But if I am wrong, if you do turn your iron against my people, there is nothing in either world that will protect you from the consequences." And without further ado he launched himself into the air, a skeletal silhouette growing smaller and smaller against the darkening sky.

Just as I was seriously considering bursting into tears, Caveat appeared, hovering in my field of vision without bothering to choose a plausible object to perch on.

"Don't worry about it anymore," she said.

"About what?" I said. I was drowning in so many worries I couldn't pick one out.

"About Tjuan," she said. "I've spoken with Shock."

"Wait. Are you . . ."

"He's agreed to link me to the facade. I'll take it to the police station, stay in it for the length of the prison sentence, and then I'll return it to Arcadia to be destroyed."

I tried to wrap my head around this. "You're going to go to prison *voluntarily*? For potentially ten years or more?"

"If the Project doesn't find a way to get me out of there sooner."

I stared at her for a moment. "That's . . . that's awfully heroic, for an Unseelie spirit."

Caveat took the trouble to manifest a shrug, clearly patterned after one of Tjuan's. "It's not altruism," she said. "It's balance. I stole a lot of years from him. Now I'm going to give them back."

"Caveat. We'll . . . we'll talk about this more. I want you to be *sure*. Don't do anything just yet. Are you going back to the Residence now? Or staying here?"

"Here, until I'm called."

"Could you . . . could you find Claybriar for me?"

"Of course. What do you want me to tell him?"

I gave the Gate a lingering look, then turned my back on it. "Tell him I need safe escort back to Skyhollow. I'm turning myself in."

44

As bad as I needed to pee by this point, I didn't dare step through the Gate, even for a minute. I ducked behind the thick scrubby brush those guards had used for a hiding place instead, put my portable toilet to use. Then I ate an awful protein bar from my backpack and drank the entirety of my small canteen of water, even though there was a whole refrigerator waiting just on the other side of that Gate.

I knew if I saw Residence Four—the cat hair, that drippy faucet in the upstairs bathroom, the peekaboo graffiti, all the ugliness that now meant *home* to me—I'd never be able to muster up the courage to come back.

By the time Claybriar found me, dusk had turned to night, and I was lying back on the sand, pinned like a butterfly by the depth and brilliance of the Arcadian stars. These were no random assortments of burning matter flung haphazardly across the galaxy; they looked placed by an artist's hand. Maybe they had been.

Claybriar said nothing in greeting, just helped me to my feet and then gathered me against his furry chest, holding me close. He was *alive*, and warm, and smelled like forest. For a moment I couldn't even breathe and held him tightly enough to make it hard for him, too.

"I thought maybe you'd died," I said brokenly. "Alondra said you were okay, but—"

"Shhh. I'm fine."

"Is the queen all right?" I said. "Skyhollow?"

"They're both still breathing," he said. "Best to leave it at that. Caveat says you're going to turn yourself in?"

"Yeah," I said. "Give it to me straight, doc. How bad is this going to be."

He shrugged. "I'm biased," he said. "Seelie trials are meant to discover the truth of someone's character, her motivations. So I think you'll do great."

"Won't she just think I'm lying? I'm getting a lot of that from fey lately, when I try to tell the truth."

He shifted his weight. "Ah, well, see . . . you kind of grabbed the queen's scepter and ran with it? And also escaped prison and disabled a couple of ancient wards? So . . . you've forfeited the whole consent thing, as far as reading your mind goes."

"Who's going to be doing the reading? Is there a judge?"

"Lucky you—the queen has decided to oversee your trial herself."

"Gulp."

"Come on," he said. He slipped his hand into mine and began to walk with me along the road. "It'll be all right," he said confidently. I tried not to think about the fact that he could lie to me if he was lying to himself.

Holding hands, it was easier to stay in step along the enchanted path, and somehow less disorienting. The nighttime landscape of Arcadia lurched crazily past us, a thousand steps at a time, as we walked.

"I love you," he said.

"And you know I love you too, right?" I said. "In my own weird way."

"Every human loves in their own weird way," said Claybriar. "That's what's so interesting about humans."

"It's not the same with fey?"

Claybriar shook his head, looking troubled. "Love is a very specific thing to a fey. Different, maybe, between species. For me, it's like a hunger. For the *sidhe* . . . it's something else. I don't even know what."

I let my gaze drift up to the stars for a moment; they, at least, seemed to hold still as we walked.

"Clay," I said. "I saw the two of you. You and Dawnrowan."

"Yeah," he said sheepishly. "I knew that was a possibility. I just couldn't think of a better way to distract her."

"Do you love her?"

"In my way, yes."

"Hunger."

"Yes."

"But I know you care for me, can make sacrifices for me. I'm not just a sex toy to you. Is it the same with her?"

He glanced at me, seeming uneasy.

"I'm not trying to trap you here," I said. "I know you think I'll be jealous, but I just want to know the truth. If you don't really love her, then don't fuck with her, because she seems like a crazy bitch. But I also don't get to tell you who you should love. And if you do love her, I don't want you to give up on her just because you don't think your kind of love is good enough for her. Let her decide that."

"I'm pretty sure she's already decided." Immediately he seemed to regret having spoken. "I'm sorry," he said. "I can only hurt you by talking to you about this. And I'd rather die than hurt you."

"You sound like some emo college kid," I said, raising his hand to my lips briefly despite the pain I knew it would cause him. "Hard to believe you're like a hundred years old or something."

"More than that," he said. "I mean it, though. I never want to hurt you. You're part of me."

"When you say things like that, it's hard for me to feel jealous of anyone. Whatever you feel for her, she's not your Echo. I am. I'm as secure with you as I'll ever be with anyone."

He nodded, exhaled as though he'd been bracing himself for an injection that was now over. "You're everything to me," he said. "That drives her crazy."

"Dawnrowan?"

"Yeah. But what I can't tell her—what she would misunderstand—is that in a certain way I do love her more."

That stung a little, despite my promises. But I didn't want to punish him for being honest with me. "I'm everything to you, but you love her more?" I said as casually as I could. "What's more than everything?"

"Well, 'more' in a . . . certain way. What you'd call a 'romantic' way, I guess. I'd step in front of a truck for you, no hesitation. You're always the first thing in my mind. I'd fuck you if I could, believe me. But with her, it's that—you know, that breathless thing where you don't even feel quite safe. Like you're falling."

"It's always like that for me at first," I said. "And then it mellows. Or goes away altogether."

"I've known her for a hundred years," he said. "And still I get weak kneed around her. I thought maybe it was because she was queen, but supposedly I'm her equal now, and I still just . . . looking at her is like looking at the stars. Makes me feel small, but in a good way. I know I'm not making any sense."

"No," I said, squeezing his hand. "I think I get it. And . . . I'm sorry you felt like you had to hide that from me. I know I flip out over stuff sometimes, but I do get over it. You can always tell me anything, and I'll never stop being your Echo."

He squeezed my hand back. "I love her," he said, seeming to marvel at hearing himself say the words. But he quickly sobered. "Unfortunately, she only loves me when she has me on a leash."

"Then that's not love," I said, "no matter what she tells herself. I am no expert on healthy attachment, but even a dunce like me knows that if it comes with conditions, it's not love. Listen, though," I added when he started to look downcast. "You've got a long life ahead of you, and you're a hell of a catch. If you ever do find someone who makes you see stars, and really loves you back? You have my blessing. I promise."

He stopped then and bent to kiss me. Carefully, bracing himself against the pain. Then he took my hand, and we resumed our stroll under the night sky.

"Be careful at the trial," he said. "Dawnrowan can't lie, but I speak from experience—she can trick the shit out of you."

The royal guards were gentle when they found us at Skyhollow Estate. I could tell Greyfall wanted to break a few of my bones just on principle, but King Claybriar insisted on accompanying us all the way to the White Rose prison, right up to the point that they locked me back in the same damned cage where I'd so recently employed two people and a spirit to spring me out.

"Be careful," Claybriar said again, giving my hand one last squeeze through the twisted boughs of the cell.

I watched with a sense of dull resignation as he and the guards ascended the stairs, leaving me without even a glimmer of light.

There wasn't much to do but lie down on the floor and close my eyes to shut out the darkness, and I was so exhausted that I dozed off almost immediately. I woke with a start when the prison doors opened again, letting in a wide, gentle shaft of starlight.

Queen Dawnrowan brought her own radiance; her golden skin, hair, fur, and feathers were surrounded with an aura like candlelight. I watched her white-swathed shape glide down the long stairway, feeling once again the raw power of her grace. Her palace was rubble above us, and yet nothing in her demeanor even hinted at defeat. She made the desolate cavern a palace just by walking into it.

"Good evening," she said as she stopped in front of my cage.

"You're . . . speaking," I said stupidly.

"Your blood is still with me," she said. "Will be with me past dawn. As for the words, since you have broken the laws of courtesy yourself, I no longer require consent to find them in your mind."

"Is it time for the trial already?" I said.

"It is."

"I wish justice moved this quickly in my world. Can you tell me how it's going to work?"

She tipped her head thoughtfully. "Think of it as a dream, if you will, a dream that I can observe as you make your way through it. What you do in that dream will tell me your character. What you reveal about your character will tell me your guilt or innocence in the crimes that have occurred here."

"Couldn't you just ask me? With access to my mind, you could know if I told the truth."

"I am in your mind already. I already know your answers to any questions I might think to ask. But these are only the answers to what you *believe* about your motivations and intentions. Deeper answers are hidden within you, waiting to be revealed. Conversation is for those who seek the surface; I wish to know the truth whole. You may not understand what I do as an interrogation, but all the same, it will give me answers."

"Before we start," I said, "may I propose something? Can I attempt to secure a promise from you?"

"You are here to undertake a trial, not to make an agreement with me."

"Can't a girl do two things?"

Something about this seemed to amuse her. Good. An amused Dawnrowan was a merciful Dawnrowan. She took a half step closer, her golden eyes as intent and curious as a cat's. "I will hear you," she said, "but I can make no predictions of agreement."

"At the end of all this, it sounds like you'll know me and my motivations pretty well. Better than you know Dame Belinda."

"I have never put her through a trial; it is true."

"So if what you find proves to you that I want the best for Arcadia, will you withdraw your support from Dame Belinda and give it to my faction, instead? Will you take some time to listen to what my side has to say about the spirits, and how you might harness them in spellwork without enslaving them, the way that Claybriar does?"

She had seemed on the verge of outright refusing until I said his name, and then she hesitated. "And if you do not pass the test?" she said.

"That's your demand to make," I said. "Whatever makes it worthwhile to you to bind yourself to this promise."

She thought it over for a moment. "If you do not pass this trial," she said, "your death will give me all that I require, except for the return of my palace. For that there is no remedy. But I see in your mind the Unseelie prince who stole from us. I see that he can make more like you, with iron in their bones. If you fail, before you are executed, will you arrange for him to meet with me, so that I may find out what he wishes to trade for this information?"

I cringed. I hadn't realized that her full access to my mind would implicate everyone who had collaborated with me. "I can't promise to make him appear, but I can promise to do my best. You won't hurt him, will you?"

"That is not my way. I only want the knowledge that he possesses. There is a war coming, and if this weapon will be used against us, I would like to have it to defend my lands as well."

"And I'll be dead, so I guess it's no skin off my back either way. You have my word, then. If I don't pass the trial, I'll do everything in my power to arrange a meeting between you and Prince Fettershock of the Unseelie Court."

Queen Dawnrowan carefully, ritually rephrased both sides of the promise in unambiguous words and then withdrew a by-now-familiar wooden key from somewhere inside her diaphanous garb. Someone needed to speak to Earth's fashion designers about those pockets.

The queen turned the key in the lock, then swung the door to my cage wide.

"Come," she said. "Let us begin."

45

I stepped out of the wooden cage and into . . . the office of Professor John Scott, on the UCLA campus.

"Oh Jesus," I said out loud, and did an abrupt about-face, walking back the way I'd come.

But when I walked through the door, I found myself simply blundering into Scott's office again. There was no sign of the prison anywhere; it was as though I'd awakened from a dream of it.

Scott was sitting right there at the desk, his ash-dusted ginger head bent, red pen in his hand, scribbling on a stack of paper. He hadn't yet noticed me.

It was all there: the magic-hour sunlight slanting in horizontal stripes through the blinds on his west-facing windows, the smell of paper and mid-priced cologne, the clutter of his desk, the sleeves of his pastel button-down rolled up to reveal the gilded hair of his forearms. This was not a dream; it was real. It was real.

I tried again to leave the room, only to find that an exact copy of it still lay on the other side of the door. I stood in the doorway, looked back and forth between them. Identical, down to the angle of the sunlight, the soft *shhhp!* as Scott turned a page.

Feeling dizzy and sick, I stepped through and closed the door behind me.

"This is a dream," I said out loud. "No matter how real it seems, this is in my mind."

Scott looked up, his expression vague. It had always been vague. The man was as difficult to read as Caryl had been when I'd met her.

I had a type, to be sure.

"Millie," he said. His voice was higher pitched than you'd expect from his lanky frame: a reedy tenor. "Is there something you needed?"

"You tell me," I said. "This is my trial."

"Right." He exhaled, looking back at the paper. Circling something, making a note. "The trial. It wasn't my idea."

It was exactly what he would have said, exactly the weary, slightly amused tone he'd have used to say it. Did I remember him this clearly? How was that possible? The pitch of his voice had surprised me; I'd forgotten it. Or had I? How else would Dawnrowan know how he sounded?

"Is it really you?" I said. "It's not, is it? I'm . . . I'm dreaming."

"Can we get on with whatever this is?" he said. He gestured to the paper on his desk. "Once I finish this, I've got three more just like it."

"I don't know how to 'get on with it,'" I said. "I don't know what I'm supposed to do. I've never done a trial like this before."

He set down his pen with a resigned, long-suffering sigh and gestured to the chair on the other side of his desk. "If you're staying, have a seat."

I moved carefully toward the desk, aware of the imperfections in my stride, wondering if he'd notice. What was it about him that instantly made me desperate to impress him?

"This is a dream," I said.

"Obviously," he said. "But is it yours, or mine?"

The idea struck me hard; I felt a wave of vertigo.

"Do I show up in your dreams?" I said. "Did I matter that much to you?"

"You were a student of mine who killed herself. That's going to leave a mark."

"I don't even know where to start with how fucked up that statement is."

"Just get on with it, Millie, seriously. Pick a place to start and have it out. Obviously neither of us gets to leave until you do."

"Okay, 'killed herself' first of all. You do know I survived, right? Did you . . . I mean you must have followed the news on it. Tell me you had at least that much human decency."

He leaned back in his chair, crossed his arms over his chest, looked at me challengingly. The way he always had during office hours, the door safely open behind me. I'd desperately wished he would close it, show some sign that he valued that time with me and didn't want it interrupted, wanted me to himself badly enough to break protocol.

"What do you think?" he asked.

"No. Answer me. Do you know that I'm still alive? Are you being your usual evasive self? Or are you refusing to answer because this isn't real; I'm not actually in your head somehow, interacting with the real you. This is all a projection inside my own mind and nothing more. And so you can't answer what I don't know the answer to."

He held my eyes for a moment, and then looked away as though in surrender. God, the way that had always felt like a victory, back then. Now it was nothing but a reminder of the many ways I'd misread him.

"I know that you survived," he said. "I didn't go seeking out the news, but everyone was talking about it. People asked me about it. Because they knew you'd—been fixated on me. They wanted to know how I was handling it."

"How you were—" Rage smothered me for a moment. Of course they'd all have been concerned for him. He was the wonderful John Scott. Who the fuck had I been? "You're a piece of work, Scott. Unbe-fucking-lievable. Playing the victim after what you did to me."

"I didn't push you off that goddamned ledge, Millie. And even so, you could have taken my career with you."

"Oh, right. Like that's ever how it works."

"That is very often how it works, Millie. There were people who took your side. Took your side on principle, because you were the student, and female, and I was a man in power. Yes, don't look so fucking surprised. People did defend you. Just . . . no one who'd ever met you. What does that tell you?"

I sat back in my chair as though he'd fired a cannon at my chest. It took me a moment to find my train of thought again. The other thing that had bothered me about his original answer.

"You called me 'one of your students.' As though there was absolutely nothing between us other than that. Does that mean you're still pretending we didn't fuck, or does that mean you fucked so many of your students that I don't even fucking stand out?"

He spread out his hands on the desk, almost as though he

intended to push himself to a stand, but he remained seated. "You weren't the first, Millie, but it wasn't something I exactly made a habit of."

"I wasn't the first? That sounds like a habit to me."

"It happened once before, just once. But it was a different situation, and she was able to keep her goddamned mouth shut about it, and after my egregious misjudgment of you it won't happen again."

The instant gut-wrenching regret I felt was interrupted only by a frisson of alarm.

I hadn't known about the other student. How could he be telling me something I didn't know? Was I making an educated guess? Or was I actually talking to some astral projection of him? Was he experiencing this same conversation somehow, in what he thought was a dream? I couldn't decide if I found this idea comforting or horrifying.

"How did you 'misjudge' me?" I said, eyes stinging with unshed tears. "I don't understand it. You initiated sex—don't tell me you didn't. I was there. And I was willing. And then suddenly you avoided me. Wouldn't even speak to me. Why? That's all I ever wanted to know, was why."

"I really don't think you do. It will not help you."

"Don't tell me what will help me."

He rubbed his forehead, then dropped his hand back onto the desk. "You said you loved me."

"I—what?" That I didn't remember.

"In the middle of it all, you said you loved me. That—before that, I thought you were playing a game with me. A thrill seeker. I was a prize. I thought if I gave you what you wanted you'd settle down. But then you said you loved me, and I thought, *Shit*. I realized this wasn't going to go away. That it might have ended my career. So I figured the best thing to do was end it cleanly."

"But you didn't end it cleanly! You didn't even tell me it was over!"

"Honey, I'd known you long enough to know how that conversation would go. I was afraid that would send you off a roof. Crazy of me, right? I thought if I avoided you I could forestall a confrontation and you'd just . . . take the hint and move on."

"It's bad enough that you just pretended it never happened, in your own head. But to actually say that to other people? Make me out to be a liar? Destroy my reputation?"

"The truth would have destroyed both our reputations, and in my case it would have destroyed my career as well. Was it fair that I'd never get a decent job again because I gave in to you, gave you something you obviously wanted, pursued relentlessly, in fact? The only reason your reputation got destroyed was that you went around telling everyone."

"I told one person, and only because I didn't understand why you were avoiding me! I thought I could trust her!"

"You are not exactly the poster child for excellent character judgment. Anyway, we both would have been fine if you'd just kept it to yourself and moved on. If you'd treated us as though we were both adults who were present in the same room and made the same horrendous mistake."

"Did you even care when you heard that I jumped off a roof?"

"Mostly, to be honest, I was angry."

"God, what kind of monster are you? How can you be angry at someone who hated herself that much?"

He spread his hands, weary, his expression strained. "I don't know what else to tell you, Millie. I'm spent. By the time you left that hospital, I'd dealt with it and moved on with my life. It was just one mistake in a life full of them, for me."

"You *destroyed* me."

"You destroyed you, but whatever, Millie. Want revenge? Here." He pushed a gun across the desk at me. Where had that come from? Dream logic. "There you go," he said. Against my will, I found my eyes drawn to the veins on the back of his hand; his human frailty made my pulse race.

"John . . ."

"It's loaded," he said. His voice was rough, but when I glanced in alarm at his eyes, they were dry. "Blow my brains out. Or shoot out my kneecaps and call it even. Just end this, please. I wish I'd never met you."

I leaned forward, wrapped my hand around the weapon. A blue steel revolver. I shuddered.

"What you did was wrong," I said. "It's not debatable. Even if you didn't know I was unstable, which I didn't exactly hide, I was your fucking student. You shouldn't have invited me to your apartment, no matter how 'adult' I was. You shouldn't have had drinks with me. You shouldn't have let us even get to that point. That's on you, and you know it."

"So shoot me."

I'd actually never held a gun before. In a dream, it should come naturally, right? It shouldn't have felt so heavy and awkward in my hand as I pointed it at him. If I pulled the trigger, would I get closure? Would I be allowed to leave this room?

I held the gun, held it, held it . . . then laid it back on the desk.

"The truth is," I said slowly, "I can't hurt you, even in a dream. I didn't mean to, to begin with. What happened was your mistake, but knowing that doesn't make me happy. It doesn't stop me from wishing we'd met under other circumstances. Wishing we could have . . . connected, without it being a mistake. I shouldn't feel this way about you, but I don't know how to stop."

"We didn't connect, Millie. Not the way you thought. I never came anywhere close to being in love with you. So I'll ask what I asked when you came in, what I asked of you every damn time we met, and never got a decent answer. *What is it that you want?*"

I looked at the gun on the desk, briefly considered turning it on myself. Realized how futile it would be.

"At this point?" I said. "At this point I just want to forget you."

"As I understand it, you've made some friends who could probably arrange that for you," he said. "Barring that, I imagine time will do the trick."

I stood, leaving the gun there on the desk. "Good-bye, Professor Scott," I said. "I hope you meant what you said, about never doing that again."

I went to the door and opened it, and this time there was something new on the other side.

46

The open door let in the muffled, stormy sound of Rachmaninoff, played live at a small upright piano. I stepped into the living room of my childhood home, dark red curtains hanging over two-story windows, a cold, cathedral-like space that had somehow once seemed like home. Now it made me feel exposed, nauseated; I turned to go back through the door, back to the office, where at least I'd had some semblance of agency, but I found that the knob was suddenly at chest-height, and on the other side of the doorway was just the same room again. Before and behind me, my father, nowhere to turn.

I looked down at myself, and as I did so, a raggedly edged sheet of hair fell forward over my right eye. My eyes felt sandy, sore. One brass-colored pigtail trailed forward over my left shoulder, over my collarbone, tied with a dark blue bow. It matched my skirt. School uniform. My right fist was clenched; I looked down, and in it was my other pigtail, a matching bow at one end, a red rubber band carefully doubled again and again around the other end to hold it together.

Following the memory as I would a script, I approached

my father where he sat at the piano, his back to me. His iron-gray hair had recently been cut, almost military short. He had loosened the collar of his shirt; his tie was untied but still draped around his neck. As I came around to the side of him, circling like a wolf in the shadows, his angular profile rotated slowly into view. He did not look at me or stop playing.

I tried to speak, but the words lodged in my throat. I silently laid the braid on the piano keys. An offering.

That stilled his hands, and he finally swiveled to look at me. I'd forgotten that his eyes were so blue, that his nose had bent in the middle. Except, I hadn't, or it couldn't have been shown to me. I'd forgotten how kind those eyes could look.

"I don't want to argue anymore," I said. Fresh tears leaping to eyes I'd thought drained.

He looked at me for a moment. "I wish you were more your mother's daughter," he said, "and less mine."

I held still. He never talked about her. This was important. If I moved, I would break whatever was happening. I had done something magical, laying my braid on the keys. I had passed his test.

"I was closing a deal on a rental property in Mississippi," he said. "She was at the house next door. Pinching the dead blooms off the petunias on the porch. Wearing something that looked like it had come from the Salvation Army. Three dogs lying near her feet. The sun was low, on the other side of her, and I couldn't see her face clearly, but I remember all three of the dogs were watching her with the same look, as though her every move was the answer to everything. And I knew in that moment that she didn't belong there. That she deserved so much more. I've never felt anything like that, before or since."

He turned back to the keys. His left hand climbed up, then back down, the notes of a scale. Harmonic minor.

"Children were important to her. She thought she'd finally feel at home here, if she had them. And there's nothing I wouldn't have done to make her happy. But she . . . we had some trouble. It took years. When it happened, it was like a miracle for her."

"You didn't want me," I said. I probably hadn't said that, at ten, but part of me was still me, still grown, still looking back on this with all of my new understanding.

"The two of you loved each other like nothing I'd ever seen," he said. Hand wandering up and down another scale. Natural minor.

"The way you wanted her to love you," I said.

"I wasn't good with babies. I let her handle everything. But she was so tired, and then one day she had this . . . strange rash on her legs. These bumps. She almost didn't go to the doctor about it, but she was so determined to be at her best for you."

"It was cancer," I said. "I forget what kind. Something rare."

Because I couldn't remember, neither did my father. "She was dead in two weeks," he said.

"I don't remember her," I said. "Not even a little. I know I should feel sad about this, but I don't. I'm sorry."

"I never let you keep a nanny more than a few months." This part I was sure he hadn't told me as part of this long-ago conversation. We'd gone off script, mixing memories.

"You never *let* me keep them? I thought they all quit."

"You know they didn't," he said. He turned, met my eyes.

I thought it over. "They always quit right when I started to get attached. Eventually I wised up and stopped getting attached."

He gazed at me with a quiet sorrow.

"Except they didn't quit," I realized. "You fired them because I started to love them. Because it made you angry that I could just . . . forget her, and you couldn't."

He turned away from me then, rested both of his hands back on the keys, just to the left of where I'd laid the braid. But he didn't play.

Something flared up inside me, hot and bright. I snatched the braid back, clutched it against my heart.

"You didn't want me yourself. But didn't let anyone else love me either. What the fuck did you think you were going to turn me into, Dad?"

He stared at the keys, looking bowed, broken, he and the piano both getting subtly, physically smaller somehow. It only made me angrier.

"You drove me away! You don't get to play the lonely victim here!"

"How can you be angry," he said to the keys, "at someone who hates himself so much?"

He looked smaller because I was myself again, fully grown, standing on prosthetic legs, my braid still clutched in my right fist.

"You never let me feel safe," I said. "You demanded my love when I wasn't in the mood, rebuffed it when I was. Just so I would always be sure to know whose story this was, who was the main character in this tragedy. And when I moved to L.A. to clutch desperately at a chance to center my life around myself, you jumped off a fucking building just to make it your tragedy again, once and for all. You made yourself the martyr."

"You broke my heart," he said to his hands.

"No! Bullshit, no, you'd already ruined your own life. But I still had a shot! You hadn't killed me yet. You just killed my love for you, *on purpose*, and then suddenly you wanted it back? Fuck you! I had a chance at happiness and I fucking leaped for it!"

He swiveled, sharp, in that way that had always filled me with such fear as a child. Even now I couldn't help but step back. All the gentleness gone from those eyes, blue as Alaskan ice. "You leaped," he said, "and you broke yourself to pieces. Look what you've done with this 'shot' of yours. Look where you are."

"Do you even know where we are right now? Do you even know why? You're a figment of my imagination, Dad. You're not even you; you're my memory of you; you're *me*."

"This is so typical of you. Trying to have control, trying to be the director."

My eyes filled again. "Dad, can we not do this? We're both dead now; what does it matter?"

"Both of us?"

Why had I said that?

"They're going to execute me," I explained to him. To myself. "We're both ghosts now. Let's not fight anymore. Can you just— will you play me another song? Can I just pretend I have some kind of closure here? The aria, from the *Goldberg Variations*. That's what you played, after I gave in about the haircut." I laid my braid back on the piano. "This is my mind, isn't it? Can't I make you play it?"

My need to hear that song was so sharp, so strong, that I realized I'd lost. There was no victory to be had over my father here.

He began to play the *Goldberg* aria, its notes so tender, so slow and speculative. My heart unfolded like a morning glory. I began to shrink again, into my childhood self.

Sometimes he'd made milk shakes from scratch, in the kitchen, I remembered. Almost boozy tasting with vanilla extract. Sometimes he'd held my hand when we walked to the school bus together.

"You'd have been hit by a car if I hadn't," he said calmly, as though I'd spoken aloud. "You were always lost in your own thoughts. As for milk shakes, I loved them, but the recipe I learned was meant for two people, and they don't keep in the refrigerator or in the freezer." As he spoke, he continued to grow, until I was looking up at him from a toddler's height. "I'm sorry," he went on, watching his hands and not me, "but I never really cared for you, even when you were small and appealing. And now? Look what you've made of yourself. How do you expect me to feel now?"

I staggered away from him, through the suddenly huge room, my legs as wobbly as a two-year-old's. This time, the door let me leave.

I stepped out of it at my full height, blundered into Daystrike Forest, wintry and haunting. I shivered; the air felt so real, and it was uncomfortably cold. Even so, I had no desire to turn back as I heard the door close behind me.

"What's next?" I said, hearing my voice get lost in the

soaring expanse of trees. "Caryl, right? This is where I find out she never loved me either?"

"No," said a voice behind me and to my left. A voice that was familiar in an intensely creepy way.

I turned and saw not Caryl standing there—but myself.

47

"Oh, I know what this is," I said, backing away slowly in the snow with awkward, jerky strides. It was cold, and I was exhausted, and I stubbornly clung to the idea of my prosthetic legs and the way I tended to lose my finesse with them when my mind was otherwise occupied.

"Do you?" said Millie. The other Millie. Me. Face as smooth as a baby's, not a scar in sight. She was wearing a sweater and jeans, a hooded jacket over them. Clothes I couldn't remember ever owning.

"You're going to try to get me to admit that I love myself or some garbage like that, make me face Past Me and forgive her for what she did to me on that roof."

"No," said Millie, continuing to advance toward me. From the way she moved, it was obvious that she had her natural legs. I realized there was no way I could outrun my able-bodied self, so I just stopped, let her come and stand in front of me.

She reached for me, explored my scarred cheek with her fingertips, and there was something very alien, very not-me, about the careful way she touched me. I felt a sudden sense of deep revulsion, felt the urge to shove her away. To be contrary, and maybe to entertain Dawnrowan, to remind her that I knew I had an audience, I grabbed the illusory me by the collar of her sweater and kissed her. She didn't resist.

"So that's what I taste like," I said. "Always wondered. Or is it just what I think I taste like?"

"Should we take a little break?" Millie said. Did my eyes really go all sultry like that when I was kissed? Were there really faint olive-green stars around the pupils? "Do you want to find somewhere warm," she said, "and find out more about how you taste?"

"Wow," I said, letting her go with a slight shove away from me. "Past Me is a tramp."

"I'm not Past You," she said. "I'm Future You."

"Beg your pardon?"

"I'm what you could be."

I shook my head, let out a weird, panicky laugh. "You're trying to convince me that Seelie magic could heal me. That somehow, even though no other fey spell can touch my body, Queen Dawnrowan or someone can just . . . grow me some new legs. Fix my scars."

"No," said Future Me. "Even without the iron in your bones . . . there is no magic ever known that can heal a wound the mind has already accepted. But with your blood, we could make another you. An unscarred you."

I tipped my head and squinted. Whatever the point was of this test, I was missing it. "And do what with it? How would that help me? What would be the point of it?"

"It could replace you."

"Replace me where, at the Arcadia Project? I'm still not seeing what the point of this would be. What would that free me up to do, exactly?"

"Are you ready to hear me?"

"I . . . yes, what a weird-ass question."

"I have come to you with an offer. Not an illusion, but a true offer, binding in the real world."

"Which real world?"

"Both. I have seen into your mind, Millie, and I know why, after you survived your fall, you have never again tried to take your own life."

"Because thanks to my damaged liver, I can't get drunk enough anymore to think it's a good idea?"

"Humor will not deflect me."

"You thought that was funny?"

"You don't wish to leave a hole in the world, Millie, or cause pain to others. But what if there were no hole? What if a Seelie spirit were to access your mind, absorb your memory, your education, your experience, everything that makes you what you are? Then it could animate this body, return to your life, and do whatever you would wish."

I stared back at Future Me for a moment and started to shiver uncontrollably. The cold was only in my mind, though. This was all only in my mind.

"You could work for the Arcadia Project," Future Me said. "You could travel freely in Arcadia, just as other Project members do."

"I wouldn't be useful against spellwork anymore, and wasn't that the whole point of me?"

"Not at all, Millie. That has long stopped being your primary value to the Project. They look to you for ideas, for leadership. In truth, your 'gift' has done more harm than good. You destroyed Countess Feverwax, mobilizing her wraiths. You released Shiverlash, leading to the need for a Third Accord, and now, with her help, you've destroyed the White Rose. How much more damage do you want to do?"

"This isn't—but it wouldn't be—"

"The new you could step in, take all your knowledge, fill your role. And the new you would be functionally immortal. You could continue to accumulate knowledge and experience, apply your unique mindset in service to the Arcadia Project, and end your life only when you choose. You could live long enough to become director of the entire project, ushering in a new era of prosperity for humanity, and still have time to retire and make films."

"But it won't be me experiencing any of that."

"That is the most beautiful thing of all, isn't it? An end to experience. You could stop carrying the weight of all your failures. You know that weight is what keeps you from joy; that is why you long for death, to forget. This way you can rest."

"But if the new me has my brain, wouldn't it just be the same fucked-up mess?"

"The Seelie spirit would be drawn toward the joy in life, not the pain. It would forgive your mistakes in a way you cannot, and so this new Millie would be you at your best. You could have the relief you desire from your pain, without abandoning your responsibilities."

Tears started to my eyes, warm against the chill. "I'm more than my responsibilities," I said, but my voice sounded faint, uncertain. "I'm not so down on myself as to think that people wouldn't miss me."

"They wouldn't have to miss you. You'd still be here. You'd have the same opinions, the same memories, the same wit; you would react to everything the same way. Claybriar could finally touch you, fully realize his desire for you."

With a pang, I thought of all of the times he'd looked at me longingly, the guilt I'd felt at not being able to give him what we both wanted, what he, in a sense, needed. And the new body could be healthier, less scarred, more able to wrap its limbs around him as he stayed safely inside the human facade that most appealed to it . . .

"Wait," I said, snapping out of my daydream. "It wouldn't be my exact body. And it also wouldn't be my exact . . . soul or whatever. Animated by a different force. So, would touching me even help him anymore? Would I even still be his Echo?"

Future Me was silent, looking down at the snow.

"I wouldn't be. He'd be losing his Echo."

Future Me looked up again, meeting my eyes solemnly. "All fey do, in the end. Is it really worth continuing to suffer, to tear yourself apart every day for who knows how many decades, just to delay that inevitable separation?"

I shifted my weight. The logic wasn't unreasonable, but something was nagging at me. "If he loses his Echo, he'll lose his memory, his reason. How is he supposed to rule the Seelie Court if he— Wait just a goddamned minute here."

Future Me was looking down at the snow again. I advanced on her, grabbing her by the collar of her sweater again.

"That's what this is about, isn't it?"

"No." Future Me shook her head, meeting my eyes again with panicked earnestness. "It's about you, Millie. Your pain is a scar on this world. I'm offering you what you wanted when you climbed onto that roof. I'm offering to take your pain away and carry forward everything that's valuable about you."

"Meanwhile Claybriar loses his throne, his Echo, his memories, everything. No. Fuck that. Get thee behind me, Dawnrowan. For you to use my own fucking personality disorder against me, just to try and get yourself a less problematic king? That's downright Unseelie of you. You should be ashamed of yourself."

Future Me lowered her eyes and this time did not raise them again.

"I'm done with this sham of a trial," I said. "Get me out of here, and confront me face to face, you fucking coward."

As though waking from a dream, I found myself sitting once again in the oaken cage beneath the ruin of the White Rose. Queen Dawnrowan sat before me in the unfinished wooden chair from the guard's station, emanating a soft radiance that revealed the bleakness of the prison surrounding us.

"You have my congratulations," she said, "on passing your trial."

I heaved myself awkwardly to my feet. "Bullshit," I said, wrapping my hands around two of the branches that formed the walls of my cage. "This wasn't some test of my inner strength or honor or resolve or any of that garbage. You were trying to fuck things up for Claybriar so he couldn't be king. So you could make him your leashed pet again."

"Cannot a girl do two things?" Dawnrowan said. Echoing me from earlier, the little diva. I hadn't realized she had any capacity for sass. Under other circumstances, she might have been starting to grow on me.

"You're nothing but a scheming bitch."

"A scheming bitch who is now, as promised, your ally."

"I still don't get it," I said. "How was what I just did a victory? I fucked up at every possible turn."

Dawnrowan shook her head, gazing at me tranquilly. "I underestimated you," she said. "I designed the trial to play on what I thought were your weaknesses: your selfishness, your rage, your self-pity. I wanted to prove how tainted you had become by your experiences, to justify removing you humanely from your and others' misery."

"You were literally trying to kill me."

"You know that the crimes of which you were accused were subject to a sentence of death. Why does it shock you that a trial might end in your execution?"

"But it didn't. I changed your mind somehow. I still don't know why."

"What did all three of your tests have in common?"

"That I folded like a cheap table? Except I didn't, the last time."

"Beneath your pain, the foundation of you is love, has always been. Even when people are unworthy of it, you give love with your whole heart. Even if it tears you to pieces. You have hidden this fact so well, even from yourself, that I nearly missed it—only the greatest stress brought it to the surface. And the last test!"

She stood, approached the cage, wrapped her hands gently around mine where they gripped the bars. There was something so sure, so tenderly maternal in the gesture that it quieted the objections I'd been lining up in my head.

"Millie," she said warmly. "You refused my offer not out of desire to keep living. You never argued that life's joys were worth enduring pain. Because you do not yet fully believe that. But despite your desire to die, you chose life simply because you couldn't bear to cause pain to your Echo . . . to my Claybriar."

"Your Claybriar?" I said, drawing my hands from beneath hers. "The man you love so much you won't let him rule unless he agrees to do everything you say?"

"That isn't why I fight him as king," she said.

"Then why?"

"Because in days past, when there was a Seelie King and Queen, they were true mates, not simply equals in rule. They were bonded together in love."

"And this gryphon? Arrowface? *That* guy, you think you could love?"

"No. But with Claybriar I would be acting out a loveless mockery with someone to whom my heart was unrequitedly bound. That is more torment than I could bear." She closed her hands around the cage as though it were she who were trapped, trying to get out. Her golden eyes filled with tears.

Despite myself, I felt a sudden wrenching sympathy for her. "Stop it," I said. "Don't cry; it makes me nuts."

"You will never know the love that the *sidhe* feel," she said, a single picturesque tear slipping free down her cheek. "We are made to pair with only one for eternity, but cruel fate bound my heart to a faun, whose loves are as many as the stars."

"Wow," I said softly. "Does that happen a lot? A *sidhe* falling for someone who isn't *sidhe*?"

"Only rarely, and the tales are always tragic. You will never know what it costs me to share the one true desire of my heart with so many. With a human! But what choice do I have? He cannot be other than he is, and I cannot be other than I am. And I cannot love another, any more than he can love only me."

She drew back from the bars, seemed to collect herself a

moment. Then she withdrew the wooden key and unlocked my cage. As the door opened, a full realization of my victory fell on me like a rain shower. I had the Seelie High Court at my command. Dame Belinda had nothing left to her at all.

Realizing this, I felt a sudden surge of generosity toward everyone in both worlds. I stepped out of my cage and looked at Dawnrowan, really *saw* her, not as an intimidating monarch or a too-beautiful rival but as a woman with a crack in her heart that I was better positioned than anyone to help put back together.

"It might not be as bad as you think," I said, "to rule at his side. I think you mean more to him than you realize."

"He has spoken of this to you?" Her glance was furtive, hopeful, like a child's.

"He has. But you need to speak to each other. I'm not going to play translator, and we're not in the eighth grade, either. Show him the truth of your heart, and he will show you the truth of his. If he doesn't, I'll personally kick his ass."

Dawnrowan tipped her head. "I will never understand you, Iron Child," she said, "but I begin at least to understand what Claybriar sees in you."

I knelt to her as I had once before, at our very first meeting, just as stiffly and painfully. This time, though, I meant it sincerely. I pressed my forehead to the stone floor of that cavern, showed her that for all my venom and quills, at heart I was Seelie; at heart I was hers. There was no magic in the gesture other than the meaning I brought to it, but it was enough to light her face with a radiant smile.

"Your Majesty," I said, "you will never regret our agreement. We will build a new Seelie palace and a new Arcadia Project, and this time it will be built from love, not from fear, and not from slavery."

"So be it," she said. "I have much to learn about these spirits that hide at the heart of a magic I thought I understood. But I have pledged to you that I shall learn, and the fey are bound by their words. Together, the leaders of your world and the leaders of mine will bring into being a Third Accord."

48

The dominoes fell so fast after that it was hard to keep track for a little while. Dame Belinda got through about a day and a half of denial before it became evident that she had lost both High Courts, the Medial Vessel, and every vial of blood the Project had been storing since the Renaissance.

Also, said the grapevine, if you wanted to deal with either Seelie monarch, you now had to go through Alvin Lamb in New Orleans. And neither of the Unseelie monarchs, apparently, were even taking calls anymore. Since most of the world's Project offices hadn't even been fully informed as to Alvin's reasons for rebelling, panic spread like a pandemic. Poor Alvin was fielding calls day and night trying to calm everyone down.

New York redeclared its loyalty to Alvin pretty much immediately. Within a week, Dame Belinda agreed to meet with us in Los Angeles to negotiate the terms of her surrender, which threw the London offices into absolute chaos. Besides Dame Belinda and her predecessors, there had never been a "UK Head" of the Arcadia Project; it had never been assumed that such a position would ever differ from Head of the Whole Shebang. It was a huge mess, but, luckily, none of it was my responsibility to mop up; Alvin was reaching out to other national heads and trying arrange a summit to decide the Project's next steps.

My primary responsibilities in the aftermath were to oversee the transfer of Caveat into Tjuan's facade and to get Brand set up with an Arcadia Project contract. I was riding such a wave of competence and normality that I even remembered to text Zach to tell him I wasn't dead.

He responded, *ok*

When I got that text, I rolled my eyes so hard they almost fell out. *Unfortunately I'm now awaiting trial for obstruction of justice,* I added.

After about five minutes, he texted back, *u r a piece of work girl*

But then, not long after, *let me know what u need, i'm around.* He was all right, sometimes.

What I needed, at least for now, was to bury myself in work. Shock was as good as his word about helping Caveat with the facade—he even knew where Qualm had stashed its weapon—but he refused to tell us anything about what was going on with his father. Apparently, he'd already made a binding promise to that effect.

Shiverlash, as far as any of us could tell, had vanished off the face of the earth. I didn't expect to hear from her again. I'd thrown in with the *sidhe*, and so our alliance, such as it had been, was null and void. I could only hope that she would at least hear about my efforts to free the spirits and be pleased enough not to turn on us the minute she was finished with Winterglass.

One small bright spot was that Brand and Naderi got to spend some quality time together as we fully initiated him into the Project. It was going to take me some time to get used to the radiant smile she wore with that bird perched on her shoulder, but she would need that serenity to deal with the media onslaught she was about to endure when she finally went ahead and rehired T. J. Miller as her supervising producer.

But first things first.

Once Caveat-Tjuan was fully operational, she/he walked into the police station carrying the same blue steel revolver and wearing the same clothes as in the infamous security video. She/he confessed in detail to the crime, but refused to show any ID or give the police a name. A run of the body's prints turned up nothing, since fingerprints aren't genetic. "John Doe" exploded into the headlines, his identical mug shot shown next to Tjuan's as American social media lost its collective mind.

And still, even with John Doe locked up, they wouldn't just let Tjuan out. Another day or two, they said. Dot the fucking *is*, cross the fucking *ts*.

I was about ready to assault someone with a deadly weapon myself at this point.

My only comfort? They had to withdraw some of my charges, as I was no longer aiding or abetting anything. Obstruction of justice, though? On that I was still fucked. Lying to cops is lying to cops. Alvin said he'd see what he could do to influence the trial, but either way, March was not going to be a fun month for me.

All in all, I decided I preferred Seelie justice.

It was a beaten, tired Dame Belinda who met with us in Los Angeles to negotiate terms at the Omni. Alvin had asked that

Caryl and I attend the meeting; also in attendance was Tracy Wong from New York, who turned out to be a portly, middle-aged man with shaved temples and an almost distressingly dapper suit. Somehow I ended up sitting between him and Dame Belinda; Caryl was across from me, seeming much too far away.

"We're not out for revenge," said Alvin to Belinda once everyone was settled and introduced. "All we want is for the Arcadia Project to be run successfully and humanely, and for you not to interfere with us any further."

"You make a grave mistake if you do not keep me on as a consultant at the very least," said Dame Belinda. "My experience—"

"Hold your tongue," said Caryl in a voice so icy we all turned to look at her. The expression on her face made me wish I hadn't. It was as cold and empty as uncharted space.

Even Dame Belinda faltered in the face of that look. She turned to Alvin with equal parts affront and entreaty.

"While I, uh, am not exactly comfortable with Miss Vallo's choice of tone," Alvin said, "I think, given that you've outright lied to the people under your command to hide your crimes, your words have lost a lot of weight with the people in this room. So I wouldn't waste more energy on them than necessary."

"Very well then," said Dame Belinda. "If you have already decided what you intend to do with me, by all means inform me."

"First let's look at the facts. You not only ordered the abduction of Caryl Vallo at the age of eleven months, but you also oversaw the execution or outright murder of everyone aside from Vivian Chandler who knew about the abduction, including Martin Reyes, the last Western regional manager."

"Soon enough," Dame Belinda said, "you will understand

why it was necessary to make certain sacrifices in order to keep the Unseelie Court under Project control."

"Right," I broke in. "Always important for the good guys to torture babies and inflict pulmonary embolisms on innocent men so that nothing *evil* happens."

"Millie," said Alvin in a warning tone.

"May we please proceed with whatever punishment you have decided?" said Dame Belinda wearily. "I have never been an avid fan of suspense."

"Obviously," said Alvin, "we will require your immediate resignation from the Arcadia Project. What's up for discussion now is whether we remove the related memories."

For the first time since Qualm had revealed her crimes last autumn, I saw Dame Belinda look frightened. "And just what would that leave me with?" she said. "I have given my entire life to the Arcadia Project. I have put aside thoughts of family and outside interests for more than sixty years."

"It wasn't charity," broke in Tracy Wong of all people. "You've enjoyed a seat at the apex of supernatural power on this planet, and you've operated with godlike impunity. If King Winterglass hadn't stumbled across Caryl and just *happened* to be the sort of person who thought he should return her to where she belonged, we still wouldn't even know about that. Which leads to the question, what have you done that we don't know about?"

"Anything you'd like to share?" said Alvin. "This would be a good time to come clean."

"It will make no difference," said Belinda, all the life draining out of her eyes as she sat back in her chair. "You have decided to crucify me for all the sins of—"

"*No,*" Caryl broke in. Her tone had a wobbly edge that caused everyone to turn and look at her. Her eyes had gone flat and glassy. She took in a deep breath, steadied her voice. "No. I will not sit here and let you *compare yourself to Jesus Christ, of all people. You are a liar, a torturer, and a murderer.*" As she spoke, I felt an odd pressure behind my ears, as though I'd ascended to a higher altitude.

"Everyone take a breath," said Tracy Wong firmly enough to bring attention back to him. "We can't force Dame Belinda to feel remorse for anything she's done. All we can do is make sure she doesn't do it again. To be honest, I was in favor of execution by lethal injection. I know a guy."

"But that isn't how the new Arcadia Project is going to do things," Alvin said firmly, giving Tracy a steady look.

"If you plan to take all my memories away," said Dame Belinda, "you may as well execute me. I see little difference."

Alvin leaned forward on his elbows. "Is there any other way you can reassure us that, even if you retain your memories of the Arcadia Project, you will in no way attempt to use your old contacts or influence the Project's activities?"

Dame Belinda looked at him blankly.

"Why are we even considering letting her go with all her memories intact?" I said. "Anyone who gets let go from the Project gets their memory wiped, right?"

"Those were the old rules," said Alvin. "But the old rules, in themselves, are so heavily wrapped up in the idea of tyrannical control of information by an elite few that I'm not even sure they're valid anymore. We're going to have to rethink the entire thing from the ground up, but that's not the issue right now. My main source of hesitation here is that Belinda's knowledge and experience *are* unique, and if we—"

"Do you like the smell of cedar?" said Caryl.

Everyone turned to look at her. She seemed remarkably calm; it was only my intimate knowledge of her various stress levels that made the hairs rise on the back of my neck. This was that bitterly cold level *past* 10 that I didn't even have a name for. A name occurred to me now, though. *Unseelie.*

"I beg your pardon?" said Alvin.

"Do you like the smell of cedar?" she repeated. I felt it again, that sensation as though my ears were about to pop. "Most people find it pleasant."

"I . . . guess I do," said Alvin uneasily.

"If I catch even the slightest whiff of it," said Caryl, "I vomit. The cage they kept me in was carved from cedar, because the smell of it helped mask the smell of my urine, I suppose."

"Caryl . . . ," said Alvin with infinite compassion. "I know—"

"*No,*" she growled, cutting him off.

A pale light flickered in her eyes, a greenish glow like swamp gas, swift as heat lightning. A ringing began in my left ear.

"You don't know," she said. "You don't know what I've hidden from all of you, for your sakes. Barker isn't the only one who can keep secrets. You don't know that I had to put a poster of an open field on the back of my front door so that I could close it without screaming. You don't know how many years it took for Martin to cure me of the idea that anything moving was on its way to cut me, or to splash icy water over me to cut the stench, or to prod me with thorny branches and make me cry just to feed off of my misery. You don't know what I, and Martin, and my therapists had to go through just to make me fit to mingle with the likes of you."

"You're right," said Alvin. "I don't. I'm sorry. And if I could go back, if I could undo everything that was done to you—"

"The person who did it is *right there*, and you're considering slapping her wrist and letting her walk away because she has *useful experience*."

Tracy cleared his throat, gave Alvin a significant look.

Alvin rubbed his forehead and sighed. "If I—if I agreed to Tracy's idea," he said. "I'm not saying I can. But if I did, if I agreed to give her a lethal injection, would that satisfy you?"

"No," she said.

Alvin blinked.

"Not at all," Caryl said firmly. "You would euthanize her, like a faithful pet who deserves an end to its suffering? Let her drift peacefully out of a world she has held in her iron grip for half a century?"

"Caryl," said Alvin. "You can't be asking me to deliberately hurt her, to torture her."

"People can survive torture, can't they?" There was an edge of hysteria in her voice, and the room's pressure dropped again, sharply. Now everyone noticed; I saw them noticing. "Torture is something we can all just move on from, heal from and become productive members of society again, throw away like a stained coat. Let's give her a chance to prove that, shall we?"

"Caryl," I said, sliding my hand toward her on the tabletop. "No. If you can't control yourself, you need to—"

She leaped to her feet, chair stuttering backward behind her and then falling onto its side. "Don't tell me what I need. I know what I need."

The room filled with a choking, soporific haze. My eyes watered; I yawned; everything tilted crazily, and I nearly slid out of my chair. Only a strong grip on the table kept me upright.

When I dragged my gaze back up to Caryl, I saw her standing wreathed in pale fire, her eyes blank glowing voids. She stared at Dame Belinda as though everyone else in the room had vanished.

"You did not flinch," Caryl said, "from sowing the seeds. Do not flinch from the harvest."

She began to recite something noxious in the Unseelie tongue, and Dame Belinda lifted her hands in horror. At first I thought she was trying to ward something off, but no. The flesh was rotting off those hands as we watched. This was no illusion; we could all see it, smell it. Alvin retched, and Tracy pitched forward onto the table in a dead faint.

I struggled to my feet and went to Caryl, grabbed her wrists, but she was still droning God knew what. Dame Belinda began weeping blood, hands still dropping bits of rancid flesh onto the table.

Belinda made a faint mewling sound and fell from her chair, crawling toward the door on her ruined hands. When she tried to rise up onto her knees to turn the knob, I heard a horrible crunch, and she fell over onto her side with a cry. Her eyes were wide with pain, still dripping crimson tears.

"Caryl! Stop!" I sobbed. "Just kill her!"

Caryl ignored me. I put my hand over her mouth, and she struggled, silent now. But she couldn't undo what she'd done, and I knew she had no intention of ending the woman's misery. I held Caryl the way I'd hold a plagued corpse, wanting nothing but to keep it away from other people.

Dame Belinda's bleeding eyes met mine from across the room, a silent plea for me to *do something*. It occurred to me that I would likely never hear her speak again. And yet in this moment, it was me she looked to, not Caryl and not Alvin, who had somehow found the courage or numbness to approach and kneel helplessly next to her.

Why me?

You are every bit as clever and stubborn as I was at your age.

Something gave way inside me, broke, releasing some homemade narcotic into my system. A weird calm settled over me, and I spoke in Caryl's ear, softly.

"Kill her," I said. "Quickly. Or you and I are finished."

Her hesitation broke my heart. But finally, vengefully, spitefully, she detonated the woman's skull as though she'd held a gun to it at point-blank range. Alvin was splattered with gore, and he sat stunned, past screaming, past anything. He looked as dead as the corpse that fell, limp as a doll, across his knees.

49

Dissociation can actually be fairly useful, under the right circumstances, which may be why Borderlines experience it
to begin with. For a weird ten minutes or so I was the only
calm person in the room. Belinda was nothing but a mess that
needed to be cleaned up, Caryl was nothing but an inert, sobbing obstacle that had to be carefully placed in a chair before I
could attend to the two humans in the room.

Tracy was the first to recover; Alvin was busy dry-heaving
when I finally got Tracy to help me move Belinda's head-
less body aside so that the door could, in theory, be opened
eventually. I tried to minimize the amount of blood I got on
my clothes in the process, but even that decision was very
detached; it was simply an unpleasant-smelling red substance
that I didn't want all over me.

There was a pitcher of water and some napkins on
a table against the far wall, so I went to Alvin next and
cleaned the unpleasant red substance off his face as well as
I could. There was nothing to do about his clothes, but the
cold water seemed to calm him. As I started to move away,
he closed a hand gently around my wrist. I glanced to him to

see what he needed to say, but he just looked up at me, mute.

"We're going to call someone," I said. "I know the Project must have cleanup people. We've disappeared gory bodies before. I just need to find out who to call."

Alvin just kept looking at me.

"Caryl," I said. "Who took care of Teo and Vivian? Can you call them?"

"You should kill me, too," Caryl said in a strange voice.

"For fuck's sake!" I said, my voice breaking. "I can't do this by myself. Is there one adult in this room? Caryl, I need you to call Elliott."

"After what I just—"

"Do it."

She spoke his name, but nothing more. In a moment he projected his illusion into my mind.

"Elliott," I said. "Caryl fucked up again. Bad, this time. She's— We put her in a room with Dame Belinda, and she didn't have you."

"I understand," said Elliott.

"The spirit she used," I said. "Can you get its name, so that someone can call it home?"

"There are several," he said. "I am already talking with them."

"Oh," I said. "That's—okay. Um, then I'll need you to take Caryl's emotions for a little while, so we can get this mess cleaned up."

"All right," said Elliott. He paused, then: "I shouldn't have left her. She wasn't ready. This is my fault."

"Not really," I said. "But if it motivates you to help, fine."

He disappeared, and in a moment Caryl rose from her chair, as cool and composed as the day I'd met her.

"Well, this is a nightmare," she said blandly.

I blinked at her. It was like facing an entirely different woman from the one who'd made a bloody mess of the wall.

I cleared my throat. "Do we know someone who can . . . who can make this all go away?"

"More or less," she said. "It will be complicated, and require misdirection of the hotel staff, but it can be done. I have handled worse."

"I— Really. Wow."

"I shall stay here until the cleaners arrive. Alvin should remain here also, as he does not seem well enough to travel, and because as my superior, he should decide what becomes of me. Tracy, take Millie back to the Residence."

Tracy had the foresight to take a plastic bag out of the empty trash can for me to hold before we got into his rental car. It was a good thing, because getting the smell of vomit out of leather seats can be a bitch. Don't ask me how I know.

I never got a full report of what Alvin and Caryl and the "cleaners" did to get that body out of there and the blood out of the carpet, but I'm pretty sure that nobody at the Omni had a clue about the grisly murder that had taken place in that little meeting room, given that they still let us hold our international summit at the hotel the following day.

We met in one of the Omni's larger conference rooms; I sat on a raised platform behind the podium where Alvin stood; on the other side sat the King and Queen of the Seelie Court in their human facades, looking like a supermodel and her scruffy bartender boyfriend.

Seated in the audience were more than two hundred people,

in theory representing the Project heads of the nations who were able to attend, along with translators where necessary. A dozen leaders had refused to come, and about thirty more were unable to travel to L.A. for various reasons, but more than three-fourths of the national Project heads were right there, in a single room. One thing that struck me was how alike they all dressed; I spotted two turbans and a hijab, but aside from that it was a sea of suits that might have all come from the same store. Something told me this was Dame Belinda's influence.

"We're going to be doing some reorganizing, obviously," Alvin said, after he'd summarized the events of the past month and answered questions to everyone's satisfaction. If he was shaken up from being showered with his boss's blood and brains the day before, he was damned good at not letting it show. In fact, I was having to struggle to keep from dozing off at what felt peculiarly like a generic business conference.

"Los Angeles seems like the best location for an international headquarters," Alvin said, "especially as our fine king and queen"—here he gestured back to them, and Claybriar gave a little wave—"are temporarily living at Skyhollow Estate. So there will be a new international structure. I won't be the one running it, though."

Once the translators had caught up, there was a general murmur of surprise.

"My goal here was never to supplant Dame Belinda," said Alvin, "only to remove her. Unfortunately, Caryl Vallo, upon hearing that we were considering keeping Dame Belinda on as a consultant, killed her with Unseelie magic. Miss Vallo is currently in custody at Residence Five."

Even though he said this in the same business-conference

tone he'd said everything else, it took a few minutes for the tumult to die down. I felt strangely removed from the events he was summarizing, as though I hadn't been there, hadn't given the order that ended Belinda's life. When Alvin had the room's full attention again, he continued.

"Obviously it would be helpful to have someone to continue coordinating things between nations. We'll have a vote later in the month to choose which of you will move to Los Angeles and fill that role. I think it's best that we keep the role independent of national operations, which is one reason U.S. National will continue to be based in New Orleans. The other is that I don't want to move."

A handful of people were kind enough to laugh at that.

"But there will be a lot of changes in the way this Project is organized," he said. "I won't go into all of them today, because a lot of it will be up to whoever moves into the shiny new office we're going to build at Valiant Studios. But I've already decided one important thing."

He leaned closer to the microphone, sweeping the audience with a very serious look.

"Everything that was based on some neo-feudal system of unquestioning hierarchy, with an Emperor of the Supernatural overseeing it all? That's done. That's history. I am an *American*."

He let that word fall; I saw people shift in their chairs uncomfortably.

"I notice your reaction, and that's exactly what I mean. I am an American. I am not Nigerian. I am not Indian. I am not French. I toured Europe once in my thirties; I've never been anywhere in Asia, and I've seen New Zealand exactly once. I know America. That's what I know. You know your countries, and you know what's best for them. Maybe the way Dame Belinda ran things was fine for you. Maybe not. Maybe you want to look to a central international leadership, maybe you don't. If you want help coordinating with other countries, great. If you want to be part of a bigger structure, great. L.A. will be here for you. I'll be here for you, until we get someone more qualified."

"And if not?" someone called from the back of the audience. I wasn't quick enough to catch who it was.

"If you just want to be left alone," said Alvin, "to deal with Arcadia the way your people deal with weird stuff best? Then I don't ever need to hear from you again."

The murmur that swept through the room this time was one of cynical disbelief.

"I'm not the head of a new empire," he said earnestly. "I'm not here to tell you how to run your people's lives and beliefs and faiths. Tell them about the fey if you want. Or don't. Whatever keeps your people safe. That's what matters to me. Safety."

"But without firm oversight," spoke up a woman in the audience, "how will you control those leaders who choose to put their people in danger?"

"I won't," he said.

At that, a few gasps.

"Look, friends," Alvin said, gently but firmly. "It's not going to be me anyway. If you want someone more hard-assed than me, that's part of what you get to decide. But since you're asking, my opinion is that the desire to declare yourself God, to unilaterally help people who never asked for your help, never led anywhere good. Of course the new Project will have rules. But they'll work more like rules in the mundane world: arrived at by consensus, imperfectly executed, changed as needed. Any rules that require flawless worldwide compliance—for example, absolute secrecy—they're just not tenable. I've seen what it takes to enforce flawless worldwide compliance, and I'm not okay with it. Bad things will happen sometimes. We'll deal with them as they come, but we will not abandon basic human decency."

Everyone was talking to one another now; some people seemed on the verge of firing their translators. Alvin waited for the hubbub to die a bit.

"All I ask," he said then, "is that you let me know by the end of April what your nation intends to do, so that we can count heads and work on restructuring. I hope that many of you will join us in an international structure, because I think we're stronger together. But if you have trouble trusting a foreigner after what you've just found out about Dame Belinda, I don't blame you."

There was a long pause, and then someone started to applaud. It caught on quickly, and soon the room was filled with the sound of approval.

We were actually doing this. Less than a year after I'd even heard of the Arcadia Project, we were remaking the whole thing from scratch.

"Before we take a break," said Alvin, "and have some drinks and start networking and all that, there's one more person I'd like you to meet." He turned back to me and smiled.

Oh shit.

Alvin beckoned, and I got up to stand next to him at the podium. My hands were distressingly moist.

"The fey call her Ironbones," said Alvin, "because she had a terrible accident, and her doctors had to put her back together with steel. She can destroy any spell she touches with her bare hands. This has caused all sorts of problems, but it has also allowed us to accomplish all sorts of wonders.

"But more valuable to us than the accident that makes her a weapon is the intelligence and courage that cooked up a plan to win back the Arcadia Project for its employees, for the people who work every day for its success. She won the Arcadia Project back for the spirits of Arcadia, powerful living creatures who have been used as slaves by the *sidhe*.

"No one believed her when she tried to tell us about the spirits, because we'd been brainwashed by tradition for so long that we never even questioned the way things were done. This young woman does nothing but question. She mobilized a small team to utterly shatter the status quo, and to take back control of all of our lives from a woman who had been keeping our blood in storage *just in case* she needed to exert control over us.

"Please allow me to introduce Millicent Roper, Echo to the King of the Seelie Court. Millie, would you like to address the people whose lives you've given back to them?"

He stepped back, and there I was, in my worst nightmare. How the hell was I supposed to live up to *that* introduction?

I stepped forward, opened my mouth in front of the microphone . . . and nothing came out. I searched myself and tried to find the director, the bullshitter, the heist planner, but she was gone. I was just Millie, the girl with one pigtail who didn't want to fight anymore.

The silence got awkward.

"This is like a bad dream," I finally said. "Except in the dream I'd have no clothes on."

After a pause for translation, there was enough of a ripple of laughter to give me some confidence.

"Look," I said. "That was nice of Alvin, all that, but I didn't really give you anything. I've been gut-feeling my way through this, tripping over things. I set loose the Beast Queen; that was me. I lost us King Winterglass and the Medial Vessel. It's my fault the White Rose fell. There's a civil war brewing in Arcadia, and that's my fault too. I'm more of a shit stirrer than a hero, pardon my F—uh, my profanity.

"But now, mostly by accident, with the help of Alvin and the king and queen here and everyone at the Los Angeles Arcadia Project—even Caryl Vallo—I've tasted what it might be like to be a hero. And I think I want to try it. I want to help, any way I can. If you need me to come where you are, I will. Just, uh, understand that I get pretty bad jet lag, so give me a day or two before you ask me any hard questions. And . . . that's all I have to say, I guess. You should probably all have some drinks."

There was some scattered laughter, and then the applause started again.

I don't know who stood up first. It seemed to be several people. Maybe they were just eager to get drinks, or maybe my legend had preceded me. But then people started standing up because their neighbors were. Some of them clearly weren't sure why they were standing but went ahead anyway.

Before long I was looking at two hundred people from all over the world who were on their feet applauding me. So I stood there and I let them do it, even as their faces blurred and smeared into one brownish glob, because I knew that the display was as much for them, to chase hope and drive away fear, as it was for me.

50

They let Caryl come see me. I don't know if she did it on purpose, but she wore the same suit as on the day we met: a trim, lightweight beige number with a shell-pink blouse underneath. She even had the same flats on. The only difference was her shorter hair: sleek dark waves with tarnished-brass highlights framing her indescribable face.

I memorized every line of her as we stood in the living room of Residence Four, the shadow of her lashes as she failed to meet my eyes, the nervous way she pulled at her gloves.

"Alvin says they've decided to send you to Arcadia after all," I said. "After all the times you fought it. He says we're not even allowed to contact you."

She sighed softly, still not looking at me. "Better it should be execution?" she said. "Barker was right about one thing. That I'm—"

"Don't," I said. "Don't say it."

"Then you say it. I think you need to say it."

"I won't, because I don't believe it."

She looked up then, met my eyes, grave. "Millie. You saw what I did to her. A human being."

"It's no worse than what she did to you."

"That isn't how being human is supposed to work."

I had never been more aware of her humanity, her frailty, the blood coursing underneath her skin. "I don't care what anyone else thinks," I said. "I'll never believe you're dangerous."

"And that," she said, stepping forward to lay a hand at the scarred side of my face, "is why I am more dangerous to you than to anyone." She traced a finger over my cheekbone, and my insides were a cold soup of helpless longing.

"This is your fault," I said around a sudden blockage of tears. "I didn't want things to go this far between us. You kept pushing."

"You were right," she said. "I shouldn't have, and I am sorry. You were right, and Barker was right, and many people were right. I was a stubborn adolescent who refused to listen to any of them. But that stops now. I will make it right."

"How, by abandoning us?"

She gave me a strange look, withdrew her hand. "Do you think everything that leaves a room you are in ceases to exist? Have you no sense of object permanence?"

"Don't be an asshole," I said. "Not right now. Just tell me what you're going to do."

She turned away, took a few steps toward the front window, gazing out.

"I'm going to the Unseelie High Court," she said. "I am not dangerous there. I'm going to advise King Winterglass, and I'm going to try to bring the Unseelie back to the Arcadia Project."

"Caryl—"

She pressed onward without looking at me. "We've seen that the Unseelie can have productive relationships with humans. I believe that eventually I can find some way to bridge things."

"You're walking into a war zone, and I'm supposed to find this comforting?"

"*I* am a war zone," she said calmly, turning to look at me again. "But my hope is that together, I and the Unseelie Court can find some sort of peace."

"The Unseelie Court is what broke you."

"The one who rescued me will be there, looking after me."

"He'd better," I said. I held back tears until my head throbbed; I didn't want her last sight of me to be a blubbering mess.

She came to embrace me, and I held her close as long as I could stand to, then pulled away.

"When it's done," she said, "I'll come back to you."

She was still human, after all, at least for now. She could still lie, when I needed her to.

Alvin drove Tjuan's car to pick him up, so that he could have the option of driving himself back. That's the kind of thing Alvin always thought of. I stayed and waited in the passenger seat when Alvin went in, thinking of a thousand things I could say, epic things.

What would Tjuan do? Would he hug me? Would he *cry*? It seemed plausible, but unimaginable. If he did cry, what would I do? How could I prove that I knew exactly what my partner needed? Because I was racking my brain, and I honestly had no idea.

When I saw the two of them approaching, my gut clenched in fear, and I wasn't even sure why. From their trajectories, it appeared that Tjuan had decided to drive. I was riding shotgun, so that meant Alvin had to get in the back.

"Hey," I said when Tjuan got in next to me.

"Hey," he said, and started the car. Once he was driving, he had a pretty good excuse not to look at either of us or say anything.

I secretly checked him over for bruises. If he had any, they didn't show. I was on fire to know if anyone had hurt him, if he'd been scarred by the experience, if I was supposed to treat him any differently. I couldn't tell. He was distant, but not that much more so than usual. He drove with his usual care, never exceeding the speed limit by more than five miles an hour. I knew because I was watching the speedometer.

I nearly choked on all the unsaid words I'd rehearsed in my head. But they all felt wrong. He wasn't talking, so he must have needed silence. I gave him that, not knowing what else to do.

When we got to the Residence, Alvin got out; his rental car was parked on the street. He clapped Tjuan on the shoulder. "Give me a call if you need anything," he said, and Tjuan nodded. So easy. For Alvin, anyway. Tjuan headed for the house.

Alvin came around to give me a hug.

"I'm going to miss you," I said.

"I'll send you annoying texts at three a.m. Pacific time," he said. "And remember, until we sort out who's the new regional manager out here, I'm still the boss of you." He gave my arm a squeeze, then walked to his car.

Tjuan was already opening the front door. I hurried to catch up. If he went into his room, shut the door, I might not see him for *days*.

"Tjuan," I said. "Wait up."

He held the door open for me, then closed it and locked it behind us. All the locks. There were a *lot* of locks.

I'd half expected Song to arrange some sort of welcome-home party, but I guess she knew Tjuan too well. The living room was suspiciously deserted. Everyone was giving Tjuan space.

Everyone except me.

He ran a palm over his hair; it needed cutting. "Look, Millie," he said. "I don't know how to write scenes like this. I always just leave 'em out."

"I know," I said, wringing my hands. "I know you probably just want to be left alone. I'm sorry I can't just—I'm bad at subtlety. I don't know how to be stoic. I know I drive you crazy. I'm sorry."

"No," he said. "Don't be like that. This is me, too. You and I . . . aren't well suited. And it's not *all* because of you. I've got shit too. Everybody's got shit. Our shit just doesn't—" He gestured vaguely, lacing his fingers together.

"Should we—you're a senior agent; you can work without a partner. Alondra doesn't have anyone. I can—"

And then I started crying. Jesus fucking Christ.

He came over, quick, and hugged me. It was the hug of a man who knows a hug is called for, but has no fucking idea how it's supposed to work. But he did hug me, promptly, and for a decently long time. Then he held me out by the arms and looked me straight in the eye.

"Just because we don't get along," he said, "that doesn't mean we're not partners. You've got my back. Now, half the time I don't want to know what the fuck it is you're doing behind it, but I know you're there, at least. That's not nothing."

"I just—I wish you *liked* me better."

He laughed and let me go. "I wish I did too," he said. "But liking isn't everything. I'd rather have someone I can count on."

I nodded, wiping my eyes. "That'll do," I said. "I'll take it."

He started off toward his room, but then he stopped, turned.

"You know you can count on me, too, right?" he said. "You don't have to . . . hover all the time the way you do. Like you think I'm going to disappear. You know I'm not going anywhere, right?"

A knot inside my chest loosened a little, and I felt myself smile.

"I do now," I said.

I went back into therapy at the end of March. Not the whole full-on DBT thing again, just weekly therapy with Dr. Davis to try to sort through some of what I'd realized during my trial. I told her they were dreams I'd had, which wasn't exactly a lie.

Things started settling into order after that. Phil got promoted to regional manager, leapfrogging right back over Tjuan, who didn't want the job. Phil helped find me a decent lawyer who argued me down to a pretty negligible fine for obstruction of justice. But of course Phil then took both the fine and the lawyer's fee out of the bonus that Alvin had paid me for my help in restructuring the Arcadia Project, netting me a grand total of eight dollars for the whole ordeal. Somehow, that seemed about right. *Thanks for leading the revolution; here's eight bucks.*

Alvin himself was too busy to answer most of my admittedly frivolous texts, but progress toward a new international structure seemed to be going more smoothly than we could have hoped, to judge by the messages he did send. Nayantara from New Delhi got voted in to come to L.A.; she was set to arrive once we'd finished making part of Valiant Studios into a

Project office. Alvin said he was pleased; Nayantara had always been a shoo-in to be next in line after Belinda, and she and Belinda had always hated each other's guts. An ideal candidate, in other words.

Claybriar and Dawnrowan didn't exactly have a wedding ceremony, but they did start shacking up together at Skyhollow Estate. I never quite got up the guts to ask, but I figured they and the duke probably just shared one big, very sticky bed.

And of *course* Naderi's show got a massive ratings boost from all the infamy surrounding its briefly fugitive supervising producer. Tjuan, of course, refused all interviews, without exception, but Inaya and Naderi basked in the media attention and rolled around in giant stacks of money. Money coming into Valiant was money coming into the Arcadia Project, so everything was good.

Almost everything.

To be honest, some of the magic walked out of my life when Caryl left, and even keeping busy wasn't always enough to distract me from the loss. The ache of grief was like the graffiti in the upstairs hall, poorly covered over and mostly ignored. It took way too long for me to stop pulling out my phone to text her, to stop wondering if the tires I heard pulling into the driveway belonged to her SUV. I sent messages to Shock asking about her, but he only ever said that she was fine, and that she loved me.

It felt unkind to him to keep asking. So I stopped.

Things hurt, and you keep living. You keep going, not just because there's no other decent choice, but because honestly? You never know. Caryl didn't even walk into my life until I'd already tried once to end it. So I knew for a fact that sometimes the movie keeps going, even after you think the credits have rolled.

And sometimes it doesn't keep going. You don't get hints about that, either. Life doesn't fit the Hollywood formula; there are no act breaks to orient you, no running times printed helpfully on the back of the box. So you do your best to line up each shot, each frame. You make sure that if this shot ends up being the last, it's damn well going to be bold or bittersweet or beautiful enough to go out on.

ACKNOWLEDGMENTS

This is, in a sense, a continuation of my words at the end of *Phantom Pains*—which themselves were a continuation of my words at the end of *Borderline*. I continue to thank all of those people; those words remain in my heart just as they do in libraries: an enduring testament to my gratitude. Here, I'll add what applies uniquely to this book and no other.

This book was written under trying circumstances. There were times when I worried I might be incapable of finishing at all. Even more than *Borderline* and *Phantom Pains*, *Impostor Syndrome* owes its existence to the support of others. I must thank Wren Wallis in a new way, because she is what glued me together during its final birthing pains. I must thank my editor Navah Wolfe in a new way, because she took on the role of friend as well as editor. I must thank my agent Russell Galen in a new way, because he revealed reserves of compassion that I'd always suspected were there, but had not yet fully witnessed.

I'd also like to add another list of names, similar to the one in *Borderline*. People whose support allowed this book (and me) to keep going, even during the worst, whether they knew it or not. These are newer friends and supporters who didn't get named in previous acknowledgments but who have since then (on a particular crucial occasion or repeatedly) given more than I ever would have asked. I know I'll forget many of you, but let me at the very least thank Daniel Barker, John Bates, Ryan Boyd, Didi Chanoach, Amal El-Mohtar, Jack Gregory, Charlaine Harris, Blair Imani, Derek Kunsken, Ellen Kushner, Yanni Kuznia, Marissa Lingen, Ken Liu, Katie O'Vary, Shaelyn Pham, Logan Rose, Michael Damian Thomas, John Trager, and Christina Vasilevski.

Thank you also to my daughters, old enough now to read "Mishell Baker" on the spines of books and express a pride so visceral and luminous that it at times stood in for the absence of my own.

My gratitude to you, as well, reader, for staying with me. I'm sorry if I've hurt you from time to time, but I hope you understand, overall, what I'm trying to communicate. I hope you understand that dragging ourselves through occasional misery is worth it, because we never know what gleaming and magical thing may be waiting on the far side.